MERCENARY'S DREAM
PETRELLAN SAGA 6

Gordon A. Long

AIRBORN PRESS
Delta, B. C.

Mercenary's Dream

Gordon A. Long

Published by
AIRBORN PRESS
4958 10A Ave, Delta, B. C.
V4M 1X8
Canada

978-1-988898-19-3

Printed by Amazon

Cover Design by Mihaela Voicu

A Matter of Grammar

Anine pushed through the farmhouse door and reported the fight to Lukin and Lord Trenet, who were sharpening their swords by the dim light from the fireplace.

"Which squire was it? I'll deal with him in the morning."

"I'd rather you didn't, your Grace."

"Why not?" Trenet frowned. "He is trained to do better than that."

"No, your Grace, he isn't."

"Pardon me?"

"What you mean, your Grace, is that you have tried to train him to do better than that. If he doesn't do better than that, then you didn't train him to do better, did you?"

"Don't play logic games with me, young lady. That lad has besmirched his honour and betrayed the trust placed in him."

Anine straightened her shoulders. "And he's bin dealt with in the way he shoulda bin. We're gettin' into a military situation, your Grace, and this here's a matter of military discipline."

The duke was about to rise when his daughter's voice stopped him. "Did you hear it, Father?"

"Did I hear what?"

Lady Talia merely nodded towards Anine. "I told you."

"Oh." He sat back and looked at Anine, whose puzzled glance went from father to daughter

"Oh." He relaxed more, and a grin began to form. "She did, didn't she? Just like last time."

His daughter nodded. "Just like I said. And you know what it means."

"Yes. I understand." The duke turned to the stunned woman. "I'm sorry, Anine, you are right. It's a military matter, and I'm sure it's better for the two of them that you handled it the way you did. Come to think of it, it's better for the whole troop if you treated them equally. I bow to your judgement."

Lukin leaned forward in his chair, as puzzled as Anine. "Have I missed something?"

Talia laughed. "Probably. It's Anine. I warned my father already. You have to listen to her grammar."

"Her grammar?"

"When she loses her posh accent and starts sounding like a mercenary, it's a military matter, and time to listen to her."

"Oh." The old soldier looked from one to the other. "Well, I don't pretend to understand, but it seems to have solved a thorny little problem. We're all honed too sharp and stretched too thin, and I'm glad we got through this with nobody hurt."

"A little spat like this, handled well, is good for morale, sir. Sharpens 'em up."

"I agree, Anine." He glanced towards the duke. "Begging your pardon, your Grace, but saving her Grace's presence, I'd be happy if they did attack. We're at top readiness for battle. We'll never be better prepared."

The old Warlander returned to sharpening his sword, and after a moment, so did Duke Trenet.

CONTENTS

The Mercenary's Quandary:
May my children grow up in a time when their father has no occupation.

... Sarasha the Lame

A man without a dream is somebody dead walking around.
... Pagris

PROLOGUE — THE PLAIN MAN

The man rode into town, and no one noticed. He rode a brown horse, not exceptional in any way. But those who knew, had they concerned themselves, would have noticed the restrained power in its gait. The man himself was of average height. His shoulders were not broad, nor was his waist slim. The sleeves of his brown leather jacket were folded back to reveal forearms well muscled, but not exceptionally so. His hair, curling from under a faded hat of no particular style, was brown and of a medium length. His face was neither handsome nor ugly. It contained just enough cheekbone that it would never be considered lowly in origin, yet no one of noble birth ever had such a nondescript nose. He was not in the flush of youth, yet the few lines on his face seemed to come from character, not an excess of age. Not quite homely: slightly friendly. That was all.

His gear was also normal. Nowhere on his person or on his horse was there any ornamentation. Every piece of equipment, each weapon, was precise in its sturdy simplicity, perfect for its task. There was no waste; nothing extra showed.

Those who should have noticed, had they been so keen, would have realized that the very plainness of the man was exceptional. The meticulous simplicity of his appearance should have set the alarm bell ringing. But they did not notice. He rode, virtually unseen, into the city: past the gates, past the watch, even past the perceptive eyes in the streets whose job it was to notice everything. He even made it past the discernment of the ladies of the Street of Dreams. Those who catered to the rich felt him to be too lowly to afford their business. Those who looked to the poor for their patronage would never dare to approach.

The brown horse's head drooped, understandable for the time of day and the heat, but the quickness of its hoof warned the barking dog that there was still a good supply of energy in reserve. The cur kept its distance.

Even so, this small disruption had attracted the attention of an urchin of indeterminate gender secluded from the afternoon sun in the shadow of an empty merchant's stall. There was a keen appraisal by a professional eye. *This one is different. Haven't had much luck with the locals, lately. Maybe some hope with a stranger.* Reaching out a dirt-lined hand, the waif tried to look pitiful and small.

With no noticeable signal, the horse paused.

The brown eyes, neither gentle nor cruel, swept the ragged figure. "You're too old to be begging, boy. There's work in the fields, this time of year."

"How would you know, stranger?"

The horse, again without obvious instruction, moved on.

Marel shrugged back into the meagre shade. The stranger was right. *I'm too old for begging. Lost my touch. It's either the cripplers for treatment or the fields for hard work.* The empty feeling in his middle, combined somehow with the vision of the competent, casual air of the stranger, decided him. Life as a deformed beggar no longer held its earlier appeal.

Marel glanced up the street, where the stranger was disappearing around a corner. He straightened up to his full height and followed at a cautious trot. *He's headed for the castle. Even better. He's here for a reason, and I got the contacts to help him.* Keeping the rump of the horse just in sight, the boy followed.

1. THE MARCH HOME

She thought like a man. That was Anine's problem, and she had known it for a long time. How could she avoid it? Brought up on a hill farm with five older brothers, her mother dead of overwork before the only daughter reached her teens, she had fitted in as well as she could. When she left the farm to seek her fortune in the mercenary troops, her huge size and plain features made it easy for the men around her to treat her as an equal.

Well, she was fine with that. *At least, I ain't complainin'.* Sure, she knew she was missing something when the tavern girls moved in on their table as they always did. For a while she had toyed with the idea that she was really a man in a woman's body, but she felt nothing towards the girls in the bars, willing though some of them might have been.

No, she wasn't complaining. At least, not out loud where anyone might notice. *I'll never be a beauty like men want, so that's that.* She had seen other girls and what love did to them, mooning and sighing and falling all over themselves. All very well if you were a milkmaid. A spilled pail was soon forgotten. *In my profession, a moment's inattention is likely to result in spilled guts, and that's a little harder to get over.*

She marched down the mountain path with the rest of the Clan, striding easily in spite of her bulk. Chasing Inari around the mountains was developing more than her fighting skills. She glanced over at the young soldier slogging beside her.

"Whaddaya think, Varli? You gonna get through this?"

The lad grinned. "Oh, Zoysana never really puts us in any danger of dying on the road. She'd sooner save us to get killed in a fight."

She smiled back, her trained eye going over his face for signs of real fatigue. "You look a bit hot, my friend."

He shrugged as much as the heavy pack would allow. "I didn't say I was happy. But I figure I'll survive." His glance became calculating. "If I was just a bit more tired, would you take the tent for a while?"

She laughed out loud. "I don't think so. Nice try, though."

They strode in companionable silence, the troop strung out evenly along the road, heads up, eyes moving, as proud and alert as

3

any fighters in the kingdom. A warm glow suffused her: nothing to do with the late fall sunshine. It had been a good campaign for the final part of the summer, harrying the few Inari that snuck down over the passes, putting the pressure on so they had no chance to do more than minor damage to the hill farms of the area. With the coming of fall, the tribes had pulled back into the fastness of the Upper Plains, and Zoysana's Clan was headed back to Arlyn Castle for a well-deserved rest.

"Whaddaya think's on the order slate for this winter? Didn't sound like she was gonna be payin' anyone off."

Varli shook his head. "Not likely. You lot are too well trained to let go. The rest of us will be back to our usual positions. I have to go home to the Inner Duchies for a while," he grinned again, "to prove to my father that I've not completely gone native out here on the frontier."

She nodded. It was easy to forget that the next soldier in this strange bunch could be a squire, a well-trained mercenary or a rough hill farmer. "Well, I got nowheres to go, so I guess it's the castle for me for the winter. I'm not really lookin' forward to it. I mean, it's nice to be gettin' paid and all, but winter sentry duty ain't exactly fun."

The boy gave her an evil grin. "Oh, it'll be worse than that, count on it."

"What?" She looked across at him. "I ain't heard nothin' about any dangerous jobs comin' up."

He shook his head. "Not dangerous. Worse. Do you know how to read?"

Only the years of mercenary training kept her from missing a step. "Read?"

"Aye. You know, words on a page."

"I know what readin' is, Shrimp. I just don't follow what yer talkin' about."

He sighed mightily, as much as one can sigh who is breathing heavily from the exertion of striding at a ground-eating pace with a heavy pack. "I mean that if you're in the castle for the winter, and you have any brain for it, you'll be learning to read."

"Read? You gotta be kiddin'!"

"Nope. Every one of the regular Guides learns to read. Useful, you know. Messages and that."

"But I'm not a Guide. I'm just a regular soldier. In case you didn't remember, I come off of a farm. I can't read. Well, not much, anyhow. I know all the letters 'n' how to write my name 'n' that."

"After this summer, you're not a common soldier any more. You're one of Zoysana's Clan. You don't stay where you are."

She paced along, wiping the sweat from her forehead. "That's for sure."

A quick, scoffing laugh. "You know very well that's not what I meant. You have to make progress, get better at everything." He regarded her, then seemed to come to a decision. "You're not as dumb as you act."

"Thanks a lot, Shrimp. You lookin' to get around me, all this flattery?"

He didn't laugh. "You know what I mean. Sure, you come from a farm, and my father's a noble in the Inner Duchies. But that doesn't mean you have to pretend to be stupid. You pick up things as quick as the rest. Quicker, most times."

She walked on, then made up her mind. "You put that in your report?"

"What report?"

She had her own sly grin. "If I'm smarter than I act, then mebby I notice things you don't think I notice. You and Zoysana bin together a while, right?"

"She trained me for years."

She nodded. "So all that complainin' you do, and she knocks you around for it, I figger that's a warnin' to the rest. They know what she could do to any man in the troop if she wanted to. So you're the company sleeper."

"The what?"

"Mercenary slang you never heard. The sleeper is the man in the ranks that reports to the Commander what's goin' on with the rankers."

"Like a spy?"

She shrugged. "In some of the rag-tag companies, I guess. In a good company, everyone knows who it is. There's always some guy who's got a personal relationship with the brass. Can't be helped, can be useful. In Zoysana's Clan, it's gotta be you."

Now he looked concerned. "Do all the others think the same?"

5

She shrugged her bulky shoulders. "The mercs, probably. Most of the others have some idea. You don't exactly hide it."

"Oh."

She reached over and clapped him on the arm, staggering him out of line, although he recovered his balance quickly. "Don't look so disappointed. Like I said, nobody minds. In fact, if they trust you, most of them like it. If they got a legit complaint, they make sure you hear it. They know you'll pass it along, without nobody bein' singled out as a whiner."

"And do they trust me?"

She laughed again, louder. "I'm gonna let you figger that out yerself, lad. I said most of them like havin' you around. I don't mind it myself. At least with the company snitch, you know where you stand!"

"Thanks. I thought you said it was called the company sleeper."

"That's only if they like you."

"Great."

She laughed again at his glum expression, and slapped him on the shoulder once more.

"Hey, Anine. You makin' up to Lord Varlinden, there?"

She turned briefly to glance at the grinning face behind her. "That's right, Beken. I'm pushin' for a soft job in the Duchies this winter. While you're standin' sentry in a snowstorm, I'll think of you fondly."

"Don't let her turn your inexperienced head, lad. She's slyer'n she looks!"

Varli laughed. "That's funny, Beken. I just said the same thing."

"Well, there ya go. If me and you said it, it must be true, us bein' the smartest heads in this bunch. Savin' Herself, there, o' course. So you watch it, youngster. She'll be tryin' her wiles on your innocence, and who knows what could happen."

The boy grinned over his shoulder. "She keeps shaping up like she has this summer, and that might not be too bad an idea." He glanced up at her and his face paled. "I mean…I'm sorry, Anine, I didn't mean anything by that, really!"

She strode ahead until the heat died from her face. Varli scrambled to catch up, putting distance between them and the pair behind.

"I'm really sorry, Anine. I didn't mean to talk about you like that. Zoysana says I'm always opening my mouth when I shouldn't. I didn't really mean it."

Seeing his distress, she felt better. "You didn't? That's too bad."

"What?"

She could smile, now. "I don't know. I sort of hoped you meant it. It sounded like a compliment."

"Oh, it was, it was."

A snicker erupted behind her, and she spun, walking backwards and raising her fist. The soldier held up his open hands. "Anine, I ain't laughin' at you. I'm laughin' at the youngster there, tryin' desperately to drag hisself out of the hole he dug, and slippin' in deeper at every word."

She stared at Beken, then nodded and turned back into the column. After a while, she looked over at Varli, who was walking just a bit farther away from her than the proper order of march allowed. "So what did you mean?"

He glanced up suspiciously. "What?"

"Well, every girl likes a compliment, but she just wants to be sure. What did you mean, 'shaping up'?" She half-turned as hurried footsteps approached from behind.

"Oh, we gotta hear his answer to this, Anine. Please don't get mad and spoil it."

She turned to glower at the young squire. "Well, Varli, the troops need to be entertained on the march. Looks like you have to explain. With all of us listenin'."

"Aye, Varli, this better be good. Ya know, Anine's a friend of ours. We wouldn't want to hear her gettin' upset."

The boy glanced back with a frown. The soldier looked half serious. "What I meant, Anine, was that...well, you're pretty big. You don't mind if I say that, do you?"

She considered this. "Whaddaya think, Beken? Another compliment?"

The soldier snickered. "He's doin' great so far."

Varli smiled. "Well, when you started out this summer, you were just big. Like one of the other big guys. But you didn't have much...well..." He fumbled for the words, looking sideways at her, then over his shoulder at the soldiers behind. They only looked on

7

with interest. Finally, he screwed up his courage, and the words came out in a rush.

"Well, I don't mean to offend, Anine, but you didn't have much shape."

There was a burst of laughter, which showed how many of the marching troops were listening. Anine joined in. Varli looked so worried she could almost forget he was talking about her. She stared at him with mock ferocity. "You're not gettin' too far out of the hole with comments like that. In fact, you're slidin' back pretty deep. Wanta quit now?"

He grinned. "No, no, now we get to the good part."

"Ya mean the punch line." Beken chuckled from behind.

"I sincerely hope not. What I meant was, we've all had a tough summer, climbing and training and fighting and chasing the Inari all over. Most of us have lost weight. And I think Anine has lost quite a bit. And if you don't mind my saying…" he glanced up at her, and she nodded "…in the right places."

Another burst of laughter from the troops around, and she surprised herself by blushing again. She knew the only thing to do was keep going. "Why, thank you, sir. You practised that sort of thing in lordling school, did you?"

He was immediately indignant. "I did not. I meant it, and it's true. Ask Beken!"

Beken raised his hands again. "No you don't, kid. You got yourself into this. I ain't stupid enough to jump in with you. Please, Anine, don't ask me!"

"Don't worry, Beken. I'll just let it remain a mystery. I've already got young Varlinden, here, in my debt; I'll take my winnings and quit the game."

She strode ahead, ignoring them, but she couldn't stop the warm glow that filled her. She always loved being included in the rough joshing and insults, but this was different. Varli had meant what he had said.

Probably.

For a moment, she was suspicious that he had another reason for the jest, but it was unlikely. He had spoken too thoughtlessly and been instantly sorry. He could have no reason to play games like that with her. There wasn't a mean bone in the young lord's body, and whatever role he played; jester, complainer, company sleeper or mascot, he was loved by the whole troop.

They strode along in companionable silence, the faint jingling of their gear a pleasant counterpoint to their steady march. Even in full kit, Zoysana's Clan moved with little fuss. The fall sun slanted lower in the west, and soon they came into a small dell with a spring running through it. The cook tent was already pitched, and they set their own tents with a will, to the smell of fresh venison roasting over the fire. Two of Zoysana's Inari scouts were tending it, accepting the troop's jesting thanks with quiet pride.

"We quit early."

Varli grunted as he hauled on a guy rope, fastening it securely with a practiced twist of the wrist. "No sense rushing. The war's over for this year, and we've got the supplies. Might as well use them before they spoil."

Maura hauled the next rope to him one-handed, her scarred fingers covered only by a heavy leather glove.

"How's the wound healing, Maura?"

The older mercenary looked down at her left hand. "Feels fine. No more pain. Just two fingers with no grab. Tendons were cut, for sure. The third finger gave me some trouble, 'n' Zoe said that tendon was probably nicked as well, but it's loosened up now."

Varli grinned. "That's good. I'll be real glad to have you training us, now, instead of her."

"Who says I'll be trainin' you?"

He shrugged. "Word gets around."

She was instantly in front of him, her good hand hoisting him by his shirtfront. "You know somethin' I don't, Shrimp?"

He laughed and twisted free; he'd had lots of practice with that move. "Nothing that you'll get upset about, that's for sure, and I'm not allowed to say."

She made towards him again, but he held up open hands, a serious look on his face. "I mean it, Maura. I don't know much, and I'm not allowed to tell anything I heard. I just figured it out. We're short one Arms Master at the castle, and Gerth said there would always be a place for you."

The woman looked stunned. "Arms Master?"

Varli shrugged. "You see why I can't say anything. If I blab and then you didn't get the post, you'd be real upset."

9

Anine reached out and cuffed his shoulder with the back of her hand. "But now you have said somethin', you dummy. How are you gonna get out of this one?"

He flinched away, but she knew he wasn't hurt. "I'll have to talk to Zoe, I guess."

"Did I hear my name mentioned?" The Clan Leader had an unerring ear for any disturbance in camp, reading stirred emotions over the usual hubbub. She and Patu strode up, the soldiers all standing to greet her. It was strange to see her without her Guard of Life at her shoulder, but Tadeo's father was ill, and he had returned to Kyabra to support his family.

Anine read the Leader's mood in the leisurely sweep of the armigerent's shaggy tail, and responded with a smile.

Varli was less impressed. "Aye, Zoe, I was talking about you. Maura's been left hanging long enough, don't you think?"

The small, dark, woman reached up and ruffled his hair, then grabbed a handful, pulling his head down while she stared into his eyes. "And you have taken it upon yourself to decide when the announcement should be made."

"He was just makin' guesses, Lady Zoe. He didn't speak out of turn."

Zoysana released the boy and turned to Maura. "He always speaks out of turn. Don't stand up for him. How am I ever going to get him to discipline himself?"

The older woman smiled as well. "Oh, I think he's doin' all right. Sometimes he's even useful."

Anine took her courage in her hands. "Aye, Lady Zoe. Now that he's brought the subject up, do you have some plans for Maura?"

Confronted by three serious faces, the Clan Leader relented. "Of course, and I'm sorry I didn't tell you sooner. I knew you would be concerned. Gerth needs another Arms Master at the castle, and he thinks you should apprentice."

Anine caught a triumphant glance from Varli and tipped him a wink.

"Apprentice? Me? I'm thirty-four years! Way too old to apprentice. Besides, where would I get the fee?"

Zoysana shrugged. "I don't see what age has to do with it. You can't fight in the line anymore, so you'd have to take a new trade anyway. You might as well get your papers. Your apprentice fee is your compensation for a wound received in battle. We'll start your four-year term from the day you signed on with us last fall." The small woman's face crinkled in a grin. "I'd say you've learned a few things in the past year."

They all laughed ruefully. The summer had been a learning experience from the first day.

"So you report to the Armoury when we hit the castle. They'll find you a room, and we'll talk to the Armourer about your training."

A touch of moisture glistened in the woman's eye. "Thank you, and thank His Majesty, Lady Zoysana. It's more than I expected. Way more."

"What about the rest of them, Zoe? Are they just going on guard for the winter? I heard Gerth say you're not letting anyone go."

Zoysana shook her head. "Again, the Mouth of the Troop reminds the Leader of her duties. I suppose everyone is worrying about that." She looked up to see an expanding circle of mercenaries around her.

"All right. The plans are pretty well set, and you deserve to know. After supper tonight we'll have a talk. You," she pinned Varli with her glare, "I will talk to now!"

She spun on her heel and strode off, the huge armigerent glued to her side as usual. Anine clapped Varli on the back, reassuring him but shoving him in the right direction at the same time. He glanced an appeal over his shoulder at her and trudged off dejectedly, to the laughter of the watching troops. Anine was pretty sure he was in no trouble; it was just his usual act. The kid certainly did have his uses.

Strange that she always considered him to be young; she only had two years on him. He had grown over the summer. Now the lad looked down on her, and the constant sword work had broadened his shoulders. However, her time had been spent with a mercenary troop, and it aged you. She thought of her blush at his jests, back on the road, and wondered if she really was that mature after all. *Life certainly does hand out the twists and turns.*

"Guess your little boyfriend's in trouble, now!"

She turned to face Beken's vacant grin. "Beken, if you had a brain in your head, you'd be grateful to him. Now we're gonna find out what's happenin', and all because he opened his mouth. So don't make a complete ass of yourself, hey?"

There was an appreciative chuckle from the audience. The two women returned to setting up their bivouac, and the rest strolled

11

back to their own tasks. *Beken is all right to have around, but sometimes his constant stupid jokes bother me.* "Is it just me, or is he gettin' worse?"

Maura straightened up from her bedroll. "It's just you."

"You mean it?"

The older woman shrugged. "I ain't noticed him any worse or any better. He's just Beken, and you put up with him, just like you put up with the rest of us. He ain't smart and he ain't pretty, but he's a good man to have at your back in a brawl."

She sighed. "I guess you're right. He just bothers me today, that's all."

"Because of what Varli said on the road."

"That's right. How did you know?"

Maura grinned. "Because everybody in the troop knows, of course. It was a borin' day of marchin', and anythin' that spices it up is fair game. This time it's you. Take your turn, Anine, and put up with it."

"I suppose so. But it won't end tomorrow."

"You're right, there. These men have to have some shelf to put you on, some excuse to deal with a woman. You either have to be an old witch, like me, or young, innocent, and plain, like you were. Now, that's changed. Varli told 'em you're a woman. Their little male brains can't forget that. Now they gotta find another title for you."

"Another title?"

Maura stretched out on her bedroll, her sore hand cradled. "Sure. They useta treat you sorta like a little sister, protect you, that sorta thing. Now they realize you're a woman, they gotta find another name. The kinda women they usually have, you don't want to be. Do you?"

"Not for sure! So, what do I do?"

The woman shrugged. "I dunno. Be tough, is all I can say. This is a hard bunch. Oh, sure, they're the right kind to have with you in a scrap. But you hang out with a tough troop, you pay the price in camp. They don't fight all day then turn into bunny rabbits at night, you know."

"Hah! Bunny rabbits I don't need right now."

Maura had a wicked grin. "Din't mean it that way. But th' fact remains…"

The big girl sighed again. "I know. It means they're all gonna be testin' me, just like they did when I first joined up. Dammit, is it always this way for a woman?"

"Till you get old and ugly, it is."

"You're not ugly!"

"Mixed blessing, believe me. I'd rather not be pretty, thank you very much." A pleased smile crossed the weathered face. "And now I'm gonna be a Arms Master! Thinka that! With papers and everythin'. With Arms Master papers from Petrella, I could work anywheres."

"You wouldn't leave!"

Maura's smile became thoughtful. "No, guess I wouldn't at that. Arms Master at a king's castle is top o' the heap. But it's nice to know I could. Gives you a feeling of freedom, ya know?"

Anine's shoulders fell. "I guess. It'll be a while before I get that kind of freedom."

Maura sat up straighter. "Look, girl, you bin sighin' like you was in love or got the chest heaves or somethin'. It ain't that bad. You just gotta get out there. Chin up, stare 'em in the face, and give it to them straight if they crosses you. You're a Fighter of Zoysana's Clan, and they can't forget that."

"Give it to them straight, hey? I tell you, Beken mouths off one more time, I'm gonna paste him."

Maura grinned. "That's the attitude, girl. If that's what it takes!"

Hiding another sigh, Anine stretched out on her bedroll to await the dinner gong. When she had been starting out, she hadn't looked much past learning to be a mercenary. After that, her main objective became survival. But now...*what if I do survive? If I'm lucky, ten years of this, and then what? I gotta start lookin' farther down the road. I dunno what for, but I gotta start lookin'.*

2. THE BROWN MAN

They made good time the next day: the mercenaries buoyed by the prospect of a full winter's easy work, the hill farmers peeling out of column to their homes and the others keen to get on with their lives. They overnighted a few candles' march from the castle and arrived near noon the following day.

It was a cheerful scene, although there was a crisp chill to the breeze that snapped the Arlyn colours streaming from the castle walls. Zoysana rode at the head of her Clan with Varli carrying their banner proudly. A surprising number of people turned up to cheer them through the town, and a contingent of mounted Warlanders waited on the parade ground to greet them officially.

Gerth himself came out of the main gate to bring them inside to the roar of the assembled citizens. Anine, who had been through her share of victories, stared around in amazement.

"What are they all so worked up about? We didn't win any great battles or anythin' like that."

Maura smiled. "Popular leadership, Anine. They love the king and they love Zoysana. Or what she stands for, anyways."

"What does she stand for?"

"Petrella's got a lot of followers of the Lady."

"Oh, that. I guess so."

"What I heard, She appeared Herself at Gerth's coronation to bless him in Her Defender attribute: Kyabran robe, armigerent and white kid and all. Oh, everybody knows it was only Zoysana and Patu and that nasty little goat from the stables, but still, it's hard to stop a legend."

"Well, more power to her. Whatever works."

Maura grinned. "Seems to work fine for her. Listen to that crowd!"

With so much noise there was no point in speeches, so they strode proudly up to the main gate and through, to disperse into the organized hubbub of the bailey. Maura headed straight to the Armoury, and Anine was left wondering what to do. Maura was settled. She had a chance to achieve her dream.

14

Wonder when that's gonna happen to me? My luck, it'll be the point of a sword that settles my future. What good are your dreams then?

As her attention slid across the crowd, it was arrested by a man sitting on a cart against the wall. She glanced his way again. What was it about him? He was dressed in plain brown leathers; impossible to guess whether he was a tradesman in work clothes, a forester just in from his paths or a noble back from the hunt. Not wanting to stare, she allowed her eyes to pass on and scanned the crowd again. Nothing seemed to be organized for the mercenaries, so she lugged her pack over against a nearby wall and stood by it, happy to be resting in the warmth of the sun reflecting off the weathered stone.

"Do I know you?"

She spun, startled at the soft approach. It was the man in brown. He was taller than she had expected. She stared into calm brown eyes the same level as hers. Then she grinned. "Now, that's an old play, even for one as young as me. Do you know me? I don't think so. Who are you?"

"Then why did you pick me out?"

"Sorry, my friend. I don't want to hurt your feelin's, but I ain't picked you for nothin'." She started to turn away.

"Yes, you did. You were scanning the crowd and you looked directly at me."

She turned back with a warning frown. "I suppose a person is allowed to look where she wants. Last time I heard, King Gerth was quite free with the sunlight in his demesnes."

He grinned. "Sorry. I deserved that. But it was a serious question. It would please me if you could try to think back to that moment, and tell me what attracted your eyes to me. Oh," he held up a hand defensively, "it's not that I'm trying to elicit a compliment. Quite the opposite. I'm not used to being noticed."

She regarded him, taking in the worn leathers, the sword at his side. This was either the strangest invitation play she'd ever heard, or he was serious. She shrugged. "You were still."

"Still."

"Aye. Everybody in the whole place was tearin' round like a hive of bees with a bear comin' up the tree, and there you was, sittin' dead still."

"Ah. That would explain it. Thank you. I will remember." He sketched her a brief 'pupil to teacher' bow and started to turn away.

"Wait a minute."

"Yes?"

"What kind of game are you playin'? This is just about the strangest conversation I ever had. Who are you, and who are you hidin' from?"

He laughed. "Oh, I'm not hiding from anyone. I'm just hanging around, waiting for the people in charge to see me, and I guess I was getting bored. That made me careless. So when I saw something that interested me, I reacted without thinking. Sorry. I hope you don't mind talking to me."

"So it was a invitation play."

"I'd prefer to call it an excuse for an introduction. I know. Same thing. Would you like to find someone to give us a formal presentation?"

She smiled. "No, that's all right. I'm not too worried about my honour, here in the middle of my troop. Nobody messes with one of Zoysana's Clan. Especially in the bailey of Gerth's castle. So you go ahead and talk, Sir Mystery Man. I'm not bored. Yet."

"You're one of the famous Clan, are you? I have business with your Clan Leader as well. I wonder if you could point her out to me."

She grinned. "Oh, c'mon. You pretend to be an intelligent sort. Check out the group. You should be able to see who's in charge."

It took him five breaths, by her count. "That one? The little one with the round face? Yes, that's her for sure. Look at how they circle her like drones around the queen bee. Amazing, isn't it?"

She was about to respond when a voice broke in from behind her.

"Well, well, well, and if our little lady hasn't got herself a boyfriend. And only just got into the castle. Wish I was so lucky. Wanta share your techniques with the rest of us, Anine?" Beken finished his comments with a slap on her shoulder and a raucous laugh.

For a moment she stood there, registering the amused interest on the face of the man in brown. Then her teeth ground together. She spun and planted her fist, almost as hard as she could, into the soldier's wind. To her surprise, instead of the rock-hard muscles she had expected, her fist sank into a completely unprepared stomach.

16

The breath went out of him with an audible 'whoosh,' and he sank to the stones of the courtyard, gasping.

Hiding her dismay, she reached down, took him by the shoulder and flipped him on his back, pushing his knees up to his chest. When his breathing evened, she bent over him again. "In case you didn't notice, Beken, I'm tired of that joke. Find another one."

She straightened, to find those calm brown eyes regarding her with humour. "Don't even think of laughing. You heard what I said."

The leather-clad man backed off, but his grin increased. "Not to worry, soldier. You have made your wishes known. Forcibly, I note."

As she strode back towards her pack, he matched her pace. "Is he usually a problem?"

She shook her head. "Not really. He just pushed too hard, once too often."

"Well, no harm done. At least you didn't knock any of his teeth out."

She glanced over her shoulder to where his laughing comrades were picking Beken up off the flagstones. "No harm, I suppose, but Zoysana's gonna have somethin' to say about it. See? Here she comes now."

Sure enough, the Clan Leader's unerring ear had picked the vibrations out of the general noise, and she was slipping through the crowd towards them.

"Anine. Did I really see what I thought I saw?"

Anine paused. Zoysana didn't look angry, and Patu's ears were up, his mouth hanging open in what could have been a laugh. "I don't know, Lady Zoe. What did you think you saw?"

Zoe actually grinned. "I think I saw as sweet a sucker punch as has ever been so well deserved. However," her brown eyes grew serious, "I will be talking to you about it later. We can't have brawling in the ranks."

Anine winced. A talk with Zoysana could be worse than a full, public dressing down by many another officer.

"And may I be introduced to your friend?"

She realized with a start that the brown-clad man was, indeed, standing forward. "Well, Lady Zoe, I could introduce you to this gentleman, but he hasn't had the good manners to introduce himself

17

to me. Only told me that he has business with you, and asked me to point you out. As if anyone needed that."

Zoysana sighed. "Ah, yes, I seem to be noticed, no matter what I do. The Sivan would be so disappointed." The dark eyes shot to the stranger's face.

"Ah, the Sivan. Yes, he might be a topic to discuss."

Zoe regarded him a breath or two. "All right, then. You have my attention. Who are you, and what do you want?"

The man in brown laughed and shrugged. "I should have known not to expect elaborate courtesies. Straight to the point, Lady Zoysana, as I have been led to expect."

"Then you will not be surprised to find that I have very little time for enigmatic strangers. I will speak with you. Briefly. Anine, would you escort us? Varli will see your pack is taken to the barracks."

Settling her sword more comfortably, Anine motioned her new acquaintance forward. He smiled serenely and stepped out beside Zoysana.

"I'm sorry, Lady Zoysana. You are right. I had chosen your large friend, here, hoping to get her to introduce me."

Zoe grinned wryly at Anine. "Thought she looked just slow and plain enough to be grateful for the attention of a handsome man. I gather you have been disillusioned on that account."

He nodded. "Yes…yes, I would say so. However, in the process of learning that little lesson, I rather drew more attention to myself than is my usual habit."

"Yes, if you do come from the Sivan, he would be disappointed in you."

The man smiled sadly. "Gravely, I'm afraid. I seem to have made several misjudgements." His face brightened, and his head came up. "However, I am a fast learner, and I am very willing to make amends for my mistakes."

Zoe turned in her office door and stared at him a breath. "And don't bother with the boyish charm, either. I'm beginning to wonder if you have any idea who the Sivan is, let alone have instructions from him. Surely he would have prepared you better."

"Oh, I assure you, Lady Zoysana, I have the appropriate credentials. I have merely learned that, especially with the Sivan, the truth is stronger than the story I was told. Considerably stronger."

She sat behind the table and extended a hand. "All right then. Let's have them. The credentials."

The man glanced pointedly at Anine. "Are you sure...? I mean, this could be very delicate."

Zoysana stood. "I become less and less sure I have any interest in you. Anine, will you escort this gentleman to wherever he is staying? Deposit him there and leave him. Return at mid-morning tomorrow to collect him and bring him to me. Impress upon him how inadvisable it would be for him to return to the castle before that time, or unescorted at any time."

"But Lady Zoe..."

The small woman spun back to face him, and he flinched. "My friends call me that. Anine?"

Sometimes it was useful to be large. She imposed her bulk in front of the man, forcing him to turn towards the door. Without touching him, she chivvied him outside and down the stairs to the courtyard.

"Where are you staying?"

"At the *Angry Bear* down in the city." They turned and began to walk. She matched his strides, only careful, not really on guard. "I overstepped, didn't I?"

"Good guess."

"What did I do?"

She shrugged. "Think about it."

"But all I meant was that it might be more appropriate to give her such sensitive material in a more...private situation. I do not mean to offend, Anine, but it is not the kind of thing a common soldier should be party to."

She merely looked at him.

"What? What have I said now? I assure you, I had no intention to offend you."

"I'm not offended. You just made the same mistake."

"I did?"

She held her silence.

"Do I have to figure this out myself? Drat, it's just like being with the Sivan again."

"First smart thing you've said so far."

"All right. So I've got to figure it out. My mistake was in suggesting that you leave. So I shouldn't have presumed to tell

Zoysana how to handle the situation. And the second mistake was in calling you a common soldier. I begin to get it."

"Fine. You've got it figured out. So tomorrow, when I take you to Lady Zoysana, you'll do a lot better."

"Oh, yes. You know, I never really believed. Not till now. Not till I met her."

"Believed what?"

"The stories. They talk about her all over the Inner Duchies." He shook his head. "I didn't think it was all real, you know? Like these stories go around, and they get changed. And then the Sivan. You know how he feels about her."

"Do I?"

"Let's just say he holds her in high regard. Even he can't hide it. I figured he was exaggerating, as well."

He laughed wryly. "So I'm sitting in the courtyard, watching you all come in, and first thing, you spot me. Well, that shook me a bit, but then I thought I could use it to my advantage, make myself known, subtle-like. Hah! Some chance. First I get you into a fight, and then I insult Zoysana and she throws me out."

He swung towards her. "She will see me tomorrow, won't she?"

Anine let him stew before relenting. "She said so, didn't she?"

His shoulders slumped in relief, and she revised her opinion of his age downward. "I should know better than to doubt her word."

They turned into the inn, and she stopped short of the door. "There you are. I'll see you after breakfast. That way you can be waitin' when she's ready to see you."

"Thank you, Anine. I'll be ready."

"And...?"

"Yes?"

She smiled sweetly at him. "It would really be a good idea to give her your name. She ain't one to put up with silly games. You want to give her a false one, go ahead, but don't mess about."

"Oh. Oh, certainly. Arvent. My name is Arvent. From Llandres."

"Thank you. Good night, Arvent of Llandres. Sleep well." She turned and strode back up the street to the castle. She knew she would be expected to report immediately. She stepped out, her head high, the fatigue of the journey forgotten. *If this is what it's going to be like, working at the castle, I could really get to enjoy it.*

3. The Sivan's Mistake

She stood in the inn doorway, scanning the late breakfast crowd. Finally, she saw him over in the corner with three tradesmen, involved in serious conversation, blending perfectly, his hand motions matching theirs. *Probably his accent as well.*

She waited on the threshold, and once he noticed her, she stepped back outside. If he was really from the Sivan, no sense in breaking whatever cover he had created here. As Zoysana taught, you never wasted an advantage without cause.

He caught her after a few paces. "Good morning, Anine."

"Good morning, Arvent. I trust you slept well."

"You know, I did. The inn is not prepossessing from the outside, but it's quite comfortable and reasonably clean."

"Another thing you better learn."

He hesitated. "What's that?"

"There's a lot of different types around here. Everybody's valued for what they are. You don't make any friends puttin' on airs."

"What airs?"

She glanced over, to see him honestly puzzled. "A big vocabulary is hardly prepossessing to someone who has spent the summer beatin' the Inari at their own game, no matter what kinda bad grammar she has."

"Oh." He grinned again. "Seems all my resolutions of yesterday just fell to pieces. I've put my foot in a puddle again, haven't I?"

She laughed. "Not really. Nobody's askin' you to change who you are. Seems to me you'll get along famously with Varli."

"Is that Varlinden, Gerth's squire?"

"And that would be King Gerth to you."

"Yes, of course. King Gerth's squire. Is that who you mean?"

"That's him."

"Oh, I'm quite looking forward to meeting him. We're sort of related."

"Sort of?"

"Yes. I believe second cousins-in-law. There's quite a lot of intermarriage in the Duchies, you know, among the lesser nobility."

"And I'm supposed to gather from this that you're of noble blood?"

He threw his hands up in frustration. "No, you aren't. I'm just trying to make conversation. Is everybody in Petrella this touchy?"

She considered the accuracy of his complaint. "No, I'm just tryin' to straighten you out a bit before you talk to Zoysana. There's been too many people around who aren't what they should be, and we're all a bit jumpy about strangers. Also, she don't like people puttin' on airs. She talks to everybody equal. It bothers some, of course, but with her position next to the king and his mother, they can't say nothin' about it. The rest of us like it."

"I can imagine. I don't like being spoken down to, myself."

She nodded. "And hidin' your true background like you do, I imagine it happens a lot."

"That's right. But I try not to let it bother me. I consider it simply a weakness on the part of the person who is speaking." He grinned again. "Not to recognize my true worth."

She shook her head. "And you call that fair? You take a lotta trouble to hide what you are, and then look down on people when they don't give you credit for what you are."

"I hadn't looked at it quite that way before."

"Don't let it bother you. I'm just a Petrellan farm girl. What do I know?"

"Right." She caught a sly smile. "And a common soldier."

She laughed. "Point well made. I call truce."

They had entered the castle through the main gate, wide open as usual. "Wait here, please, and I'll see where Lady Zoysana is."

"Is she really a Lady?"

She held up her hands in a helpless gesture. "I dunno. From the stories, she's a Lady twice over, here and in Kyabra. Top of that, she's the king's best friend, and got a bunch of religious clout as well. I don't know any of it for sure, 'cause she never mentions it to anyone. Oh, don't worry. If you call her Lady, you won't be breakin' any rules."

She strode up the steps into the castle and found Zoe in her usual spot, on a stool in Loreline's office. Both of them seemed intent on some papers, and Anine stood respectfully just outside the door.

Zoysana looked around. "Oh, there you are, Anine. Have you brought our spy along?"

"Do you think he's a spy, Lady Zoe?"

Zoe grinned and glanced a quick communication of some kind to Loreline. "If he comes from the Sivan, he better be. If he comes from anywhere else, then he is for sure. What do you think? You've had a chance to spend some time with him."

Anine shook her head. "I don't know. I never met the Sivan, but from what everyone says, I expected more from one of his pupils."

Loreline leaned forward. "What do you mean?"

Anine shrugged. "Dunno. He seems to be a lot younger than he looks. Sounds like Varli at his worst sometimes."

Zoe laughed. "That sounds strange, coming from you."

"I know." She found herself uncertain. "I don't know why he bothers me, but he does. He's actin' like he needs a sister to keep him straightened out, and I got no thought of playin' that game. And I don't think he really needs one."

Both older women laughed. "Well, bring him in, and you can stay, too. We'll see what you think after we've heard what he wants."

If the stranger was bothered by an interview with three women, he didn't show it. He marched forward, introduced himself properly, and was introduced to Loreline in turn.

He immediately reached into his shirt and removed a small packet. "I am very pleased to finally meet you, Loreline, and I have been instructed to give this to you personally." He looked to Zoysana, as if for permission. "I suggest that you open it in private."

The older woman went red, and the package disappeared.

Wonder what that's all about? This is gettin' more interestin' by the minute.

Arvent then turned to Zoysana. "I have been instructed to ask you, Lady Zoysana, that moving water will be found, but did you need to create a cataract?"

Zoysana laughed. "All right, Arvent. Your credentials are established. What can we do for you?"

He looked at the three who confronted him. "You know, I was sent here by someone we all know, with the intent of furthering my training. I wondered what I would learn here, and I am beginning to understand."

Anine snorted.

All eyes turned to her, and she shrank back.

"No, go ahead, Anine. Your opinion, clearly expressed, is as valuable as that of anyone in the room."

She shrugged. "I've been hearing this sort of thing all morning. I'm sorry, Arvent, but you haven't proved anything to me but that you're a smooth talker." She looked hesitantly at Zoysana.

The smaller woman nodded. "Fair assessment, if perhaps harsh. What have you to say to that, Arvent?"

He spread his hands helplessly. "Not much, since a good defence will convict me."

They all laughed at that.

"So, what did the Sivan have in mind, besides broadening your mind?"

"Well, nothing, really."

This time there were two incredulous snorts.

"I mean it. He told me to come and introduce myself and deliver that package, and that's it. He said it would be to my advantage to stay here a while. That was all." He scanned three disbelieving faces. "That's what he said."

Zoysana chuckled. "Oh, we don't doubt that's what he said. The question, as usual with the Sivan, is what else he meant."

The man nodded. "Ah, I see what you mean. Well, if he had any other plan, he didn't tell me."

Loreline smiled. "He rarely does."

Zoysana leaned forward, her elbows on the table. "So, what do you suggest?"

The brown man shrugged. "I don't know, really. I assumed King Gerth would find me some minor position in his household, and I would work at whatever was required." Again that engaging grin. "I'm quite at the mercy of those of you who might guess what my master wants me to learn."

"Or do."

"What could I do?"

Loreline regarded him. "Either what you haven't told us or what you don't know."

Zoysana nodded. "That's the Sivan's style. He puts people that he knows into situations where he can guess how they will act. It's a risky trick if you want short-term results, but over the years it has been highly successful. Note," she held up a finger, "although he himself was long gone, his machinations put the proper people in the proper places to settle the Time of Troubles two years ago. Note," a second finger, "it is almost certain that his advice to Lady Talia ended her up in Petrella at exactly the right time, with exactly the right resources, to make a great impression on Gerth."

Loreline laughed. "Not that that blasted carriage didn't almost get her killed on the way here."

Zoysana shrugged. "I'd say, going by that evidence alone, that perhaps our sneaky friend is losing his touch." She shot a sharp glance at Arvent. "What's the chances this is our second bit of evidence?"

Loreline stared at the man as if reading an oracle. Finally, she shook her head. "No. Too general. He's either here for some specific deed which he won't tell us about, or for some more general situation he may be useful in at some later date."

"To us or to the Sivan?"

Loreline shrugged. "Until I hear otherwise, I assume we're still on the same side."

"Is it safe to assume that?" The younger woman peered hard at her friend's face.

Loreline's hands slapped the table. "By all the Gods, Zoe, how can I tell? You know what he always said. Emotional involvement is the first thing that messes up a good plan."

Zoysana smiled ruefully. "Well, if we're going against him, it will be by using all the techniques he taught us. Is that an advantage?"

"Who knows?" The taller woman turned to stare at the leather-clad man again. "It doesn't help us much with the question of the moment, though. What to do with him."

Zoysana turned, and her gaze took in Anine, standing at parade rest just inside the door. "Anine, do you have anything specific planned for the next few months?"

"No, Lady Zoe. I was waiting for orders." A light dawned. Her heart fell. "What did you have in mind?"

Zoe chuckled. "Don't look so worried. You are already involved. You seem to have a good handle on his behaviour. Why don't you take charge of him for a while, see how he turns out?"

Anine thought furiously. "I don't know what use I'd be, Lady Zoysana. What do I do with him?"

Zoysana shrugged. "I don't know either. We haven't been given much to guide us." She smiled up at the younger woman. "I hear you got pretty good at improvising, out there in the mountains this summer. Figure it out as you go along."

Anine drew herself up to her full height. "You can count on me, Lady Zoysana, to do my best to check out this recruit. I will have a full report of his capabilities and my impressions in one quarter-month. I guess we better fit him in somewhere. The Castle Guard? You don't want him in the Clan."

"Not the Clan. Ask Varli. Tell him I said to help. He'll find a position."

Anine could tell when an officer was finished. The decision was made; the problem was hers. She didn't need to be dismissed, but she did a parade turn anyway.

"Come on, Arvent. Let's get you settled in." She strode off, buoyed with a new sense of purpose, assuming he would follow.

A moment later he was beside her. "Well, I certainly wouldn't like to go through that too often."

She grinned. "What? Don't like bein' talked over like a side of beef or a bolt of cloth, and by two women, yet? And you bein' ignored like you ain't even there?"

"Something like that."

"Ah, don't let it bother you. Far as they're concerned, you're just a minor problem to be solved. Notice they dump it on the first person handy. Now you're a major problem for me. So far, my only one."

"Well, I'm sorry. As you noticed, I didn't have much choice."

"Don't be sorry. I had no idea what they was gonna do with me this winter. Trainin' recruits is part of the merc's life. I ain't what I'd call finished, myself, so I got a real good memory of what it's like. Course, you probably got a whole lot of experience at fightin' and the like."

He nodded. "Oh, yes. All sorts of training."

"So, the best thing we can do is run you through a bunch of the standard routines, see what you know, what you can do. I got seven days to do that, then I'll have to report to Zoysana and Loreline. Maybe that'll give them some ideas."

"And what now?"

"Siddown here on this wagon and we'll think a bit. Now, you aren't a regular recruit, so we won't worry about you callin'

26

everybody 'sir' or anythin'. If you're a spy, that won't do no good at all. So we'll have to have a story. Best stories are the ones that're mostly true. Got any ideas?"

"Sure. Say I'm a back-fence relative of Varlinden's, and you're helping out by showing me around."

She considered, shook her head. "True, maybe, but that puts too much on him. How about just someone he knew back home?"

"Fine with me. Doesn't help me figure out my status with everyone, though."

She grinned. "First lesson. Your family name don't mean a whole lot around this bunch. Too many mercs, Guides, and women doin' men's jobs. You take your hint from Zoysana. She treats everyone with respect and gets the same. Worked real well with her Clan and with the Inari this summer."

"What exactly is this Clan, anyway? In all my studies, I never heard of anybody from Petrella having clans."

She chuckled. "Nobody ever heard of a lot of the things that Zoe does. What happened was, she went up over the Barrier Range, took on the Inari in their own camp and gained some followers up there. Then, when Gerth needed somebody to counter the Inari raids, she and Jhanes and Varli put together this bunch that all had experience at Inari fightin'. Her tame Inari joined us, and we got down to business. Shoulda bin a bad year for raidin'. Three of the Inari tribes was pushin' for a full-scale invasion. Lucky for us, Zoe impressed Chuko the Great Potentara – that's their big leader – that tradin' was better for both of us than fightin' against each other. So both sides got richer and Zoysana's Clan kept the rebels off the backs of the farmers for the summer. Worked out great all round, and managed to make a real tight fightin' unit at the same time. Great troop to be in, Zoysana's Clan. Great leader, fine morale. Hope I stay in till I get killed."

He shot her a glance. "Till you get killed?"

She shrugged. "Sure. I'm a soldier. How many old mercs do you see around? Not too many. Actually, my odds of survivin' bin goin' up lately. The first year is the worst, 'n' then it gets better. If you can get some extra trainin' of some sort, you got a much better chance, of course. You don't have to hire out for the shock troops, you know?"

"So, you might not get killed after all."

"You laughin' at me?"

"No, no, I certainly was not. It's just such a different way of looking at your life. I've always assumed I was going to live. Not really much use in going on if you're not, it seems to me."

She shrugged again. "Well, that may be so, but it's also a great attitude for creatin' a coward."

"I hadn't looked at it from that point of view."

She grinned. "Second thing you've learned today. This may work out after all. Hey, there's Varli." She waved to the squire as he crossed the bailey, and he swerved in her direction. "Varli, I'd like you to meet a relative of yours."

Varli looked over the older man. "What side of the family?"

Arvent rocked his hand side to side. "Well, sort of your mother's, but I believe there's a connection on your father's side as well. My father is of the Kunuth family of Lladres. My mother is a Kelner of Velikii. I'm pretty sure they're cousins of yours, but a long way back."

Varli nodded. "Somewhere down the line. Not my specialty, I'm afraid. But don't worry about it. Who you're related to doesn't make too many waves around here, anyway."

Anine pursed her lips. "He also got connections to the Sivan. Apparently."

Varli looked again at the stranger. "Apparently?"

Arvent frowned. "They were good enough for Lady Zoysana and Loreline."

Varli caught on immediately. "But not for Anine?"

She shifted uncomfortably. "I bin told off to check him out. That means I don't take nothin' for granted. Zoe wants you to find a position for him, just temporary-like till we got a handle on what he's good for."

"Sure. I'll look into that." He pretended to write. "Number eighteen on my list."

She grinned suddenly. "We're not supposed to talk about him as if he isn't here. Makes him feel left out."

Varli pointed a finger at her. "They tend to do that to you, don't they? I've always figured that makes it easier for them to send you out to get killed."

Anine looked at the squire in surprise. "You've bin hangin' around the mercs too long, kid. You're gettin' your brain contaminated with all sorts of low-class ideas."

The boy shrugged. "Say, I was just headed to the kitchen for some grub. Want to come along and talk philosophy over a tankard? I find I think much better that way."

"You think you think much better. Well, I never turned down a mug of ale, so let's go. Step in line there, raw recruit, and we'll get you started down that long, steep, slope towards overweight and lazy. Happens every winter here. They got real good cooks."

Arvent shook his head and chuckled, and the three started across the bailey.

* * *

Varli took a long pull at his mug, then slammed it down and smacked his lips. "Now, that was a good lunch. What's on for you two for the afternoon?"

"We're gonna run Arvent through some trainin' routines, check out his fightin' level. What about you?"

Varli shook his head. "Once upon a time, I'd be after you like a rabbit with a fox behind. Unfortunately..."

She ruffled his hair. "Bein' the king's squire don't leave a whole lotta time for that kinda fun, hey?"

He nodded. "You got it. He's given me seventeen things to do before dinner. Eighteen, now."

"So why aren't you doing them?"

He grinned again, happily. "Oh, but I am. I'm seeing that the newcomers get settled." He shoved his stool back and rose. "But that leaves seventeen others. See you at dinner." He was gone before either of them could reply.

"Sort of a whirlwind, my cousin."

"You get used to him. Gets a lot done."

"And what about us?"

"You ready for some sword work? Let's see your blade."

She watched how easily he handled the heavy sword, laying it with proper respect on the table. She took a moment to regard it. It was similar to Zoysana's, but much larger: a long blade, narrow-tipped and sharp along half the back. A semi-basket hilt told her that he used the tip as well as the edge and didn't expect to have mailed gloves in every fight. An unusual element was a wider plate on the back of the blade, down near the hilt, probably for use with the left hand. In all, a serviceable and versatile weapon.

"Very pretty." She stood. "Put it away. We practise with wands here. Good ones. Proper size and balance. Hurt a bit when you score, so it keeps us honest. Any other weapons?" She glanced sideways at him as they left the kitchen. "That you'll admit to, anyways?"

He motioned towards his high-topped riding boot. "I have a dagger, but I don't usually use it. I'm not really strong enough to use this big blade the way it should be done, not in any long battle, so I support with my left hand in several moves. The dagger's easy to reach if I need it."

"Hmm. Unorthodox, as Jhanes would say. Fair enough for the kind of work you'll probably be doin'. Staff?"

"I use a staff. Double sticks, too. I've worked with a lot of stuff you just find lying around."

She nodded. "Good idea, for a spy."

"Who says I'm a spy?"

She stopped, forcing him to turn and look at her. "Look, let's get this straight right from the start. You're somethin' outa whack around here. We don't know exactly who you are, or why you're here. You gotta be ready for a bit of suspicion, because as long as you won't say anythin' more, you're gonna get lots of it. That's the way it's gonna be, and there's nothin' anyone here wants to do about it. That clear?"

He held up his hands helplessly. "What can I say?"

"Nuthin'. 'Cause anythin' you did say, nobody's gonna believe. Trust is somethin' you earn, and comin' from where you did, the way you did, you got a long way to go. So, let's not worry about it, let's just do today's work today. Ask me in a couple of years if you've made any progress on the trust part."

He grinned as they turned out the postern gate to the practise field just under the castle wall. "Only two years in purgatory? I can take that."

She laughed and kept walking.

Sword practice was no surprise. She could tell from his warmup that he was a superior swordsman, and from the moment they first touched practise blades, she knew he was far in advance of her. They sparred for a few parries, then she stepped back and grounded her tip.

"All right. I've got that figured out. Where did you learn to fight like that?"

He grinned, saluting with a special twist of his sword, a move she recognized.

"Oh. With family in Llandres, I might have known you'd bin at Pertin's school. I'll do my best to give you a workout, at least."

She gritted her teeth and prepared herself. This might not be fun, but it would be at least instructive. She enjoyed working with a good swordsman because it improved her own skills. As long as it didn't hurt too much.

To her surprise, it didn't go that badly. She took his hint about the strength of his sword arm and used her weight to full advantage. She anticipated the unusual double-hand moves, and worked to find a position where he couldn't use them. It seemed his lower right was the open spot, and, having received only three or four serious pokes from his tip, managed to score a decent slash to the outside of the thigh. She pulled the stroke at the last moment, but she knew it hurt.

He battled on as if nothing had happened, and she pushed back, trying in vain to get his guard to loosen. It was useless; any time she thought she had an inside line developing, he countered with an attack that drove her back.

Then her opponent came on the offensive, and she had to mind her footing. His attack was rapid but not flashy. Serviceable and competent. Very competent. He scored several more times to her arm and legs before they both stopped, dripping sweat.

"Good round." He saluted her casually with his free hand.

Maybe his sword arm is as tired as mine.

"Very good. I haven't had that much fun since I last sparred with Jhanes."

"Who's he? I've heard his name a few times."

"You're about to find out. I only mentioned him because he's headed this way. Hey, Jhanes. I thought you'd be down the road to your precious Sarha last night."

The big soldier grinned. "Soon's I can, Anine. Soon's I can. Who's this?"

"Arvent, this is Jhanes, second in command of the Clan. Former Inari, former mercenary, former hill farmer..."

31

"...and former second in command. I'm an innkeeper again, starting as soon as I get everything cleared up around here."

"And this is Arvent. Some kinda old friend of Varli's, sent out from Llandres for trainin' where the fightin' is real. You want any more than that, you'll have to ask the Lady Herself."

Jhanes regarded the newcomer. "I might just do that. Anine checking you out?"

Anine answered. "Aye, but I'm not competent in swordplay. Could you step in?"

The big man grinned. "I saw you working him over pretty good. I guess I could match up, now that he's tired." He took the practise wand that Anine offered and stepped back, saluting formally. Arvent replied with his characteristic salute, and the former mercenary nodded as he moved in.

This exchange did not go as it had with Anine. These were two top fighters, testing each other without holding back. Anine watched the play closely, then with more interest. Jhanes was certainly the more experienced swordsman, but the man in the brown leathers had a few tricks of his own.

When they had sparred a short while, Jhanes stepped back and saluted. Arvent mirrored the gesture.

"I always said Pertin trains 'em well. You've picked up a bit since, though."

Arvent grinned. "Pertin always said his training was only a start."

"Thanks for the workout. No more time for fun. See you around, Arvent. You too, Anine."

"Say hello to your wife for me, Jhanes. I never met her, but you told enough stories about her, I feel like I know her."

"Nothing more boring than a newlywed on patrol, hey?" He grinned sheepishly, then strode away across the practise field.

"Newlywed?"

"Aye, it's some love story. He got hooked up just last spring with an innkeeper woman out north of here. Can't say enough about her. Her brother Ferlen's in the Clan, too. Good type. Trapper. Keeps to himself usually, but a good man, specially for trackin', of course." She nodded thoughtfully. "Jhanes is probably the best officer I ever had. Always knows what the troops are thinkin'. He'll be goin' home for the winter, now, and good luck to him."

"So are we going to try anything else?"

She considered. "No, that was enough for today. I'm not gonna kill myself, now that we're not fightin'. I'll bring a coupla staves tomorrow. I got a special one, myself, and I'd like to use it. Let's find Varli again. I forgot to ask him about puttin' you up. Now you're signed on, the king'd go for your room at the inn, but not if we can put you in the barracks."

"Well, like I said, I liked the inn fine, but I'm sure there's lots of room at the castle."

She caught the confident grin, and it grated somehow. "You won't be in the castle after curfew till we got a better handle on you. There's plentya places outside the walls."

He did not respond, and they walked the rest of the way to the castle gate in silence. When they reached the courtyard, she turned to him. "I've got some things to take care of. Why'n't you take a break, and I'll see you at supper."

He nodded, and she strode up the stairs into the administrative wing of the castle. Once she was in the shadow under the arch, she turned to make sure he was gone back down the street into the town. Then she continued to Loreline's office.

Sure enough, the older woman was at her desk. She looked up and smiled. "Got a preliminary report already?" She took in Anine's expression and sobered. "What's up?"

Anine shook her head. "Why did Zoysana give that guy to me?"

Loreline smiled again. "Probably because you don't like him."

"I don't dislike him! Well, not exactly…"

"I didn't say you disliked him. I said you didn't like him. That means you'll do a much better job at checking him out. Found something already, haven't you?"

Anine nodded hesitantly. "It's just a feeling, you know?"

"And you don't want to say, because it might be dislike, and not fair to him."

"Somethin' like that."

"Anine, I'm in charge of the safety of the whole kingdom. It's my job to be suspicious. You bring me the information, I'll tell you if it's suspicious or not. What is this feeling you have?"

Anine stepped over to the tall stool Zoysana usually used. "Fine, since you put it like that. I've always bin a bit careful around him from the beginnin'. You understand, that may be just a girl's reaction to keep herself from gettin' involved with a handsome man."

"You think he's handsome?"

She grinned. "He ain't, but he's handsomer than any man I'll ever get." Immediately, she became serious. "But I was watchin' real close, and I hope I'm not seein' what I thought I might. I think he's connin' us."

"You do?"

"Yes. I wondered why Zoe was so hard on him, but I think she's pickin' up the same thing. Could be he's playin' some game, deep or not, but he hasn't come near to showin' us who he really is."

Loreline smiled. "Isn't that what you just said you'd been doing with him? Holding back, not giving out, keeping your defenses up?"

"I know. That's what made me worried I was makin' it all up. But sword practice today made it all clear."

"What kind of a swordsman is he?"

"Excellent. He's so good, he can make himself look average and nobody'd ever know."

"What do you mean?"

She shook her head. "You got no trainin' so it's hard to explain. When he was fightin' me, it was obvious from the first touch that he was superior. So he was holdin' back, or he'da beat me quick. I can see that. But then Jhanes come along, and I asked him, casual-like, to have a go. And you know, the moment he figured how good Jhanes was, he changed. He changed his style and his speed and everythin'. He made himself just good enough to be a little worse than the officer.

"But I'd already fought him, so I knew. He made a coupla mistakes that I knew he knew better, if you follow what I mean."

"I think I do. Did you get a chance to talk to Jhanes after?"

"No, he was busy, so he took off. He's headin' home real soon."

"I think this is a bit more urgent than that. Can you check around, and bring him here?"

To Anine's surprise, when she returned with the big soldier in tow, Zoysana was in the office as well.

"So, Jhanes, what do you have to say about the Sivan's new protégé?"

The big man grinned. "This is another of the Sivan's tricks, is it? Well, he just may be losing his grip after all. Saving your presence, Loreline. There's definitely something going on, there."

"What do you mean?"

"I'm not used to being patronized. Especially on the practise field."

The two women looked at each other. Zoe spoke. "Patronized? You're going to have to explain."

"He's some kind of expert swordsman, and he doesn't want us to know it. Sure, he trained with Pertin, but he's done a lot of work with several masters of far higher level. I could tell."

Loreline nodded. "That jibes with what Anine said."

Jhanes turned to her. "You noticed it too? Good for you. It wasn't that obvious."

She shrugged. "Well, I'd just sparred with him, and somethin' didn't look right."

Zoysana slapped the table. "All right. So this is getting interesting. Well, if the Sivan's involved, that's no surprise. And – saving your presence, Loreline – I guess that maybe speaks to whether the Sivan is losing his grip."

Loreline grinned. "Stop worrying about my feelings, you two. And don't look at me like that. I don't know any more than you do. The package was personal."

Zoe grinned. "I'm glad. For you." She turned to the other two. "Jhanes, there's no need for you to hang around for this. It isn't your problem, and there are plenty of soldiers here if we need them. Go home to Sarha. She needs you more than we do. I'll be out in a couple of quarters. It's a month or more before the rains get serious, and I have a lot of ground to cover in that time. With Tadeo back home in Kyabra, I have to do it all myself. We'll leave this little problem in Anine's capable hands.

"Anine, you can report to Loreline. This is her problem anyway. Keep on as you have been."

Anine knew that tone, and figured she had time for about one question. Better make it a good one. "Do we give him a position in the castle? I was gonna barrack him outside."

"Good. Until we know more, that's the place for him. Loreline can decide to move him if we need him. Figure out some position that gives him enough money to live on, and that's all."

Anine grinned. "Swordmaster. We're short till Maura's hand heals up completely, and it'll keep him on his toes, tryin' not to show himself."

They all chuckled, and the meeting broke up. As they were leaving, Zoysana stopped Anine with a hand on her sleeve. "Oh, I just remembered. Talia is going out to Codding the day after tomorrow. She asked for you to go along."

"Me? Why?"

"It's sort of a formal occasion but social, too. Probably some hunting, riding out, that sort of thing. She doesn't know any of these people very well, and I want her to have some protection of her own. She said she feels better with one of her friends along," Zoysana grinned, "especially someone bigger than her."

"What do I do with Arvent?"

"He's an adult. He can take care of himself for a couple of days."

"Great. I could do with a holiday."

"Is child-minding getting you down already?"

"No, but a change is good any time."

Anine chuckled to herself as she strode out into the bailey. *A career as a lady in waiting to a princess ain't quite my style, but at least the food'll be good!*

4. PACKING

As the weeks went by, Anine grew more comfortable with her charge, but became more and more convinced that he was hiding something. It wasn't only his swordplay. He seemed so practised at disguising himself that he never showed anything like his true personality to anyone. He blended in with every group, but was careful not to get involved in any real friendships. He spent exactly enough time with Varli to support their story that they were casual acquaintances from the Duchies, but no more than that.

As a result, he was thrown into Anine's company more and more often. She was the only one he could let down his guard with, because she knew who he was.

Well, I think I know who he is.

In fact, though he did talk more openly with her, she still felt a barrier around him, like slick stone. He spoke freely until the questions reached a certain personal level, then he simply changed the topic. He allowed a certain amount of physical contact, then slipped out of the way if it got too close. The situation got more and more frustrating, because she was thrown into his company as well. Most of the Clan had returned to their real positions in the realm. The mercenaries were spread around on their duties, as was Maura. Anine realized that she was lonely, so she mentioned it to Loreline one day.

"I thought I oughta warn you."

The spy mistress looked up, concern in her eyes. "I didn't think a bit of loneliness would bother you that much."

"It ain't that. If I'm lonely, and I spend all my time with Arvent...well, I just don't think that's such a good idea, you know?"

"Oh, I see. You think it weakens your effectiveness at your duties."

"Weakens? I'd say worse than that."

"You falling for this guy?"

Anine shot her a look, but Loreline seemed to be serious. "Naw, I doubt it. But I am startin' to enjoy his company a bit too much."

"Want a break?"

"Well...I didn't come here lookin' for a holiday..."

"I know that, but I've got some important messages need taking, and I want two messengers for security."

"But if Arvent and me take the messages…"

"Not you and Arvent. I'm already sending Ferlen. You could ride herd on him."

"Ferlen? Why would he need me?"

"Well, maybe I'm just being my usual cautious self. Or maybe there's some strange things happening up in the hills. But I have the impression I'm missing some information. Nothing serious yet, but I get this hunch something's not getting through. I've done pretty well at this trade, paying attention to feelings like that.

"I don't want to advertise that I've got agents out. So, instead of Ferlen by himself, I'll send you along as protective colouring. Why don't you two go out in a wagon, like a couple travelling? Take your time, look around, see what you pick up. It'll give you a nice holiday from your chore here."

Anine nodded. "Fair enough. Ferlen's a good man. It'll be a pleasure to watch his back. Anythin' I can do to help."

"Yes, he's a good man. With the winter rains coming, it won't be an easy trip; I've at least routed you past his sister's inn, so he gets a family visit out of it."

Anine laughed. "And I get a holiday, so I can't complain either. You're about as sly as Zoysana."

Loreline smiled. "If it keeps the troops happy…"

"You know what Varli says about that."

"No, I don't. Should I?"

"He says if the troops are happy, they march off to get killed easier."

"Sounds like Varli, all right. Ever wonder what it's going to be like when he has to take on his responsibilities instead of playing the fool?"

Anine shook her head. "He's already way past that. You didn't see him in camp this summer. He's what mercs call a 'facilitator'. Gets things done, finds stuff you need, knows where everythin' is." She grinned. "Includin' where the hideout daggers're hid."

Loreline nodded. "I suspected as much. He's been with the common troops too long, though. He's got to learn leadership."

"He's learnin' from the best."

"Zoysana? She's unconventional."

"Aye, but Jhanes is pretty straightforward: years of merc trainin'. If I had a new kid who was officer material, I'd want him with that pair."

"His father will be glad to hear that."

"Wait a bit!" Anine held out a hand in warning. "You ain't sendin' my opinions to Varli's father, are you?"

Loreline smiled again. "Don't worry. I'm not using you to spy on your fellow troops. It's just that his father's been wondering how he was doing."

"So you dig around and come up with me. Say, now that's a turnaround. I was accusin' him of makin' a report on me, and now look what's happened."

Loreline smiled, then regarded Anine. "You don't miss much, do you?"

"A girl's gotta keep her eyes open." She shrugged. "But I doubt if any lord of the Inner Duchies is gonna listen to anythin' I say."

"You'd be surprised. Varli's father understands soldiers. He'd be happy to hear an opinion from a trusted fellow trooper of Varli's. However, I won't be putting it to him exactly that way. I can present it in more general terms."

"Probably better that way," she paused, "if I had anythin' to say about it. Which I don't."

Loreline merely smiled. "So, get in touch with Ferlen, and I'll let you know when I've got the messages ready."

Anine restrained herself from saluting and left.

She took a new look at Ferlen as she sat across from him at dinner that night. Spare and dark-haired, about her height. Heavy eyebrows shading deep eyes with a twinkle she hadn't noticed before. He had spent the summer scouting for the Clan, so he hadn't been in camp much, and she'd had no chance to form an opinion. He didn't look like he'd cause her any trouble on the road, but you never knew.

"So. We're takin' a trip together."

She nodded. "I guess you know more'n me."

"Not much. Loreline just gave me the general idea. Whataya think of this idea of us goin' out as a couple, travelling?"

She grinned and speared her eating dagger at him. "As long as you don't get any ideas about makin' it too realistic!"

He raised his hands in defense. "No problem. I've seen you work with that big sword. No, I mean the idea of a couple travelling."

She shook her head. "I dunno. Why are we travellin'? Folks of our class don't just go on trips. We gotta be goin' somewheres, comin' home from somewheres…"

"…or have a reason for travelling around."

"Like pedlars or somethin'?"

"I don't know if we want to get that fancy. I'm not a pedlar, and we could lose a lot of the king's money if we tried actually trading. As well as looking pretty silly."

She nodded. "Who do we chat up to see if there's anythin' that really needs deliverin'? Somethin' they'd be sendin' out anyways. Maybe for the outposts."

"Good idea. There's that new outfit quartered with my sister since the summer, and that's where we're headed. I'll check around tomorrow. Why'n't you talk to Loreline on the same thing?"

"Sure. We'll need some cash."

"We already have that arranged." He grinned. "Don't you worry your pretty little head about the money, my dear."

She waved the knife again with a mock scowl. "And don't you go patronizing me, my darlin'. I picked that 'patronizing' word up this summer, and I figure it's a real good one."

He nodded. "Nice to have that straight, anyways. Shall I be the complete apron-tied husband, then?"

"Naw, I don't want to play any games. Let's just be who we are and see how it goes. It's gonna be hard enough to fake the rest of it."

"Right. I have no idea about becoming a spy. Let's not try to be too good at it."

"I'm with you on that. This outfit, you don't wanta look good at anythin' you don't like doin', 'cause you'll end up doin' it, you wanta or not."

"Egalitarian bunch, aren't they?"

"What's that 'egalitarian' mean? Anythin' to do with 'equal'?"

He nodded. "That's what it means. They treat everybody equal. Unusual, out here in the southern wilds."

"Sounds like a good merc outfit to me. Let's you and me work the same way. Egalitarian. I like that."

"Suits me fine. I have no doubt you always carry your share."

"Oh, I do that, all right. Say, where do you get big words like that? Most the time you sound like me."

"Books."

"You read?"

"Aye. My dad ran an inn. There were always a couple of books around. I had to learn to read, write and figure a bit. For running the inn, you know. Then I went trapping, he died, and my sister took over the inn. I still carry a few good books in the winter. Helps when you're snowed in, weeks at a time."

He glanced over casually. "You?"

"Just a bit. I bin tryin' to learn. Winters, half-pay duty, you know? Zoysana's got me started with some books from her Archives, and Loreline's real good about helpin' when I don't understand."

"If you want, we can keep it up on the road."

She smiled. "I'd take that real kind, if you don't mind."

He shrugged. "Lots of time, nothing to do."

"Good enough."

She left the meal in high spirits. *Sounds like an interesting trip. Ferlen seems a good companion.* She was surprised to feel a pang of distaste when Arvent stepped in beside her as she crossed the bailey. She glanced at him, feeling guilty.

"I guess nobody told you. Change in plans."

He raised his eyebrows. "What kind of change?"

"I gotta run an errand for Loreline. Goin' out on the road for a few quarters. I'm not sure who's gonna work with you."

His smile didn't make it to his eyes. "Considering how little we're doing together, I guess that won't be too difficult."

She slapped his shoulder. "Hey, call it progress. Loreline doesn't think I need to keep such a close eye on you."

"I guess I could look at it that way." He glanced over at her. "Where are you going?"

She shrugged, trying to sound casual. "Just deliveries, I think to some of the troops stationed around."

"Going by yourself?"

"No, with Ferlen."

"You mentioned him. The trapper?"

"Well, he used to be a trapper, but he signed on with the Clan this spring, and I don't see him makin' any move to the hills this fall. His sister's the innkeeper Jhanes's married to."

The brown man nodded. "I remember. Trust him, then, do you?"

"Trust him with what?"

"You know, on the road together, all that."

41

She stopped and looked at him straight. "You really think I'd have that kind of problem?"

He glanced away. "You never know."

"Thanks, but yes, I trust him. This is business, and Zoysana trusts him. He's one of the Clan. He'll treat me all right."

They walked on, and she glanced at her companion. It was the first time he had said anything even a bit personal to her. *Makes you wonder what's goin' on behind that placid face.*

"Want a little swordplay?"

Stranger and stranger. "I don't think so, not against you, right after a meal." She found a smile for him. "My stomach don't work so good when I'm in pain."

He smiled back. "Another time, then." A moment later, he stopped.

"You know, the next time, if they send you out? Maybe I could go."

"Gettin' itchy feet?"

He shrugged. "I don't mind teaching the recruits, but I could use a break. It would be easier with you, because I wouldn't have to be so careful."

She looked directly at him. "Don't look to me like you're any less careful around me. Can't get a direct piece of information out of you. If I ask, you close up like a clam. Whatever a clam is."

"It's a creature that lives in the ocean. Got two halves, like this," he demonstrated with his hands, "a real hard shell. When danger threatens, it closes the shell together, and nothing can hurt it."

"Oh, two shells. Now I know what that means. Thanks. Yep, that's you. Any danger of givin' away information, and you clam up tight."

He shifted his feet uneasily. "Well, I've been trained, you know, and I don't know who to trust. So I just keep my head down."

"Well, sooner or later, you have to trust someone or you're gonna be very lonely. You're also not gonna get a whole lot of extra trainin' here, because if we don't get somethin' out of you soon, Loreline and Zoe ain't gonna trust you as far as you can spit, and that's it. You'll be a couple of years sittin' here on the doorstep of the castle trainin' the recruits until you get tired of it and run back to your Sivan with your ears pulled back and your tail down."

"I don't know what to do."

"Look, I seen you fittin' in with everybody, but only enough to be allowed into the group and no more. You never let anybody close, never hold out a hand. You're accepted by everybody, but you gotta be the loneliest guy in the whole city. You been tryin' so hard to not be noticed that you succeeded way more than you ever wanted to."

"So, what do I do about it?"

"Go make some friends. Talk to people. Tell them somethin' about yourself. Better if it's true, but it don't matter. Better to be figured as a liar than not figured at all."

"I thought maybe I had made a friend."

She thought. "Me? How can you call me a friend? I don't know nothin' about you. All right. You're a fine swordsman, and you're supposta be a friend of this Sivan, who I never met. I suppose you're a pleasant guy, but I don't really know if that's just an act, too.

"You know, I hear there's this animal they got, out east of here. Lives in the desert. Never seen one myself, so I don't know if it's real. They say it can change the colour of its skin to match the rocks around it. Not sure I believe in it, but that's what you're like."

"A chameleon. Yes, I have tried to be like that."

"But when it comes to people, if they don't notice you, then…they don't notice you. And there you are."

"I see what you mean."

"So, I'm takin' off for a few quarters. Try it out on somebody. Talk to people."

"Thanks, Anine. Maybe I will." He turned and strode down towards the village.

Anine reviewed the conversation. Could anyone really be that dense? Maybe. *Or is it like his swordplay with Jhanes? Is he setting his skill level just below mine, so I won't see him as a threat?* She shook her head and turned back to her room in the barracks along the inner curtain wall. *For a month or so, he ain't my problem.*

* * *

The next day the two new partners met in Loreline's office.

"Here's the map. You take a swing to the northeast, as far as Jaspen. Either of you been out that way?"

They both shook their heads, and Loreline continued. "So nobody knows you, and you can keep the 'married couple' disguise. Then

43

you turn west towards Lanil's Rock. When you get near the inn, you'll have to change your story. Maybe Anine can be a mercenary, going out to join up with the soldiers stationed at The Rock."

"And what happens once we get to the inn, and I don't join up?"

Loreline grinned. "If I tell you, it won't be half so effective as something you think up yourselves."

"You sound just like Zoe."

"Learned from the best." The woman's face became serious, and Anine knew where that thought had taken her. "After that, you can come back south again, and Anine can be the reverse: a soldier coming in off a tour of duty. Make sure you keep your stories straight. We might send you out again."

"I'm not gonna get in the habit of spyin', Loreline, I'm too easy to remember. Plus, I don't like it."

The spy mistress smiled wanly. "Maybe you'll enjoy it so much you'll want to go back. In any case, remember who you were and where as well as you can."

"Fine. We'll have plenty of time to go over our plans, once we're on the road." Ferlen leaned forward. "What kind of a cargo do you have for us?"

"Winter supplies for the troops. Jam, pickles, cured hams, blankets, that sort of thing. Too late in the season for a heavy freight wagon, but a light load in a small rig should get through, and we need those supplies out there before the rains mess the roads up. You'll be coming back empty, so as the roads get worse, you'll have less trouble."

"What kind of rig have you got for us?"

"A light freight wagon with room to sleep in, if you need to. Team of good horses, not pretty, but with stamina. You'll like them."

Ferlen nodded. "How are you with horses, Anine?"

"Brought up on a farm."

"Excellent. You're in charge, then."

"Wait a minute. Who says?"

Loreline broke in. "That's one point we better get straight. This is a military operation, and somebody has to be in charge. Who?"

Everyone looked with surprise at the pointing fingers.

"All right, both of you chose the other." Loreline grinned. "No officer material, here?"

The trapper shrugged. "I don't do so well talking with people."

Anine shook her head. "I wouldn't mind, but when it comes to dealin' with the local folk, they're gonna expect the man to be in charge. Too complicated otherwise."

Loreline raised her eyebrows in a question to Ferlen. Finally, he nodded. "I see your point. All right. I guess I've been doing this messenger bit some already, so I've got more experience. But Anine, you can deal with people most of the time. That's not unusual."

"Sure." Anine nodded, then grinned. "Best leader is the one who didn't want to lead."

"Sometimes. Just remember you're second in command."

She laughed. "And last." *Yes, this looks to be an interesting trip.* Then she remembered their true purpose. "Now, what are we really lookin' for?"

Loreline knitted her fingers together in front of her. "I've been doing my analysis, and I've figured out what was bothering me. We've been losing more of our messages than usual. Not that strange, with our most trusted messenger chasing Inari all summer." She grinned at the trapper.

"However, we've also had some bandit raids; again, not a whole lot more than you might expect, with the king's attention on the South. However..." Loreline looked at the two across the table.

Anine leaned forward. "Let me guess. They match."

"Exactly. I checked the times, as near as I could, and if we're about to have a raid, then the information is cut off for a few days. No messengers messed with, you understand. Just held up a while, or their gear stolen, or any of a number of things that could naturally happen."

"So you figure there's a pack of bandits has real good reconnaissance."

Loreline shook her head. "It's not so simple. These have been happening all over the northern half of the kingdom. There isn't a bandit group that big, or we'd know. Not that organized. Zoysana has been out checking, and her methods are pretty thorough."

Loreline got up and walked over to shut the door. When she returned, she sat forward and spoke a bit softer. "Now we get to the point where you have to make a decision. This isn't just an easy drive around the country."

45

"We knew it would be dangerous. That's not a problem."

She shook her head. "That's not all, Ferlen. To do this task properly, you have to be told things that most people don't know. You've already been in this situation, running messages this spring. Anine, you understand if you decide to stay in this, there are things which you will not be allowed to tell anyone?"

Anine nodded. There was nothing to say.

"Are you still willing?"

"Of course."

"Ferlen?"

"Certainly."

"I thought so. Well, here's what the king thinks, and we all agree. There are quite a few people around who are not happy with Petrella's recent successes. Think about it from their side. If a realm which is already renowned for its warriors and its war horses manages to deal with the barbarians on its frontier, make an alliance with its nearest neighbour, subdue its closest enemy and form a lucrative trading partnership with a powerful realm nearby, what might it do next?"

"Expand."

"Exactly."

"And are we gonna expand?"

Loreline smiled. "Anine, if we were, I certainly wouldn't give that information to an agent about to be sent out into the countryside. As it happens, we're not, and you can believe that as you like. Gerth and Kenna both think that trading superiority, brought about by less war rather than more, is in our best interest. The Sivan and Zoysana agree. Around here, that makes it official policy."

"How do you feel about it?"

Loreline stared at the trapper, then at Anine again. "You're going to be a fine pair, I can see. Each one more insubordinate than the other."

"You didn't answer the question."

"Did you hear what I just said?"

He shrugged. "Sure, but I didn't pay it any mind. Zoysana's Clan is the most insubordinate bunch you ever run across."

"You couldn't run a merc outfit like that. It'd fall apart in a month."

Loreline sighed. "And well I know it. And I will answer your question. I agree as well, of course. Now, back to business.

"We think one of the nearby duchies, or maybe a group of them, has sent their agents in to find out what's going on and stir up a little trouble. Maybe a few troops disguised as bandits. Nobody's too upset about that, mind you. It's what I would have done."

"But that's no reason to let them get away with it." The trapper's slim face took on a predatory look.

"Exactly. Zoysana can't be everywhere at once, so you're going to cover the area I showed you. Remember, you're not out to solve any problems. Just bring back the information. We don't want to tip them off that we know about them."

"So, we ain't takin' any action. Bring the information to headquarters, and let the brass make the choices."

Loreline smiled. "And that may be one reason why I'm sending you, Anine. The trapper, here, may be too independent. We need a mercenary's discipline to combine with his leaning towards improvisation."

"Then why isn't she the leader?"

Loreline looked at him. "I'm going to let you figure that out yourselves. For the moment, everything is organized. You can load the wagon tomorrow and leave the next day. Any reason that's a problem?"

They both shook their heads.

"That's fine, then. I wish you luck. With your combined abilities, I don't think you'll run into any problems you can't handle."

Anine turned in the doorway. "Clothes."

Loreline snapped her fingers. "Of course. I don't think Ferlen needs anything other than his normal wear. You'll need some women's clothes, and I bet you have no idea where to find them."

"Huh. I was just wondering if it would be a bad idea to go out and get them myself."

Loreline considered for a slow breath. "I don't think it would cause a problem. We have to assume there are spies around the castle, but they have no reason to be watching you. It's only after you leave that they might get suspicious."

"Fair enough. Ferlen, darling, do you have enough cash to buy your dear wife a dress or two?"

Loreline laughed and pushed them out the door. "I don't get in the way of married people when they quarrel."

"Who says we're quarrelling?"

"Aye. Wait till he sees the cost. Then we'll quarrel."

He reached into his belt pouch and took out a purse, spilled coins into his palm. "Take what you need. We'll need the rest for travel money."

"What about food, cooking supplies?"

"Already taken care of."

"Good. You take care of the cooking, and I'll take care of the horses."

"I help with the horses and cook, you clean up after."

This was the sort of bargaining that happened in every mercenary troop, and she felt, again, that it was going to be a good mission.

She picked a coin from his hand, then glanced up at his face. "By the time I get a coupla dresses from this, there won't be enough change to rattle."

He stowed the rest without comment.

Later, as she strode through the marketplace, she allowed herself a private laugh. Here she was, Big Anine the farmer's plain daughter, going with the king's money to buy herself two dresses. More than she had ever owned at one time. Maybe even three. She considered the coins in her belt pouch and the length of the journey, and decided on two.

Thinking of the money set her usual wariness into play, and her eyes scanned the market around her. Was that a small brown head ducking behind the jeweller's stall? She walked on and, sure enough, a slim figure followed her. She wove through the market, making sure to visit several different booths. Once her pursuer had relaxed, it was easy to set a trap. She disappeared behind a hanging carpet, then sprinted three steps back and came around the corner to see Marel standing, looking around with a puzzled frown. Her hand closed on the nape of his neck and he froze.

"And what are you about, young man?"

"Nothin', Anine." His head shook so hard it looked like it would fall off his scrawny neck. "I was just in the market checkin' out prices."

"You was checkin' somethin' else out. Who for? Arvent?"

48

His eyes dropped, his look turning sullen. "I was checkin' the prices."

"Or were you lookin' to finger somethin'?"

She caught a sly look that disappeared as soon as it crossed his face.

"I wouldn't do nothin' like that."

"Sure, you wouldn't." She released him. "I'm workin' for the king, you know. I see you doin' anythin' wrong, I gotta turn you in. You scram, now."

He disappeared into the crowd so fast she couldn't be sure which way he went. As she continued, she thought it through. The boy had been following her, and Arvent was the only one she knew who would have hired him. She doubted that Marel would admit to being caught, so she was one ahead in that game. She would tell Loreline before she left, and leave it at that. Watching her backtrail, she proceeded to the clothing stall she had in mind. There she purchased, for a fair price, two plain brown dresses of good quality, which had belonged to a large, short, woman. This meant a length of cloth to adjust them to her height, and some thread to match.

She chuckled as she thought of Arvent and his nondescript clothing. So this was how spies worked. Then she thought of Arvent in terms of what Loreline had told them. What if he wasn't from the Sivan at all? Worse, what if he was from the Sivan, but allied with the enemy? No wonder Loreline and Zoe were being so cautious. She slapped the hilt of her sword. *By the Lady, I hate spying.*

First thing thenext morning, she hit the stables to check the horses. Ferlen found her there going over their hooves. They were shod with old but serviceable iron as she had expected. Likewise, the horses themselves were not anything to look at twice, but similar to any of a score or more teams you might find pulling the lighter freight wagons up and down any road of the realm on a given day. A pair of mismatched bays, too small for the big freight wagons but cheaper to feed.

"They'll do."

She nodded. "They'll do fine if we don't pack too heavy."

"Wagon's around the corner. Want to show me how to harness up and we'll take it over and load?"

In spite of his jesting, Ferlen did his share of the harnessing job, and soon he was skillfully weaving the team up the busy street behind the castle to the quartermaster's warehouse. Their load was waiting: a small pile of boxes and bales, not too heavy, each labelled clearly with its destination. Ferlen checked over the list and climbed into the wagon bed.

Without comment, Anine stepped over and hefted the first bale. He had done a good job of backing the new team in close to the pile, so the loading went quickly. As soon as everything was in the wagon, she joined him in the bed.

"How have you arranged it?"

"The cargo: last out, first in. Our daily supplies are here, in this locker. Camping equipment on the other side. Cooking stuff in the box hanging under the wagon bed. Here's the wagon tarp. Ties in this box."

She nodded. "Personal space?"

He showed her two small trunks, tucked on either side near the tailgate. "Easiest to get at here. At the inns, we can bring them inside."

"Weapons?" She was already moving forward.

"Under the seat, close to hand." There were two half-spears and a good bow, a short, rider's recurve with a sheaf of arrows. Barbed war heads, she noticed.

She approved. "Looks about right. I'll keep my sword there, too. No need for anyone to realize it's mine."

He grinned. "Once they do, we're long past worrying about what they know."

"Right. Anyone has to find that out, either us or them's gonna be dead before too long."

They swung up on the seat and laughed as they both reached for the reins. He took them. "We'll have to straighten that out."

She shook her head. "Any couple carryin' freight are gonna share the work." She grinned. "You did a fine job of backin' that team in there next to the goods. You sure you don't wanta take a turn with the horses?"

"I don't know. Can you cook?"

"I'm a farm girl, remember?"

"Oh. I do tend to forget."

"A compliment?"

"You can take it as such."

She raised the pitch of her voice. "Oh, my, I got me a flatterer for a husband."

He chuckled and slapped the reins on the horses' rumps. The clatter of the iron-shod wheels on cobblestones drowned out further conversation.

Of course, they sat together at supper, there being plans to be made and details to discuss. It was only after they were almost finished eating that she noticed Arvent seated one table over, by himself.

Feeling a bit guilty, she caught his eye and nodded a friendly greeting. After a moment, he got up and strolled over.

"Arvent, I don't think you know Ferlen. One of the Clan's scouts."

Arvent held out his hand. "Glad to meet you, Ferlen. I've heard about your tracking skills."

The former trapper ducked his head, perhaps embarrassed. "Thanks."

"So, you're taking Anine out on the road for a while."

"Seems like."

"Well, take good care of her."

Ferlen looked at the brown man, bemused. "Oh, I intend to." He regained his usual composure and grinned. "Actually, I'm hoping she takes care of me."

Arvent smiled wanly. "Aye, she can do that. She's getting pretty good with that sword."

"You going to sit down?"

"No," the swordsman turned partly away, "I've got a few things to do. I was just leaving. Thought I'd stop by and say, 'good luck,' that's all."

Anine took the hand he reached out. "Thanks, Arvent. We'll see you in a month or so."

"Good enough. Nice meeting you, Ferlen." He made a casual salute and turned away.

"Seems decent enough."

Anine nodded, thinking. How much did Ferlen need to know? Enough to be a bit on guard. "He's sort of on probation around here."

"How come?"

"Well, he comes with some kind of recommendation from some friend of Loreline's, but she's not so sure of him. I been keepin' an eye on him for her, you know?"

"I wondered, seeing the two of you together so much."

"You mean you noticed?"

He grinned. "Sure. Believe me, every man in the Clan knows what every other man is doing. The women, it goes double."

She felt warmth creeping up her neck. "I guess so."

"Sure. You know what would happen, some guy started messing around with one of you?"

"I always figured you guys thought of us as just another soldier."

He shook his head. "Anybody who thinks that doesn't know men. Oh, sure, you and Maura, for example. You aren't what most people would think of as romantic or anything. And both of you more than carry your share. But the guys still keep their eyes open, you know?"

She sighed. "I know. I mean, we fight like crazy to be treated as equals, but I guess I should be pleased, somebody like me..."

He smiled and reached over and slapped her shoulder. "Hey, don't sell yourself low. Varli was right."

The heat seeped into her cheeks.

"I can see it bothers you. I won't give you trouble about it, you can count on that." And he turned the talk to more practical matters.

She felt relieved but disappointed at the same time. The point was usually unspoken, but the women in a mercenary troop did have a special position. There were certain rights that had to be protected, despite the fact that the women usually felt they had to be twice as tough as their male fellows, just to keep it straight. She sighed. Life was complicated.

Well, better than the simplicity of the farm. Here I am off on a journey that will take me farther in a month than most farm wives travel in a lifetime. This is what I wanted.

Her heart lighter, she went to her barracks to finish packing her simple possessions and turned in early, wanting to be sharp for the next day.

5. Teamsters

"The thing that bothers me most," she stared out over the horses' rumps as they jogged along in the early sunlight, "is how we're ever gonna get any information that Loreline wants."

"How do you figure?"

"Well, I been thinkin' about it. Loreline's messengers are havin' trouble. Here we are, supposedly a coupla carters, and maybe we're travellin' the same roads, but that's about all. Nobody who is botherin' with the messengers is even gonna notice us. Unless we actually see a messenger in trouble, we ain't gonna learn nothin'."

He slapped the tails of the reins against the footboard. "I thought of that. We have to stick our necks out somehow. Any ideas?"

She thought a while, as the wagon jounced over a rutted part of the road. "I dunno. First, we just keep our eyes open. According to Loreline, the messengers stay at inns. She gave me a list. We'll stay at the same places. We got enough money for that, ain't we?"

"No problem there. I guess then we just keep our eyes open. See who seems to be legit travellers, who's just hanging around."

"I guess if we're lucky enough we'll be able to watch any messengers we see and check who pays attention to them."

He nodded. "That's pretty iffy. I don't think they pass through that often."

"If we see one, do we identify ourselves?"

After a moment's consideration, he shook his head. "I don't think we want to advertise ourselves, even to the messengers. If one is in trouble, we can give him the password, so he knows to trust us. Otherwise, we keep our distance," he tossed his free hand, palm up, "which doesn't help us with getting any information."

"How much do you think we can get away with, askin' questions?"

Ferlen shook his head. "That's where you'll have to take over. I'm pretty awful at that kind of socializing."

She grinned. "I guess I can handle that. I'll be the young and talkative type. Maybe sort of stupid, as well. Like Varli acts, you know? I'll be worried about bandits, and all that. Oughta be able to get some tongues loose."

"As long as you don't get too friendly."

"What do you mean?"

"Anine," he turned to look directly at her, "I had a talk with Loreline before we left. I figure it's only fair to you to tell you what she said."

"What did she say?"

"Well, she reminded me that you're pretty young. You went straight from the farm, where you were completely protected, to the mercenaries, where you had it tough, but, again, you were protected in some ways. She doesn't know how good you'll be at dealing with...you know...the big wide world out there." He ended with a sweep of his hand and a smile to take any bite out of his words. Then he looked at her anxiously, waiting for her response.

For a moment, she stared straight ahead, trying the reconcile the conflicting emotions that passed through her.

"Is that a hard thing to hear?"

She turned to him, measuring his attitude. "Aye," she finally answered. "It's hard to hear. I always pride myself on my independence, you know? And now you tell me that some man's always been lookin' out for me. But...well, it's nice to think I got friends lookin' out for me. I dunno."

He slapped the reins again, and the horses sped up slightly. "I wouldn't take it too hard, if I were you."

"Aw, I don't, really. I already knew."

"You did?"

"Every new recruit gets taken care of. Oh, sure, they tell you how rough they are on you. And they are. Your first year is a big test, and you have to make it through. You can be proud of that.

"But the women?"

"Well, that never changes. A woman is still a woman, no matter how good she is with a sword."

He slapped the reins against the horses' rumps and was silent a while. "It's been really interesting, talking to all the different types I met this summer. I find the mercenary troops fascinating. From what I heard, they like to have a few women in the unit."

"I heard that, too, but the guys would never give me a straight answer why. If they even knew."

"I gather the units with women in them have a different attitude. They obey orders better, they stick together, they take better care of each other. Some even say they fight harder."

She tossed her head. "Well, I suppose it's nice to be appreciated, even if it's only as a mascot."

He let the reins go slack and stared at her. "Anine, I don't know you very well, and this is very early in the trip for me to risk making you angry, but that is the stupidest thing I ever heard you say."

When she didn't respond immediately, he shrugged, his hands held helplessly in front of him. "I don't hang around with women much. The only experience I have, really, is my older sister. So you'll have to pardon me, but I'm going to treat you like I would her. And if she ever said anything like that, I'd tell her off, quick as anything."

She dragged out half a smile. "I guess it was pretty stupid. It's just hard to think I'm gettin' special treatment, when I thought I was holdin' my own."

"That's just the point, Anine. You are holding up your end of the bench. Each person gives what he or she can to the group. Women give a little different from men. I'm a good tracker, so I scout. You're bigger, so you hold the centre of the line, or whatever it is you call it. Is there anything wrong with that? How about Varli. Think what he gives. Do you really believe that he held his own place in the battles at the beginning, and there wasn't somebody looking out for him?"

"I suppose."

"Of course there was. He's nobility, he's young, he wasn't very strong and he's a good friend of the Commander. Sure thing nobody wants him killed. He'd probably be upset like you if somebody told him, though. I didn't mean to bother you. It's just that you were starting to sound pretty sorry for yourself, and you've got nothing to be sorry for."

Now she could really smile. "I think that's a compliment."

He shrugged and turned his attention back to the horses, which had slowed to a stroll. "Take it that way if you like."

"I think I will." *I got some things to think about. That's one thing about travelling: plenty of time to think.*

Ferlen glanced at her, then glanced again.

I wonder what's coming now?

55

"There is one more thing we should get straight. About the reality of our roles."

"Oh. That."

"Yes."

She shrugged. "I think that's simple. We decide, here and now, how it's gonna be, and we stick to it."

"That sounds simple. Too simple. People's feelings are involved. Things change."

She stared ahead. "Not if we decide they won't." She turned to look at him. "This is an assignment. We're on duty. We don't get to let our feelings get in the way. That's our duty. That makes it safe for both of us. We lay out the deal and we stick to it. That way, nobody gets hurt and we do our duties."

He nodded. "Fair enough."

"So?"

He grinned. "I think that was about it. You laid it out clearly. We're on duty until we hit the castle again, and that's it."

She glanced at him again. "Aye. That's pretty much it."

He nodded and clucked to the horses.

He didn't say nothin' about after we hit the castle. I guess we play that the way it falls. Not that it's likely to fall anywhere. But it's good to have it straight. I could work with this guy. Then she grinned at herself. *Aye, and I know what that sounds like.* She returned to her duties, watching their surroundings for danger.

The weather was still warm, and they were close enough to the castle that there would be no information to collect, so they decided to camp that night. They pulled in at one of the roadside sites where there was good water and a meadow for grazing.

After they had eaten supper and settled the stock, Anine started her work. There was another wagon there, a heavy hauler headed in the opposite direction.

"I think I'll go over and try out my new personality. They're carters and they oughta be a good source of information. If they notice anythin' wrong with us, they'll be just takin' their suspicions to the castle for the winter."

"Fair enough. Let's go."

"You don't have to come."

He grinned. "I said I didn't want to talk. I'll come along. Don't worry; it's not to protect you. Two sets of ears."

She mirrored his smile. "Yours won't be much good if I take a swing at one of them. I know you weren't thinkin' of protectin' me. Don't treat me like blown eggshells."

"Fair enough. If we're finished with our first marriage quarrel, shall we go?"

They laughed together and headed across the clearing to the other wagon.

The inbound wagon was teamstered by a huge, brusque man with a scar that started in front of his left ear and ran down his neck, disappearing under his collarless shirt.

His swamper was more talkative. In fact, he made up for his boss' taciturnity. Probably due to having to spend all day and night with someone who never spoke.

"Where did you come from?"

"Alderly."

There was a pause. When it became obvious that the man was not going to say any more, Anine filled in.

"Oh! That's where we're headed. Isn't that on our list, dear?"

Ferlen merely nodded.

Anine smiled privately, thinking of these two wagon masters meeting if they were alone with their charges. If they contacted at all, they would spend candles of silence between comments. Fortunately, the apprentice was more forthcoming.

"We left there six days ago. Roads're pretty good. Long as the fall storms don't hit us, we'll be at the castle tomorrow, no problem."

He looked very relieved at this idea, and Anine couldn't blame him.

"What are the roads like farther north?"

"They ain't so good up there. Once you're over the border into Velikii, they get worse for a while, but then they get better as you get into the Inner Duchies. They keep their roads real good in the Duchies."

"Well, that's too bad, because we're not going that far."

"Good thing." The apprentice nodded sagely. "There ain't time to get in a Big Swing before the winter rains. You doin' the Small Swing?"

Anine looked to Ferlen, received no help. *Oh, well.* "What do you mean, 'Big Swing'?"

The apprentice gave her that look of pity that comes from the newly initiated speaking to the complete beginner. "The Big Swing is a circle route that takes ya through the south of the Inner Duchies, then back to Petrella. The Little Swing only goes through the northern part of Petrella, from the castle to Tsalk, cuts over to Jaspen, back through Lanil's Rock, across to Alderly, then back to the castle."

"Oh. We're taking the Little Swing, then."

"Great. Ya should be able ta get back before the rains come, if y're lucky."

She sighed. "I hope we're lucky, then. I hate the rain."

He grinned. "Me too. But that's just onea the things ya have ta put up with, if y're gonna be a carter."

She shrugged. "I suppose. Say, any word of problems through the Little Swing? Any bad stretches of road, any bandits, any inns we should stay away from?"

"Nope. So far this fall, the road's rough, but all right for a light load. Five-six daysa rain and it'll all change, though. Bandits're more of a problem. Word's out they're causin' more trouble than usual. Gerth's troops bin chasin' 'em, but no luck so far." His voice dropped a bit. "Far as I've heard, nothin's gonna happen till the Lady comes."

"What lady?"

"The Lady. You know." He made a circular motion with his hand. "She's out there, ya know? She supports King Gerth. The bandits got no chance, once She shows up."

Stifling her smile, she nodded seriously. "When is she going to show?"

He leaned closer. "That's just it. Nobody knows. But she always does. Anyplace there's trouble, She's sure to show up. Then the bandits got no chance. She'll wipe 'em out, just like that." He clapped his hands, ground the palms together, then pushed them away and grinned.

She nodded again. "Well, I hope She shows up soon. I don't like the idea of bandits."

"Aw, you won't have any problem. Single wagon like this, they won't bother ya. They're lookin' for bigger prey."

"What do you mean?"

58

He hunched even closer, with a quick glance over his shoulder at his wagon master, who seemed not to be listening. "I heard somethin'."

She let her eyes widen. "What?"

"I heard they're waitin'"

"Waiting for what?"

"I dunno. Word has it they're waitin'. When the time is right, they're gonna show their hand. Folks're worried plenty, believe me."

"And when's the right time?"

"When Gerth's lookin' the other way."

"The other way?"

"Aye. I dunno what that means, but that's what they say. When Gerth's lookin' the other way, they're gonna take over. Believe me, I don't wanna be anywheres around when that happens."

She did not have to invent the shudder that moved her shoulders. "I don't either."

"Don't scare the woman, Ched." The teamster's harsh voice cut through the silence.

The lad shrank, but his voice still rose. "She deserves to know. She's goin' in there."

"Pah! Gossip 'n' lies. The bandits're always makin' big threats." The teamster patted the sword that curved away from his waist. "You notice they never bother us, no matter how big they talk."

Ferlen finally chimed in. "So you don't think there's any real problem?"

"Bandits're always a problem. You got a tough rep, they don't bother you."

Anine faked a worried glance at her 'husband'.

Ferlen shook his head. "Like the lad says. We're small coin. Wagon's lightly loaded, not worth losin' a coupla men over."

Anine straightened her shoulders. "That's right. And if the Lady comes to save us, that's fine. If She comes to take us Home, that's the way the Wheel turns, and what can we do?"

The carter and his apprentice nodded as if she had spoken the wisdom of the ages. Thinking about it in the silence that followed, she figured maybe she had.

There was no more information to be had from this unlikely pair, so they soon returned to their own camp.

"Do we set a guard?"

Ferlen took a moment. "What do you think? We're pretty close to the castle. This is peaceful country."

She nodded. "Tell you, we won't set a guard, but the weather looks good. You bed down under the wagon like normal, and I'll crawl in there, but once it's good and dark, I'm gonna slip over into those trees and find a soft spot. If there's any trouble, we can get them from two directions."

He nodded. "Sounds fine. I'm happy to sleep in the trees, if you like."

She chuckled. "That's right. I forgot you was a trapper. Why don't you take the trees over there," she pointed, "and I'll take that big bush near the horses."

"Great. As long as the smell doesn't bother you."

"Smell? Horses? I guess they smell. A whole lot better than a tent full of mercs, that's for sure."

"Hadn't thought of it that way, but I suppose you're right." He banked the fire, now burned down to glowing coals, and they made a show of creeping under the wagon and arranging their bed.

Their caution turned out to be needless, although the bed of leaves Anine slept in was quite comfortable, and the bush kept the worst of the heavy autumn dew off her. She woke to the cool mist of the morning well rested and ready for the trail. Ferlen was up before her, and the smell of breakfast wafted across the campsite. It took a while to get cleaned and packed, harnessed up and on the road, but she knew they would soon develop a smooth routine.

They left camp just as their neighbours were backing their horses into position, and she waved cheerily. Predictably, only the apprentice waved back. His silent boss merely nodded to Ferlen, and the other wagon soon faded in the dust behind them.

It was a decent road, following the gentle winding of a small valley, so they rolled along at a good pace. Anine took it easy on the team; they would do better if they hardened to the journey in gentle stages. There was little traffic on the road, so they passed a pleasant day in the cool fall sunshine and made good time.

"Should we stay in a town tonight?"

He nodded. "Can we make one of the inns Loreline mentioned?"

"I think so. We're two days from the castle, and the messengers probably travel twice as fast as we do. The first one is at the next village."

He glanced up at the sun. "It's really too early to stop, but if it takes another couple of candles to get there, we could quit for the day with nobody asking why."

Sure enough, they reached the inn at a reasonable hour and pulled into the spacious yard. It was simple to get a room, there being few customers this early, and they secured the wagon tarp tightly over the load, stabled the horses and moved their belongings upstairs.

Ferlen nudged open the door to their room. "One bed."

"You expected anythin' else?"

"No, but I hadn't really thought what we'd do. Should I sleep on the floor?"

She shook her head. "Naw, I bed next the other soldiers all the time."

"But that was in barracks tents in the field. This is just the two of us."

She punched his shoulder lightly. "What's wrong, soldier? You afraid to sleep with me? You can keep your clothes on if you like."

He grinned with some relief. "If you aren't worried, I'm not."

"I ain't worried, but thanks for the thought."

They gleaned nothing from the inn's patrons that night. There were few travellers, none of whom had anything to add to their knowledge. The locals who dropped in for a mug of ale had even less to say. The picture they formed was of a realm at peace, with the usual petty problems, the usual small fears.

It was the same for the next two days as they moved northeast towards Jaspen. Easy travel, decent roads, and no information.

"Well," she sighed mightily, "I was askin' for a holiday. Looks like I got one."

He glanced over. "Feels kind of useless, doesn't it?"

"Aye. Do you think we're doin' anythin' wrong?"

"I don't think so. We weren't expecting anything to come easy."

She swung down to walk alongside the off horse, but he had only stumbled and didn't seem to be limping as a result. She was about to vault back to the wagon seat when Ferlen's hand stopped her.

"Stay down a moment."

She turned as if to check the doubletree, but her eyes were moving. A man stood in the road ahead, with the obvious intention of stopping them. She noticed the trees on either side of the road, close enough to hide an ambush.

"Is my sword handy?"

"By my right foot."

"Stop a few strides back of where he wants."

Ferlen pulled up. "Good morning, stranger. Is there a problem?"

The man stayed where he was, his eyes shifting to left and right. "No real problem. You goin' to Tsalk?"

"Passing through there, yes."

"Could you give me a ride?"

Ferlen pretended to think, taking in the man's ragged clothing, spare enough to hide no weapons. "You got coin?"

The man shook his head. "I was walkin' in, but I got a sore leg. Bin out lookin' for work."

"For an injured man?"

"It ain't serious. Just slipped and banged my knee real hard gettin' a drink at that last crick back there."

Ferlen glanced at Anine, and she gave a small shrug.

"Tell you what. You just walk on ahead for a while. I'll think about it."

"Sure." The man limped ahead and Ferlen clucked to the team. Anine stayed down by the horse, her hand on the side of the wagon near her sword.

Farther ahead, the trees cleared away from the road and there was no longer an ambush point. Anine swung up on the seat and kicked the hilt of her sword out of sight. Ferlen moved the team faster, then pulled the horses to a stop as they came up to the limping man. "Jump in here beside me. Hope you don't mind. A man can't be too careful, travellin' with his wife and all."

The man sighed and stretched his sore leg over the footboard. "No complaint from me, sir. I wasn't lookin' forward t' spendin' the night in the bush."

"Glad to give a hand to someone who needs it. You live around here?"

"I got a farm up the road this side of Tsalk. Got my early wheat crop in, thought I'd see if I could pick up some coin at the bigger farms closer to the castle."

Ferlen grinned. "I won't ask you how well you did, because only a fool would tell me if he was carryin' cash."

The man laughed at that and looked a bit more comfortable. "That was a good trick, makin' me walk a ways."

Ferlen nodded. "That place was too good an ambush spot. Plus it gave me a chance to watch you walk. Carters have to be careful, you know."

"Hey, I'm ridin', I'm not complainin'. With the bandits around like they are…"

My chance to play the worried woman. "Are there bandits?"

"Well, there's always bandits, ma'am. I wouldn't wanta worry you overmuch. But the word's gone out to be careful. That's another reason I wasn't lookin' forward to a night on the road."

"Well, I'm glad we picked you up. We need all the news we can get, don't we, dear?"

"That's true. How long do you think it'll take us to get to Tsalk?"

The man looked ahead. "Well, these here horses o' yours are movin' along right smartly. I figure well before sunset."

"Good. So we've got lots of time. Fill us in on what's been going on in the area. I've never been through here before. I was thinking I might do a regular run, next summer."

"Well, now, you might do all right at that. There's lotsa new trade all over. Most o' the stuff we see comin' through is from farther away. Big freighters, ya know. Three or four together, with a coupla guards, some of 'em. Roads're gettin' beat up."

"I'm not looking to compete with those big fellows. What about local, town-to-town stuff?"

They whiled away the rest of the afternoon draining their passenger of every bit of information he had about carting in the area, which turned out to be not much, since it wasn't a trade he had anything to do with. However, he did bring them a better picture of the feeling of the locals. Gerth was a great king, peace was a lot better than war, and prosperity seemed to be around the corner. He talked on with little prompting from Ferlen, and Anine slipped in a compliment now and then. When they dropped the man off at the lane to his farm just outside the village, he invited them to spend the night, but they politely declined, on the excuse that they didn't want to take the loaded wagon up such a narrow lane.

Ferlen slapped the reins and the horses picked up speed. "So, there's more bandits but there's more peace. I don't know."

Anine nodded. "No real evidence." She sighed. "Well, I guess we'll just have to keep movin'. A bit frustratin'. Like we're just goin' through the motions."

Ferlen glanced her way and smiled. "Patience catches mice."

She snorted. "If it was mice you wanted, why'n't you tell me?" She flicked the trailing end of a rein at the haunch of the near horse, which had a habit of lagging.

"Got any other ideas?"

"Nope. I'd just like to have something to show for our little trip."

The trapper shrugged, stretched. "Well, if we don't find anything, that says something as well."

"I s'pose."

The horses jogged on. Lulled by the jingle of the harness and the motion of the wagon, they passed another candle. Then they rounded the corner of a hill, and the village was in front of them.

"This place looks a bit bigger. Oughta be more action."

"We ain't lookin' for action. Just information."

He grinned over at her. "You know what I mean."

"Aye." She frowned. "If we don't get some information soon, we might have to stir up a little action."

"What do you mean?"

"I dunno. But I'm gettin' frustrated."

"Me too. But let's not do anything stupid."

"And I was supposed to be the professional in the group."

He clucked the horses to a faster pace. "But I'm in charge. That lets you be a little less responsible."

"You serious?"

"Sure. I know what it means to be the leader. You take on the responsibility for the task."

She slapped his shoulder with the back of her hand. "Well, don't worry I'm gonna pick a fight with someone, just to blow off some high spirits."

"I didn't think you would."

"My flatterin' husband seems to be gettin' less enthoosed."

They kept up this prattle as the wagon rolled through the town, but it didn't stop them from watching and listening. Tsalk looked older and more prosperous than the smaller villages they had so far passed through. Slate roofs covered some houses, and the barns that backed the fields around the town were taller, in better shape, and several looked new.

"Note the barns."

The trapper nodded. "Prosperity seems to have struck."

"More'n that. They pretty well fill in the gaps in the outside walls. It wouldn't take much to defend this place, now."

"You think it's on purpose?"

"Of course. These towns are all laid out with defense in mind, and lately somebody's done a bit of improvin' on this one. Let's see if we can figure out who."

It wasn't hard to find out. The inn was a three-storey stone building facing the road, with a slate roof and two levels of storage and stables surrounding the courtyard in the back. As they drove through the narrow opening, Anine nodded at the heavy gates that were pulled back to allow them in.

"This place looks pretty sturdy."

"Figure on the innkeeper?"

"He's got to be part of it." She looked around, noting the angle of the windows, allowing archers to stay concealed yet cover the gates. The stable doors were of thick planks and not overly wide. Inside, all was clean and airy, if dim. They left the wagon in the courtyard and stabled the horses before swinging their trunks to their shoulders and entering the inn.

The stooped, balding man in the faded apron who took their money was certainly not the owner. Following his directions, they hiked up to the top floor to a small room with a dormer overlooking their wagon. Anine opened the window, leaned out and nodded in satisfaction. She turned back inside to see Ferlen watching her with raised eyebrows. She gestured.

"I don't like the top floor. Too hard to get down to the wagon if there's any trouble. It's all right, though. The roof slopes down to the lower level, and you can slide down to that post over there and shin down, no worry."

He looked out. "You'd slide down that roof, hoping to hit the lower level before you went over the side, then try to catch that post as you were going over the edge? In the dark? What if it was raining?"

She grinned. "Then I'd just get there faster. Come on, Ferlen, this ain't nothin' compared to the climbin' we did this summer, chasin' the Inari." Then she sobered. "But if you're the one has to do it, don't slide down the first part. You'd have to run across to the corner, there."

He winced. "I guess. Let's hope we don't have to."

"I never thought we would. I'm just checkin' out the lay of the land. A smart fox never dens up without a back door."

"Have to agree with that. You finished?"

"Sure. I'll check the other ways out when we go down to eat."

"Hungry?"

"Any time. You armed?"

He turned to show the long knife slung on his belt. "You?"

She showed her hideaway dagger, in a drop sheath on her inner thigh. "That's all I have, besides my eatin' knife. Any trouble, I'll just pick up somethin'."

"Such as?"

She considered. "Well, I like a stool with a good, thick top. Hold off a sword pretty good with one of those, and lots of heft when you hit with it. A bench is next best, if it's not too long. Coupla heavy beer mugs'll do, if the handles don't break off."

"I see."

"You don't do much brawlin'?"

He shrugged. "Not the kind that needs weapons."

"That's another reason for usin' what you pick up. Don't look like you started it."

"Well, I'll be sure to check the heft of the stools before I sit down."

"I ain't jokin', you know."

"I never thought you were."

He held the door for her, and they descended the stairs to the common room on the lower floor. It was a large space, with rows of tables along either side and a big fireplace at the end. Ferlen caught her eye to let her know it was her choice, and she went to sit at an unoccupied table near the door but not close enough to be in a draught. The food was straightforward: stew, bread, and ale, but it was plentiful and well seasoned. They kept watch through the meal, but only saw the old barman and two serving girls. By the time they had finished eating, the room was half full, with teamsters, richer

66

pedlars and one official messenger who ate by himself in the corner by the fire.

Making it look like a sudden impulse, Anine got up and approached him. "Excuse me, sir?"

He looked up. He was an older fellow, long and lean, with a weathered face and a cautious smile. "Yes, my dear?"

"If you was comin' in from the north…?"

"Yes?"

"I was hopin' you could tell us if there's any troubles on the road. You know, mudholes, washouts…" she paused as if not wishing to say it, "…bandits?"

His smile widened. "Are you travelling north?"

"Yes. My husband and I are taking a load of freight out to Jaspen."

He frowned. "A bit late in the season for freighting. Bad for the roads."

"Oh, it's only a light load. We'll be coming back empty. I'm sure we won't hurt the roads."

He relented. "I suppose. No, there's no trouble you need worry about from here to Jaspen. There was a bandit attack three quarters ago, but that was a rich merchant with three big wagons and no guards." He shook his head. "Sheer stupidity." He looked up at her again. "You have guards?"

"No! Should we?"

"I wouldn't think so. You're too small to bother with. They do stop you, just give them the load, and they'll let you go."

She frowned. "But then we'd lose our fare."

"Better than losing your life."

"Oh."

He shook his head. "I wouldn't be too worried, my dear. I'm sure your husband knows what he's doing."

"But I don't understand. Why would the bandits let us go? Wouldn't they kill us?"

He shook his head. "Not if you don't put up a fight. If they just take your load, nobody will come after them. Not worth it. If they kill someone, or do them…" he paused and gestured awkwardly towards her, "…harm, there'd be soldiers all over in half a quarter."

"Are they that thoughtful?"

He smiled. "I'm afraid so. The bandits seem to be very organized these days."

"But that's terrible! Can't King Gerth do something about it?"

The man shrugged. "It's a big country, and the king has a lot to look out for. It's too late in the season to send out a lot of soldiers unless somebody gets killed. Don't worry; King Gerth knows about the bandits."

"Oh. That's good. Thank you for the information."

He turned back to his ale, already forgetting her. "Have a good trip."

"The same to you, sir."

She returned to her stool, shaking her head. "It don't add up, Ferlen."

"In what way?"

"Well, I don't know. It seems like everybody's worried about bandits, so that means that there must be more bandits. But everybody's tellin' us that we're not in danger, because the bandits don't want such small pickin's."

"That's true." Ferlen's brow wrinkled. "What do you think it means?"

"We seem to have bandits that ain't acting like bandits."

"So, according to Zoysana's logic..."

"...they ain't bandits."

He nodded, and they sat in silence. Then he grinned. "At least we're making progress."

"Of a sort, I guess."

"You expected the bandits to fall into our laps the first quarter-month on the road?" He shook his head. "The only way we'd get that kind of first-hand knowledge wouldn't be pleasant. I'd rather pick up news the slow and difficult way."

"I suppose, but I don't think this will be much news to Loreline. She already had somethin' like this figured."

"Then we're bringing her confirmation. Don't worry, Anine. We're out here doing what we were instructed. We'll either get the information or we won't."

She stared at him, nodding. "So, when you're out trappin', you set your traps and either you catch the animals or you don't."

"Something like that."

"But if you don't catch any animals, don't you try somethin' different? A different type of trap, or work a different area, or somethin' like that?"

"I guess. But I don't get all worked up over it."

"Well, I guess that's the difference 'tween me and you. I'm given a task, I want to get results, and if I don't, I'm gonna figure out why." She sighed. "I never thought I was gonna like this spyin' business."

6. Sarha's Inn

After all those days on the road, Anine thought she knew her companion. Quiet to the point of reticence, calm, competent and undemonstrative. It didn't prepare her for the reception he received at his sister's inn.

They pulled into Lanil's Rock, which consisted of a narrow, muddy street between high-walled houses, opening onto a small, equally dirty area she supposed, earlier in the year, was the village green. The rock outcropping for which the town was named rose above the surrounding forest like a thumb through a torn glove. The first building to the right would be the inn because of the raw colour of the new construction on the upper floor.

As they approached, a door burst open, and two large, grey-and-brown hounds bounded out, heading at full bay towards them. Ferlen tossed her the reins of the nervous horses and slipped out in front to intercept the charging beasts. He staggered as he caught the first in the chest, and the second, hitting him just above the knees, knocked him sprawling on the dirt, laughing. The two dogs worried at him, alternately barking and whining, each trying to push the other aside for his attention.

A hearty laugh drew Anine's eyes to the woman standing in the doorway of the inn. "Come on, Ferlen, control those dogs of yours. What kind of trapper can't bring his own dogs to heel?"

She was tall and thin, with a loud voice and a softness in her eye as she watched her brother. Her hand rested comfortably on the shoulder of a small boy who grinned shyly from behind her, his eyes mostly hidden by a mop of straw-coloured hair.

Ferlen finally got the dogs calmed down and signalled Anine to bring the horses forward. He strode in front of the woman, his finger pointing accusingly. "You set them up for this, didn't you? You held them in there and got them so excited they were fit to tear the door off its hinges, and then you set them loose on me. You've spoiled them completely. I knew it!" He ended this tirade by taking his sister in a quick, tight, hug. Then he turned, motioning Anine off the wagon seat.

"Come down here, Anine, and meet my least favourite dog trainer."

The woman pushed him away. "You want your dogs trained your way, you keep them. You leave the poor things with me, how can I help but treat them the way they're supposed to be treated?"

He slapped critically at the ribs of the animal nearest him. "Yep, put on enough weight to slow her down by half. Probably no wind left. I'll be reduced to hunting wild sows and piglets. This pair couldn't run down a deer if it had two legs broken."

He gestured again to Anine. "This is my sister, Sarha, the one that keeps the family in food while I'm off gallivantin' around with the king and his lackeys. Sarha, this is one of my summer playmates, up in the mountains: Anine, professional soldier."

Sarha grinned. "Another professional soldier in my inn? This is getting to be a bad habit."

Anine mumbled something about being pleased to meet her, but was overwhelmed by the general riot.

"Speaking of soldiers, where's that husband of yours?"

"Oh, he's around somewhere. Last I saw, he was headed up the street to the smith's."

Anine looked around. There was hardly a street, only the passage between the houses to the open fields. The dogs burst away and bounded around a corner, to be met by a stream of mild cursing.

Soon, Jhanes strode into sight, spurning the leaping dogs with his free hand, the other carrying a large piece of iron. Seeing the wagon, he quickened his stride, his smile expanding.

"Hey, there, Ferlen, Anine! Got word you were coming in. How was the trip?"

Ferlen reached out and grasped the soldier's arm. "Good road, good company, passable horses. Can't complain."

"Anine! You keepin' this fella under control?"

She couldn't help but smile. "I tried, but my efforts are going to be destroyed if he spends any time with this lot."

They all gathered around the wagon, chatting and jesting as they unloaded the personal supplies. Then Sarha nodded to the small boy, who jumped up on the wagon seat and slapped the reins on the horses' rumps. Startled at this sudden development, they threw their shoulders into the traces as if they had every intention of running away. The boy called out to them and hauled mightily, holding them to a reasonable pace.

Ferlen chuckled. "Take them over to Mussef at the camp, Frey, and let the soldiers unload their own supplies. Anine, is there a manifest?"

She started out of her amazement and pulled the sheet from her satchel, jogging alongside and handing it over to the lad. He grinned down and turned his attention to the horses again.

As he pulled away, she glanced at him one more time, then turned back to Jhanes. "Isn't he a bit young to be handling a wagonload with strange horses?"

Jhanes shrugged. "Ask Sarha. Surprised me, too. He's good with animals. He's been handling horses for the inn patrons all summer. Guess somebody had to take over, since I was busy elsewhere."

They trooped inside, everyone carrying something.

Sarha turned in the main room, just at the bottom of the stairs. "You can have any room you like." She regarded her brother. "One room or two?"

He laughed. "I'm sure Anine would be happy to have some space to herself. That wagon's all we've had for half a month."

Anine felt the need to contribute. "Aye, this pretendin' to be married is a bore. I'm holdin' out for the real thing." She slung her travel trunk to her shoulder and headed up the stairs, her face warm with the realization of what she had just suggested.

The burst of laughter behind her, fortunately, seemed to be at her companion's expense.

"There you go, Brother, you've messed it up again."

The soldier's deep voice came on top of his wife's. "You've had your chance, lad. Half a month to practise, and you still haven't got it right."

Their voices faded as she fled up the narrow stairs. She turned the corner into the hallway and considered. It had been a hot day, so she figured the shady side of the building would be better. It overlooked the inn yard, and she could keep an eye on the wagon, as well. She chuckled to herself as she looked out the window of the first room. Not that she had much to worry about in this inn. The room looked fine, so she tucked the trunk into the corner and thought about her clothing.

She was dressed in soldier's garb, since the last two days they had adopted the story that she was going out to join the troops. She reasoned that there wasn't much point in trying any story here, so she thought she'd stay with what she wore. *Too many changes, too much complication.* She busied herself with opening the window wider, checking escape routes and fields of fire, which didn't matter much, since she didn't have a bow. If they were needed, she'd bet Jhanes had a couple in the house.

She could hear the thumps and bangs as Ferlen established himself in the next room. On his way back downstairs, he stuck his head in her door. "Nice work. You've picked the best room in the house."

She jumped to her feet. "Oh! Was this supposed to be yours?"

He laughed. "There. That makes up for the trouble you got me into a moment ago. The rooms aren't that different, although this one is usually taken first in the hot weather because of the size of the window. I took the next one down the hall. Force of habit."

"You're actually part-owner?"

He slapped the new wood of the wall beside him. "Yep. Just the new part. That's where last year's furs and this summer's pay went."

"Must be nice."

"What?"

She shrugged as she headed down the stairs. "Havin' a place to come to, makin' money for you, whether you're there or not."

His voice drifted in from behind her. "Haven't you got a place to go home to?"

It was easier to talk with her back turned. "Not really. I tried to go back to the farm after the first year, but it didn't work, really."

"Why not?" He seemed more interested in talking now, selecting a comfortable corner in the common room of his family inn.

She slung a leg over a stool and propped her arms on the table. "I just didn't fit in. My home town's a stolid bunch. There's no place for a mercenary in their little world. Especially a female one. My brothers didn't know what to do about me. I think they were a little scared, actually."

He laughed. "I can imagine. You show up with that big sword of yours, and they start rememberin' every little time they teased you."

She smiled back. "Somethin' like that. Oh, I know if I needed to, I could go back there. But it wouldn't be my first choice." She leaned back and stretched her legs out in front of her.

"From what I hear, every merc has somewhere he'd like to go. It's sort of a tradition. They tell about them when the booze is flowin', or the night watches are long. Some of them hardly exist, as far as I can figure out. I'll find my own, some day. Or make it up. Since most mercs don't really figure on lasting long enough to get there, it's sort of a dream, more than anythin' else, anyways."

"And here's the man who's found his."

Jhanes strode into the room, purposeful as usual. "Talking about me?"

Ferlen nodded. "Aye. The lucky mercenary. Found his place to settle before a sword settled it for him."

Jhanes moved efficiently, filling tankards from the barrels behind the bar. "Settle is a relative term."

"What?"

"I'm settled, all right. Then I go spend the summer fighting the Inari, and half the winter running errands for King Gerth."

"That bother you?"

The big soldier slapped a mug in front of his brother-in-law. "Not at all. I'd be bored silly just bein' an innkeeper. In the winter especially."

"So, what're you doin' for the king, these days? If you can tell us simple workin' soldiers."

Jhanes slid Anine's mug over to her and sat down as well. Sarha had appeared from somewhere, and stood beside him, her hand on his shoulder.

"What I'm doing includes you two."

They hitched forward, elbows on the table, tankards forgotten in their hands.

"It's like this. Some decisions were made after you left the castle. I got a report down from Loreline two days behind you, came the quick route, sealed for me only. You know about the messenger problem with these supposed bandits. We thought at first that they might just be waylaying or delaying the messengers, to keep us from knowing what was happening, just when they were about to make a big move."

"Loreline told us about that."

"Well, we're beginning to wonder. It's possible that some of the messengers have been more than waylaid."

"Killed?"

"Nothing that clean. Persuaded."

Anine sat up straighter. "Bribed?"

74

"It's a possibility, and it fits the pattern too well to be dismissed."

They sat, considering the implications.

"What can we do?"

Jhanes shifted forward. "In the first place, of course, you'll write up a report of anything you found out."

The two exchanged glances. "Not much, I'm afraid."

He made a negative gesture. "Don't worry about that. You know how Loreline works. You send whatever information you have, and whatever opinions you have about the information. She'll figure it out. After all, you don't really know what she's looking for."

Anine looked at the soldier, puzzled. "Yes, we do. She told us specifically."

He grinned. "I doubt it. She told you what you were looking for."

Anine was about to respond when she caught his meaning. "I see."

"Right. So don't try to second-guess what she wants. Give her what she told you."

Ferlen nodded. "I like that. I don't want to get into the twist of figuring out what's in somebody else's head."

"Exactly. Then, we'll play a few other games." The soldier ticked off points on his rugged fingers. "First, we'll send your report back through the regular messengers. When you get back to the castle, you'll check to make sure the same report got through."

They nodded.

"Then, we'll send some other, very specific, information through the regular messengers."

"And you'll send the same with us, again to compare them?"

"Right."

Anine thought she was starting to get the idea. "Why don't we send slightly different information through different messengers, and see what gets through straight, and what gets changed or lost?"

Jhanes reached out and slapped her shoulder. "You're catching on. But we can't do that."

"Why not?"

"You figure it out."

She thought. "I don't know."

He grinned. "Don't worry. You're not expected to match the Sivan's training in the first month on the job. If we followed your idea, what information does that make available to the enemy?"

She tried to follow that. "Umm…if we send a message, and it's obviously wrong, they might catch on to what we were doing…" her words came faster, "…and if we send different messages through two different messengers…"

Ferlen leaned forward as well. "…and they've paid off both those messengers…"

"…then they'll know we're on to them."

Jhanes sat back, with a pleased smile at Sarha. "They're both pretty good, aren't they?"

Both of them sat upright, sharing an alarmed glance.

"But we don't want to be spies!"

He grinned. "If you're in Zoysana's Clan, you'll end up doing all sorts of things you never thought you would. Oh, don't worry. If you don't like it, nobody's going to force you."

Sarha smiled. "But Lady Zoe has a very persuasive way of asking."

Jhanes pressed both hands to the table, palms down, in a business-like sort of way. "Anyway, that's the plan. You two are our guaranteed messengers. That's all you need to do. Other than that, continue with your original mission."

They looked at each other, nodded. "Sounds fine."

Ferlen glanced slyly over at his brother-in-law. "And are we right back on the road again?"

Jhanes laughed. "I don't think I'd get peace around here for a month if I sent you away this soon. Let's just say we need a couple of days of consultation. And those horses could use a rest before they head out into wet road conditions. Maybe their shoes should be checked."

Anine got into the swing. "I've been worried about the wagon. It's developed some new squeaks. Do you have somebody who can check it out?"

"Of course. Since the soldiers arrived, all sorts of people moved in. A wheelwright set up shop just down the other side of the parade ground. We'll have him look it over tomorrow."

"The town is growing?"

Sarha grinned at her brother. "Concerned about your investment?"

"Right you are. If I'm going to become a rich merchant, I have to be sure I've got my money in the right place."

"Well, if you're going to be a rich merchant, you'll be interested to know what went on at the castle, just before I left."

They leaned forward.

"There was another meeting. I got called; I'm not sure why. I thought it was going to be strategy, but King Gerth showed up, and they got talking about money. I just sat there listening. Interesting to see how they think."

"What were they talking about?"

"They were talking about how to finance the road repairs. In the past, each lord was responsible for the roads through his demesne. He was allowed to charge fees to the merchants to pay for them. Of course, many of them charged too much in fees and didn't keep the roads up well enough. In order to attract the merchants, Gerth persuaded all the lords to let the merchants through for free, because it would mean the goods would be cheaper for everyone."

Ferlen nodded. "That was all happenin' last year."

"Right, but then how was Gerth to repair the roads? He has to get the money somewhere."

"What's the solution?"

"Well, Gerth told the merchants they had to pay something, but that if they paid it to him, it would be collected more fairly, and the roads would be kept up more evenly for lower fees. They could see the logic of that, but one of them apparently asked why they should pay at all.

"Gerth was telling this tale at the meeting, and I could see he was leading up to something. He said that he told them he needed the money to repair and patrol the roads. The only other way he could get it was to go into business himself. He paused, he said, to let them chew on that.

"Then he hit them with the clincher. 'If I have to do that, I'm thinking of putting Lady Kenna in charge.'

"Well, we all burst out laughing at that. Except for Lady Kenna, of course, who just sat there, a little grin on her face. She asked him, all innocent, if that made any difference. He just laughed again and tossed his head like he does.

"Then Zoysana pipes up that he's going to have to stop threatening people that he'll tell his mother if they don't do what he wants. Then we all start laughing some more."

77

The soldier grinned wider. "Tell you, being in a strategy meeting with those people is like nothing I've ever seen. They're laughing and teasing each other, and they sound like any other family around the dinner table. Then you walk out, and you realize that the policy of the kingdom just got set."

Ferlen looked thoughtful. "So the king collects the fees. He uses the money to fix the roads. Who takes that money and fixes the roads?"

Sarha slapped her husband's shoulder. "You know, I think my brother's got some of that merchant blood in him."

Jhanes nodded. "You've put your finger on it, Ferlen. There is going to be a whole new demesne set up. There has to be. But it won't be based on land. It'll be based on doing the task of road repair, over the whole kingdom."

"Who gets the demesne?"

The soldier shrugged. "Whoever proves he can repair the roads for the kind of money the king is willing to spend."

Ferlen's hands flattened downwards. "For a moment there, I thought I might be interested."

"What's the problem?"

"That 'willing to spend' put the bull in with the heifers. What the king decides to spend will never be enough to repair the road to the level the merchants want. The man who takes on that task will spend his life listening to the complaints of the merchants and trying to persuade the king to spend more money. He won't get any time to actually work on the roads."

Anine couldn't help but agree. "Sounds like a perfect job for one of those courtiers who spends all his time talking to people. He doesn't actually have to do any of the work. From what I've heard, you got that kinda guy in charge, most of the money ends up in his pocket, not on the road."

Jhanes nodded. "You've put your finger on the problem. But remember, you're dealing with the Arlyns here. Can you imagine anybody getting money from Gerth to do a job, and not coming through?"

Ferlen smiled. "Let me guess. With Lady Kenna overseeing the operations?"

"You're getting the picture."

The trapper shook his head. "Sounds like too much trouble to me."

"What do you think, Anine?"

Anine started. She hadn't really been listening. "What?"

Sarha looked at her. "What do you think of the idea? Getting someone to oversee the road works."

Anine took a moment more. "I was just thinking about that. How you'd organize it, I mean. You couldn't exactly run it like a mercenary troop, you know, because the guys workin' for you wouldn't be soldiers. But they'd soon enough get to be specialists, sort of, in the type of work they did, and you could get a sort of feelin' goin', you know, like you do with the mercs.

"You could set it up like a merc troop, with different guys responsible for doin' different jobs. There'd have to be a quartermaster who got the right materials for the workers. You get the right man in the quartermaster's job and you'd save the king a lot of money, right there. You know how everybody thinks because it's goin' to the army, they can charge more? A good quartermaster'd settle them pretty fast." She looked around at the group in front of her. "Sorry, I've been blatherin' on, haven't I?"

Jhanes shook his head. "I wouldn't call it blathering, Anine. It sounds like good sense to me."

"Ever fixed a road, Anine?"

"Me? A farm girl? We owed the lord seven days of road repair every year. Next you'll be askin' if I ever forked hay."

Jhanes nodded. "So you might be interested."

She realized that there had been a pause, and her mouth was wide open. "Just a moment, there, soldier. I didn't say anythin' about fixin' roads. I'm a mercenary. The only shovellin' I do is camp defenses." She paused, then grinned. "Latrines if I screw up somehow."

"Nobody is asking you to do any shovelling."

"Hah! The only ones who don't shovel is the officers...wait a bit. I ain't officer material. I only been in the mercs for three years...well, comin' up four. I don't even know how to read proper!"

Jhanes merely looked at her.

"All right. I'm learnin' how to read, and I do figures all right. It still don't fit, makin' me an officer. I'm a farm girl!"

79

"And I'm a farm boy. From a hill farm, yet. That didn't stop Zoe from putting me in charge up on the mountain this summer."

He stopped, and a sly grin crept over his face. "Unless, of course, you'd rather be a spy."

"Hah! You never quit bein' an officer, do you? I mean, here you are, paid off for the winter, comin' home to be an innkeeper, but you ain't really, are you? You're still on duty for Zoysana."

Anine turned to Sarha, sitting quietly now at her husband's side. "How do you stand it, knowin' he's not really yours?"

Then she felt the warmth creep up her neck. "I mean, if I ain't too forward, askin'."

Sarha smiled. "We're just family around here, and anyone of Zoysana's who comes in is treated as such. To answer your question, I don't mind it at all. I mean, you never really have another person completely, you know? If I'd married a carter, he'd be on the road all the time. I married a soldier, and now the stuff he's doin' is a whole lot safer'n' fightin'.

"Besides," a sly look to her husband, "I been alone a lotta years before he showed up. Gets nice to have it my own way for a while." Then she relented and placed her hand on his arm. "But it's sure good to have him back."

Anine nodded and turned her attention to the big man as well. "Did She put you up to this?"

He shook his head. "No, I guess I'm just learning to think like an officer. I keep looking at people and listening to them talk, and I start getting ideas where they'd fit, you know, if I was running the show."

"I see. So, if I don't want to be a spy, I gotta go lookin' for somethin' else to be useful for? Speakin' as soldier-to-officer, you know."

He laughed. "Officer-to-soldier, I have no orders for you. But speaking as a friend and knowing how things go, I'd grab any path to advancement in this bunch, because you're going to get a chance here you'd never get anywhere else." Another thought struck him. "Speaking officer-to-soldier, do you mind us discussing your future with Ferlen here?"

She glanced over at the quiet man, his hands folded around his mug of ale, eyes regarding her calmly. "Hell, no. We're all just family here, ain't we?" As their smiles died again, she spoke to the

80

trapper. "How does it hit you, Ferlen? What are the rest of the mercs gonna say, I go runnin' off to build roads instead of stickin' with the troop?"

He did her his usual courtesy of thinking before he answered. "In the first place, I don't think you'll actually be leaving the troop. Just like the Innkeeper, here, when the next trouble comes, I figure I'll be hauled off my trap line or wherever I went for a rest, and you'll be yanked off the road crew, quick as beaver grease down a pole, and we'll all be lined up with the rest of the Clan to go and do whatever needs to be done. Sure, a few might be jealous, but most will just keep acting like they always have. I don't know how it goes with mercenaries. What happens when a fighting man gets moved up to officer?"

She shrugged. "Nothin' much. Usually everybody's already got it figured, and the guy's been doin' officer work. The next time there's a shuffle, he slides in to where he's best suited. After all, next shuffle, if he hasn't been holdin' up his end, he might slide right back out. Doesn't happen often, though, unless somebody in the upper end is playin' political games, promotin' his cronies. Doesn't happen at all in a good troop." She looked around the three of them. "I mean, can you imagine Zoysana lettin' anythin' like that go on?"

Jhanes nodded. "If there was any slogan for Zoysana's Clan, which there isn't because we're not really a mercenary troop, it would be, 'Get the Job Done'."

They all smiled, then the trapper's laconic voice slid in, "No, it would be, 'Get the Job Done – or Else'."

They laughed out loud at that and talk turned to other matters, but Anine didn't join in much. Too many ideas were whirling around in her head. *An officer. But not really an officer, because a road crew ain't a merc troop. But like an officer. I could do that sorta thing, I figure.* She hadn't thought of advancement with the mercenaries, because she didn't have the battle experience. *But anybody can fix a road. No, wrong. Anybody with the kind of experience I have can fix a road.* Besides, she would have people who knew roads better than she did to take charge of the individual crews. She would be busy bargaining for materials, organizing shipments, talking with the merchants…*talkin' with the merchants.* Another thought hit her, and she spoke before she realized she had.

"Ferlen, how come you speak so different from Sarha? If you don't mind me askin'. No offense, Sarha, but you speak sorta like me. I noticed it before, especially with a lot of the others around, he don't say 'ain't' and he speaks like he's been educated somewheres. How did that happen?"

They were all looking at her.

"What? What did I say? I'm sorry…"

Ferlen raised a hand to stop her. "No, Anine, it isn't that. It's just that you were obviously off in your own little corner, and suddenly you come out with a question like that. Takes a while for us to catch up to your pace, you realize."

"Oh. That's all right then. So?"

He shrugged. "I told you about the books."

"Sure, books give you the right grammar, but you sound different when you talk."

"Once I learned what proper grammar sounded like, I started listening to other people when they spoke, and," here he ducked his head a bit, "I have to admit, I practised on my dogs when I was trapping. Speaking like other people spoke, you know. It was fun, and it kept me from going nuts, up there in the mountains all winter."

"I guess I better learn to read real fast, then."

Jhanes looked interested. "And what does that have to do with whatever you were thinking about? I assume it was the road work idea."

She nodded. "I was thinking about all the people I'd have to be dealin'…dealing with. Merchants and lords and such, and how they'd be takin'…taking me for a hick who didn't know nothin'. I couldn't serve the king very well that way, so I guess I'm gonna haveta learn to speak good."

Ferlen grinned. "You mean you guess…"

She thought, and spoke slowly, "I guess I must learn how to speak…well?"

He nodded. "I suppose you are."

"Will you help me?"

He really laughed at that. "You're asking for language lessons from a trapper who was brought up in an inn. You're really desperate, aren't you?"

She shrugged. "You know us mercs. We make do with what we have." She had a moment's thought. "By the way," she closed her fist and looked at it meaningfully, "you wouldn't be thinkin' about teachin' me anything that was wrong, now, would you? Just for a joke?" She shot him a hard glance, then smiled slowly.

He held his hand up in a defensive gesture. "Anine! I'm hurt that you would even think of such a thing."

She nodded. "I didn't think so. But I gotta be on my guard. I'm only a young girl, just startin' out, you know."

"Aye. A young girl with a fist the size of a small buckler. You know, Beken still winces and rubs his stomach any time your name comes up."

Her head went side to side, sheepishly. "That was a bit of a sucker punch. I apologized to him after. He took it pretty good."

Jhanes shook his head. "From what I heard, he took it flat on his back with the wind knocked out of him."

"Just what is this all about? What have you been doing, Anine?"

And so the two men had to tell Sarha the whole story, with Anine chipping in to straighten them out when the facts slipped too far into fantasy. When they had finished, Sarha turned to Anine.

"And he took it well, did he? I assume you meant the apology."

"Aye. He admitted he'd been riding me a little hard, and he apologized for that. He's not a bad sort, Beken. Just gets the bit in his teeth and keeps on goin'. You know the kind."

Ferlen agreed. "Actually, Beken got more attention out of that than he's had in months. It's sort of a badge of honour for him, now. Tells the story himself sometimes. Of course, it's a highly personal version, but you come out quite well, Anine."

"That's good, then. I don't want anyone in the troop with a grudge against me. I mean, we're all soldiers together in a fight, but you still gotta live together."

"And your final solution to that problem is to become an officer."

"Why is that?"

Jhanes raised his eyebrows. "Well, in the first place, a new officer needs a reputation. Beken seems quite happy to start yours. It also helps him, because that makes his getting floored not such a knockdown, if you'll pardon the expression."

"Because he got dropped by somebody good enough to be an officer?"

"That's it. If, as you say, he's not really a problem, just a bit thoughtless, you'll find him one of your best troops. His reputation will depend on your success."

"I never thought of it that way."

"You would have. You've got that kind of mind."

"I do?"

The soldier smiled that slow smile. "Yes, Anine. You don't fool your friends. You're always playing that 'dumb farm girl' role, but then you ask all these questions that most of the others wouldn't have realized existed."

"Oh."

Sarha's voice cut in, and she sounded less amused. "All right, Jhanes. You've played your officer game. Now leave her alone for a while."

He looked over at his wife, puzzled. "What do you mean my 'officer game'?"

"I mean you've discovered a way to keep control of your staff. In this case, you toss her compliments. She falls apart, red as an apple, and you're on top of the heap again. You oughta be ashamed!"

He grinned, unabashed. "But I'm not. Whatever works."

Anine made eye contact with the other woman. They both smiled. It was a moment Anine was to remember later. It was another step, she knew, this feeling of being accepted. Into another group, another class.

Later that night she lay awake going over the evening's conversation. It was just like Jhanes had said about the king's family. They sat around and joked and teased each other, and all at once a major decision was reached. *Was that what happened to me tonight? Have I been tested somehow?* She certainly felt that she'd passed some sort of barrier.

It was a good feeling, and like any good feeling, she was wary of it. *I can't see how it could be bad for me, but a girl's gotta be careful.* Maybe in her innocence she was somehow being used. The tough summer she had just spent in these people's company told her otherwise. That was one thing three years in the mercenaries had taught her. If you fought beside someone and lived at close quarters with him, you knew him as well as it was possible to know another human.

No, the message was clear. The 'officer' conversation had not been by accident. If she took on this road work and she got called back to the Clan, it would be as an officer. If she matched up. Zoysana played no politics. *It's all up to me.*

Now her mind wandered. She wondered what it would be like to go back to Menchal to fix the roads. Picking up local labour, giving the farmers a chance for some extra cash between seeding and harvest. She could imagine strolling into the meeting, seeing her brothers' disbelieving faces when they realized that she was the one leading the operation, the one they had to come to for work.

She could just feel their consternation, mixed with fear. Would she hire them? *Standis, for example. He's a good man with stone. I know where I'd put him. The bridge at Valder would be crumbling as usual. I'd send Standis off to Manistee to choose the stone. He'd soon have that bridge in proper shape. Good enough to last for centuries. Omer would help him. A good helper, Omer, but not a good leader. That's fine. Good helpers have their place.*

Then Osgad. He's no asset. I wonder if I could, with all good conscience, hire him for the king's work. Oh, he's the strongest of the lot. When he wants to be. That's been his problem ever since I can remember. He always finds it easy to do things. Too easy. He finishes his work ahead of the others, then lies around. Always careful to do his share and no more. Always keeping track of what's fair.

But am I just getting my own back, or is he really that difficult to work with? I couldn't afford to be seen playing favourites. Maybe I would send him back to the farm, where Dad would need some help, anyway. That would put him on his mettle. Maybe Dad would get a little extra help out of him. Or else he'd go into a blue funk and not do anything all summer. Well, I can't help that. That would be his problem, not mine. My problem would be to get the road fixed for the king.

She chuckled sleepily to herself. Here she was with her family all hired for the summer and she hadn't even asked for the assignment. She drifted off, dreaming of swanking around in officer's braid, giving orders to the men, fighting battles that would never happen, accepting accolades she would never earn. At least, not the way she imagined them. That was fine. A girl was allowed to dream. And while she was at it, maybe there would be a man, someone who didn't mind her size, who admired her uniform and her power. No...she was vaguely disturbed by that idea. That was the last kind of man she wanted. Oh, well, for tonight, anyway...

Then she slept.

7. THE ROAD BACK

It was a bit hard after that, hanging around the inn, watching Ferlen and his family enjoying conversation, jokes and comfortable, quiet times with each other. So she spent more time with the soldiers, who looked a pretty sorry lot, by mercenary standards. Once they found out she was one of Zoysana's Clan their interest rose, and they plied her with questions about the summer's activities, the fame of which had spread to every outpost, it seemed. The kidnapping of Lady Talia and Gerth's rescue party topped their demands; she had to tell the story three nights in a row at the inn.

In all her talk with the soldiers, she had her ears open. The common men often knew things the officers didn't, so she kept her mouth shut, trained with the soldiers when they asked, and listened a lot.

The training was the fun part. In all her mercenary career, she had always been the one learning, always been a poorer fighter than the others around her. Now, with this average bunch of soldiers, her size and experience put her way up the list. The first time she dropped her guard, stepped inside a slash and threw her opponent over her hip into the dust, there was a general exclamation, immediately followed by demands for another demonstration. She complied, and soon had them all practising the basic Weaponless techniques Zoysana had taught her Clan.

That evening in the inn, she sat for supper with Jhanes's family and the officers from the king's troop: a lean old sergeant who had seen better days, and the lieutenant, a younger son of one of Petrella's minor houses.

"Tell you, Jhanes, I've never had the men take to training with such enthusiasm. Even when you come to lend a hand."

Jhanes nodded. "Zoysana's people always train like that. Hard, but plenty of fun. You never know when the move you just learned is going to save your life."

The old sergeant winked at Anine. "Naw, it's bein' taught by a woman. They couldn't wait for a chance to get their hands on her."

Anine found she was able to accept this dig with no embarrassment. "I made sure they didn't get the chance."

He nodded. "If I wasn't crocked up in the leg like I am, I'da traded a few throws with ya. I done somea that stuff when I was in the mercs."

Talk turned to the various techniques of different mercenary companies, and Anine noticed a hush along the tables nearby, as the soldiers and townsfolk listened in. She and Ferlen were sitting at the main table, being treated as officers. She caught the trapper's eye, and he grinned at her.

The next morning they were on the road. The messages had been composed and compared, ready for the next official messenger to do his part. The empty wagon rolled southward again, heading straight for the castle, and Anine's heart lifted at the thought of what new tasks might be waiting there.

The weather cooperated, and they were only five nights on the road getting back, overnighting at inns along the way. The king's messenger overtook them on the third day, staying in the same inn, paying no attention to the poor carter and his wife who sat in the corner nursing light ales.

The next morning saw them on the road early, their harnessing procedure having smoothed over the past month. They were moving along at a good pace, the empty wagon rattling easily over a road dampened by a night of rain, when Ferlen grabbed the reins from her hands and hauled the startled team to an unceremonious halt. Anine's eyes were scanning the surrounding brush, her hand hovering over her sword hilt, when she realized that the trapper was looking back at the damp dirt at the side of the road.

"What is it?"

He leaped from the wagon seat and circled some scuffmarks in the mud like a hound with a new scent. "What do you make of this?"

She tied off the reins and joined him. "I can't see much. The ground is too hard. Somebody definitely pulled a horse to the side of the road here. Is that a footprint, there? Right where a man would step if he swung off the horse."

He nodded. "Not bad, for a farm girl. See anything else?"

She shook her head. "The rest is all scrapes in the gravel."

He pursed his lips thoughtfully. "It was the messenger we saw last night. They have horses shod at the castle, with cleats for traction on icy roads. This horse has cleats like that. Tall horse, too: long and light, like the messengers' horses." His head swivelled.

"Now, from the way he pulled up, we want to look at the other side of the road...yes, here. Two horses. Waiting. One man stayed on, the other came forward on foot. They trust each other, or they'd stay mounted. Their tracks are lost in the middle, but I'd have to say that it was a meeting, not a fight. Figure the messenger's horse stood there for some time, then he probably went on. The others left..." he gazed around, "...that way."

She could see the line of hoofprints leading to where a faint trail broke through the roadside brush and disappeared up a small gully. A sudden prickling of her spine sent her back into the shelter of the wagon, her hand again close to the weapons under the seat.

His eyes scanned the area as well, but nothing moved. "I imagine they're both long gone. No reason to hang around, every reason not to be seen here."

They jumped onto the wagon and moved on.

The rest of the trip was uneventful. Anine held Ferlen to his promise to help her with her speech, and he in turn regaled her with imitations of how various people talked. His ability moved far past style of speech and into individual mannerisms that were easily recognized, and sometimes he sent her into spasms of laughter with the accuracy of his imitations.

"Ferlen, you're so good at this. Why don't you ever do it in camp? Everybody's tired of everybody else's stories, and here you have this ability, and no one knows about it."

He shook his head immediately. "No, I never liked doing that sort of thing. I like to sit back and watch and think, and have nobody notice me."

"But how do you make friends?"

"I have friends."

"I never noticed you hangin' out with anybody."

"I guess it worked, then."

She pushed his shoulder. "C'mon. Who are your friends?"

He shrugged. "You."

"Me!"

"I reckon. I mean, here I've been sleeping with a woman nigh on a month and I never laid a hand on her. If she isn't a friend, then she's sure enough an enemy by now!"

She laughed to cover her confusion. There was a long silence as the horses trotted along. "Tell me, Ferlen, and you don't have to answer if you don't want to. But if you're my friend, I guess I can ask this…"

There was a pause, and finally he broke it. "I think I know what you're going to ask, but ask it anyway."

"Well…if you know what I'm gonna ask, then maybe I don't need to ask it."

He threw up his hands with a bark of laughter. "Hey, now, if that isn't a completely useless exchange of information. If you've got a question, ask it. If not, don't. Let's have no misunderstandings."

She sighed. "All right. You know we made a deal at the beginning of this trip. That was when we didn't know each other very well. Now you say we're friends. Has something changed, or is the deal still on?"

As usual, he thought before answering. "Yes. It is."

"Fine."

"It has to be."

"Why?"

"Well, it's this way. We had the conversation before, about a woman's place in the mercenaries. Before we started this trip, as you say, we didn't know each other very well. So we made a bargain to keep things businesslike. That was the right thing to do, then.

"I don't think anything has changed. We made that bargain to protect us both. Sure, I know you think it was to protect you, but it suited me fine, too. One thing it was supposed to protect us from was our own emotions. Our attitude towards each other has changed. It was bound to. Our bargain keeps us on track. We're on duty, here, and we stay on duty until we hit the castle, stable these horses, and report in to Loreline."

"And after that?"

He grinned. "After that, I'm going to have to be damned careful."

"Why?"

He held his hands up, open. "Because you were a mercenary before you joined the Clan. I'm only Clan. If any of your old merc buddies think I've got around you, my hide isn't going to be worth goat spit."

"Would they think that?"

"Oh yes. 'I'm just a poor farm girl.' That role worked so well with your friends, they all believe it. They're going to have to see you as a woman, first. Then they'll accept the fact that you could have a friend who isn't just a friend. Then, it might be safe for me, if you and I decide I should come calling with posies. Otherwise, I'm just going to be careful that everybody knows I'm just another one of your buddies. Which I am. Right?"

She nodded glumly. "Great. You're tellin' me I gotta completely change my relationship with all the mercs before I can even look at a man sideways."

He shrugged. "That's life. Simple for me to say, complicated for you to do." He took the reins from her. "My turn to drive for a while."

He glanced sideways. "Say, I just got to thinking. Does that boyfriend of yours back at the castle fit in here somewhere? The one in the swordsman's leathers you introduced me to?"

Her mind jumped. "To tell the truth, I haven't thought about him since we hit the inn. What do you mean, swordsman's leathers? I've seen him in a padded jacket while he was teaching."

"No, not while he's teaching. It's his regular clothes. They look like normal leathers, like you or I would wear in the bush. But there's some extra padding stitched in where you wouldn't see it. More protection in the chest area. I always figured it must be pretty hot, come summer."

"You've got a very sharp eye. I never noticed any padding."

"Skins are my business. If I know what people are going to do with them after they buy them, I can do a better job of selling them. I always notice what people wear, especially if it's leather or fur."

"Anyway, to answer your question, I don't think he fits in there at all."

"You don't think."

"Well, he certainly isn't supposed to. I'm not letting on any secrets when I tell you he was assigned to me."

He shook his head. "That was obvious."

"Good, because from what you just told me about the mercs, it could have got him into a lot of trouble. I guess I can also tell you that one reason he got assigned to me was that I didn't like him a lot."

"Oh. Why not?"

"I don't know. I like straightforward people. I don't like to be messed around with poor information."

"He lie to you?"

"Yes and no. He's never said anything false that I've caught him on. But he's not said a lot of things that I could have caught, either. He just doesn't say anything. So I'm supposed to be checkin' him out, to make sure there's nothin' un-to-ward goin' on."

"And is there?"

She thought about it. "It's not up to me to be tellin' you." She swivelled to face him on the seat. "You can see that, can't you?"

He nodded. "You've reached the point where your assigned duty takes over and it's none of my business. Fair enough."

She stared at him. His voice had been light and easy, his face calm. She turned to the road again. *One thing about Ferlen; if he says it's fair enough, he means it.*

"My turn for a question."

"All right."

"I've never known anyone called Anine."

"Probably not."

"So, where does your name come from? I mean, it's a pretty name, but I'm just unfamiliar with it. I always figured it was some kind of version of Ann."

"My real name is Anna."

"Oh."

"But Anine was what my brothers called me when I was little." She blushed a bit. "It means 'Little Anne'." She was careful not to look at him.

"Little Anne."

"That's right. In our local dialect, 'ine' on the end of anything means 'little'. So a 'housine' would be a little house, and a 'nipeen' would be a really small drink."

"I see. So how did you end up with that name in the mercenaries? I doubt if any of them know what it means."

"A bunch of them do. One of my dratted brothers come to check on me, my first year, and he called me Anine, like usual. The guys asked him about it, and the bugger told them."

"And they thought it was hilarious, and started to tease you with it."

She shrugged. "The mercs are like that. They don't mean no harm."

"And also, they were a bit afraid of you, and it gave them a handle on you."

"Afraid of me? I was only a recruit."

"A big, smart, female recruit. Embarrassing if you hurt them physically, but you could do them much more damage in other ways."

"I'm not sure I understand what you mean."

He shrugged. "You probably do."

"You mean that old 'how to treat a woman' we were talkin' about a few days ago?"

He nodded.

"Aye, could be. Anyways, I let it ride, because they seemed happy with it. If I'da bin upset, they'da let it drop, but after a while, when they saw it didn't bother me, they just kept doin' it. I didn't see no harm, since I was used to bein' called that, so I always responded quick enough to it, if there was danger. And here I am."

He looked at the sky. "And here we are, about to get wet."

She glanced up. "Don't think so."

"Farmer wisdom?"

"Trapper wisdom?"

"Got a bet on it?"

"Cook and cleanup tonight?"

"You're on." He glanced at her. "I'll be glad to lose."

"Unless we stay at an inn."

He grinned. "I already thought of that."

"I'm havin' trouble with the next part of that book you gave me. Buncha big words."

"Let's look at it, tonight."

The weather remained dry until they hit the next village, and Ferlen laughed as he pulled up beside the inn the messengers used. "Duty takes precedence."

"I won't forget." She glowered at him. "You owe me one night's chores."

The next two days and nights were comfortable, except the rains did begin, with a light mist that turned to a slow drizzle as they ploughed southward. They knew that this close to the castle they were unlikely to pick up any new information, and they didn't.

Huddled under the tarp as the horses splashed up the road, they discussed what they had learned, but could come to no conclusions. There was something going on; that was certain. Only the double message trick and Ferlen's sign reading on the road seemed to have any possibility of turning up anything useful.

So, they were not exactly happy as they pulled in — a bit tired, a bit damp and a whole lot unsatisfied — to the stable yard below the castle wall. Ferlen grinned wryly as he expertly backed the wagon into the narrow slot assigned by the head hostler.

"At least this trip's been good for something."

She shrugged. "Sure. I got a couple of dresses out of it. I should be happy."

He slapped her shoulder, then passed down her trunk. "Let's get our belongings settled and go see Loreline."

They helped the boys rub down and stable the horses, out of habit and perhaps a desire to put aside the meeting as long as possible. Then they split to their quarters in the castle, meeting outside Loreline's room half a candle later.

The door was open as usual, and Loreline beckoned as soon as she saw them, a broad grin on her face.

"So, my two favourite carters have finished their Swing. Bring back any interesting loads?"

They glanced glumly at each other, then Ferlen spoke. "Not much, I'm afraid. Here's the messages Jhanes made up for you. Hope they work."

Loreline held the package, looking from one to the other. "Something wrong?"

Anine shrugged. "Not really. We just don't think we did very well. We haven't come up with anything; not really. We talked it over, the last couple of days, and we don't see that we have much that might help. Unless those messages worked."

"You're doing too much thinking. That's my job. Your task was to get me information. I'll let you know if it's worth anything." Loreline motioned to the stools that sat by her table. "Sit down and start from the first day."

She sat back in her big chair. "And make yourselves comfortable. This is going to take a while."

And a while it took. Suppertime came, and Loreline had Anine grab a passing page to find them something to eat. As they talked, the older woman wrote notes, jotting quickly, sometimes asking for more details, sometimes holding them while she pondered what they said.

Anine wondered at the amount of time she took with the information from the soldiers at Lanil's Rock. "Soldiers always gossip, you know. It's based on hearsay and what they would like to happen. You gotta discount most of it."

Loreline leaned back, interlaced her fingers and cracked her knuckles. "You'd be surprised at what the common soldiers know. Often more than they think. For example, those soldiers have been out there all summer, right? Made some contacts with local women, no doubt?"

"Aye. The Troubles a couple of years back took a lot of the men. There are a few eligible widows, some with decent farms, lookin' to find a man. Some of those soldiers are close enough to muster-out, they might find just what a soldier's always lookin' for."

Loreline nodded. "The information they have is not just gossip of their own. They talk to the women, they listen, and a lot of real information gets spread in there with the gossip. For example. In any one of the stories you just told me, was there even one hint that there was a local bandit involved? Any romantic, 'good lad driven to crime by the bad landlord'? Any, 'local bully finally goes over the line'?"

Anine thought, then nodded. "I see."

"That's right. The absence of that kind of story tells me a lot that all the other stories don't. Do you have any evidence at all to tell me that this force we are dealing with doesn't come completely from outside?"

After due consideration, they both shook their heads.

"Next point. After the Troubles were over, there were plenty of deserters, bandits-made-soldiers and general rag-tag left out in the forest. A bunch of them gave Jhanes and Lady Talia trouble last spring. When there's a group like that around, usually there's a few that don't really belong. They soon get disgusted with the rough life and the nastiness and slip away. They can't make it in the forest alone, so, since they're basically decent people, sooner or later they turn up looking for honest work. In the end, they find places for themselves and settle in. Have you seen any evidence of that?"

Again, they both shook their heads.

"So that simply confirms, one more time, what we are dealing with. We have a force from outside the realm. It is not a rag-tag bunch of criminals. I have tallied up their take from all their reported attacks and, as far as I can see, they have not made enough to support the size of force they seem to have. My conclusion is that it's a well-organized group with backing from the outside. We also suspect that they have enough cash money to suborn at least one of the king's messengers. We weren't sure which one, but your sign reading, Ferlen, and I hope the contents of this package, are going to change that."

She smiled, more a showing of teeth than an indication of humour. "It so happens that I have information that the same messenger was met the following day by two unknown horsemen. The meeting was not observed, but the conclusion was obvious."

Ferlen nodded. "He gave them the messages, they took them away and they met him later on his trip to give them back."

"Or ones like them."

Anine mirrored Loreline's grim smile. "Are you going to confront him?"

Loreline shook her head. "Oh, no. We wouldn't want to do that."

"Why not?"

The spy mistress gave Anine one of those looks that she had become used to over the summer.

She put up a hand. "I know. You have a messenger who gives your messages to the enemy. A direct line to send information to the enemy. Whatever information you like."

"That's right. And that's all you need to worry about. I only told you what I did because the two of you came wandering in here like your favourite kitten just fell in the millpond. Your information is very useful, and I'm quite happy with your success in your task. Do you have anything else I need to know?"

They exchanged glances; both shook their heads.

"Well, now you have a better idea of how we are thinking about this. Go away and let it mull in your heads for a while. I don't need to tell you not to discuss it in front of anyone. If you come up with anything else, let me know right away. There has been a lot of action out there recently, and we think something is on the move."

"A lot of action?"

Loreline grimaced. "Oh, yes. When the reports started coming in, we were worried about you two. A big merchant convoy was wiped out on the road east of Jaspen, two quarters ago. You must have gone right through there about that time."

96

"We didn't see anything!"

"Exactly."

Ferlen stood. "We were part of the bait."

Loreline looked up into his face. "Yes, you were. We assumed you knew that. We had to know who the targets were."

He nodded. "We knew. We don't mind. It's part of being a soldier." He turned and headed for the door. Then, suddenly, he spun back. "By the way, do you have anything else planned for me for the next little while? Like maybe all winter?"

"I don't. Why?"

He shrugged. "Because you can't just start trapping any time you want. If I'm running my lines this winter, I need to get out there before there's too much snow on the ground," he grinned at Anine, "and I have to rescue my dogs from that sister of mine before they're completely spoiled, and run some of the fat off them before I need them for real work."

Loreline smiled. "Why don't you check with Zoysana? Tell her I said you were free, as far as I'm concerned."

"Good." He tipped his finger to Anine and strode out the door, leaving her flat-footed in surprise. It was the first she'd heard of trapping plans. Probably he'd been thinking of it, and it was only the completion of this task that had set him towards the next one.

"How about you, Anine? What are your plans for the winter?"

She started out of the fog of thought. "Me? Well, I thought I'd be going back to my duties here."

"Good enough. Your special project has been wandering around looking forlorn, lately. Looks like he needs a friend. Will you take up where you left off? Your first report didn't give us enough to work on. I'd like to hear something from you in, say, a quarter?"

Anine nodded. "Certainly...right, I'll report then. Thanks."

"Thank you. You two did a good job. Did you get along all right? No...problems?"

"No problems at all. He's a good man to work with."

"Right, then."

8. VARLI

Dismissed, she left smartly, only to falter into a wandering pace as she moved down the stairs. Her whole attention for the past month had led up to this meeting. Now it was over, Ferlen was gone, and she was at a loss.

The first thing was to stay away from Arvent. It would be too easy to find his company pleasant, to fill the empty spot. What to do?

She headed out to find Varli.

Even as she walked, it occurred to her that it wasn't a logical move. *He's younger than me and a lord's son in the Duchies. He's the king's squire and a friend to the king's family. What's he gonna say about my little problems?* Still, she needed his cheerful assurance that everything was all right with the Clan.

She found him easily, because all she had to do was wander a few of the castle's main halls, and sooner or later he would come running by. Actually, he was striding. The boy had put on length over the summer, and he moved with more assurance, less hurry.

"Hey, Anine. Back from the road are you? How'd it go?"

She swung in beside him. "Better than I thought, actually."

He grinned. "Had your talk with Loreline, and you're feeling dry, are you?"

"Oh, yes."

"Well, I tell you. I can't get much done at this time of night anyway. Why don't we head down into town and get a drink?"

Her heart lifted. "Really?"

He looked at her strangely. "Of course."

"But aren't you busy?"

He laughed. "Always. But I can do all that tomorrow. I see another of my jobs is more important."

"And what's that?"

He grabbed her arm, swung her out the door and towards the castle gate. "Troop morale."

"Huh! Am I that obvious?"

"Only to those of us who know you. I spotted you before you spotted me. You were...drifting. Anine doesn't drift. You're one of the more settled people I know."

"Hah! You mean one of the heaviest!"

He punched her shoulder lightly. "I am definitely not going to respond to that. Last time I got into a discussion of your weight, I wasn't allowed to forget about it for a month."

"Fair enough."

They strode across the parade ground and down into the town. "So, you're off the road and back to your old job, and it's a bit of a letdown, is it?"

She nodded, then realized he couldn't see her in the growing dark. "Aye…Yes. How did you know?"

He chuckled. "I could take it as a compliment to my sensitivity and intelligence, but Zoe told me to keep an eye open for you and Ferlen when you got in. How's he doing?"

"No problem there. He's itch…itching to get back to his trapline."

The boy nodded. "Good. That'll put something positive on his mind." They paced a while, then he cocked his head at her. "How did you like the journey?"

She considered. "It was interesting. Certainly different from what I'm used to." Then she rounded on him. "But I am _not_ gonna take up spyin'. It just ain't me."

He grinned. "So you gonna become a teamster?"

She snorted. "Varli, I started out farm…ing. I'm not likely to take up a job that involves looking at a horse's butt all day.

He glanced at her. "You're working on your speech these days."

"You could tell?"

"Only when you correct yourself in the middle of a sentence." That old Varli grin. "Any specific reason?"

She explained about the road crew, and he nodded enthusiastically. "That's the way to do it. There's new stuff goin' on, and you haveta push yourself ahead."

She, in turn, punched his shoulder. Lightly, she hoped. "You, Varlinden, are going to have to watch your speech as well. You sound like a common soldier."

"Couldn't help it, all summer with you lot." He stopped, then sketched a bow. "Shall we practise our etiquette this evening, my Lady?"

She lightened her accent. "If you were to make a jest of me, my Lord, I would make certain that you obtained some practice in retrieving your teeth from the dirt. My Lord."

He gaped at her. "Where did you learn to talk like that?"

"Ferlen."

"Ferlen?"

"That's right. He's a great listener, that one. He knows how everybody talks. Nobles, commoners, farmers, Inari, you name them, he can mimic them."

"Hmm. Interesting. I never would have known it."

"Well, don't you go spreading it around. He wouldn't thank me. You know what he's like."

"It could come in handy, you know."

She turned into the door of the inn. "If you mean it would make him a better spy, I wouldn't count on it. He didn't like that bit any more than I did."

"Surely." Varli led the way to a couple of stools along one wall. "I'll let Zoe worry about that."

He signalled to the barmaid, and the topic was closed.

"How's Jhanes doing?"

"Fine, so much as I can see. He and Sarha seem really happy. She's quite a woman, isn't she?"

He nodded soberly. "It would take a really strong person to tie up with Jhanes. He's been so many things, I don't think he's sure which one he really is."

She lifted the mug that the barmaid clunked in front of her. "He seems to do all of them pretty well. But I tell you this; now that he's an officer, he's changed."

"How?"

"Hard to put your finger on. I didn't know him that well before. But he seems to be more intent. I don't mean he's unhappy. In fact, he seems really pleased, out there in the sticks being an innkeeper. But he hasn't forgotten that he's an officer. He's got that town so well arranged that I would pity a group of professional soldiers who tried to take it. That rag-tag bunch of soldiers King Gerth sent out there are just about ready to fight a real battle. I worked with them, and they've got that attitude, you know? They want to learn.

"We actually had a good time training together. They made a big fuss about me getting them enthused, but I could see that they were already prepared."

"You figure Jhanes will be a good officer."

"Hah! He's been a good officer ever since I've known him, so he must have been before that. He just moved into the position officially, that's all. Happens in the mercs all the time."

"I guess so. You want another?"

She looked into her mug. It was empty already.

"Of course you do. You've been on the road for quarters, and you need to wet down all that dust."

She held out her mug. "I got enough wettin' to dampen a lot of dust today."

"Wetting."

"Right. Wetting. I would be happy to be wetting my throat again, thank you, my Lord." She caught the barmaid's eye and spun her finger in the age-old signal for another round.

"You want to tell me more about this road work?"

She considered. "I don't know much more than what I've told you. Jhanes only gave me the basics. I gather King Gerth's gonna...going to take over the road work. Stands to reason he's going to have to find somebody to do it for him."

"He could let the job out to local groups."

She shook her head emphatically. "He can't do that. He's been promising the merchant traders a more regular maintenance than the local lords have been providing. He can't take their money then go back to the old system."

Varli shook his head. "That will cost a lot of money."

"There are a lot of merchants on the roads, and more coming in the spring, according to Jhanes."

Varli considered the bottom of his mug for a moment. "Tell you. You come up to the throne room tomorrow, right after the king's public audiences. There's a small council after that, and I think he and Lady Kenna will want to hear your ideas. I'll slip you in on the list of topics."

She dropped her empty mug on the table in surprise. "Whoa, now, wait a minute. I don't have a plan to present to the king. Varli, I didn't come looking for you, just so you could put a good word in for me with the king to get me the position I want. I came looking for you because...well..."

"...because your infallible instincts told you I was exactly the person you needed to see. And you were right. A chance to celebrate getting in off the road by hoisting a few jugs...I guess it's my turn to order them...and a chance to get going on this new idea of yours."

"It wasn't my idea. It come from Jhanes...came from Jhanes."

He shook his head. "I was at the council before he left. They had things sketched out, but nothing as detailed as you've been telling me. Are you saying he thought all that up and briefed you? Why?"

"Well, no, it didn't work that way. He told me the general stuff, and I got thinking, and then we discussed it some more."

"So, a lot of the ideas are yours."

"Aye, well, I sorta approached it like organizin' a troop of mercs, you know, and I got lots of experience with that. In fact, if these bandit raids keep happenin', we're going to have to arm the workers, anyway. At least their camps. Which means soldiers, or some trainin', at least."

He slapped the table, just as the barmaid brought their mugs back. "Right. I never thought about that. Sounds just like the old Kyabran army I learned about from my history tutor." He gazed at her in wonder. "You know, I never thought anything that dry old stick told me would be any use at all. I'm almost sorry I set his robe on fire that day."

"Varli! You didn't!"

"Well, not really. I just knew how he was going to swirl around like he always did when he got going on ancient Kyabra. So I put a candle in the right place. It was just an experiment, really, and I was pretty surprised, myself, when the smoke started curling up. Then I couldn't figure out what to do, so I just sort of sat there, fascinated. He really got going, then. I guess he thought he finally had my attention." He took another pull from the mug. "And then he noticed the smell, and that spoiled it all."

"All right. I knew you were a rotten kid. What did he teach you about the ancient Kyabran soldiers?"

"It was their way of moving across hostile territory. They actually built a new camp every night. Palisade wall, ditch, parade ground, the whole thing. Every soldier carried a shovel along with his sword. There was something about how they fought, too. All foot soldiers with big shields to make a wall. I can't remember exactly how they did it."

"Is that all you can remember?"

He grinned at her. "Yep. I was very young and very uninterested. If you want to know more, Zoe's probably got a book on it in that library of hers up in the southwest tower, where she and Loreline spend all that time."

"She does?"

"Probably. They got… I mean, they have a lot of books up there."

"Varli, I have to leave."

"What?" His bleary eyes looked up at her.

"I have to go back to my quarters."

"But we've just started!"

"We've had three large mugs of the Mercenary's best dark ale, and you've started telling me stories of your badly spent youth. Thanks, Varli, but I have to get some sleep, and then get up early in the morning and get Zoysana or Loreline to let me into the library. I've got to find out more about those Kyabran soldiers. Curse it, I wish I could read better. Maybe Loreline will help me, at least to find the right book."

He looked up at her, his brow furrowed. "Why all this rush, Anine?"

She leaned down to face him. "Varli, don't you see? This is my chance to do somethin' with my life. This is what I've been lookin' for. Somewhere I can use my abilities to get ahead. Up till now, I thought I was gonna be a merc until I got killed or invalided out. Now I got somethin' better'n that. I got a dream, Varli!"

His face brightened. "Well, I guess you're all right, then. Zoe told me to see if I could find something to get you going on. Hah! A lot of work that was. You had it already figured out."

His usual smile played crookedly across his face. "And once again I get credit. Damn, am I good!"

She hauled him up by the arm, dropped coins on the table, and headed for the door. "Take all the credit you like. I want to see the king tomorrow."

He followed, stumbling and moaning. "Just when I was starting to have fun. Couldn't we have just one more?"

Then the cool fall air hit them, and they straightened. "Thanks, Varli. That was just what I needed."

"Obviously. Your steps are twice as long as they were when we came down the hill. Can you wait up a moment? I don't have your capacity for ale."

She hoisted an arm around him. "Come on. You hit those a little fast, didn't you?"

He flapped his arm around her waist, and they staggered up the hill. After a while, she realized his hand was moving.

"Hey, I was right."

"What?"

"You do have a waistline."

She straightened, pushing him away. "Varli! What do you think you're doing?"

He held his hands up defensively. "No offense, Anine. I wouldn't dare try anything. I was just checking to see if I was right this fall, when I said you were getting some shape."

She balled her fist. "Varli, if you weren't so drunk, I'd take serious offense at that."

"Aw, come on, Anine, I was only joking. Well, not really joking. But you know I didn't mean any harm. I wouldn't dare. Your bastard boyfriend with the two-hand...No, I mean your boyfriend with the two-hand bastard sword would chop me into little bits and pieces."

"Varli, he is not my boyfriend. He's my assignment. You've known that since the beginning. You are either way more drunk than I thought, or..."

At that thought, she grabbed him by the shirt and hoisted him up against the nearest wall. "...or else you're way less drunk than I thought. What are you getting at?"

He grinned up at her lopsidedly past the bundle of shirt that was half-choking him. "And you're never going to know, because you're much too nice a person to beat it out of me, and if you don't let go, I'm going to pass out from lack of air."

She dropped him with disgust. "Ah, you ain't worth the hassle it would be, explainin' why I thumped a twerp half my size. Just you keep your hands to yourself."

He straightened his shirt, the grin firmly in place. "Sure, Anine. I won't tell anyone."

"Tell anyone what?"

He motioned towards her waist. "It'll be our little secret." He made a circle with his thumbs and fingers, waist-height. "Little! Get the joke? Too bad, though, to waste it. Hah! Waste it. Waste, Waist. Get the joke?" He went off into gales of laughter, staggering up the street ahead of her.

She shook her head, trying to get clear what was happening. If this latest stupid joke was meant to show that he really was drunk, it was doing the job. On the other hand...

With Varli, you never know. Finally, she gave up and followed him across the parade ground into the castle. As long as he got her into King Gerth's council tomorrow, and as long as she could find a book that would give her something to say...

9. NEW ASSIGNMENT

King Gerth paced the room twice, and Anine had to force herself to breathe. Finally, he turned to her.

"You've been reading about the Ancient Kyabran Army."

She expelled her breath. "Yes, your Majesty. Varli told me about them. Some of their ideas seemed exactly what we need."

Gerth shot a glance at his mother. "What are you looking so smug about?"

Kenna maintained her perfect poise. She always did. "I was just thinking how you complained about your history lessons."

"Fine, Mother. Would it make you feel better to know you were right?"

"I always knew I was right, dear. It is pleasant that you realize it, though."

Gerth slapped his hand to the side of his head and turned to Talia. "I've been putting up with this all my life. Can you imagine how I turned out as well as I did?"

The lady matched Kenna's serene smile. "And I hope you'll be putting up with it for a long time to come."

He threw up his hands and turned to Anine. "How am I supposed to run a kingdom with this kind of aggravation?"

Anine, startled to be included, thought furiously, and came up with nothing. "I'm sure you're doing a fine job, your Majesty."

A peal of laughter from lady Talia stopped him from answering. "Now you've really been put in your place, Gerth. You make a pathetic plea for support from the only person in the room who cannot refuse, and you get exactly what you deserve: empty platitudes."

"It so happens," Gerth drew himself to his full, impressive height, "that I value Anine's opinion, on this matter as well as general policy. I'm sure she meant exactly what she said. Didn't you, Anine?"

"Don't put her on the spot like that, Gerth."

Anine pulled her scattered wits together. She had some idea of this kind of interaction from watching them this summer. "It's all right, Lady Talia. I assure his Majesty that I meant every word."

He stopped and looked at her, his head to one side. "Please. Don't tell me I detect sarcasm! Not in Anine." He shook his head sorrowfully. "I had counted on you, Anine."

"I'm sure you can always count on me, your Majesty."

Both Kenna and Talia were laughing now. The king spun on his heel, and returned to his chair. "All right. I can see I'm not going to get anywhere with this. Why did I ever consent to a meeting with three women?" He shook his head in mock sorrow.

He raised a finger without turning. "And don't you even open your mouth, Varli. You're my squire, and a squire is a piece of furniture, to be treated like one and to act like one. Silent and useful."

Varli subsided, rolling his eyes.

After a moment the king looked up, his smile gone. "Anine, I like your ideas. You need to look into this more thoroughly over the winter, and we'll see what we can organize in the spring. The harvest reports aren't all in, and we won't know exactly how much extra coin we'll have for a month or so, yet. That gives you time. Consult with whoever you think can give you good ideas. Keep in touch with Lady Kenna, Captain Lukin and Loreline. I'm sure there will be connections with all their areas of influence. Any questions?"

"No, Sire. I'll get on it right away."

"Not right away, Gerth."

Both Anine and the king turned to Talia, his eyebrows raised.

"The hunting, Gerth, remember?"

"Oh, yes. The hunting, of course." He turned to Anine. "Do you have anything important planned for the next quarter?"

She hesitated a heartbeat, then took the plunge. "You are the king, Sire."

His voice rose, to cover the splutters of laughter from the others. "I'm quite aware of that, Anine. Once you have been released from the dungeon, do you have any duties which preclude you accompanying Talia on a hunting expedition in Karnan? It will be like that jaunt out to Codding last month, but this time there will definitely be hunting."

"No, Sire, as long as the length of my sentence has not left me too weak to perform my expected duties."

"If you refrain in the future from poking fun at your monarch, we might see fit to commute your sentence."

Anine dropped in a mock curtsey. "Thanking you from the bottom of my heart, your Majesty, I await your further orders with great anticipation."

The king nodded. "Varli, when you can keep a straight face, take Anine out and fill her in on the hunting."

He took each one by the shoulder as they approached the door. "Go. And there will be no laughter in the hallway." He pushed them out, then added, "At least not in my hearing."

Grinning at each other, they strode down the hall. Varli obviously didn't trust himself to speak, but after they had rounded two corners, he let a large burst of air out of his lungs. "Anine! I never knew you were that funny."

"I never had the chance."

He glanced over at her quizzically. "You never had the chance to what?"

"Make fun of a king. It seems to bring out the worst in me."

"Take a hint from a friend, and don't try it on any other kings."

"Not likely to get the chance. We're going hunting in Karnan?"

"Right. Lord Rost has a new stag showed up in his demesne. A huge one, in his prime. No idea why he'd be changing territory, but there he is. Rost figures there'll be too much fighting with this huge newcomer, and he's worried he may lose too many stags, especially the young up-and-comers. He sent a message, asking Gerth and Talia if they'd like to give him a hand."

"We're going trophy hunting?"

"Oh, no. He doesn't want the big one killed. He needs that blood in his herds. He wants us to take out a few of the medium-sized ones, just to keep the number of battles down."

"Has he considered how that stag showed up?"

"What do you mean?"

"What you said. If that stag is so wonderful, why did he move his range? Maybe there's something wrong with him."

"Oh, you mean like he isn't interested in does, or something?"

Anine grinned. "Who knows? He's still a gamble."

Varli sobered. "Still, you bring up a good point. How come you know so much about this?"

"The word is 'why', Varli, not 'how come.' And you know the answer to the question."

108

The squire snorted in disgust. "You're starting to sound like the rest of them. Correcting my speech, playing Zoe games. Farm girls are better behaved where I come from."

She reached over to cuff at his shoulder, missing as he slipped away. "Not farm girls who make fun of the king."

He laughed and strode on. After a moment, he spoke as if none of the preceding repartee had happened. "We're taking Lateda, as usual, but she doesn't ride to the hunt. At least I don't think so. Lateda has a lot of talents we don't know about. However, Talia needs a lady to ride with her."

"A lady to ride with her? Who says I 'ride to the hunt,' whatever that means?"

He glanced at her with an evil grin. "It means you throw your horse through the brush, over logs and ditches, jumping the streams you can, splashing through if you can't."

"Oh. You mean like in a cavalry skirmish. I can do that. I've been on horses plenty." She paused thoughtfully. "Usually without a saddle, though."

"Without a saddle?"

"Oh, sure. When we were kids, we used to ride the plough horses around. Through the brush and stuff like that. No saddles, of course. You had to be pretty good, 'cause…because those horses are smart. They'll run between two trees or under a low limb, try to scrape you off."

"Really?"

"Oh, aye. The one my younger brother used to ride was the worst. We'd be trotting across a field, and she'd stop and have a roll, scratch her back. Nothing he could do would make her quit. He learned to wait until she was finished, when she raised up on her forelegs to stand up. Then he'd jump on her back and grab her mane. When her hind end came up, there he'd be."

"You figure you can handle hunting."

"Sure. As long as I don't have to be in the lead. I'll just watch what everybody else does, and my horse will probably follow along. I'm not much on jumping. Plough horses don't jump."

"I think as long as you stick to Talia, you'll be all right. She's a fine rider."

"Great. Knowing Talia and Gerth, that means they'll be out in the lead."

"Hmm. I never thought of that."

"Don't worry. It'll be less dangerous than a lot of assignments I've had."

A sudden thought struck her. "What about Arvent? I'm supposed to report to Loreline, and I never see him anymore."

Varli shrugged. "This takes precedence. You'll have to ask Loreline, but he's been no trouble. I think he's fine on his own."

She was pleased that she did not feel especially relieved or especially sorry at this news. "Good for him. When do we leave?"

They got to discussing schedules and equipment. When they had a rough idea of what they needed, they split up, Varli to discuss their escort with Lukin, and Anine to see if Loreline had any information that might affect the safety of the royal party.

As it happened, she had none.

"I know I have a reputation for seeing a threat in every shadow, Anine, but in this case, I don't expect any problems. The king is going, well escorted, to the demesne of a family well reputed as firm supporters of the Arlyn dynasty. Except for the usual precautions, especially since hunting is a dangerous pastime, I expect everything to go smoothly." The older woman grinned at her. "Guard duty isn't fun, but it isn't always a chore."

Anine nodded. "Don't worry. I'll take all the usual precautions, no matter how safe it looks."

"That's the only reason I dare tell you that I don't see any difficulties. I know you'll be doing the best of your duty anyway."

As far as Anine was concerned, it was the highest praise she could receive.

* * *

A half-month later, as she peeled away from the court procession to her own quarters in the castle, she figured she had earned that praise.

She had only had time to scrub off the road dust and change into something more comfortable, namely her usual leathers, when Maura was banging at her door.

"Is her ladyship too snobby to open the door for people who used to be her friends?"

"I'm coming, I'm coming. I just have to finish dressing."

The voice through the door responded sharply. "My Lady has to finish dressing, does she? I'll just take a proper pose of subservience out here until my Lady is ready to see me."

Anine jerked the door open a slice, just enough to stick her head out. "If you only want to insult me, why are you here?"

Maura grinned. "That got you moving."

Anine made a guttural sound of disgust, and opened the door. "I'm almost ready. Come on in."

Maura entered, looking around curiously. "I always wondered what a lady's bedchamber looked like."

Anine rounded on her. "Look, Maura, do me one favour? No jokes, no wit, no repartee. All right?"

The older woman peered at her friend. "You mean that, don't you?"

Anine's shoulders slumped. "Do I ever."

"All right. I figure sooner or later I'm gonna find out why."

"As long as I got a good big mug of ale in my hand, and nobody's watchin' to see if I spill it, you got a good chance."

Maura grinned. "Sounds like the Mercenary's Rest to me."

"Great idea. Just you and me. Some of the stuff I'm gonna say ain't for polite ears."

She refused to give any more until she was, truly, seated in the Mercenary's Rest with a mug of ale in her hand. She leaned forward, and they clashed mugs, bottoms and tops, heedless of the foam that sloshed onto the table and flew into Anine's hair.

"So, what's goin' on? Did you have such a terrible time? Not so enamoured with the upper classes no more?"

Anine ran a hand through her hair. "No, I didn't have a bad time. Most of it was a lot of fun. It just ain't me."

Maura's head flew back, and her laugh rang out. "I coulda told you that without you wastin' a half-month findin' out. Can't handle the hoity-toity?"

"No, it's not that. I can put up with it. I can even fit in enough that I don't bother everyone."

"But it ain't you."

"That's right. I can do it, and I can even have a good time sometimes, but after a while, it gets pretty boring."

"Boring! All those parties and dances? Boring?"

"Aye. All those people are doin' other stuff besides eatin' and drinkin'. You know, they got their plans and their dreams, and they're workin' through them at the same time as they're havin' the parties. But not me. I'm just stickin' in there, playin' a role because that helps Talia and King Gerth. Sure, the food's good and the music's well played, but after a while, there's nothin' left to do. I stand and watch what's goin' on, try to figure out who's courtin' who. More important, who's tryin' to stick a knife in whose back. Actually, that part was pretty fun."

"Could you figure it out?"

"Sometimes. Of course, there'd be lots I missed. I probably only noticed the novices. The ones that do it for real are probably so smooth you wouldn't notice the knife until you recognized your own blood on the floor."

"Any of it fall under your duty?"

"None of the really nasty stuff, no. There was a few who thought they could make fun of Talia, subtle-like, you know, but we mostly laughed at them," she paused, grinning, "or just stood and looked at them a while. Has an interestin' effect on cutesy little lords and ladies, that does. They try to stare you down, you know, but you just look at them as if they're bugs you find interestin'. I amuse myself by figurin' out which button I'd cut off first. After a while, they just seem to fade. Next thing you know, they're gone."

"Sounds as if you were some use to Talia, then."

"Oh, I suppose so. She and I had some good times, no question. It only took about three days to weed out the nasty ones. They got the picture and left. There was a few more come in later, but we already had the high ground, and they hardly tried."

"How about the huntin'? Did you fall off your horse?"

"No, I never fell off. Came real close a couple of times. Tell you, Maura, some of them ladies are braver than you'd think. Throw their horse at anything, and usually get over or through it. Lotsa places I'd never have thought about goin' 'cept Talia went first. Gerth made sure I had a good horse, or I'da bin fried a coupla times. Horse knew more'n I did, that's for sure."

"It sounds like you had a fine time. So, it was boring at times. Guardin' always is. What're you so down on jokin' for?"

"That was the real bad part. I never shoulda done it, let me tell you. Never shoulda done it."

112

"Done what?"

"Made fun of the king."

"You did what?"

"Oh, we was jokin' around, just before we left. I don't know if you ever heard them, but the king and Talia, and Zoysana and even Loreline. Sometimes Lady Kenna. They get tradin' jokes with each other. They're good at it, you know, witty like, and sometimes they say things that'd get a glove across the face, if it wasn't they're family, or like family."

"And what did you do?"

"Well, they was makin' fun of the king. He turns to me, to try to send the trouble my way instead." She shrugged. "I sort of turned it back."

"You turned it back? On the king? Are you losin' your mind?"

"He thought it was pretty funny. They all did."

"He laughed?"

"Of course he did. Then he tried at me again, so I turned it back on him again, all polite-like, of course. And everybody laughs again, includin' him." She shook her head. "I shoulda known. I shoulda known."

"Shoulda known what?" Maura was leaning forward eagerly, her mug forgotten in her hand.

"I shoulda known that you don't beat an Arlyn down. They'll get you back, every time. Sneaky buggers."

Maura stifled a giggle, and looked around the room. "That's pretty close to treason, my girl."

Anine nodded glumly. "That ain't nothin' compared to what I said to him, and them all laughin'. But he got me. Mighta known it."

"What did he do?"

Anine took a gulp from her jug, slammed it down on the table. "He hit me with my own stick, is what he did. He decided that I was so funny, he and I was gonna be a comedy team."

"What?"

"That's right. Me and the king. Every time he gets the chance, he picks on me. I gotta respond. Then everybody laughs."

"I don't understand. Is he mean to you? Does he make fun of you?"

"Oh, no, nothin' like that. He's as polite as can be. So, I'm polite as can be right back. If you wrote down what we say, it sounds completely normal. You gotta hear the way we say it."

"Give me an example."

Anine thought. "All right. We was out huntin', and the hunt was over for the day. We'd got a good stag, not a real big one, but a decent trophy. We wasn't supposed to be takin' the real big ones, because Lord Rost is tryin' to improve his herd. So everybody's laughin' and shoutin' at each other.

"Finally some smart politician asks the king what he thinks of this idea of killin' off the up-and-comers to protect the ones in power. Double meanin', you see. I doubt if Gerth really wants to get into a discussion like that, so he looks around and he spots me.

"He says, 'Oh, I couldn't do a thing like that. Anine wouldn't let me. Would you Anine?'

"And I say, 'Your majesty, you're the king. You can do anything you want. I would never dream of getting in your way.'

"And he says, 'But what if I try to do something that's wrong?'

"I come back with, 'You're the king, Sire. If you say it's right, then it must be right.'

"And the king says, 'My, Anine, you are such a loyal subject. Maybe I won't throw you in the dungeon after all.' And everybody's fallin' off their horses laughin'."

"That's it? That's all you said?"

"That's all. I tell you, you gotta be there."

The older mercenary shook her head, took a drink, then shook her head again. "I don't get it. It sounds mostly like nonsense. Why would anybody find that funny?"

Anine sighed. "It's like this. You gotta know what's really goin' on. That guy, the one who asked the question, he wasn't just makin' a joke. He was tryin' to tweak the king for some sort of political policies that are goin' on. Now the king can't respond to him, because he'll look like he's on the defensive. So, he turns the attention to me, because I'm no threat to anybody.

"Then, while we're makin' this silly talk, I remind everybody that he's the king, and he can damn well do what he likes, and nobody better say nothin'. Now, in the first place, it's a bit funny, because it sounds like I'm gettin' away with twittin' the king, because I sound so naive, they all know I must be bein' sarcastic. But for those who know what's goin' on, they're laughin' twice as hard, because they know this smart fella has just been put in his place, maybe even threatened with prison, if he steps out of line."

"You're kiddin' me. All that's goin' on, and everybody knows it, and nobody says nothin'?"

"Not quite. Most of them know what's goin' on. Why would they say anythin'? Most of them are on Gerth's side. They love seein' somebody like that put in his place."

"But it's hard for you?"

"Oh, it sure is. Every time he starts on me, I gotta be as quick on my feet as a sheep-dog runnin' across a herd's backs. I gotta play all the levels of the game as best I can. So far, I ain't messed up, but I'm worried I might."

She took another swig and blew foam off her lip. "I figured I had messed up, now that I mention it. When I challenged him to a duel."

"You challenged the king to a duel?"

"Not really. I just left him an opening, so he could pretend I had. That gave him the opportunity to choose. He chose a duel."

"How did that happen?"

"Same as I said before. These social occasions, there's always about five different levels of conversation goin' on. When somebody says, 'there's word going around that such-and-such', you know that this guy, or somebody who's put him up to it, is really concerned about the topic, and wants an answer from the king. Usually it's somethin' nobody would dare ask about to his face."

She shifted forward, checking to make sure nobody was listening. "This one young fella makes some kind of comment like that 'some people are worried' about 'other people' making a whole lot of cash, and getting 'extra powers' because of it. Dumb bastard. Everybody knew he was talkin' about the king and those who have sided with him on this tradin' bit. So Gerth turns to me, and asks me what I think about people getting extra powers over everybody else.

"I say, 'That's what we have a king for, isn't it, your Majesty? To keep people from getting extra powers over other people that they shouldn't have?' or somethin' the like.

"And he says, 'What if the king was the person getting the extra powers, Anine? Don't you think somebody ought to bring him up short as well?'

"By now, everybody knows how the game goes, so they turn on me, and I'm feeling like a lame deer with the wolves lookin' on. And I'm gettin' tired of it all. So I says, 'I don't know, your Majesty. Taken one way, that kind of comment might sound like an accusation of treason, and that might even be enough to cause challenge.'

"He frowns and puffs himself up. 'Challenge?' he says. 'Have I been challenged?'

"I look innocent as usual. 'I don't know, your Majesty. You were here listening, just the same as everybody else. Were you challenged?'

"Then he frowns and looks at me. 'I think you're getting above yourself, Anine. You shouldn't be challenging the king.'

"And I say, 'Your Majesty, if you feel that you've been challenged, then I, as a loyal subject, can do nothing else but oblige you.'

"And he says, 'Right you are, Anine. Swords in the bailey in two candles.' And that's it. We're having a duel."

"With bare swords?"

"That's what he said, so that's what we did. Sends a message to everyone how serious he is."

Maura grinned. "And also tells them that he trusts his friends a hell of a lot."

Anine shrugged. "I never thought of it that way. Anyways, we have at it for a while, and, as I suspected, he's not playin' around. This is a real training session, and I've gotta skip lively, or he's gonna clip me one.

"We trade blows back and forth for a while, each gettin' in a couplea minor touches, when suddenly he does a reverse on me. Just came outa nowhere, I swear, so fast I didn't even see it comin'. Catches me on the side of the helmet, high, and glances off. Tell you, my left ear's still ringin', and that was five days ago. He stands back, grounds his sword. 'How are you, Anine?' he says.

"I puts on my best, educated-in-the-Inner-Duchies accent, and say, 'If your Majesty deems that the insult has been sufficiently repaid, I would concede to end this travesty.' And once again, everybody laughs.

"But he isn't done. 'No,' he says, 'I have only chastised the head that produced the treason. I must also deal with the body that supported it,' and he whales away at me again."

Maura's fist hit the table. "I got that one! He's sayin' that if anybody commits treason, then he won't just take down the leader, but anybody who helps him."

Anine paused for another drink. "You're catchin' on."

"What happened next?"

"Nothin' much. We slam on each other for a while, each showin' off some fancy tricks, and I notice the king ain't so spry as he was. I bin hittin' it pretty hard, with the Inari fightin' all summer, and the trainin' with you this fall. Plus, I've picked up a few tips from Arvent, you know? He's not that heavy, so he knows a whole lot about not usin' up your energy until you need it. The king's got no time for trainin' so he's not on top of his style right now, and he's gettin' tired. I back off just a hair. Not so anyone'd notice, but he can tell, and he knows I'm ready to quit.

"Now, he's tired, but he's got reach on me. He uses that damned double-figure-eight he has, startin' way out where I can't really reach, then workin' in every once in a while with the tip, you know. I never did figure out how to counter that. He's just too big and too strong. But I thought I found a flaw. Every time he comes over his left shoulder, on the downward slice he comes in just a hair closer than on the right. The next time he comes left, I really lean into it, and try for an outside bind."

She paused to stare at her friend in surprise. "What are you laughin' at?"

Maura controlled herself. "I got a right to laugh because I tried the same trick last month, and I know exactly what happened. When you leaned in real hard, his sword wasn't there, was it?"

Anine shook her head ruefully. "Nope. It wasn't there. And I'm leanin' real hard on fresh air. So, of course, I fall over. Nothin' else to do. But just as I'm goin' down, I notice that he's steppin' sideways, and I take a swing, catch him on the greave just before he puts his foot down. Kicked his leg way sideways, just as he's about to put his weight on it. He just about went down, Maura, I just about put the king on his duff."

The other mercenary's grin widened. "But you didn't."

"'Course not. He's better'n that. He dances around a bit, gets his balance, but it gives me time to get back up and on guard. 'How are you, your Majesty?' I says."

"'Fine, Anine, but my footing is less sure than I thought.'"

"I says, 'Some people might say that anybody who gets too big for his armour ought to have his feet kicked out from underneath him.'"

"Then he grounds his sword, and pulls off his helmet. 'Anine,' he says, 'your logic is even stronger than your swordplay. I think I better quit while I'm ahead.'"

"'Course, they all fall apart laughin'. But I can see some forced laughs and some serious faces. They all got the message. Anybody who starts throwin' his weight around is gonna be sorry. For a lord, havin' your feet kicked out from under you means one thing: losin' your demesne."

"He's usin' you to entertain everybody, and to lay some serious discipline on anyone who objects? That man is smarter than I thought."

"Oh, that's just one part of him."

"What do you mean?"

Anine tried not to make it obvious that she was checking the nearby tables. "That's just another level. Sometimes, he plays that 'simple boy-king' act, and it fools a lot of people. Then sometimes he plays it 'simple boy-king who doesn't know any better than to bash your head in.' That one doesn't have to fool anyone. He's just bashed someone's head in. Then, if he really wants to mess everyone around, he listens to his mother."

They shared a laugh. Gerth had early on proved himself a power in his own right, but Kenna was known to be his strong left hand.

Maura leaned back and drained her mug. "Sounds like you had a pretty good time."

"That's your say-so. Anyways, it's all you're gonna hear about it tonight, 'cause I'm gonna order another mug of the dark ale, and I'm not gonna be responsible for anythin' I say after that stuff goes down."

10. Conference

Anine pulled gratefully into the shelter of the castle wall, spitting the water that had run down beside her nose and over her upper lip. Her horse, knowing that the stable was near, stepped forward briskly. At the stable door, she dismounted and led the dripping animal into shelter, rubbing the ears of the small white goat that pattered out to greet her.

"How's life in the stables this winter, Bunt? No strangers to ambush?"

The lad who came to help her with her horse grinned up at her. "I've been trying to train him, ma'am."

"Aye, but train him to do what, Ardu? Only to attack the people you tell him to?"

He just grinned and turned away to hang the bridle up, and returned with a scoop of grain for her horse. "Do you want any special treatment for him, ma'am?"

"No, once I've rubbed him down, he should be fine. He only got wet, not cold. Keep an eye on him until tomorrow, just in case, though."

"I always do, ma'am."

"I know you do, lad."

He glowed at the praise and went to get another cloth to help rub down the parts of the tall horse he could reach.

Once she was finished, Anine slung her saddlebag and bedroll across one shoulder and strolled up into the castle. Her usual room in the officers quarters was vacant, so she tossed her equipment in and went to clean up. One thing about the castle, there was always plenty of hot water in the kitchens.

Once she felt human again and had removed the deep chill from her bones with a hot drink, she snagged a page. "Where's Zoysana?"

"I don't think she's here, ma'am."

"How about Loreline?"

"She's in her rooms, ma'am. I was by there just a moment ago."

"Thanks, lad." She turned towards Loreline's office.

The woman sat in her usual position behind the big, worn table, writing on one of the sheets of paper that overflowed onto the floor beside her. "Anine! How's the weather out there?"

"Wet."

"I thought it might be. It is winter."

Anine hauled up a stool. "You oughta get out in it yourself, some time. Get some first-hand information."

Loreline smiled. "No, I think your reports are reliable enough on that topic, same as any other. Actually, you don't look too bothered."

Anine thought, then shrugged. "No. Not especially. Happy enough to be warm and dry, though."

"Things going well in Lanil's Rock, I gather?"

"You could say that. Very well, you could say. I've got a written report for you and Lady Kenna."

"Fine. We'll look it over and talk to you later."

"So, where's Zoysana? I thought she was the one wanted to see me."

"She's just out of the castle on a small task for the king. Back late tonight, or early tomorrow I think."

"Good to know somebody else has to be on the road. It makes me feel a whole lot less like a martyr. Anything else?"

Loreline shook her head. "Until Zoysana gets back and certain other developments... develop, I think you're on your own."

Anine nodded. "Good. I've got some friends to see. I'll be around the castle, or maybe down in the Mercenary's Rest."

Loreline inclined her head, and Anine shifted off the stool and left.

At the armoury practise hall she could see that the young recruits and squires were having no problem with the winter chill. They were in the middle of sword drill, and their concentration was complete. Maura strode through the mêlée, her wooden sword always moving, lifting a point here, correcting a leg position there, and her voice rose and fell in counterpoint to the clash of wood and the grunts and cries of her pupils. When she saw Anine grinning from the sidelines, she glanced around at her charges, then slipped over to grab her friend's arm and pound her shoulder.

"Anine! Come to help us out with the trainin'?"

Anine returned the embrace. "I'm just here for a day or so, Maura. How's the new duty going?"

The older woman shrugged, grinning. "Can't complain. I'm warm and dry and workin' for my bread."

"How's the hand?"

Maura lifted her left hand. "The two cut fingers are a bit floppy, you know, so I had this glove made that keeps them together. The rest of my hand is back to normal. The fancy handle on that dagger Zoe made for me makes up for the weakness, so I got no problems. You don't mind helpin' out? I like to have a real soldier in once in a while to remind them what they're really trainin' for."

"I'd love to."

The Swordmistress turned and let out a shout. "Hold!"

There was instant silence, as every fighter froze.

"Down points. Gather here."

She swung her hand in an arc, and immediately a semicircle of young men – and two women – sat on the floor at their feet.

"All right, you've been workin' pretty hard today, but I think you're just doin' it outa habit. I don't mind that habit, because good habits are useful. But habits ain't good enough. You gotta have more. You know what you gotta be? You gotta be scared a little bit."

She bared her teeth in an evil grin. "So, I have arranged a little experience for you. Geral, you skip over to that rack an' bring me one of the big wands there that you use for two-hand work. That's right, the long one. Come on, lad, it's only wood, hold it properly!"

The poor squire was trying to hold the heavy practise wand steady with one hand, but the point wavered.

"A little heavy, Geral?"

"Yes, ma'am. Too heavy for me."

"Then give it to Anine, here."

The boy passed the wand over and Anine hefted it experimentally. True, it was heavy, but not as weighty as her own sword. She ran through a basic warmup as her friend talked.

"Now, lads and ladies, you are supposed to be training to be fighters, and I don't think you realize what that really means. For example, you all fight against each other, and some of you think you're doin' pretty good. But what if you get into a real battle? You think all your enemies are gonna be skinny little weaklings like you are? What you gonna do if you suddenly come up against somebody like Anine, here?

"I tell you what you're gonna do. You're gonna take your wands and you're gonna form a line here, in front of Anine. Do it!"

They scrambled to comply.

121

"The man in front, you just step up, like you was in a battle, and take a swing at Anine, here, and see what it feels like."

Anine knew what was expected of her. As each young fighter approached — some hesitant, some calculating, some bold — she was to take them out as quick and as hard as possible without breaking any bones. It wasn't much of a challenge, but it was good practice in control.

As they attacked, their teacher kept up her running commentary.

"Come on, lad, step up. Now SWING! That's right. Hah! That didn't work, did it? Nice try, girl, but brace your wrist with your other forearm next time. Oops! How's the head? Good man. Keep it up! Don't let her beat you down like that...well then, duck! Don't just stand there and let her take your head off when you lose your sword."

After the full group had been through, the splinters of several practise wands littered the floor. Maura sent them to get new weapons and ran them through the drill again. One of the young squires, a hulking giant a hand taller than Anine, brought one of the two-hand wands like hers. He was almost strong enough, and when their weapons clashed, it was Anine's that broke. She merely grinned and stepped in, bashing his wrist with her forearm guard and twisting the sword from his hand. She tossed it away and took the next five attackers using Weaponless, blocking and parrying with her arm guards, attacking with fists, feet, elbows, and knees.

Finally, Maura called a halt.

"All right, you lot. Now come and sit down, and tell me what it would look like if that had been a battle. Yes, you, Jaica. What just happened?"

"Well, ma'am, if somehow, in a battle, we had to attack her one-to-one, she would have killed or wounded about forty soldiers, with minor injuries to herself, if any."

"Good girl. And that's not so unusual a situation. They always put somebody like that guarding a gateway or a trail where it's all one-to-one."

Anine nodded. "Think of a situation where you had to defend a narrow pass. If half of you were guarding, and half attacking, what would be the result?"

A hand went up. "We'd pretty well kill each other off, ma'am." There was a chuckle, but Anine nodded again.

"That's right. Do you begin to see the usefulness of highly trained mercenaries for special situations? In a pitched battle, on flat ground, with no protection for my back, I would be hard-pressed to defend myself against any two or three of you. Placed in a position I can command, I'm worth all of you."

"Could I ask Anine a question, ma'am?"

"Go ahead."

"Aren't you tired, ma'am?"

Anine grinned. "That was only a half a candle, lad. Sometimes a battle lasts all day."

"But do you fight all day, steadily? Surely nobody can do that."

"No, that's not possible. The battle moves and changes, and there are moments when you can rest, but never for long. You get so tired you think you can't lift your sword, and then somebody comes at you with a spear, and suddenly you find the energy. As Maura was just sayin', fear creates ability you didn't know you had. But talkin' tactics, think what difference a troop of fresh reinforcements can mean, near the end of a battle."

Maura stepped forward. "Thanks, Anine. All right, that's enough for today. Tomorrow, I expect a whole new enthusiasm."

They bounced up and headed for the door, talking energetically.

"Looks like a good bunch."

"Pretty normal. I've had them for a month now. A few dropped out, some doin' better than they ever figured they could, some tryin' to get through on the minimum. You know how it goes."

"That little one, the girl. She's pretty smart."

"I don't know what she's doin' here. She's too small to be a soldier, smart enough to be an officer, but how does she ever survive to get the experience? Fights like a wildcat, mind you, but her size is against her."

"Zoe is smaller."

"That's a thought. Maybe she should be gettin' more Weaponless."

"She'll never be a front-line soldier, that's for sure. There's always staff officers."

"I wouldn't wish that on anybody."

"I guess some of them are useful."

"No denyin' it. What ya think of the big fella?"

"He's strong, all right. Moves pretty clean. Nobility?"

"Aye. Don't know what sort, didn't ask. Name's Dalija. I treat 'em all the same in my classes. Well, not quite. I push him harder. He just knuckles down, pushes back. I ain't beat him down yet. Close a coupla times, but he's still got a grin at the end. Pleasant fella, too. Helps the weaker ones."

"Sounds like he's got it all. Reminds me of the king."

"Same upbringing." The older woman raised a hand, palm up. "It don't spoil all of them, I guess."

"How do you like teaching?"

"I don't mind it at all. When you get a bunch of good ones, you know, and they get goin' hard on an exercise you set them up for, it feels pretty good. Plus, you know for sure that what you're teachin' them is gonna keep them alive. Aye, it's a worthwhile job."

She punched Anine on the shoulder. "And I'm workin' here in a nice, dry castle, while you're out ridin' in the rain! Bet you could use a drink!"

"Never turned down a drink. Any other Clan around?"

"There's always a couple somewheres about. Tell you, I'm goin' back to my quarters to change, I'll meet you in the bailey in half a candle, see who I can roust out in that time. We'll hit the Rest and talk about old times."

"Arvent around?"

"I think he was giving an advanced lesson this afternoon. Want to ask him?"

"Not especially. How's he doing?"

Maura shrugged. "Not bad. He's hangin' out with some of the Guard."

"Good. I told him to make some friends."

"Good advice." Maura nudged her ribs, not gently. "With somebody other than you?"

"Sort of like that. He's not my responsibility anymore but you know…"

"I know. You still feel responsible. That's just merc trainin'." She slapped Anine's shoulder, pushing her along her way. "See ya outside."

A candle later, four Castle Clan and two Inari strode out of the gate into a fading drizzle, headed for the Mercenary's Rest. Near midnight, the same six rolled up the road again, slower and louder, to be stopped by the guards at the gate.

"Maura, are you out past your bedtime?"

The Swordmistress looked up at the burly guard. "Who says when it's my bedtime, laddie?"

"Well, now, if I wasn't on duty, I might be wantin' to help you figure that out."

"Ah! Go on with ya," her voice rose above the laughter this jest brought, "hustlin' old women instead of doin' your duty."

The two seemed ready to entertain their audience with more of this, but the officer of the watch came by and good-naturedly broke it up.

"There's people who sleep at this time of night, you lot of drunks. Who's causing all the trouble?"

"It's Maura, sir, and a bunch of her Clan. They bin drinkin' sir, and we thought we oughta check to see if they was fitten to enter the castle."

The officer lifted his torch. "Well, if they're Clan, we let them in, fitting or not. Who's the big fellow?"

Maura stiffened. "The 'big fella', my dear sir, is Anine, Lady Talia's personal bodyguard, and one of the Clan's best officers!"

The officer stepped closer. "I'd be pleased to shake your hand, Anine, ma'am. All the stories I've heard about you this winter, I wasn't sure you really existed."

Anine straightened theatrically and reached out a hand, hoping she wasn't wavering too much. "Thank you, my dear sir, and I apologize for not demonstrating the proper military demeanor. I have been upholding the traditions of the mercenary trade this evening, and I fear I made such a success of it, come tomorrow morning, I might not even want to exist."

There was another chuckle from the group, and the guards stepped back to allow the Clan members to stumble into the castle. They parted ways with a final back-slapping mêlée, and she pushed her way up the stairs, feeling that all was well with the world.

The next morning she wasn't so sure, but she had a good breakfast and a brisk workout with Maura on the practise floor and felt ready for the world again. As they strolled away, Anine asked a question she had been pondering.

"Do you usually get treated like we did last night? I mean the guard officer?"

"Sure. Zoysana's Clan has a pretty good rep around here. We police our own like a good merc troop, so we're never any trouble to the duty soldiers. We take our turn on guard, so we got sympathy for them, too."

"What did that officer mean, the stories about me? I didn't do anything special against the Inari."

Maura smiled. "I dunno. Must be somethin' to do with Lady Talia. You was with her while she was out there against the Inari, right? Lot of stories about that."

"Aye."

"She's well liked around here, you know. Sort of the fairy-story princess, but the Petrellan version. She hooks Gerth, she's gonna be the most popular queen for a long time."

"I don't think there's been a queen for a long time."

"Weird, ain't it? None of those Arlyn brothers ever gettin' married."

"They all got killed off too young. But what's Talia got to do with me?"

"Anine. All fall, every time they see her out of the castle, you're at her shoulder. The two of you are sort of a pair. All the girls look to you as some sort of a role model."

"What about you?"

"Me?"

"Don't they look at you as a role model?"

"What? A crocked-up old merc with a sharp tongue? Not a chance. Oh, they love the classes bein' taught by a woman. Puts the boys in line, far as they're concerned. But it's you they look up to, stridin' around, shoulder-to-shoulder with a princess, in your shiny ridin' boots, your big sword, your hair all braided in the merc's halo, disappearin' on secret errands for the king."

"Do they realize I'm going to disappear next summer to build roads?"

Maura laughed. "Naw, they don't want reality. I give 'em enough of that on the practise floor."

Anine shook her head. "I don't know, Maura, I never would have thought it."

"That's weird, too. Whoever thought we'd be heroes?"

"Doesn't make much difference, does it?" Anine splayed her hands out. "We still got a job to do."

"But when you got respect, it makes the job easier, and it don't hurt your social life, either."

Anine looked down at the older woman. "Social life?"

"Oh, aye. I got friends."

"Well, that's nice, Maura."

"Nice? Mercs don't talk about 'nice', Anine. You bin hangin' about with princesses too much. What about you? Any prospects?"

She shrugged. "Life's pretty good. I'm too busy to worry about a social life."

Maura shot her a shrewd glance. "Some day, girl. Some day."

* * *

She had just finished changing when she received a message, brought by a properly respectful page, that Lady Zoysana would like to see her. She was, it seemed, expected to know that it would be in Loreline's office, and she grinned to think of another session with those two bright minds.

Zoysana was smiling smugly when Anine entered, her elbow leaning on a cloth-wrapped bundle on the desk. "Well, Anine, you've only been here a day and already you've set the castle on its ear."

"I did?"

The smaller woman glanced at Loreline. "From what I hear, you've got the Weapons classes working double time and the Castle Guard disgusted by your drinking habits."

Anine held up her hands. "Just trying to help out."

Loreline shook her head. "Those soldiers don't need an excuse to start their tongues wagging. It's been a dull winter."

"Aw, I wasn't even that drunk. Besides, Maura did all the talking."

Zoysana raised her eyebrows. "I think that's the point. The Clan has a pristine reputation around here. You show up, and suddenly there's a hand or more of you rousing the whole castle in the middle of the night."

"Well, if that's the case, the Clan obviously needs to loosen up. I oughta hang around more often. Show them how a real merc conducts her affairs."

Zoysana grinned again. "You keep trying to turn my Clan into a bunch of rowdy mercenaries, you and I are going to have words."

Loreline straightened a few papers in front of her. "If the meeting is going like that, I think we're wasting our time. Let's get Anine's report and ship her back out into the rain before she gets you in trouble, too."

Zoysana settled her elbows on the table. "Yes, Mother. We'll be good."

Anine settled down to business as well.

"How are things out at the Rock?"

Anine gestured towards the papers. "It's all in the report. It's easy to create the plans. I won't know where I messed up until it all falls apart next summer."

Loreline nodded. "The plans look good. Of course, there won't be enough money to do everything you want."

Anine nodded glumly. "Never thought there would be."

"And a lot depends on what our adversaries have in mind for us."

"Any new information on that?"

Loreline shook her head. "Nothing from any of my sources. We must be dealing with a small group. Easy to hide."

Zoysana leaned forward. "Or a very powerful one."

Anine shook her head. "Based on what they came up with last summer, I don't think they've got that many resources."

Zoe wavered her hand. "I hate to underestimate the enemy."

Talk turned to likely sources of trouble for the summer, and Anine wracked her brains to find ways to deal with each possibility.

By the time they were finished, Anine felt that they had covered every angle they could possibly think of. She was dissatisfied with the results, but given the resources they had available, it would have to do.

The discussion wound down, but she could tell that Zoysana wasn't finished. Sure enough, the small woman dropped her hand casually on the bundle at her side.

"How's your reading coming, Anine?"

"Not bad. Jhanes and Sarha give me a hand while I'm out there."

"That's good, because I've got some practice for you." She pushed the bundle forward, slipping the cloth off it. A small pile of books lay there, their leather bindings glowing gently in the candlelight.

Anine took the books carefully in her hands, one at a time reading the titles: *Builder's Geometry* and *Kyabran Military Engineering* caught her eye. "Where did you get these?"

Zoysana's grin was casual, but it held a touch of pride. "My official position here is Keeper of the Archives, you know. I have my sources."

Anine spread the four books across the table, so she could check the titles again. "Your sources are owed a great deal of thanks." She looked over at the smaller woman. "How can I pay for these?"

"Use them well. Information's no good unless it's applied."

"In that case, I should be getting back to the Rock."

Zoysana glanced to Loreline, then nodded. "Nothing more for you here. Keep your eyes on the roads in your area over the next couple of months. Don't get so caught up in your reading that you forget."

Anine grinned. "Patrols every day: rain, snow, or storm." She became serious. "I've been covering a lot of area, checking out what needs to be done next summer. I'll make it even farther if we get a good mid-winter thaw."

Zoe nodded. "Good. We'll see you again in the next couple of months. Either I'll be out that way, or you can drop up to the castle between storms."

Anine gave a casual salute to Loreline, made a more formal bow to Zoe and went to pack her saddlebags. There was still a fair slice of the afternoon left, and she could make a good distance in that time. She was on the castle payroll, now, so she could stay at inns. When the sudden winter evening closed in, she would have candlelight to get started on Zoysana's books. She walked faster.

11. THE INARI ARRIVE

So the winter passed, with storm and frost, sun and frozen rain. Anine spent the good days travelling and the bad days either at Sarha's inn or the castle, working out her plans for the road repairs and trying to find a creative solution to the bandit problem. The road repair schedule was coming along much better, and she consoled herself with the thought that the bandits were not really her problem. *Unless they start interfering with my crews. Great. Another worry.*

She happened to be crossing the castle courtyard when the messenger galloped in, his horse lathered and staggering. He bailed off as it stumbled to a halt, and was shouting as he ran.

"They're coming! Get ready!"

Anine placed her bulk in front of him, taking his arm to steady him as he almost fell.

"Calm down, fella. Who's coming?"

"The Inari. Get outa my way, I gotta tell the king. The Inari are coming over the pass!"

She spun aside, still holding his arm, and boosted him up the steps. "Come with me." She guided him quicktime to the king's family rooms where Gerth was at this time of day, and cleared him through the guards. The man started speaking before she could leave, so she stayed.

Gerth was on his feet before the second word was spoken. "Inari? How many? Where?"

"Lots, Sire. Coming over at Broken Boulder Gap."

"'Lots' isn't good enough, soldier. Give me a proper report!"

The snap in the young king's voice steadied the man, and he drew himself up. "Report from Broken Boulder Gap, Sire. A party of Inari spotted, coming down. Mounted. Twenty or more. Two candles later, a larger party started down. About a hundred. Mounted, with supplies. All armed to the teeth. No women or children. Captain Cawber says it looks like a big war party. He took all his men out to face them, sent me post-haste."

"To face them?" He turned to Kenna. "We've been through this before. When Chuko came last summer. Turned out to be a big kafuffle over nothing."

His mother shrugged. "You've got an Inari expert here. Ask her."

Anine gulped, then straightened as well.

"What do you think, Anine? Does this sound normal?"

"This doesn't jibe with anything I picked up last summer, Sire. When they're coming to fight, they never come in the open, in a large group. I can't see Cawber confronting them in a straight battle. From what I heard, it's never happened. The only reason he'd go out to face them is if they were in a single mass, and that's never happened either. I can't see it's an attack, your majesty."

He nodded. "I agree. What's the next best choice?"

Anine thought furiously. "Zoysana always says that when something different happens, look for other differences. There's always a connection."

A wry grin quirked the king's lips, "Sounds like Zoe. What does that mean?"

"Well, if the Inari have never acted like this before, then it has something to do with last summer's activities, because last summer never happened before."

"I see. So maybe they've changed their tactics, and have decided to fight us straight out? They aren't that stupid. Cawber has a full squadron up there. Bigger horses, armour, heavier weapons. He'd slaughter them in a pitched battle."

Anine had another thought. "Of course, there's always another difference. Probably the biggest."

"I don't have time for Zoe's games. Spit it out."

Her cheek burned. "Sorry, Sire. It's the Clan. There's about twenty Inari who would have no problem riding down the Pass in a group, because they spent the summer down here with us."

"And what about the other hundred?"

She turned to the messenger. "Did it look like the others were chasing the first bunch? The smaller group?"

The man thought a moment, then shook his head. "They were both moving at an easy pace. Nobody hurrying. Just seriously covering ground."

The king smiled. "So perhaps you galloping in here shouting was a little over-dramatic? Did the Captain tell you it was an emergency?"

The man's head dropped, and his feet shuffled. "No, Sire. He just told me to get down to the castle as quick as I could, and tell you."

"I see. Well, if you don't have anything more to tell me...?"

131

"No, Sire. Captain Cawber sent me out before we knew more."

"Then you have done your duty, and we thank you. Go and see to your horse and get some food and rest. Anine!"

The sudden sharpening of his attention stiffened her spine. "Yes, Sire?"

He started ticking points off on his fingers. "Find Varli and send him to me. Where's Jhanes?"

"He's still in Lanil's Rock, Sire."

"The only fluent Inarituk speaker we have, and he's home when we need him. And Zoysana's somewhere along the Velikiian border checking out smugglers' trails." The king put that thought aside with a gesture. "While you're looking, find everyone in the castle who fought Inari last summer. Gather them in the courtyard, mounted, with supplies for a quick trip up the mountain. Any questions?"

"Full weapons, Sire?"

"Yes, but don't let that slow you down. I don't expect you'll need them. I just want every experienced man we have up there to deal with this." He grinned at her. "And woman. Off you go."

She saluted and spun away, leaving the room at full stride.

One candle later, seventeen of last summer's Inari Fighters stood beside their horses in the courtyard, packed and ready to move. Gerth strode to the front, checking faces, Varli at his shoulder. After a moment he raised his voice, although everyone's attention was already on him.

"Any chance of more, Anine?"

"I've sent messengers out, but this is all we have for the moment, Sire."

"Good enough. We can't wait for more. No officers."

"The Clan doesn't really have officers, Sire."

"Then Varli's in charge. Anine, you're second in command." He faced the two. "Any more who show, I'll hold here, waiting for word from you. I'm not going to mobilize any more troops until I hear something. Get up there as fast as you can, but don't show up too tired to be effective if Anine's wrong about the Clan."

He held up a hand to forestall Varli's questions. "She can fill you in as you ride."

Varli gave a quick nod. "Right, Sire. We're on our way."

He and Anine swung into the saddle and led their small troop out the castle gate. As their hooves drummed hollow on the drawbridge, she glanced over at Varli, to catch a slight smile on his lips. He noticed her regard and sobered, then looked at her again and smiled more broadly.

"Feels good, doesn't it?"

She laughed. "Pretty scary, actually."

His gloved hand slapped her thigh. "Don't worry. This sounds like a pretty simple assignment. Deliver the troops to Cawber up at the Pass. Take care of them until an officer shows up. Now, what's this Gerth wants you to fill me in about?"

She explained her reasoning. "...and to me, none of this sounds like an attack."

"It's almost the right time of year."

"They've never come this early before. And, from what the soldier said, they aren't acting like that at all."

He considered awhile, then nodded. "I can't think of anything more likely. I hope Cawber sent the regular Guides out to the other passes. I suppose this might be something to attract our attention while they sneak down somewhere else."

"I hadn't thought of that."

They tossed ideas up and down the line as they rode, but no one in the troop could think of another likely explanation for this new Inari behaviour. Speculation was ended when they met the next messenger trotting down the trail towards them. This one was a regular Guide, and he seemed in less of a hurry. Varli recognized him.

"Nall. What's the news?"

The Guide pulled up. "Hi, Varli. News is good, I guess. There's no attack, at least not yet."

"Who were the Inari? Clan?"

"I think they are Clan. I recognized a couple of them."

"Describe them. Old, young? Fighters? Any women?"

The Guide considered. "Definitely fighters. No women. Mostly young, but one older fellow. The bigger group, the ones coming behind, hadn't got there yet when I left."

"You made contact with the first group? What did they say? You must have had somebody up there who speaks Inari."

"Not really, but one of their youngsters talks Petrellan pretty well. They say they want to talk to Lady Zoysana."

"What about?"

133

"They won't really say. They just want Zoysana. They did say something about coming to help."

"To help?"

"That's right. They didn't say at what, but that's it."

Varli turned to Anine. "If they speak Petrellan, then they're Clan."

Anine nodded. "The older one would be Pagris. The Petrellan speaker Mantinello."

Varli turned to the Guide. "Thanks. Sounds like we don't have a problem. Just tell King Gerth everything, and pass along from me that it looks good, but we don't have any more information yet."

Nall nodded, pushed his horse through the milling troop, and was off down the trail at a quick trot.

"Well, I don't see any reason to waste our horses, but let's move along." With that, Varli kneed his mount into a steady walk up the trail, and Anine and the rest followed.

By the time they reached the mouth of the Gap, the parley was over. An unused area of the rough parade ground in front of the camp bustled with a mass of Inari, over a hundred, setting up their tents, picketing their horses and starting cooking fires. Anine and Varli dismounted a polite distance from the growing camp and walked forward.

As they approached, activity slowed until silence descended. Then Mantinello pushed out from under a tent and strode forward, smiling. Pagris appeared from the other side of the camp.

"Varli, Anine! Good to see you. We come to help Zoysana. Clan and others." He swept his hand back, to indicate the group of Clan who were gathering close, smiles on their faces, and the larger group who hung back, uncertain.

The others of Varli and Anine's troop also moved in, greeting old friends from the summer, and a general mêlée of back-slapping and shoulder-punching arose, leaving Anine, Varli and the two Inari in the calm centre.

"Help with what, Mantinello? Zoysana doesn't need any help."

He nodded knowingly. "Inari know better, Varli. King Gerth has trouble on his borders. Zoysana needs Inari help."

Varli stared at the slim Inari lad. "And I wonder how you knew that?"

134

Mantinello slapped the squire on the shoulder, turning him towards the Inari camp, the gesture including the other two as well. "Come, sit. We will talk. It is good to see old friends, yes? And we have new friends as well."

Anine regarded the circle of watchers. "Quite a few of them, it seems. Have they come to help, too?"

"Oh, yes. They ask to help. All good young Fighters; they want very much to help Zoysana."

Varli frowned. "They all want to become Clan?"

"Oh, no. Not Clan. Other clans. Allies." He indicated several saddles and packs that his men were pushing into a rough semicircle. "Come and sit. We will have *boal* and *aaruul* and we will talk."

Varli shrugged at Anine. "Sounds like a good idea." Then he turned to a nearby soldier. "I think it would be polite if we asked Captain Cawber to join us."

The man responded with a curt nod and strode towards the rest of the camp and the group of regular soldiers milling nearby, watching developments with interest.

Soon he returned with the Camp Commander, and the meeting became more formal. Varli made certain everyone knew each other, and the ritual friendship food and drink were offered. Formalities ended quickly, because the Petrellans were as eager for information as Mantinello was primed to talk. Pagris, as usual, sat silently watching.

"Zoysana sent a message. Two months ago." He turned for conformation to the young Clan members behind him. They nodded solemnly.

"Pagris and I came over the Pass last month."

"We didn't see anyone coming down."

The Inari grinned at the commander. "We didn't want you to."

Cawber frowned at that, but said nothing.

Mantinello continued. "We had a hard trip, Varli. Hard to travel and live off the land when we cannot use the farms."

"What do you mean?"

The lad grinned and explained. "Pagris says all farmers are Zoysana's people. We are Zoysana's Clan, so we cannot take food or horses from them. It seemed very wasteful, as we are in too much hurry to hunt. But Pagris says we must not. So we move fast and eat little."

The older Fighter took up the story. "We found Zoysana and the Balagueratu at your town of the Rock of Lanil, where my friend Hidden Twig has his home. It was good to shelter under the tent of my friend, although I do not like your houses. The walls are too thick, and the air is stale inside. It is also good to meet his wife and son. A good wife. Strong. The boy has – what is your word? – potential. He knows how to be silent."

Varli's eyes had been widening through this. "You mean you two scouted all the way to Lanil's Rock without anyone seeing you, and had a meeting at Jhanes' inn with Zoysana?"

He nodded. "And with the Grandfather of Wolves."

Varli rolled his eyes. "I imagine Patu approved, did he?"

"Of course. The Balagueratu is very wise."

"And what was this meeting all about?" Varli suddenly slapped his leg. "You don't mean Zoe asked your help with the bandits?"

Pagris nodded. "Not at first. She only asked our ideas. Then we talked. We made many good thoughts. King Gerth must match fire to fire, water to water, like last summer with the Inari. Your soldiers cannot get to these bandits to fight them. Your Guides can find them, but they are not fighters. Inari go where they wish, fight when they wish. I come back to raise Zoe's Clan for her."

"But what about the rest?"

"Ah. That, I did not plan. They are young Fighters from Aguilana, Credana, and Verneta Clans. They have a great difficulty, come spring. They wish to prove their manhood in battle, but they cannot fight below the Rim of the World because those are Zoysana's people. Who should they fight? Chuko, the Grand Potentara, has made it known that he would look very unhappily on the Clan that causes disharmony by fighting with other Clans. Somehow they find out about Zoysana's call."

Varli nodded, then frowned. "It's a good solution to their problem. But Zoe doesn't know they're coming?"

Mantinello shrugged and shook his head. "I have no way to tell her. I have no power to tell them not to come, and there must not be trouble between our Clans and Gerth, the Great Potentara of Petrella. So I bring them with me. They swear they will fight with great bravery, skill, and honour."

"And where does Zoysana want you?"

"She showed me a place, just outside of the Rock of Lanil. We will pitch the tents of Zoysana there and then start our campaign."

The Camp Commander shook his head. "Lady Zoysana thinks you're going to march a hundred or more Inari across Petrella and not run into any problems? With due respect, she's out of her mind."

The Inari shrugged uncomfortably. "She did not know a hundred. She asked for just us." He indicated the Clan members seated around him. "No one would see us."

Varli threw up his hands. "It looks like we don't have a choice. Zoe wants these Inari in Lanil's Rock. It's up to us to get them there. We'll have to change the plan a bit, that's all."

"What did you have in mind?"

Varli looked to Anine. "In the first place, we can't sneak a group that big through. Not even Inari."

She nodded. "Especially this bunch with no experience, or at least friendly experience, with Petrellans."

"We'll have to go openly."

Anine frowned. "Maybe not too openly. I bin lookin' at maps of the realm this winter. There's decent trails out to the east that circle past the castle. Some roads, even."

Varli nodded. "Fine. We'll just have to take back trails as much as possible and hope for the best if we meet any locals. I don't have any worries with our Clan. But how will we keep the others in line?"

"We'll have to be sure they'll follow orders. That's a tough idea for them. Mantinello," she turned to the young Inari, "how do the Inari Potentaras make their followers stick to the plan in a hunt or a war party?"

"Loyalty. If they have sworn loyalty, then they will follow the leader or dishonour themselves."

"That's not exactly the same as following orders. What do you think, Varli?"

The lad shook his head. "I think it's the best we can do. Next question. Who do they swear loyalty to?"

Anine frowned. "You, of course."

He shook his head again. "I don't think so. I might not even be going with you." He grinned. "I have to pretend to be Gerth's squire now and again, just for appearances' sake. What about you, Pagris?"

It was the Inari's turn to shake his head. "I am first Cerdana Clan, then Zoysana's. It is not correct that they swear to me. Mantinello is the same."

Varli grinned. "I guess you're next in line, Anine."

She felt her jaw drop, snapped it closed and swallowed. "I don't think so, Varli."

Varli sent an enquiring glance to Pagris, who moved his head sideways, then back. "They would follow a woman, I suppose, but this is going to be very difficult for them. I remember all the new things I had to learn last summer. This will be more."

Varli shrugged. "I don't see anyone else, Anine."

"I don't know…"

Varli grinned. "You're the one, Anine. No doubt about it."

"I ain't even really an officer, yet."

Varli laughed. "You know what they say about working with Zoysana. You never know where you're going to end up."

"All right. They swear to me. But," she fixed Pagris with a glare, "I gotta know exactly what that means. And they gotta know exactly what I think it means. Because I know how this goes. If one of them messes up, I have to kill him myself, don't I?"

The Inari nodded solemnly. "Better than to let him go home dishonoured."

"Huh! Some consolation, if one of these young bucks gets it into his head he's been insulted and gets us into a battle. Once Zoysana's finished with me, there won't be enough left for King Gerth to take his turn."

Varli clapped her on the shoulder. "Don't worry, Anine. Pagris and Mantinello will help. I'll do what I can. You'll do fine."

They decided it would be best to break the news to the rest of the Clan Inari first. To Anine's relief, there was no hesitation. They crowded around her, clapping her on the back, shouting compliments. She wasn't so sure the rest would take it so well.

Finally, she turned to Varli. "All right. This has to be done, and I'm not putting it off. Mantinello, line them up."

As the new Inari were forming a double horseshoe in their usual way, she was frantically reviewing her faint Inari, cursing the luck that had sent Jhanes in the wrong direction at the wrong time. Finally, they were assembled. When Mantinello would have spoken, she shook her head. "I'll do it from the top, Mantinello. It's better that way."

She turned to the assembled Inari and spoke, she hoped forcefully, in Inarituk.

"Some of you know me. I am Anine. I speak for Zoysana, Leader of our Clan. You wish to ally with us?"

There was an immediate murmur of assent. Fine.

"To join, you must swear to a Leader. You all know this. Zoysana is already on the field of battle. You cannot swear to her. You will swear to me."

She forestalled the expected protest by drawing her sword. "If you do not agree, you have a choice." She pointed back up the pass with her weapon. "You can go back, and none will question."

She pointed to an open space of dusty grass nearby. "Or we will make a circle, and have our discussion there. Understood?"

There was an uncomfortable stirring in the group, but no one took either of her options. Good. She turned to Mantinello and was relieved to lapse into her own speech.

"Please explain to them about going through Gerth's kingdom. Tell them how important it is that they follow the ways of the Lower Places. Make it a challenge to their abilities."

He grinned. "Good thought, Anine." He turned and spoke eloquently to the other youths. She listened, pleased that she could understand quite a bit of what he said. As he spoke, she thanked the Lady for sending this diplomat to her. The lad spoke with emotion, taking his listeners through a tale of danger and risk to honour. When he had finished, Anine was sure they were ready to follow her into the depths of their own private hells and out the other side.

Mantinello turned back to her, his voice barely heard over the roar of raw emotion from the throats of the assembled Fighters. Even her own Clan joined in. "I think they are ready, Anine."

"Nice job, kid. Let's do the ceremony now. Then we start training while we've got them enthused. I want them used to carrying out my orders."

As Zoysana had done with the original Clan, Anine started them out on the Weaponless drills she knew they had little experience with. Because of her size, she could demonstrate, but the trick of shifting weight was not obvious. She could lift any of them off the ground anyway, so the advantage was needless for her.

She spent her time supervising while Varli and the Clan Inari worked with groups of newcomers. She worked them hard, aware how important it was for these fiery youngsters to feel challenged. When she had them all sweated up, she grabbed the ropes. "All right, folks. Let's go check out the rock."

They jogged behind her over to the closest climbing wall, and soon they were swarming over it, demonstrating their skill or lack of it. Anine worked the wall herself, cursing her slack winter when her aching muscles threatened to rebel. It was important that she be able to do anything she asked of them. When they were down from the wall, she stopped them.

"All right, Clan. You have done well. You may rest, now. Prepare to ride tomorrow into the dangers of the unknown. I know you will hold high the standard of Zoysana's Clan, and the pride of all Inari."

As they charged, shouting in glee, back to their camp, she walked beside Varli, wiping sweat from her face. "I don't know. I can keep up with them physically. It's all this shouting and enthusiasm I'm gonna run out of."

Varli laughed as usual. "No problem. If you feel you're flagging, just sent Mantinello at them for another round."

"He is a truly frightening person, even if he doesn't know it yet. Think if he were on the opposite side."

The king's squire nodded. "We really have created something, there. In the normal run of Inari life, as the son of a minor Potentara he would have to work just to raise his Clan a few steps. Give him a group like this or a full-scale war, and he could make the difference between success and failure of a whole campaign."

"As long as he's helping me, we might just make it."

Later that night, a weary Guide trotted his equally exhausted horse into camp. He wordlessly dropped a paper into Anine's hands. She scanned it, and her roar of laughter brought the others running. Unable to speak, she passed the paper to Varli.

He read it. "A message from Zoysana. She says to head out to Broken Boulder Gap to meet Pagris and the Clan Inari. She says they should be here soon!"

They all chuckled. Anine took the message back and walked away, shaking her head.

Varli's voice followed her. "I guess there's no response."

For the next two quarters the Inari, holding creditable formation, rode through the farmlands of Petrella. They kept to the side roads and stayed completely away from the castle, and they made the traverse without incident. As far as Anine and Varli could tell, there was not a farmer's dog kicked, not a chicken stolen from its roost.

It helped, of course, that the Clan Guides served as outriders and messengers, cushioning the savages from the local people, and that huge amounts of food were prepared and waiting at each camp as they pulled in. Because of this organization, Zoysana's augmented Clan arrived at their summer barracks in the woods above Lanil's Rock in good time and in good spirits. There, they all swore allegiance to Zoysana herself.

It was with considerable relief that Anine turned her command over to the Clan Leader. As the ceremony closed, she found herself walking beside Pagris. "I thought I knew what you were going through last fall, with your language difficulties. Believe me, I had no idea!"

"Harder for you, Anine. You had to keep face as well. I was just stupid barbarian if I made a mistake."

"Hah! You missed an 'a' again!"

He shook his head ruefully. "If I am not careful, I always do that. Just a stupid barbarian." He grinned at his own joke.

The problem arose just before she left the camp. Mantinello came to her as she was briefing Zoysana about their trip across the country. Teaching the Inari and the Petrellans to co-exist was going to be crucial, and many small lessons had been forced on them by the journey.

Mantinello paused apologetically in the tent doorway. "I am very sorry to intrude, ladies, but I must admit to an error."

They both looked up, mildly surprised. "What is it, Mantinello?" Zoe indicated a cushion for him.

He grimaced. "When we started with the new recruits, we had a problem."

"I know. To get them to agree to swear to Anine."

"Right. I did what I could to make them feel that she was worthy."

Zoysana laughed. "You have done admirably. They seem to adore her."

The boy nodded sadly. "That is the problem, Zoysana, my Leader. I have succeeded far too well. Are you aware of the concept of *neurath* in Inari culture?"

Zoysana frowned. "Vaguely. It's a mythical war leader. A story."

Mantinello shook his head. "Yes and no, Lady. It is not a story. The *neurath* is real. He is created by the Fighters. They put all their *neurin*, all their luck, into his charge. As long as he is with them, they cannot lose a battle."

"Oh, no."

"I am sorry, Anine. I only sought to help. I did not create this *neurath*. The Fighters did. You must realize it was a very difficult passage for them. They were going where no Inari have gone before, and they needed every help."

"So they turned me into their mascot."

Zoysana shook her head. "It's not a mascot, Anine. These men truly believe that their honor and their luck is tied up in you. If you leave, I have no idea what will happen."

Anine felt that familiar sinking in her stomach. "Why do I hear the sound of slamming doors?"

Zoysana had no answer. Mantinello couldn't meet her eyes.

"It ain't fair, Zoysana. I've got plans for the summer. I got roads to build. I spent the whole winter settin' it up!"

"That's all right, Anine. You've done the basic setup. Now somebody else can work with it."

"But that's just it. It was a whole bunch of new ideas. It'll have to be adapted as the work goes on, and we find out what works and what doesn't. Besides..."

Zoysana waited, puzzled. "Besides what, Anine?"

"Well, this may sound selfish to you, Zoysana, but this was gonna be my big chance, you know? I had an idea, and I was in the right place and at the right time, and it was gonna set me up, you know, with work for the rest of my life."

Zoe smiled softly. "Mercenary's dream, Anine?"

"This wasn't a dream. It was right here, happenin' this year. Now you tell me I gotta shepherd a bunch of Inari around all summer. I gotta give the job to someone else. He'll take over and change everythin', and it won't be mine anymore. I won't be able to just pick it up when this is over. My chance will be gone. And I'll be back to bein' just a merc again."

"I thought you liked being a mercenary. And a member of the Clan. You know you've been tagged as officer material."

Anine sagged. "I know, Lady Zoe, I know. But this was gonna be mine."

She straightened her back. "But there isn't anythin' anybody can do about it, is there? A hunnert Inari is like a forcea nature, and you deal with them any way you can. Well, I guess that's it, then. Mantinello, I'm gonna take this out of your hide, you realize. And to start, you're gonna be my second in command."

"I am?"

"Aye, and don't look so pleased. You ain't been an officer in the Clan yet. I hope you slept well last night."

The boy looked puzzled. "Well enough, Anine."

"I'm real glad for you, 'cause it's the last good sleep you're gonna have all summer. From today on, you'll be up before everybody in camp, and you won't get to sleep until they're all tucked in tight. The only person gets less sleep than you is me. Got it?"

The boy took a deep breath. "Got it, Anine. Where do we start?"

"Good question. Well, Zoe? What are the orders?"

Zoysana didn't quite conceal her smile as she started to lay out the maps.

12. SUMMER WORK

A quarter month later, Anine was in the middle of her maps one afternoon, putting pins in the big board, when Mantinello ducked into the tent.

"You got visitor, Anine."

She thought she caught a strange smile on his face, but he ducked back out through the flap before she was sure. She followed.

"Ferlen!" Her spirits rose as the familiar figure stepped towards her. She took his forearm in the usual greeting, reaching out to slap his shoulder with the other hand. He smiled a bit, nodding in his reserved fashion.

"Good to see you, Ferlen. Come on in out of the sun. What brings you up here? Oh, I suppose you're down at the Rock visiting your sister. How is she? I haven't been in for a visit in ages. We're keeping pretty busy up here these days."

"She's fine. I came up to talk to you, Anine."

"Oh?" She indicated a camp chair beside her worktable. "That's good. What about?"

He opened his mouth, but before he could sit, Zoysana's voice came from outside the tent, "Anine..." followed by her head sticking through the flap. She took in the situation at a glance, then nodded. "Good. You're already working on it. See you later."

The head disappeared before Anine had time to register what she had said.

"Working on what?"

"That's what I have to talk to you about, Anine. You've got to get me out of this. I am simply not going to do it. Tell her I won't do it. Tell her it's..."

She held out her hands defensively. "Wait a bit, wait a bit. Get you out of what? What are you so worked up about that you say more than three sentences in a row?"

"This isn't something to make jokes about, Anine. This is serious."

"All right. It's serious. Just tell me what it is. We'll figure it out."

He stopped and looked at her, then peered more closely. "You really don't know?"

She threw up her hands in exasperation. "Isn't it obvious?"

"I figured you cooked this up between you, and I couldn't see how that would happen."

"Ferlen. I have not cooked anything up with you in it. I haven't even seen you since you headed out for your trapline last fall. I'd ask you how the winter trapping went, but somehow it doesn't seem the right moment. Come over here and sit down and tell me from the start. What has Zoysana, with that devious mind of hers, put you into?"

He nodded and relaxed enough to take the chair. "I'm glad it wasn't you, Anine. I was plenty steamed when I found out about it. Not steamed enough to get rude, you realize, but dammit! I spent all that time in the fall being a spy for her, and I told her I didn't like it. So what does she do? She lines me up to be head of the road repair crews for the summer. Me! The trapper, the woodsman. What do I know about roads?"

Anine sat back as the realization hit her. "My road repair crews!"

"And that's the other thing. Those are your crews. I know how important it is for you to be given that duty. So now she's stuck you up here with a bunch of Inari, and she's given your task to me and I won't take it from you. It isn't fair to you, Anine."

A tumble of ideas was running through Anine's head, and she scrambled to organize them.

"Ferlen, aside from it being my duty. What do you have against the road work? Did you have some other plans for the summer?"

"No, no plans. I figured to come down with my furs, hang around in town for a while, have some fun until Zoysana or Loreline found out I was there, because I knew sure as stink from a skunk they'd grab me and put me to work. Then I found out this bunch of the Clan was out here. That took some very close tracking, believe me. There aren't too many in Petrella who know there's a hundred Inari camped in their back yard."

"As you can probably figure out, we'd like to keep it that way."

"Of course. Anyway, I heard the Clan was out here. So when I got the call, as I knew I would, I went up to see Loreline and, sure enough, she says to come out here and see Zoysana, because she had something important for me to do this summer."

"I bet you didn't like that 'important' part. They always say that when you're not going to like what they have in mind."

"True enough, but I still figured it was going to be something to do with the Clan. Maybe leading a group of the Inari or something."

"Could you have done that?"

"Oh, I suppose. I mean, I know Zoe'd like me to do some officer stuff. I could handle that, I guess. But then I got here, and she told me. She remembered that I said something to Jhanes about doing stonework, way back last fall before you took over. Now she wants me to do your road repairs while you do the officer work with the Inari! Why doesn't she do it the other way round?"

Anine ran a hand through her hair, shaking her head in frustration. "Look, Ferlen, I'm with you on that. If you could do the leading up here and I could do the road work, I'd be the happiest merc in Petrella. Except I wouldn't be a merc and, you know, that doesn't bother me a whole lot anymore. But I can't."

"You can't?"

"No, I can't." She explained what had happened on the trip down from the Pass.

When she had finished, he sat back, his hands on his knees, and looked her up and down. "Their *neurath*? That's serious business."

"You know for sure it is. So, much though I'd like to be doing the road work, the actual work, you know, not just all the planning I did last winter..."

"Those plans look great, Anine. Zoysana showed me, down at the Inn. I think they've got a really good chance of succeeding. Although, some of your estimates on the bridges...

"What about them?"

"Well, you have the wrong kind of rock for the foundations. The right stuff costs more, but it lasts better. I didn't want to horn in, but..."

"What do you know about bridges?"

"Oh, I've never built a bridge. Just walls and houses and that."

She grinned. "And last summer, you just happened to mention that to Jhanes."

"Aye, when we were talking about expanding the inn."

"And now we know why you're in charge of the road work."

"But I didn't mean to! I don't want to take it away from you. I know you'll do a great job of that, once you get the chance."

"But that's the problem, Ferlen. I'm not going to get the chance. I'm stuck up here until this cleanup duty is over, and that's not going to happen just this month. I'm here until the Inari go home. No question.

"What was burning me up was that they were going to give my project over to some lord's son or merchant who was going to take it over, mess it around and either destroy it completely or make a pile of money off of it, and I'd be left back in the dust, back to workin' my way up the mercenary ladder if I didn't get killed first."

"I see."

"But now they've given it to you. Did you tell her you won't?"

"Did I ever. Several times. She just nodded and said I should wait until I've talked to you."

"And does it change things, now that you've talked to me?"

He grinned wryly. "In the first place, I'm not looking to wring your neck. I guess that's progress. I might have figured you had nothing to do with it."

"But now that you know I can't do it. How do you feel about it?"

He threw up his hands, slapped them down on his knees again in frustration. "I don't know, Anine. Whatever did they give it to me for? Like I said, I don't know the first thing about roads."

"Except for a month as a carter, and building a bunch of walls and houses."

"I suppose. But what does that mean, in terms of experience?"

"I don't know. I'm trying to answer your question. Why did they choose you? It sounds like politics to me. Zoysana doesn't usually work that way."

"What do you mean?"

"Well, a political type, faced with a choice between someone who knows the job and someone who is a friend who will support her, gives the job to the friend. The job suffers, but the political type has a friend, and a friend who owes her his job, in a good position to support her, should she need it."

"I see."

"Like I said, Zoysana doesn't usually work like that."

"But Loreline does."

"When she has to. But she was trained by the Sivan, and his specialty is putting the right people in the right places. That means there's a reason why you're here. You're supposed to do something that needs to be done, and this road duty is a good place for you to do it."

"You think so?"

"With Loreline, that's almost sure. I'm relieved, actually."

"Why?"

"The thought had occurred to me that they gave the job to you because you were a friend of mine, so I wouldn't be mad at them for taking the job away from me. Then I would do a better job up here with the Inari, and they could order you to give the road work back to me and you'd be happy to, because you didn't really want it."

"Is there any reason why that couldn't be true as well?"

She thought about that, looking at him steadily. "And would it bother you if it was?"

He shrugged. "Not really." Then he jumped to his feet. "Damn them! May the Lady take them straight out into the Void and dump them off within sight of the Gates of Paradise!"

He turned from his pacing. "Can you imagine the bunch of them up there at the castle with their heads together, and how pleased they must have been when it all started to fit? I can just hear it. 'He's a friend, she'll be happy, he'll listen to her, he'll never keep it from her.' I can just hear them!"

"Say, that's a good idea, Ferlen."

"What idea?"

"What you just said. Once you've set the crews up, when you get to the actual work you can check in with me any time you like. I can tell you how I meant it to go, and we can figure out any hitches that come up."

He sat back down. "And the rest of it's true as well, isn't it?"

"What?"

"The rest of that, about you being happy because it's me."

"Yes, of course. Oh, I see what you mean. Ferlen, if it wasn't for the fact that you're unhappy with this, I would be very happy. As happy as I can be, when I'm not doing it myself. I'm sorry. It makes it look as if the manipulators at the castle had it all right, doesn't it?"

He just sat there, shaking his head. "I hate to think I'm that easy to peg."

"Me too. But at least you still have a choice."

"Sure! Some choice!"

"You do! You can refuse."

"So could you."

"No, I couldn't. The Inari might go home."

"And I can? And leave you with some lord's son or merchant messing up your beautiful plans?"

"I'm sorry I said that, Ferlen. I didn't mean it to put pressure on you."

His shoulders slumped. "I guess I had nothin' to do this summer, anyway."

"You mean you'll do it?"

"Anine, there was never a question of whether I'd do it or not. It was simply a question of how mad I was going to be about being saddled with the job."

Oh. "And how mad are you?"

He ran his fingers through his dark hair, looking up at her through the locks that fell over his face. "Oh, not very, I suppose. The worst part was the thought that I was takin' it away from you. Are you mad about it?"

"Not anymore. It wasn't anybody's fault, after all. Nobody was out to get us, putting us in the wrong jobs for the summer."

"How are you doing in this one?"

She shrugged. "Not bad at all, I suppose. I'm just riding the line between Inari freedom and merc discipline. I pick the strongest ones of each, and sort of find a way to fit them together."

"You're finding places where you enjoy the work."

"I always was proud of being a merc, and a good one."

He nodded thoughtfully. "You know, what you were just saying about the Inari. That's sort of like I'll have to do with the road crews."

"In what way?"

"Well, you know. Motivate them, discipline them. They have a tough job. They have to fix the roads, but they're in danger from the bandits as well. I probably ought to do some weapons training."

"Or hire some road workers that can already fight."

"I suppose I could do that."

Anine's mouth fell open. "That's it!"

He looked at her.

"The road crews. Hire a bunch of fighters and teach them to mend roads. Your men will be spread out all over the place. They'll be a great asset to our defences against the bandits."

"I suppose. And I could train my road workers to fight. Then I pair up the fighters and the craftsmen, and they can train each other."

"Have you put out the call for workers yet?"

"I was just going to start."

"Well, the description of the duties has changed a tad."

"Right. And once we get the men, we'll be able to weed out the fighters who are too lazy to work and the workers who don't have the stomach to fight, and make a pretty good core group. When word gets around, we'll get new ones to replace the ones that drop out."

"Where are you going to muster?"

He looked surprised. "Up at the castle. I thought that was already set."

"Oh, I remember now. But once you had the men organized. Where were you going to start?"

"Same answer."

"Why?"

"Why are you asking me? You made all the plans. Are you so busy here that you forgot?"

She grinned sheepishly. "Well, sort of. But what I was thinkin'...I don't remember that we had made the decision where to start."

"I don't remember seeing it written down anywhere. That was going to depend on the road reports in the spring, some place where the need was greatest but with a supply of material available."

"Where the men could be accommodated and provisioned?"

He nodded. "I think those were the main criteria."

"So why don't you start here? There's good gravel in the cutbanks along the river over at Alderly. There's a stone quarry between here and Jaspen. This part of the road is going to be the main route between the castle and Kyabra. The roads near the castle are kept pretty well, already. It's out here near the border where they need the most repairs. For example, that bridge that Talia's wagon broke through has never been fixed."

"You think I could start here, stay at my sister's inn, quarter my men at Lanil's Rock, and fix the roads around that area, and nobody's going to squeal 'favouritism'?"

She gave him an evil grin. "You gotta start somewhere. Of course, you might not want to."

"Why not?"

"Because you'll have me leanin' over your shoulder every time you look up. With a troop of Inari backin' me up."

The grin disappeared from his face. "From the look of some of those reports Loreline showed me, I have a feeling there might be a few times this summer when I'd be glad to have you and your Inari looking over my shoulder."

"Trouble movin' in?"

"Nothing certain yet. I brought in some orders, though, that Zoysana will probably be passing to you. I think they'll tell you where to start scouting."

"That's good. I don't mind tellin' you, there's a lot of ground to cover, and I don't have that many men. They haven't hit any merchants yet as far as I know, so there's nowhere to begin."

"Zoysana will have something for you."

"You know, I just figured something else out."

He turned to her expectantly.

"You know what I said about Loreline putting the right people in the right places? Well, look at you, put in charge of the road crew, and see what that means."

"Well, I don't know much about actually fixing a road."

"Means they don't care so much about the actual fixing."

He slapped his knee. "What I *do* know has to do with travelling on them and tracking. So that's what they're expecting. I travel the road; find out everything I can about it, like a trapline. Don't rush the actual repairs, but concentrate on helping you keep order. And if I can hire some fighters on my crews, I can do even better."

She nodded. "I see it the same way, myself. Let's keep the information going both ways, save us time, covering such a large area. Another reason they put us together. They know we'll cooperate with each other. Can you imagine the trouble if two people who were worried about their positions got these two jobs?"

He laughed. "They certainly nailed that one. Neither of us is likely to be fighting for our positions, at the expense of the work getting done."

She joined in. "Since neither of us wants the job!"

Then she thought about it. "There was a time when the idea of being an officer sounded good to me. Maybe I'll find out I like it."

Ferlen shook his head. "You better not. I might end up fixing roads for the rest of my life."

13. Win Some...

A dusty troop of Inari slouched in off the trail from the main road. Dismounting a polite distance from the camp, they brought their horses in and took scrupulous care of them before they wandered to their tents. There were no empty saddles, but the men were in a serious mood.

Anine shook the dust off her helmet and flung it towards her tent, where it hit the canvas and slid to the ground. She did not bother to pick it up, nor did she take off more than her chainmail before she threw herself, deep in thought, onto her cot. There she lay, unmoving, until the supper gong rang. Then she roused herself and made an effort to clean up before she went to eat. The first person she saw as she left her tent was Zoysana.

"Glad to see you, Lady Zoe."

The Kyabran woman took a step back, cocking her head. "You don't look particularly glad about anything, and the boys aren't exactly whooping it up either. What's going on?"

"We found one of their big concentrations of men, got away without a scratch. They don't even know we was there, unless they go readin' sign real careful."

"Sounds good. Why isn't it?"

"I better tell you now, because I ain't sayin' nothin' about it at the briefin' tonight."

"All right."

"Zoe, I found out today that I ain't an officer. I ain't got what it takes, and it ain't never gonna happen."

"That's a pretty strong statement when you just came back from a successful patrol with all your men."

"Aye, but I found out somethin' about myself, and it don't make me officer material."

"What did you find out?"

"I'm too soft."

"Too soft? You?"

"Strange, i'n'it? Big, tough Anine hasn't got the guts to be an officer. You never woulda known, hey?"

"So how did you find this out?"

"Well, we found the enemy, like I told you. There was a bunch of them, but not like we couldn't handle them, you know? But I had a funny feelin'. I watched them for a while, and they didn't look right. I dunno what it was. Too many officers, not enough men, too many horses to be infantry, not enough for cavalry. So I wouldn't let the boys go in. They was a bit steamed up, but I laid it on the line, and they didn't push it, but I could tell they wasn't happy. I figured to find out what was wrong. I sent out the scouts, all directions, with instructions to be real careful. I took to the high ground myself, to see what I could see."

"Sounds like good precautions. And I already know you were right."

"Oh, yes, I was. Sure enough, the scouts come squirmin' back, huggin' the ground even more than when they went out. The rest of that troop was just around the corner, doin' I-dunno-what. Mixed cavalry and infantry, but they was all on the ground for some reason. That's why the horses were somewheres else. I gave up the idea of attacking. We wiped our tracks, backtrailed, foretrailed, did all the stuff we shoulda, and came in to report."

"What's wrong with that? We'll take a reinforced troop out in the morning, take them at our leisure and wipe them out. Or bring them in as prisoners to embarrass their masters."

"That's the problem, Zoe. I coulda taken them right there."

"But you were seriously outnumbered. You know the orders. No pitched battles with superior forces, no extra risks."

She shook her head. "They was divided. The cavalry was away from their horses, and most of the officers was away from their men. There was one canyon between them. I checked it out real careful, believe me.

"All I'da needed to do was send a small patrol down to block that canyon, go in with my other Fighters and wipe up the officers, then sit on the rocks and clean out the rest of them, with no chance of them gettin' away. Like fishin' in a mill pond."

"So why didn't you?"

"Well, Zoe, I started makin' the plans. When it came to the part about sendin' the small patrol down to block the canyon, I had to choose who was gonna go. And I couldn't."

"You couldn't?"

"That's right. I knew, and they woulda known, that there wasn't a lota chance for that patrol. They'd be in the fiercest of the fightin' and had a good chance of bein' completely wiped out. All they needed to do was hold for a quarter candle, give us time to clean out the first bunch. After that, if they got overrun, no problem."

Zoe smiled sadly. "You could have asked for volunteers."

Anine nodded her head. "I know. And you know as well as me that askin' for volunteers is just duckin' the responsibility. I'm the officer. I order them to go. If they choose themselves, they still die, and it's still my choice. And I couldn't make it.

"I'm not officer material, Zoe. I thought I might be, but I'm not."

The smaller woman nodded. "That's good information to have, Anine. I still think you did a good job. We'll walk the field tomorrow after we clean up this little mess, and I'll have a look, see if I agree."

"Thanks. That'll make me feel better."

"But I'm going to leave it to you to fix up the morale of your troop."

"Don't worry, Zoe. That I can handle."

As they joined the line at the mess kitchen, Anine straightened up and found it easier to look confident at least, if she couldn't scare up a smile. When supper was over, she called the whole camp in for a meeting.

When they were all assembled, she strode to the centre of the horseshoe and faced them. She spoke, as she always did, with a combination of halting Inari and correct, slow Petrellan.

"All right. We learned something today. We didn't have much fun, but we learned something. What did we learn?"

She waited, and finally it came, from somewhere in the middle. "To follow orders."

"That's right. You already knew that other soldiers have to follow orders. But you learned something more important, something that even the best Inari fighter has to learn. Do you know what that was?"

She had perked up their interest, at least. "You learned that fighting is not always fun."

There was a puzzled murmur. "That's right. Fun. I have the right Inari word, don't I? Up until now, you thought fighting was fun. You went out and did it on purpose, and you enjoyed it. Well, now you have learned that not all fighting is fun.

154

"You all know me. I am a mercenary. For the mercenary, fighting is work. Sometimes it can be fun, but it is always work. What we are doing this summer is not just fun. We have a task to complete. There is a nest of parasites in Petrella, and it is our duty to clean out that nest. So, sometimes our fighting is not fun, but it does the job of cleaning out the parasites better. That is what happened today.

"Let us look at today's work, and see what happened. First, I am going to give an arithmetic lesson. Inari know arithmetic.

"I had fifteen men out on patrol today. Good fighters all. We ran across a large patrol of the enemy. About eighty men, I believe. I know my Fighters wanted to attack those eighty men. So I had to do arithmetic. I think each of my Inari should be able to handle about three of those soldiers. Right?"

She could see the grins. She could almost hear the little voices in the backs of their heads saying, 'I could kill many more than that.'

"Now, let us look at the arithmetic of today's patrol. If I attack with my fifteen men, and they each kill three or even four of the enemy before they are killed, what is left? I'll tell you. The enemy has twenty or thirty men left. I have none.

"The battle is won by the side with the most men left when the battle is over." She raised a cautionary hand. "I know that the way the Inari fight, the winning of the battle is not so important. In fact, many times, nobody can say who won the battle. What is important is that the individual fighter fought with bravery and honour. Is this not so?"

A guttural agreement from a hundred voices.

"But remember, the Inari fight for fun. We have a job to do. If I allow my fifteen men to have their fun but I lose them, then I have no more Fighters to finish the task I have been given by my Leader, the Great Potentara Gerth.

"Also, it would have been very greedy of my fifteen Fighters today to keep all the fun to themselves."

A chuckle. *They're still with me, so far...*

"So, today, I had to give the order, and it is very good that my Fighters all obeyed. It is very good, because today was very hard.

"Then there is tomorrow!"

Their heads came up a fraction.

"Tomorrow, with a good battle plan, and a good number of men, we will fight. Yes?"

"Yes!"

"Tomorrow, we will all fight with bravery and honour! Yes?"

"Yes!" Louder.

"Tomorrow, we will all kill as many of the enemy as we can, will we not?"

"Yes!"

"And tomorrow..." She let her voice drop, and they leaned forward.

"It will be fun!"

They leaped to their feet, shouting. She turned away, and they dispersed to their tents. Soon the noise died to silence, broken only by the sound of weapons being honed.

Zoysana grinned up at her companion. "Not bad for a farm girl."

"I've been watching Mantinello. Set them up, pull them back a bit, then give them what they want to hear."

"Right. And about the other matter?"

"It will be good of you to walk the ground with me, Zoe, but that isn't the problem. Whether I was right or wrong about the strategy, I couldn't do it."

"But think of what you just told your men. Waiting was the right move."

"Yes, but I hadn't thought of it at that point. I had the battle planned. I had the orders in my head. But when it came time to actually say the words, nothing came out. I thought it was only my intuition telling me that something was wrong. I thought through the plan. It was still good. I tried again. Nothing.

"I could not give the order, even if it was the right thing to do."

"So you've had your first case of buck fever. It happens. You'll get over it."

"I'm not so sure about that. I'm not so sure any more I want to. I know what you mean. This was sudden, and a clean choice. Death or not. In other circumstances, I might work my way into being able to do it.

"But I'm not sure I want to. I'm not certain I would like to be the kind of person I would have to become."

"I see."

"So there you have it. Not officer material after all."

"It does limit you."

"Limit me?"

Zoysana pulled the tent flap aside, motioned for her to enter. "Yes, Anine. Limit. You don't think every officer is perfect, do you?"

"Bitter experience tells me the answer, Zoe."

"Right. What's worse than an officer who is too timid?"

"An officer who is too brave. With his men's lives."

"Exactly. And every commanding officer has to balance his command, whoever he has for officers, and try to put the right person in the right place. If sometimes the wrong person gets in the wrong place, well, that's how battles get lost. Just bad luck. You're still one of the best officers I've got, Anine." She grinned. "Not that I have very many. You're still the only officer that can fill this spot."

"Oh, I know that. I wasn't tryin' to get out of the summer's duty. Nothin' like that, Zoysana. I was just lettin' you know. For the future, like."

"Well, thank you, now I know. How's the road work going?"

"Why don't you ask Ferlen yourself? Afraid he won't speak to you?"

Zoysana laughed. "Oh, he's speaking to me, all right. Things worked out pretty much like I thought they would. Aren't you pleased?"

"I don't like to be pleased at the expense of my friend."

"I wouldn't be too worried on that account. I think he was mainly upset about being pushed around. He's not a soldier, you know. Never will be. He started too late. He's definitely limited in that respect."

"He wouldn't be upset to hear you say that, tell you for sure."

Zoysana reached under a saddle blanket and pulled out a bottle and two glasses. "I think a toast to tomorrow's battle, and then we'll get to the planning, shall we?"

They tossed back the drinks, then Anine beckoned to Mantinello, who was waiting outside. He returned with Pagris and the three non-Inari Clan from the castle who were in camp, and they turned to the maps.

"What are your plans, Anine?"

"It will depend a lot on what the scouts bring back at dark tonight and dawn tomorrow. Where they camp, how they're positioned. But I do have a rough outline.

"I don't think we'll attack at dawn. If we were dealing with regular bandits, that would be good. But this is an army, at least the officers, and they're deep in enemy territory. They'll be ready for that. I thought we'd play a game with them. We don't attack at dawn. Then they relax.

"There's a point just before they set out. First thing, they'll send the scouts along the proposed path. Once the scouts report that the path is clear, they pull in the pickets send out the day's outriders. They'll replace the sentries with the flank and tail riders. There's a point right about then, when duties are overlapping and people are moving, that things are pretty loose.

"My plan is to let the scouts report a clear trail. Then we pick up the outriders as they leave camp. We let the point of their column get a ways down the trail with a good number of the horse, strung out. Then we hit them all at once. Cut off half the cavalry on the trail, box the rest in the camp with horse and infantry all getting in each other's way, and wipe them out."

"How easy is it going to be to box them in their camp?"

"Again, that depends on where they camp."

"The wind will help."

"Why is that, Pagris?"

"The wind has blown hard for two days. To keep shelter, they will cheat on military need. The canyons are good shelter, bad defense. Like fish in a clear stream."

Zoysana nodded. "Let's leave it that way. Where do you want me?"

"I don't know, Lady. It's your Clan."

"And it's your battle. I know it's hard to have a superior officer looking over your shoulder. Why don't we just wait it out up above to keep some control of the shape of the battle? Then, when it all falls apart, we lead the final attack on the main camp together."

"I didn't say anything about a final attack on the main camp."

"You didn't need to. It would be a pleasure to fight beside you."

She nodded at the little woman. "Perhaps we should have a little drill?"

Zoysana grinned. "Pagris, Mantinello, we need someone to practise on. Get the wands."

As they walked towards the training ground, Zoysana began to stretch her arms and hands. "Nothing like a little training to loosen

158

you up, the night before a battle. Can you fight in Warlander's stance? High and wide?"

Anine grinned. "Like Gerth does?"

"Maybe we can give them a little surprise."

One of the Clan from the castle nudged his companion and whispered to him. He had obviously seen Gerth and Zoe train, and knew they were in for a treat.

The two women faced off against the two Inari, older and younger, and started slowly. It soon became apparent that neither man was any match for his opponent.

"I think you need some help, Pagris."

"If you think so, Anine. How many?"

"Tell you, Pagris. We'll take the rock, over there, and you can have as many as you like, until you get in each other's way."

The women set their backs to the rock wall, and waited. Pagris assigned the positions to an enthused army of volunteers, and soon the attack came. Anine was having little trouble because of the reach of her wand, although she was feeling the lack of weight when it came to sweeping several swords away at a time.

Zoysana was having more trouble. "I need help, here, Anine." She fended off the last thrust with a sweep of her hand that would have been risky with a sharp blade, and discouraged a side attack with a kick to the head.

"Any time, Zoe."

"Right...NOW!"

Zoysana started a standard one-two attack against her nearest opponent. However, instead of completing, she committed a break-time, pausing for the briefest moment, and Anine, with a sideways parry against her own opponent, slid her sword over and lunged instead, taking Zoysana's attacker completely by surprise. He "died" dramatically and stepped out of the mêlée.

Without missing a beat, Anine returned to her own assault, and Zoysana turned her attention to her other attackers. After a moment they tried the opposite, with Zoysana slipping a quick lunge between Anine's larger cuts.

The attackers finally backed off and grounded their wands.

"Nice trick, Lady Zoe."

"It isn't a trick, Mantinello. It's a desperation move when your partner is in trouble, and it puts you into danger yourself. Anine and

I will be working side-on tomorrow, so we needed to get our timing straight. Thanks for the workout, lads."

They went down to the stream to bathe and soon returned to their cots. Anine lay awake thinking for a while, but then her training took over and she slept.

14. Battle

She awoke before the sky began to pale and led her troop out of camp well before the first glow of dawn touched the tops of the trees. They were in position above the enemy camp and off their line of march before any serious movement started below.

As the dawn light grew and her last scouts reported in, Anine was pleased to note that the enemy officers had, indeed, opted for shelter. "Fish in a clear stream."

The enemy also provided a solution to another of her problems. Somebody had to take the unpopular position of backtrail guard, to make sure none of the enemy fled the scene and returned to their main camp. Definitely a "not fun" task, but very important.

As they watched, a troop of five horsemen lined up in front of the officers' tent with one empty saddle. Sure enough, an officer came out and got on that horse, and they wheeled out of camp towards the north.

Anine grabbed Mantinello's shoulder. "Take three-four men. Remove that party. I want the dispatches he's carrying. Be nice to have the officer alive. Let them get far enough from camp that they can't raise an alarm. As you come back, sweep the trail."

Mantinello nodded, indicated specific companions, and sprinted silently for his horse. In spite of their hurry, they left with their horses walking silently and faded into the gloom under the boulders.

Anine turned her attention to the camp below. The men had finished eating and were tearing down the tents. It seemed that the officer's orderly would wait until the others were already on the trail before his tent went down. If the troop ran true to type, he would then rush ahead to have the tent up at tonight's camp the moment the officer needed it. She was not surprised that this lot had that kind of officer.

Three scouts had been out since it was light enough to see. All three had returned, and the outriders started to line up for their orders. Anine looked around at her troop.

"Glock, you were pretty good at that silent take-down drill we did last quarter. Pick two-three friends who can do the same. You heard what I said to Mantinello. Let them get out a ways. No alarms."

"No alarms, Anine." Again, a small group flitted away.

"Zoe, unless you'd like to go and play closer in, I've got some lads who particularly want to try their hand."

"Oh, no, I'm out of practice and not dressed for rock work. You send who you want."

Anine merely had to nod to the ones who had been briefed on the timing of taking down the flank and tail riders, and they slid down through the rocks towards their quarries.

As the light became clearer, Anine and Zoysana chose their positions and sent their troops in. They had no concern that any of them would be spotted getting into their initial posts; they were too far out from the camp. If any motion was seen when they moved into their final attack positions, it would be too late anyway.

The sun broke down into the camp, and Anine sent another group to take advantage of the blindness it caused.

Soon the cavalry, and a sorry lot of horse-soldiers it seemed, was trotting merrily up the narrow defile away from camp. Because of the narrowness of the canyon, Anine had decided to let a larger group get away from camp.

"They'll have enough trouble turning around, let alone getting back to help."

Pagris nodded. "It was me, I'd go forward."

"Then take an extra bunch to make sure that doesn't happen, Pagris."

He grinned and was off, as quick as any youngster.

Anine drew her sword. Glanced at Zoysana. "How many horsemen out, Artemin?"

"Twenty, Anine." The Inari youth did not look around, his eyes intent on the trail.

"When five more have gone, start shooting."

Zoysana glanced at Anine. "You're not going to start the battle?"

She shook her head. "They don't work that way. If I try to control them, somebody will screw up, and I can't really discipline him, can I? So, I let them take care of things I can't control anyway, and I don't have any discipline problems. Very Inari. Very unmilitary. Oops, there we go. At least they didn't yell."

The battle started in a hum of bowstrings and a zip of arrows. Startled cries and screams of pain from the soldiers broke the morning's stillness. There were no horses hit in that first, organized salvo. Inari were careful of livestock that might become theirs, soon.

Anine jumped up onto the rock for a better look. There was no point in hiding, now. Twenty of the more mature Inari, the ones she could depend on the most, jumped up with her, eager for orders. In groups of five or so, depending on the need, she sent them to shore up the circle that was gradually tightening on the camp. True to her prediction, there was pandemonium down there. As the arrows whirred in from unassailable positions in the rocks, the soldiers ducked for any cover they could find while the cavalry tried to get out to somewhere they could fight. She saw three soldiers pull a mounted man from his horse and drag the beast down so they could hide behind it. The cavalryman willingly joined them in their temporary sanctuary.

When the receding noise from the canyon indicated that the cavalry on the trail had been dispatched, and her extra Fighters had swarmed in from that direction, Anine closed in on the camp below. As she started forward, her whole troop moved downhill as well. Now she took some casualties as her people moved onto more and more exposed rock, and the most accurate bowmen from below found targets. Once the attack reached a certain point, there would be no point in hiding any longer.

Anine fended off a spent arrow with her buckler. "I think we're about to that point, Lady Zoe. The horses are taking too many arrows. Hate to waste horses. Would you take the honour?"

"I appreciate that, Anine. I would be pleased."

With a sharp cry, the little woman jumped up to run down the rock face, Anine a step behind her. The Inari, silent up until this moment, gleefully joined in with their personal yells, and the horde poured over the rock, down on the startled soldiers below.

Finally given a tangible foe and freed of the arrows pinning them down, the soldiers tried to form up and fight, but they had little chance. Anine and Zoe plunged through their wavering ranks, moving purposefully towards a pair of archers who were still methodically and accurately mowing down the Inari. They set off their last bolts at the two who stormed at them, but the sight must have shaken them; the arrow intended for Anine went wide, and that for Zoysana was a hurried, weak shot that she parried with her sword. Then they were between the archers, and they economically downed each with a blow from a sword pommel.

Scooping up the bows, Anine grinned at Zoe. "Saving them till later."

The little woman nodded, and they moved on.

By the time they had achieved this objective, however, the fight was basically over. The commanding officer was setting up a valiant defense in front of his half-packed tent, behind the grim faces of four well -armed soldiers who confronted the circle of approaching Inari with no movement. Anine strode forward.

"To the death, boys?"

None of them moved, although the eyes of the one on the far left flicked to the commander.

"Good for you." She lowered her sword and stepped closer to the soldiers so she could speak in a conversational tone to the sweating man who hovered behind his bodyguard. "Well, sir, I suppose you could order these men to fight, but the end would be the same. If you have papers in the tent, it's too late to burn them, because by now there are five Inari back there, as well. Why don't you just stand these men down, and we'll be civilized about this."

"Civilized?" The man looked disbelievingly round the circle pressing in on him.

She grinned. "That's right, sir. Civilized. Or I could just back off and let it become uncivilized again. Of course, anybody who comes into a peaceful country and starts preying on honest businessmen as they go about their work could hardly be considered civilized, could they?

"Maybe I should save you from these savages and turn you over to the families of those merchants you murdered, day before yesterday. I guess we'd see what civilized was, then."

The man blanched, his eyes shifting left and right. Then he turned and dashed for the tent. He disappeared inside, there was a startled cry, and his body flew back out the door.

She turned her attention to the four swordsmen in front of her. "What do you think, boys? Looks like the payroll just dried up. How about you sheath your swords, and we can discuss this?"

The soldier to her right shifted his sword out of line enough that she could see his whole face. "Who's to guarantee our safety?"

164

She shrugged. "You didn't sign on for safety, did you? Who's to guarantee you don't steal a sword and try to get away?"

"We won't try to get away."

"Mercenary's parole?"

At that, shoulders relaxed a touch. "You a mercenary?"

"Not at the moment, but it's pretty obvious you are. Nobody else in this rabble could fight properly. Do I have your parole?"

He dropped his sword, motioning to his friends to do the same. "You have my parole, ma'am."

"Ah, keep your sword. You're not goin' anywheres for a while. How did a bunch of mercs get caught up with this lot? Code says you don't have to answer, I know."

The man shrugged. "Bodyguards, ma'am. We didn't know what they was doin' or where they was goin'. He just hired us on as bodyguards. Me and my three friends, and the two archers." He glanced regretfully to the right. "I guess they bought it, hey?"

"Nothin' wrong with them but a lump on the head."

"You took out the archers without using your sword...ma'am?"

She shrugged. "The Lady and me, we move pretty fast."

"Lady? What lady?"

"You didn't know? Who do you think this outfit is that wiped you out so easy?"

He shrugged. "Somethin' outa my worst dreams, I tell you, ma'am. Are these Inari? I never met one."

"You have now. Are they as bad as you heard?"

"Pretty much." He looked around, then closer at the body of the one dead Clan member in front of him. "Hey! These are all just kids. There ain't a beard among the lot of 'em! Not meanin' to offend, ma'am."

She grinned. "No offense taken, soldier. And you're right. These are just kids, out for their training summer. You don't want to get together with the old men."

She watched him think for a while longer.

"So, you got it figured out?"

He shook his head. "Naw, that ain't possible. They don't really exist."

"Hey, Zoe! Come over here!"

The little woman appeared instantly. Anine knew she wouldn't be far away. "This fella says you don't exist."

165

The Kyabran woman looked the soldier up and down. "Is he very sure?"

"I don't know. Whataya think, soldier? She looks pretty solid to me."

"You're Zoysana? This is the Clan? You mean we went up against Zoysana's Clan with just the six of us and a hundred irregulars?" He shook his head in disgust and turned to his friends. "Boys, I let you down. I told you this was gonna be easy money. I told you it was gonna be a fun trip into the wilds for the summer. Huntin' and fishin' and no real deep work. Don't you ever listen to me again."

The big, dark-skinned mercenary with the strange tattoo on his cheek chuckled. "Oh, I dunno, Spandrel. It's a story to tell. We're still alive, ain't we?"

"I guess so." He turned to Zoysana. "I really scre…messed up, here, Lady. We hired on as bodyguards to this officer-type." He thumbed a gesture at the body in the tent doorway. "I had no idea what he was plannin'. I wasn't even sure why he needed bodyguards until I saw some of the so-called soldiers he was bringin' along. We come through the smugglers' trails and into the bush. I gotta say, he was so sneaky about it I'm not too sure where I am. Ouida here's got a great sense of direction, says we're way in the south. That true?"

Zoe nodded. "Petrella. A third of the way to the castle."

"Huh. Figures. And then they started this bandit stuff. Now, we didn't sign on to be bandits, and I hope you'll believe we didn't have nothin' to do with that robbin' of merchants. We stayed strictly out of that, made it real clear, and he didn't seem to care."

"He wouldn't. His mission was to make it look like there were a lot of bandits in Petrella, preying on the merchants. Last thing he wanted was mercenaries showing up. That's why I believe you."

"Good. What happens now…my Lady?"

Zoysana nodded at Anine and walked away, leaving her to deal with the problem.

"Well, boys, you could hump yourselves over and see to your buddies, there. Just don't go anywheres. Safest place you could be is in the middle of this camp, in my sight. You may be able to take one of these boys in a straight sword-to-sword, but believe me, you get out there in the rocks and nothin' is straight."

"You got our parole, ma'am." He grinned. "Actually, now that we're out of it, this is startin' to get interestin'."

She stooped and lifted the dead Inari. "As long as his blood is at your feet, you better hope things don't get any more interestin'!"

"Oh. Aye. Sorry, ma'am."

She carried the dead boy over to where the others were already digging. She laid him with the three others already there, and looked around. "Mantinello?"

"Here, Anine."

"Do you have numbers for me?"

"Yes, ma'am. Just the four dead, ma'am. Seven wounded, none seriously, as long as there's no infections. No horses, of course, because no horses fought."

"The enemy?"

"Not so sure yet, ma'am. We're still bringing them in. Twelve horses down or like to be. Twenty captured."

"Anyone escape?"

"Not that we know of, ma'am. None you sent me or Glock to find. The officer's over there. I put a rope on him, because he was...uncooperative." He used the Inari word which meant 'causing disharmony,' one of their major social taboos.

She grinned as she saw the officer standing under a tree, a noose around his neck stretching him to stand at his full height. "Fine. Half a candle of that and he won't be any trouble. Line the enemy bodies in the trench with the dead horses. Prisoners?"

"Seventeen more, ma'am. Five wounded; one won't make it."

"Put them over near the officer. He'll influence them not to make trouble. Anything else?"

"No, ma'am."

"That'll keep you happy for a while. I'll take care of the sweep. Dismissed."

Mantinello sprinted away.

She strolled the enemy camp, taking in everything she could. She knew Loreline, and maybe the Sivan, would want to know. Soon she found Pagris, but he was dealing with the wounded, so she did what she could to cheer them and left him to his work.

Looking around, she tried to remember anyone she had seen doing well during the battle. She gathered a few of these and grouped them.

"Anyone for more fun?"

They grinned at her.

"It's just boring old trailing. You need to make a very careful sweep, the full perimeter, about three bowshots out from the camp. If you find any tracks, follow them. If you find anyone, bring him in, unless he fights. Then, do what you have to. Be very careful. Nobody leaves. Got that?"

"Right, Anine."

"Yes, Anine."

"Yes, ma'am!"

As energetic as if they had not just experienced an hour's battle, they sprinted to their horses and raced away.

It took all the rest of the day to sort through the materiel of the camp and select what would be kept, what burned. Then they set the uninjured prisoners to repacking the goods on the spare horses and started back to their own camp. Anine and Zoysana took a quick detour down the enemy's back trail to Anine's ambush point, but Zoysana could add no more to the details.

"I have to agree, Anine, that if they were deployed as you say they were and their forces were the ones we have seen, you would have had a very good chance of destroying them, in spite of the number imbalance. In a desperate situation, I would have tried it myself without hesitation. It is easy to look back now, knowing today's outcome, but I don't think you would have gotten away with four dead and seven wounded."

Anine nodded. "My decision is proven correct."

"That's right. I think part of your problem is that you have been too long out here with the Inari."

"I have?"

"Yes. You have been fighting and living with them for two months. You have started to think like them. That is natural. The idea of attacking a force five times your size should never have occurred to a mercenary of your experience. To an Inari, it was as natural as breathing."

"But I still couldn't give the order."

"Yes, but that might have been some normal part of yourself, telling you that an attack was not correct."

"But it might have been me, just bein' too soft."

168

Zoe swung back up on her horse. "Look, Anine, you've spent the summer trying to live up to the standards the Inari have placed in front of you. As far as I can see, you have succeeded. If, just once, your natural mercenary caution has saved you from possible disaster, I wouldn't be too upset. I, for one, have no intention of changing my opinion of your abilities."

With that, the Clan Leader kicked her horse into a gallop, and they soon caught up with the slow-moving train of triumphant Inari and their trophies.

They interrogated the prisoners the next day, but got little they didn't already know. The good news was that, as they suspected, the dead officer had been concerned at the inroads the Inari were making into his troops, and he had brought the small cells of fake bandits together for protection.

"This is interesting. The Inari were right. When you divide up into small bands, like the bandits do, then you're susceptible to attack by other small bands."

Anine grinned across the fire at Pagris. "Fire with fire, water with water."

The Inari just smiled.

"Do you think the bandit problem has been solved, then?"

Zoysana shook her head. "We have to change our tactics. You have had this group all summer. You must have some leaders you can trust."

"Most definitely."

"We have to break into smaller groups, cover more territory. We have to find any bandits that remain and clean them out or force them into a larger group that we can then treat to a similar fate to yesterday's lot."

"Sounds good to me."

"Pagris?"

The Inari shrugged. "Zoysana speaks with discretion, as always."

The Clan Leader chuckled. "You mean this is my idea, and if it falls on its face, it's all my fault."

Pagris was unmoved. "The Clan Leader shows her usual wisdom."

"Ah, the Lady protect me from politicians. All right, Anine. Can you have the new groups drawn up for tomorrow? You two know better than I do. You consider the number of Fighters in each. We'll

169

take a look at them and the map and plan the sweeps. Keep yourself to a short sweep pattern, Anine. You'll need to be here every few days to coordinate. Besides," she grinned, "what would Ferlen do, out on the roads without you to consult?"

"I think he's doing quite well, Zoe."

"Considering the kicking and screaming this spring, he's doing miracles."

"Ah, you pinned it there. That was just Ferlen, kicking against being manipulated."

The Clan Leader stood. "Well, you have some decisions to make. I'll see you in the morning. A good day, I think."

A good two days, actually. As Zoysana left the tent, Anine shared a smug smile with Pagris and Mantinello. The Clan was making progress. She reached for her own bottle and passed the glasses around.

Over the next few days, they sent their patrols out. Anine stayed in camp, mainly to clean up all the details. She and Zoysana, helped by Pagris and the three Castle Clan, took the prisoners down to Lanil's Rock for the smith to put them in irons for their transfer to the castle. Nobody who had made contact with the Inari was being turned loose to take the tale back to the Inner Duchies. Rumour and supposition were their friends. Real facts might aid the enemy.

A more complex problem was what to do with the mercenaries. Anine didn't want to send them to the castle in chains, but they could not be turned loose. A bit of work with the Inari impressed on them the impossibility of escape. However, they seemed content to stay in camp, keeping to themselves but contributing their share to the chores.

They were a fairly cohesive group, not big enough to be called a troop, but their leader, Spandrel, had pulled together this small bunch of free swords and kept them in work for the past few years. His one mistake did not seem to have shaken their confidence in his leadership, so they were a fairly cheerful group in their captivity. He expressed interest in being hired on in Petrella, but Anine had to discourage him.

"We found you in suspicious circumstances, Spandrel. King Gerth doesn't hire anybody like that. I admit, I was impressed at your behaviour in that battle, but I couldn't recommend you to anyone."

"Fair enough. It was just an idea."

She thought a while. "You know, what you need is some kind of work where you can prove yourselves around here. Let people get to know you."

The merc shrugged. "Sounds good, but without your recommendation, and since we aren't allowed to leave, I don't see that happening."

Then it struck her. "How much do you want to stay here? Would you be willing to work?"

"What do you mean, work?"

"I mean work. Hard physical labour. For pay."

He shrugged. "We never backed off from work. What do you have in mind?"

She explained the road repairs and the composition of the crews.

"You mean, you got regular crews out there, workin' the roads, and they're full of old soldiers and trained fighters? And anybody who's in trouble can call on you, and have a troop of armed rock-slingers there to help in a heartbeat?"

"That's right. We don't want it to be a secret, so you can tell anybody you want. They're a proud lot. They've broken up a few bandit attacks this summer and kept the roads safer, just because they're there. And hauled a lot of gravel in the meantime."

"And you're offerin' us work on one of these crews."

"Sure. If you're in a crew, we can still keep an eye on you. It's that and get paid, or sit on your butts here for nothin'. What say?"

"I'll talk to my people. Say, how do you know this outfit'll hire us on?"

"I'm in charge."

He grinned. "A woman of many talents."

"Aye, well, me and a friend of mine. He'll be the one you're actually working for."

Zoysana was pleased at the solution. "If they choose to work, that says a lot about them. What does Ferlen think?"

Anine looked a bit guilty. "I haven't had time to ask him, but I know he could use some workers. Especially a team like this that's been together for so long. He'll have them trained up in no time."

Ferlen, as she expected, was less than enthusiastic, but willing to try the new crew out. "So, on top of everything else, I have to act as jailer to your prisoners. How do I know they aren't just going to run?"

"They aren't going anywhere. They want to gain some credibility in this part of the world, and they've lost a lot by being involved with the bandits. Also, they're mercenaries. There aren't any wars going on at the moment, so a regular worker's pay looks pretty good. They have a choice of staying here or hitting the long road, looking for work. No merc will turn down a chance to stay off the long road."

"But can they work?"

"I imagine. Most mercs can. It isn't all fighting, you know."

"I know. Well, if they're disciplined and they're willing, I have a place for them. It's actually a ways closer to the castle than here, just south of Tsalk, where the road runs through that low mountain range. Reports I get, I think we may have a problem with real bandits there. They don't sound like the ones that have been in action around here until you ran them off. There's also a lot of small potholes that need fixing. They could take a wagon and some shovels, billet in Tsalk and work that area for a while."

She nodded. "Thanks, Ferlen, I was hoping I could count on you. I like these guys. I think they made an honest mistake and are happy to have a solution. If they're a problem, you just send word, and my boys'll jerk their chain up short in a hurry."

* * *

As it turned out, that was not necessary. Two quarters later, she was interrupted at her work by one of the Inari. "Visitor, Anine. Mercenary."

She turned to find the big black man from Spandrel's group standing in the doorway.

"Come on in, Ouida. What brings you here?"

The man entered. "Reporting in, ma'am. We've had some action, and Ferlen said you'd want to know."

"Fine. Have a seat, while I get a pen sharpened. So, what happened?"

"Well, we was workin' that stretch of road south of Tsalk, like we was assigned. Needed the work, believe me. You got potholes there it takes a day to climb down into and another day to cross."

172

She held the pen poised. "Should I write that down?"

He looked mildly abashed. "No, ma'am. Sorry. By the Lady, I'm startin' to talk like a road builder! Anyways, we'd been workin' there a week or so when this kid comes runnin' down to us. Said there was a fight up the road a ways. We asked him more, but he didn't know nothin'. Just said his dad, who's a farmer up there, heard a fight and thought we'd want to know.

"Spandrel, he's a suspicious sort, but we had to check it out. We get our weapons and head up the road. Well, sure enough, soon we meet a guy comin' down the road, bleedin'. Says he and his partner got held up by bandits. We ask where's the partner, and he says, dead. We send the guy with the kid to the farm to get fixed up, and we move on, real cautious now. Standard procedures, point and flank, you know the drill. By the time we get to the wagon, it's all over. Nobody there but the bodies. The partner and one of the guards, they've bought it for sure. The other guard's lucky. He got hit on the head and he's just comin' around as we get there.

"But it's a real amateur job. Nothin' like those Duchies guys were doin'. There was tracks all over the place. Any of the six of us coulda told you how many, what kinda horses, the whole lot.

"We decided we better check these bandits out. We tell the guard to hang in there in case anybody came along, and also so Ferlen knows we haven't gone loose on him. Then we take to the brush.

"Tell you, it didn't take long. These bandits are pretty stupid. They've made their strike within five bowshots of their own camp. There we are, leapfroggin' up their tracks, all proper and careful, and these guys have been drinkin' up the liquid part of the nab, and they're so drunk already they wouldn't be hearin' a troop of Warlanders in full armour clankin' up the valley.

"There's only ten of them, and there's six of us and we're sober, so we just scoop in, swords in front, archers on flank, cleanup on the far side, you know, and we manage to snare eight out of the ten alive, no problem. Marched them into Tsalk and turned them over to the magistrates."

He grinned. "And we made 'em carry the loot back, put it on the wagon and harness the horses up again. We sent the merchant and the one surviving guard on up the road with most of their cargo and their lives. Tell you, they was as happy as they coulda been, in the circumstances."

Anine nodded. "I've got all that. Spandrel thinks they were just a group of bandits and not connected with any organized group? How does he figure that?"

The merc shook his head in disgust. "They was real disorganized, ma'am. They fit the pattern pretty well. Too lazy or dumb to work, mess up enough to get thrown out of their town or demesne, they all get together and decide they're bandits. Some real fighters show up, they collapse pretty quick. No good weapons to speak of, not much skill, for sure. We searched their stuff, too. No letters, messages, anythin' like that. I doubt if any of 'em could read."

"Well, that's fine, Ouida. You can take a break here until tomorrow. We have a wagon going south from Lanil's Rock and they could use an escort."

"And incidentally keep an eye on me. You're a cautious woman, ma'am. I'd be happy to fight in any troop you led."

She shooed him out. "Flattery isn't one of the criteria for hirin' on here. You want to be useful, go over to the cook tent and offer to peel spuds."

She heard him muttering imprecations about how 'these hands were made to hold a sword', but he was grinning as he sauntered away.

15. WINTER PLANS

Three more quarters went by, and it became more and more evident that the rest of the invaders from the Duchies, if there were any left, had retreated back to the north, leaving behind any of their men unlucky enough to get trapped behind Anine's net.

Looking at the map one afternoon, Anine called to Zoysana.

"Zoe, I've been looking at the patterns. Want to check?"

The Clan Leader stood looking at the tabs on the map, her eyes thoughtful. "I think I see what you mean. Look at how they all fan out from here." She pointed to a spot on the border near Renalk. "They're coming in from Velikiii. Stands to reason. We aren't exactly held in high esteem by a certain segment of the Velikiian nobility, not after what Barent did to Rawden."

"All they'd need is one sympathetic landholder, here, where the road from Jaspen runs along the mountains." Anine pointed. "There's poor road from there north into the Duchies. What's the name of the Duchy north of Velikiii, over to the west?"

"Remence. We don't have much contact with them because of the mountains. I'll have to ask Talia and Varli. They'll know as much as anyone."

"Say, we've got a few Inari who haven't got much to do right now. Do you think we ought to take a little look?"

Zoe considered. "I'd really like to know where these invaders are coming from. You'll have to send a small group, and it can't be all Inari. After all, if they're lucky, they might be able to track them farther than Remence."

Anine nodded. "I guess I better not go, much though I'd like to. I've still got a lot going on here. But you know Pagris and his yen to travel. He'd love the chance to look around. I could send a couple of really good trackers with him and maybe a couple of Castle Clan. There's always a few of them down here to take a holiday from their regular duties and play Inari games in the bush."

Zoysana nodded. "Put Pagris in charge. His language has improved enough, and we need someone to keep the kids in line. He'll listen to advice from the Castle Clan if they make contact with any citizens up there."

Then she smiled. "Holiday, you say? Do you realize what's been going on this summer?"

Anine looked down quizzically at her Leader. "In what way?"

Zoysana sat down, stretching her legs out. "We've taken the Inari who normally would have been raiding us to practise their skills, and given them a whole lot better training and a reason to fight. You knew that. At the same time, we've sent a rotating bunch of our own Castle Clan, as you call them, and given them invaluable experience with the Inari."

"What? You've been usin' us as a trainin' camp?"

The dark woman made a calming gesture. "Sit down, Anine. I never mentioned it to you because it didn't matter."

She sat on a stool, but did not relax. "I thought those Castle Clan were comin' down here on their own, sort of like for a holiday."

Zoysana shook her head. "Not likely. If we'd allowed everyone who wanted it the chance to come down here and play with you, there would have been no room in the woods for the bears and wolves, let alone our quarry. No, we had a waiting list of volunteers, and we only let them come down here three or four at a time. You ought to be flattered."

"I oughta be what?"

"Flattered. You've been given the task of training our best people. Those who came down here are officer prospects, every one of them. In fact, now that you're not so busy anymore, maybe you'd write me a line or two about each one. I'm sure you can remember."

"Now you want me writin' reports."

Zoe shrugged. "Officer stuff. I didn't hit you with it before because I thought you had enough to handle."

"I guess there's thanks coming to you for that."

"Yes, well, back to the summer's work. The reports coming down with the returnees were very flattering. They all loved 'Inari tactics' as they call it, and they all think you're one of the best officers they've worked under."

"Me?"

"Certainly. They say you've got a really fine touch."

Anine sat in silence, taking this in. She considered her large, calloused hands and chuckled. "I have no idea what you're talkin' about. Me? What's a fine touch?"

Zoysana laughed. "I shouldn't have to explain it to you. It's the balance between giving orders and inspiring obedience. You've got that mercenary attitude towards obeying orders, but you balance it with the Inari method of motivating followers. I watched you in that battle. You would pick some Fighter, remind him of something he had done well, so he knew why he was picked. Then you would give him a very specific objective, which he had to complete precisely. Then you would let him choose his own followers, even the number to take. You were creating officers left and right, and you didn't even seem to notice it."

Anine shrugged helplessly. "It wasn't anythin' I figured out myself. You have to deal with Inari that way. It's the makeup of their war parties and their individual sense of honour. On the other hand, you can't just turn 'em loose. They gotta stay with the battle plan."

"That's right. And from all reports, your battle plans, simple as they usually are, tend to hold together much more firmly after the battle starts than the meticulously detailed plans of most regular officers."

A suspicion was beginning to dawn. "What's this you're sayin' about reports? Have all those people been writin' reports on me?"

Zoysana held up her hands in defense. "Not you specifically. Every Castle Clan member reported to Loreline or me when he came back. I'm sure you expected that."

"Of course."

"So that's all. If they had anything to say about you, of course we listened. And they had. Plenty."

"Oh." She sat back and thought. "You've got me slated to be an officer, then, have you? Got me on the list for quick advancement?"

Zoysana leaned forward, holding her with a firm stare. "Is there something wrong with that?"

Anine sighed. "No, I suppose not."

"You don't sound too enthused."

"Not really."

"Would you like to tell me why not? I don't suppose this has something to do with our conversation earlier this summer, after the battle in the canyon?"

"Well, yes and no. Oh, it's not that I don't like bein' in charge. I know I'm a good officer. I can look around the camp and see that.

The men are happy, they're fightin' well, they're winnin' the war. What more can you ask for? I don't have any problem with that. It's the other thing. What I discovered this summer. I don't want to become the kind of person who can send men to die. I've seen the old merc officers, even the good ones, and now I know why they got that dead look in their eyes."

Zoysana nodded. "I agree with you there. In that sense, I don't want to be an officer, either. It's much easier to send some junior out to make the on-the-spot decision about who lives and dies, and stay back out of it yourself."

Anine shook her head. "That's not right either, Zoe. You give the order, you still have to take responsibility for it. It's dishonest to think otherwise."

The other woman's brow furrowed. "I know. That's why I hope we don't have any wars. I would like to have to do that kind of thing very rarely, if at all." She brightened. "But you don't have that problem."

"I don't?"

"No. Even if we do have a war. Have you ever heard of a staff officer?"

"Of course. A good place for the useless younger sons of the nobility. Strut around in pretty uniforms and keep as far away from fighting as possible."

Zoe laughed. "But Anine, how do you think anything gets done? Surely, after this summer, you realize that if you didn't have Mantinello you wouldn't be able to function."

"Aye, but..."

"You're running a hundred Inari, who need very little in the way of managing because they do their own cooking and camp duties. You still need a staff of five, whom you rarely deal with, because Mantinello handles them. Right? I thought so. Now take that idea and apply it to an army of several thousand men, who need cooks and food and firewood and wagons to carry it all. Somebody has to organize that, and a good staff officer is worth ten lances."

"So you have me pegged as Quartermaster, do you?"

Zoysana shrugged. "Probably not. If there ever was a war, the Clan would be out in the field, doing scouting and raiding. You'd be a Camp Commander, same as now. You'd be working with Lukin, Orrick, Cawber, and the Warlanders who lead their own levies. You have the skills, you have the experience, and you have the status to function well in that position."

The Leader slapped her hands on her knees and rose. "So, don't worry about your position in the Clan, Anine. You're in the best place you can be, and I'd say your duties here are running to a close for the autumn."

"You think so?"

"That will be up to you to decide. When you figure there's nobody but a few scattered outlaws in the forest, and Pagris has come back with all the information he can gather in the North, I think it'll be time to send our Inari Fighters home to tell their war stories up over the Rim of the World, and you can get a month or two of solid road-building in before the fall rains start. You'll finally get a chance to straighten Ferlen around on how he really should be running it all. How does that sound?"

Anine grinned and rose as well. "Sounds fine to me, Zoe. Although I don't think Ferlen has had any trouble with his duties this summer. I'll be running to catch up, I think."

"How have your tame mercenaries done?"

"Very well. They're hard workers and can make decisions on their own. I'd like to have them next summer, as well."

Zoysana turned to her. "Now, that's another thought."

"What?"

The smaller woman paced away a few strides and returned. "I'll have to clear this with Gerth and Kenna, but this is what I'm thinking. If you don't want to stay fighting, it would be a shame to waste your fighting talents just building roads. But there is the second aspect to your road crews. What if we were to push their military function more?"

Anine considered. "We already pushed it, you know. When Ferlen and I started to figure out why King Gerth gave the road building to a coupla novices like him and me, we figured we were supposed to do it somehow that used our talents."

Zoysana regarded her. "And since you weren't there, how did you use Ferlen's talents?"

"Well, he's a tracker and a trail maker. We had them cover a lot more ground than any road building crew ever did. We organized regular patrols that reported on the condition of the surfaces and also checked every track and trail that touched the roads, and tried to figure out who was going where."

"That explains the quality of the map you have here, and the details in the information you've been sending Loreline."

"Information's important, Loreline says. I sure figured it was. It gave me more of an edge when I was chasing the bandits, too. We've been doing a lot more police work than we thought. How did you think to increase it?"

"I got the idea from your mercenaries. We need to hire some better talent. Spend more time training. Give your men more responsibilities for the safety of travellers." Zoe continued her pacing, speeding up as her mind worked. "What if, for example, we took a bunch of your best workers who had fighting potential, and your best fighters who had brains enough to learn, and kept them on for the winter? We use your mercs to help train them. We use the masons you already have to train them in stone work."

"Where would the money come from to support them?"

Zoysana grinned. "We pull the soldiers out of somewhere and leave you in charge of keeping order in that area."

Anine suddenly got it. "And the best place for that is in the Free Counties, where the king is responsible for keeping order."

"And somewhere we have quarters already..."

"Like Lanil's Rock!"

Zoe stopped pacing and grinned up at the taller woman. "I like people who think fast."

Anine grinned back. "Well, that was easy, once you got me going. You really think we could take over the military base at the Rock and use it for a training area all winter? All we have to do is keep order in the Free Counties? How many men do we keep?"

"I don't know, Anine. I just had this idea a moment ago. We'll have to make a solid plan to present at the castle. But think of the numbers. We have twenty soldiers plus officers barracked there. We have to keep about ten road workers available to make emergency repairs, all winter. That means we could keep thirty men without adding to the money already set aside."

"Thirty men, all winter?"

"That sounds about right to me. It could even be more."

It was Anine's turn to pace. "We could train them up, have them ready to build some really good bridges. Ferlen and me have been talkin'. We figure, with some of the books you got up in your library there at the castle and the experience from this summer, we could build some bridges that'll still be here in two hundred years. Three hundred, even!"

She rubbed her hands together. "It'll be so much easier when I'm actually down there with them. Ferlen's real good at the bridges, you know? He can concentrate on those next summer, and I'll work on the travelling repairs and the safety of the road."

"And what about the bandits, next summer?"

"What about them?"

"You don't really think this problem is over, do you?"

Anine took a moment to put her mind to this different problem. "Not really. It's hard to say. If they're being run by somebody in the Inner Duchies, it depends on the political situation there, I guess. We gave them a lot of trouble this summer. They might just give up, and decide to try something else."

Zoysana shook her head. "We don't think so."

Anine nodded. "I didn't really think so, either." She grinned. "But next summer, it's not my problem."

"How do you see that?"

A small, cold trickle of doubt began to run down Anine's spine. "Because this summer, I wasn't supposed to be in charge. I only got into it by mistake. Next summer there will be a new bunch of Inari, and I won't be their *neurath*. You can give the job to somebody who wants it, and I can do road work."

She looked at her Clan Leader, but there was no response on that broad, placid face.

"Come on, Zoysana. That's what you lot are supposed to be so good at. Putting the right person in the right place. I'm supposed to be buildin' roads. It was my idea, remember? All the plans is mine. Ferlen's done a great job with them, but it's not the same."

She paused for a breath. "You don't really want me back with the Inari next summer? I just bin workin' moment by moment, figurin' it out as I went along. You want somebody who's got more military trainin' for next year. You want a career officer, with more battle experience."

Zoysana looked up as if surprised. "You don't consider yourself a career officer?"

Anine tossed her head back and forth. "I dunno, Zoysana. Was a time I'da jumped at the chance. But it's not the same, now. I got a lotta other things planned. I go out and get an arrow through me, I won't get to do them. Tell you, if I was just a merc now, I'd be takin' my pay and pullin' out. This Clan is what's keepin' me. And the chance to build roads.

"Tell you, Zoe, I just wanta build roads. Why can't I do that?"

Zoysana rose and, taking the larger woman by the arm, led her back to her chair. "I understand, Anine. Believe me, I do. But sometimes our duty asks us to do things we don't want to do."

"And I gotta run the Inari camp next summer? Why me?"

"Anine, have you been listening to what I was saying? You're the best person for the task. You have found a way to persuade the Inari to work in a disciplined way. Nobody in the kingdom can do that as well as you have."

Anine snorted. "One thing you learn in the mercs. There ain't nobody that can't be replaced. Happens too often in a battle to think otherwise."

"Perhaps. But at the moment, our greatest chance of success is having you in charge."

"But we don't even know if there's gonna be a problem next summer!"

Zoysana leaned her arms on the table. "Look, Anine. There are three possibilities with the bandits. One: they give up and don't bother us. Two: they try the same thing as this year. Three: they try harder. What's your analysis of each possibility?"

Anine thought. "Well, if they don't bother us, we're gonna have a lot of bored Inari hangin' around the camp."

"Right. And that could be a problem in itself. You'd be the best one to handle any difficulties and, after a while, we could send them home, and you'd be free to go on with your other duties."

"Fine. And if they do the same as this summer, I'll get the boys trained up, we'll go out and round them up, and then I can go back to roadbuildin' like I want."

"Right. But what if they come on even harder? What if your roadbuilding crews aren't even safe?"

A dark cloud of inevitability settled over Anine. She shrugged. "Then I guess my best place would be out in the bush, chasin' them down."

Zoysana sat back. "That's right. Best for your road crews, best for the Inari, best for the kingdom."

Anine sighed. "And who's gonna tell Ferlen? You do have him down for leadin' the road crews again?"

The Clan Leader smiled. "I sort of thought I'd leave that to you. You did a good job of settling him down this spring. I tell you, he was so steaming mad, I almost thought he'd refuse."

"Huh! Shows how much you know Ferlen. If it's for the Clan, he'll do it. Whatever it takes. Don't mean he's gonna be happy, though."

"Oh, I don't know. He seems pretty happy with how things have gone this summer."

"Is he?"

"Surely you know that."

"I guess so. He sure done a good job. That might make it a bit easier."

Zoysana stood up. "Good. That's settled, then."

"I guess it is."

Zoysana slapped her friend on the shoulder. "Cheer up, Anine. The king is very happy with your service this summer. I'm sure there's going to be a hefty purse waiting for you at the castle, this fall."

"Aye, and what am I gonna buy with it? A pretty dress? A new sword?"

"Maybe a few books on road building?"

"Huh. I better do somethin'. By the time I get free to run this road crew, Ferlen'll be so far ahead of me, you'll realize that he's the man for the duty and you'll send me off to somewhere else where I'm 'needed more,' until I turn into the soldier you want or get killed tryin'. I seen how these things work."

Zoysana sat down opposite her, and clasped her arm firmly. "Is that what you're worried about?"

"Of course it is. Sure, it isn't so bad that it's Ferlen that's takin' over. But it's like I told you at the beginnin'. Chances like this don't come along often for somebody like me, and I see it slippin' away."

The Clan Leader shook her head. "I'm not going to make you any promises, Anine, because I can't predict what the realm is going to need from you in the future. But I can tell you that the king is very aware of your desires and your sacrifice. Gerth doesn't let his friends down. You know you will be taken care of."

"I guess. I never questioned that."

Zoysana looked up at Anine, her head on one side. "You know all this talk about honourable deeds that's so important to the Inari. Do you believe it? I mean, do you live your own life by the same principles?"

"I think so."

"What's your definition of an honourable deed? What makes a deed truly honourable?"

Anine had to stop. "I don't know. I never really thought about it that much. I suppose whatever you did would have to follow the Codes or the Inari ideals."

"Certainly. That makes it honourable. But what would make a deed more honourable than that?"

"More honourable than honourable? I don't know. I guess it would have to have somethin' to do with helpin' somebody else. I mean, an honourable deed in battle might be like attackin' bravely against a superior force. But guys who do those super-brave things just for their own glory don't get much credit. The attack would have to be for the benefit of the rest of the Clan."

"So, the most honourable deed is one which requires danger to yourself, but benefits the Clan."

"There's an old saying in the mercs. 'The more you lose by the deed, the more honourable it was'."

Zoe laughed. "That's another from Sarasha the Lame, I believe." A frown crossed her brow. "Although I think there's something like it in Haskell's too..." She shrugged. "Anyway, if you take that off the field of battle, where there is no danger to yourself?"

"I guess it would be discomfort, or the chance of not gettin'...All right, Zoysana, I get the point. Sacrificin' your own good for the good of the Clan."

"That's right. And I'll tell you something else. A good leader has to notice these things, because often the person who performs that kind of deed ends up losing on a personal level. It's up to the leader to make sure that person gets something in exchange. So don't worry. Your sacrifice has been noted."

"I didn't mean it that way, Zoysana. I bin doin' my duty the best I can, and I'm real happy it came out as well as it did. I don't want any kind of reward. I just want…well, it's a sure thing I can't have what I want, so I'll have to make the best of it."

Zoysana jumped up, slipped around the table and, in an uncharacteristic gesture, gave Anine a quick, firm, hug. "Anine, you are a true gem."

Anine smiled awkwardly. "Well, I do my best."

"You always do, Anine. I know we can count on you for that." She turned and walked towards the tent door. Then she stopped.

"You know, that Inari definition of the honourable deed? I checked it once. It's exactly the same in the Codes of Petrella. Interesting."

* * *

Anine spent half a sleepless night trying to figure out a way to break the news to Ferlen that he was stuck with the road crews again next summer. Then she gave up and went to sleep. When she woke up, the solution was right in front of her.

"Waste of energy. Who am I tryin' to be? I'll just go and tell him."

"What are you muttering about, Anine?"

She turned to Mantinello, who was organizing the map for the day's patrols. "I just heard from Zoysana. I gotta babysit you lot again next summer."

A bright smile lit his face. "Do you?"

"Aye. You comin' back?"

"May I?"

She shrugged. "I dunno, Mantinello. Nobody chose you this year. You just came."

"Not really, Anine. Zoysana sent for the Clan. We all came."

"Well, she's just sent for the Clan for next summer as well, and I guess it's you and me again. Tell you, lad, I got plans for you."

"You do?"

"Certain. I need more time next summer to work on my other duties, so you and three-four others are going to be leading more of the patrols. You can spend the winter thinking about what we need to do to improve how much ground we cover and how quick we get to any bandit attack."

He nodded enthusiastically. "We'll do that, Anine. We'll come back in the spring with lots of new ideas."

"Great. Now I gotta go tell Ferlen."

"Is that hard?"

"You didn't hear him this spring, when he got saddled with the duty."

"I think maybe he changes his mind."

"You do?"

The boy shrugged expressively. "He seems happy when he comes here."

"Huh. I'm glad you can tell."

"I think so."

Nobody could fault Mantinello's reading of a crowd or an individual. "Thanks, Mantinello. I guess you could be right."

"Don't worry, Anine. Ferlen will be happy to work with you next summer."

"Great. And I'll be happy to work with you next summer. Everybody's happy."

"Except you."

"Aye. I don't want it to sound like I don't like working with the Clan. I really like that. But I want to be road building. I'm hoping that you can take some of the pressure off me next summer, Mantinello."

"I would be pleased, Anine. Whatever I can do."

"Thanks." There was nothing more to say. Inari didn't go in for awards, honours, or money. Pride in a task honourably completed seemed to be all they required. She determined to ask Pagris about that, next time she had a chance.

Meanwhile, she had a task to perform. She saddled her horse and headed down the road. As she rode, she tried again to find a way to break the news to him gently, but once again, she concluded that the only way was to tell him straight out.

* * *

"What?"

It was as close to a shout as she had ever heard from Ferlen.

"I thought you might be pissed."

186

He settled back on his bench. "All right, Anine. Tell me the whole plan."

"You realize that nothin's been settled. It's just that we gotta be ready for two things. If the enemy gives up and doesn't attack, then we gotta deal with a hundred bored Inari. If the enemy ups their attacks, then we gotta deal with that. Either way, Zoysana wants me up in camp with the Clan. I'm sorry, Ferlen, but you done such a good job with the patrols and the repairs down here, she wants you to keep that goin' next year. Looks like we're both cursed by our own success."

He nodded, his lips pressed together. Then he glanced at her sharply. "How does this strike you?"

She shrugged. "I dunno. I had a good summer. My command has been successful, I got good reports goin' back to the castle. If I was a junior officer in the mercs, I'd be pleased as a bear in a honey tree. But I had my eye set on this road work, and that's gonna be another year off. Unless you get so good at it that they give the duty to you outright, and leave me with the Inari."

"Anine, I'm not good at the road work."

"Whataya mean? Everythin's gone great this summer."

"Right. Great patrolling, great tracking, even some good bridge building."

"You've got a talent for that. Where did you learn to work with stone?"

He opened his hands. "I have no idea. I just get a picture in my head of what it ought to look like, and I start piling the stones on."

"Some of your stone piles look as good as the ones that've been there forever. So why do you say you're not good at road work?"

"Because most of the actual work we got done on the road had little to do with me. You organized it all, got the materials lined up, and the crews did the work. I just looked over their shoulders and nodded wisely."

"You're in charge. That's what you're supposed to do."

"No, Anine, all I did was follow your plans. Don't worry, I'm not about to take over from you."

"But you don't mind keepin' on, just for one more summer?"

"Tell you, Anine, I'll make you a bargain."

"A bargain?"

"Sure. I'll agree to fill in for you next summer, but only until your duty with the Inari is over. After that, I'll hand it all over to you."

"And what do I have to do to fulfill my part of the deal?"

"Same as this year. Planning, sourcing of materials, ideas."

"And you don't mind? You'd be putting another summer into somebody else's project."

"That's right. It isn't my project. I'm a trapper, remember? I'll be heading off into the mountains well before snowfall, free as the birds, while you spend the winter planning and working." He grinned. "I think I can handle that."

She held out her hand, and they clasped arms. "That's a bargain then."

"It's a bargain."

She shook her head. "You have no idea how good that makes me feel. I was so worried, you know."

"That somebody else was going to take over your pet project? Why? You're doing a great job."

"Aye. I still say it's you doing a great job."

"Let's do a great job together. Once you get finished with these bandit problems, you can handle it easy yourself and I can go about my business."

"That's great, then."

As she rode back to camp, she realized that, actually, it didn't feel that great. She liked having Ferlen around to toss ideas at. He was a good man to work with. Did his share and more, certainly never complained. A man to climb a mountain with. She wondered idly why he wasn't married. *Too tough and independent, probably.*

Although she had seen another side of him at his sister's inn. More open, friendly. She gave herself a mental shake and a talking to. *You got a lot of work to do and you don't need to be chewin' over one of your friends. You got enough problems of your own. He can solve his or live with them.*

That put her on track, and she started to think about how she would spend the winter. The next time Zoysana broached the subject, she was ready.

"...you'll have to work a little farther into the fall, through the start of the rains, to get all the major repairs done in this area, though. With the information we're getting, I think we have to move the Clan base next year."

"I'd already figured that." Anine nodded enthusiastically. "And you're right. We'll be finished the roads around here by fall, at least the major repairs. But I was sort of hoping to set up our operations somewhere near the Clan camp again. That way, I could keep up with both. Now that it looks like the problems are going to be moving over to the east, I was sort of looking at Jaspen. In fact, I sort of had this plan..."

Zoysana laughed. "Come on, let's go back into the tent and check the maps. What's this 'sort of' plan you've got?"

Anine ran her finger across the map, east from Lanil's Rock. "It's the road from here to Jaspen. It just stops there. Why doesn't it go farther?"

Zoysana shook her head. "Roads seem to go where they're useful. Maybe there's no need for a road out there."

"Maybe there wasn't a need. But maybe, if you put in a road, it becomes needed. I took a couple of runs out through that area this summer, chasing bandits that escaped our net. There's some nice country out east. Possible for farming, although maybe not in big enough chunks to attract any of the nobility. In fact, it has been farmed, once. The trails looked too good, so we got to checking around. There's roadbeds there, all grown over, and tumbledown farmhouses in fields full of young trees. I asked Loreline. It's part of the demesne of a family that died out about fifty years ago, and the king, Gerth's grandfather, picked it up."

"You're thinking of another Free County."

"Something like that. If there was a road and a road crew who could keep order, I think you'd attract some settlers. They could start with sheep and some cattle, plant crops as they clear more land. It's long-term, of course.

"Short-term, there's the bandit problem. They never went there this summer because there were no merchants to raid. But if we made it too difficult for them this summer, they won't be so lazy next year, coming in by the shortest routes.

"I figured we'd need to run our patrols much farther out next summer, especially to the east. I figured what we could do," she took a deep breath, "is see how much road we could comfortably build out east from Jaspen in the early spring. We can start runnin' line and cuttin' trees way before the normal roads are dry, followin' the hard roadbed that's under the brush. We set the Clan camp out at the end of the new road. We run our road crews from Jaspen and our patrols from the Clan camp. By the end of the summer, we've got a new road, a safe area for farmers, and we've cut off another section of our territory from the invaders."

She hadn't realized how much this meant to her until she finished laying it all out. Her hand was shaking, and she dropped it from the map, turning to face her Clan Leader.

Zoysana frowned, a sign that she was thinking deeply. Then she looked up. "You have certainly thought this through, Anine. It would work out very nicely for you, wouldn't it? Both your duties within reach?"

Anine let out her breath. "I know, Zoe. I only thought it out from what would work best for my position. I didn't consider much else, but I did try to think of all the advantages for the king. I figure that, technically, he owns all the land that isn't in some lord's demesne, doesn't he? And his grandfather took over this area officially. So Gerth can give it or lease it to anybody he wants. If he were to lease it, he could gain rent from it to pay for the roads, couldn't he? It truly is good country out there, Zoe. I wouldn't exaggerate that."

"Oh, no, I'm sure you didn't. I've been out as far as the Caragata River, you know, one mountain range south of there and farther east. One of the reasons there isn't anyone out east of Jaspen is that the mountains push farther west there and are almost impassable. Patu, here," she reached over to ruffle the wiry mane of the armigerent pacing at her side, "is the only one I've ever heard went over them in the winter.

"Another thought: we haven't had any trouble with Lord Peple of Falticeni because the mountain replaces the border guard for us. I personally don't like the man. If we start pushing in there, he's bound to start looking over the mountain to see what he can make of it. He's that kind. In fact, if our summer visitors from the north have any thought of moving east, he's one man they'll talk to. Or Teremsla of Remence. I think he's a duke, but I haven't heard anything about him. Keeps to himself, I gather.

"Your ideas have merit for a lot of reasons. I'll be talking to them up at the castle, and I'll try it out on them.

"First, for the winter plans. I don't see that as a problem, and you'll need to know soon, so you can start figuring out your winter crew. As soon as you wrap up work, you can come up to the castle and have your say. How does that sound?"

"More than I'd hoped, Zoe. It would certainly make my life simpler."

The Clan Leader laughed. "Don't fool yourself. It only sounds like that at the beginning."

Anine followed her out of the tent, shaking her head in agreement.

16. New Duties

Two months later, Anine arrived at Arlyn Castle, where she discovered that her new plans had already been approved in principle. She endeavoured to hide her surprise, and settled in to firm up the details with the king and his mother.

Nearing the end of her second meeting with the royal family she got the feeling that their attention wasn't fully on the topic at hand. She tempered her enthusiasm and stopped her pacing up and down the War Room. She focused on Gerth, relaxing in the big chair at the head of the table. "So, your Majesty, I can go back to Lanil's Rock and start setting the camp up for the winter?"

"Actually, no, not right away."

Anine turned to Lady Talia in surprise. "Pardon me?"

"I have a small task for you first."

Anine risked a quick glance at the king, who was looking on pleasantly. "Of course, my Lady."

"It seems I must make a journey."

"A journey, my Lady. At this time of year?"

"Yes. I'm afraid so. I have received a letter from my father, and circumstances at home and also here mean I have to get there as soon as I can. I have asked Gerth for some of his people to accompany me."

The king nodded. "I think you are ideal for the task, Anine. She needs protection and she needs female attendants. Of course, she has Lateda, but I wanted someone else as well."

"Plus our similar size," the lady continued. "Just like last summer. In a fight, it might be enough to confuse attackers. That is, if you don't mind."

Anine shook her head. "Of course not, my Lady. It is always an honour."

"And there is another reason," Talia looked uncomfortable, "that is connected to your size."

Anine could only wait, eyebrows raised.

"It's this way, Anine. In my home, I have always been the big one, the clumsy one. Everything is so small, so delicate, I have spent my life feeling out of place." She looked down at herself. "You know, for my whole life I thought I was a small, shy, person, somewhere down inside this big, clumsy body." She looked up at the group of large people around her.

"I've since learned that it wasn't true at all. I was just in the wrong place, taking the wrong training."

Then her mood darkened. "And now I am returning. I think...no, I know I have changed, but I still worry about slipping back into the old patterns. I need your support.

"Oh," she held out a placating hand, "I don't mean that you are big and clumsy like me. I mean..."

"I know, my Lady. You want moral support."

Talia laughed in relief. "Exactly. I want someone from here who knows the new person I am, who will remind me that what I am is right, and what I want to be."

"And, my Lady, to show your friends and enemies at home that there are others like you in Petrella, who are big and strong and can use a sword. Are you sure I'm the example you want to take along?"

The king laughed out loud. "Anine, if I were choosing an ambassador who represents all the elements of Petrella that should impress my new in-laws, who better could I send? The ones who recognize your worth will be impressed. Those who don't, I expect you to slap them into shape."

"Is that an order, your Majesty?"

"Most definitely." He turned to Lady Kenna. "You see, Mother?"

The lady nodded. "Yes, I see, Gerth. She will be ideal." She turned to Anine. "I would be pleased to see you accompany Lady Talia on this journey. The roads will not be easy, and there are dangers. Once you reach Trenet, the dangers will not be over. Do you understand this?"

Anine nodded. "Of course, my Lady. I am not practiced in politics and intrigue, but Lady Talia can always count on my sword and my support."

Kenna leaned forward earnestly. "It may be that, but it may be more personal, you understand. There will be those who wish to use ridicule and social censure as a weapon. Can you stand firm in the face of that?"

"Ridicule?" Anine laughed in relief. "I was a farm girl who wanted to join the mercenaries, my Lady. You can only ridicule someone who is sensitive about her position. Can you imagine me being upset because somebody thinks I am not as graceful and polite as his standards require? What is that to me?"

"Good. You do understand. I could tell that you were trying to change your style of speech. I thought that perhaps you felt the need to be that which you are not."

"If I am to do the king's work, my Lady, it is important that others don't see me as a complete rube. I like the way I speak. I can adjust for others who don't."

The king's mother turned to him. "She will do admirably. All the qualities of Petrella that we wish known abroad."

"Don't talk about her as if she weren't here, Mother. It bothers people."

Anine risked interrupting this conversation. "Don't worry, Sire. It doesn't bother me half as much as it does Varli."

All eyes in the room turned to the squire, who reddened. "Well, you and Zoysana do have this habit, which I find very disconcerting…"

"I know, dear, I know. We will try to mend our ways and follow your wise teachings." Kenna turned from the boy, leaving him spluttering. "Now, Gerth, Talia, who shall we send to help Anine at this task?"

"Perhaps Anine has some ideas?"

Put on the spot, Anine thought quickly. "I assume the lady will have her original retainers?"

Talia nodded.

"So we have one other female attendant, skilled in close quarters work?"

Gerth chuckled. "Appropriately put."

"Is that enough women to suit you, my Lady?"

"I think so."

"And your coachman and two footmen are experienced with weapons? And your butler?"

Talia smiled and shook her head. "Arderton is an experienced, steady hand, and an expert bowman. Ranill and Albier are young but well trained. Gavess is an expert at provisions, materiel, and etiquette. His fighting skill is limited."

Anine nodded, thinking. "I suggest Pagris, the Inari friend of Jhanes. I think he's still around the castle and I know he yearns to travel. He is a cool head, an excellent scout and a fierce fighter."

"Anyone else?"

She shrugged. Ferlen came immediately to her mind, but he seemed intent on going back to his trapping. She hesitated a breath. "If we are looking for fighting skill, how about Arvent? He would probably welcome a chance to visit his home, wherever that is, and his swordsmanship is without peer."

"Do you trust him?"

She wavered her hand before her. "The Sivan trusted him enough to send him to us. That was enough for Loreline and Zoysana."

"And you...?"

"I have learned nothing to change that opinion."

The king nodded. "Good enough. That makes a party of nine. Any larger and it will be difficult to find lodging. You might also attract more attention than you wish."

"I agree, your Majesty."

"That's settled, then. Consult with Gavess about provisions, Loreline about safety and travel details. Inform the others who are going. Lady Talia will make the final decision about when she leaves."

She could see that he was about to dismiss her, when a thought occurred to him. "And while you're in the Inner Duchies, keep your eyes open for what they do to keep their roads up."

Kenna looked up from her desk. "Don't be afraid to ask questions out loud. We wouldn't mind word getting around that we are improving our roads."

"Thank you, Mother, you always think of those subtle things."

"I do my best, dear. Now let the dear girl get about her business."

He drew himself up to his considerable height with mock dignity. "I am the king, Mother. I know what to do!"

Amid the laughter, he nodded to Anine, who bowed and left the throne room.

As she hurried down the castle hallway, her mind was ticking over the recent meeting. *The king's new in-laws. That wasn't a slip. They're getting married: word isn't official yet, but he wanted me to know.* She smiled. *Good for Talia. And she'll be good for Petrella.* She was so preoccupied that when Arvent matched stride with her, it took her a moment to register.

"In a hurry?"

"A big hurry. I've got a task to perform for the king. So do you."

"Me?"

"Aye. We're goin' on the road."

"Could be a tough slog."

"That's what I said, but it's gotta be done. Guard duty. That bother you?"

He actually smiled. "A chance to get out of this castle? Not a worry. Where are we going? When do we leave?"

"I'll let you know when I know myself. For the moment, just think about leavin' in a coupla days."

"I can be on the road in a candle length."

"We aren't in that much of a hurry."

"Who's coming with us?"

She bridled a bit. "You'll know when it's time. Right now, I got a lotta stuff to do."

"I get the message. I'm off to pack my meagre belongings."

"You do that, and wait for orders."

He nodded, gave her a half-salute, and peeled off to his quarters outside the gate.

Pagris was as enthused, with only one question. "We go to Inner Duchies?" When she agreed, his face lightened. "I am ready."

She laughed. "Not right now, Pagris. It takes a coupla days to get somethin' this big organized."

He nodded sombrely. "If I can help, you ask."

She looked at him seriously. "On the road, Pagris, we will count on your experience."

"My life is for the Clan." With this traditional response, he turned and left her, a bit in awe at this indication of the powers she was dealing with. It occurred to her that with the bad roads, the bandits, and the distance they had to travel, his offer of his life might not be merely words.

She hurried off again, a stronger resolve lengthening her stride.

* * *

They left the castle with little fanfare three days later. The king, of course, was there to see them off, as was Lady Kenna. Loreline and Zoysana stood on the steps to observe. They had run Anine and Pagris through their assignment the night before, and did them the honour of not interfering with useless additions.

196

The morning was just becoming warm as they cantered down through the town and out onto the road north. It was a pleasant enough fall day, with a bit of wind and a scattering of clouds that suggested rain but had yet to realize their threat.

They did not travel with any kind of military precision, but the fighters in the group naturally took appropriate positions, and Anine was pleased with the front they presented. Few bandits would bother a party where seven of the nine were obviously well armed, and all were well horsed. The two pack animals were sturdy beasts, and even Lateda rode a larger steed than the pony she preferred.

Anine wore her light helmet, mainly because the easiest place to carry it was on her head and it was waterproof. Her sword hung at her waist and her tabard covered a mail shirt. She had decided to carry a buckler as well, because she often used one when fighting on foot and for once she had a horse to carry it. The arm-strap slipped firmly over the head of the saddle, ready to hand at an instant. It also kept her left knee dry; she had no illusions about the weather they would be meeting. Arvent looked his normal self, his brown leathers unchanged, but he, too, had a helmet, neatly capping one end of his saddle roll, easy to hand.

Pagris carried everything he owned in an oiled leather box fitted low behind his saddle, and his lithe, long-limbed plains strider jittered a bit, either from the extra weight or anxiety to be off at a faster pace. The Inari grinned and let the horse sidestep, then brought him under control with a firm hand. He had no armour, no shield, only his straight, short sword slung at his shoulder, and a tough, versatile rider's bow at his right knee, a quiver of arrows at his left. She knew that he could hit full gallop, string the bow and loose his first arrow before most soldiers had realized there was danger.

There was no danger now, however, on this breezy fall morning in the heart of Petrella. Everyone was glad to be out and moving, in spite of the prospect of bad-weather travel ahead. At least there would be no thought of canvas. They would be covering ground and staying at the biggest towns and manors.

They eased the horses into the journey and did not try for a whole lot of distance the first few days. The towns spun out behind them in sun and rain, the road mostly sloppy, so their main problem was getting themselves and their horses clean every night. However, they could afford the largest inns, and were able to order up plenty of hot water when they wanted it.

Evenings in the common rooms were pleasant, with new companions and new stories to hear. Travelling minstrels and other entertainers frequented the larger inns, so they were amused each night by professionals.

Still, there was plenty of time for talk. She was pleased to see her group getting to know each other, and encouraged the war stories that inevitably surfaced. It was difficult for a new troop to learn to fight together when there was little opportunity to train. Hearing how the others had fought in the past was a poor substitute, but all she could think of. Even Arvent contributed to these stories, she was glad to see.

"So, Arvent, you were in the army. Which one?"

He shrugged. "Nothing special. Just the local call-up for Llandres."

"Oh?" She waited. They had spoken again of his reticence, just that day on the road.

She could see a tightness around his lips, but finally he spoke. "Yes, I'm the second son of minor nobility, you know, so it was that or running the family business." He glanced around the table. "As Anine will tell you, the talents of a merchant do not suit my personal tastes, so it was the army for me. I spent a few years there, but I was not happy being an officer, so I moved on."

"When did you take your sword training?"

He shook his head. "That was the stupid part. After I left the army I learned to fight properly. I don't know where I thought it would lead me, but I enjoyed the training more than anything else in military life. The money was there to support me. I think my father was happy that I was doing anything constructive with my life, so there I stayed until Pertin threw me out."

He glanced at the looks on their faces. "I don't mean there was a scandal or anything. He just said he had taught me as much as he could, and if I wanted to hire on as one of his instructors, that was fine, I just had to go out and get some different experience first."

"And that's what you're doing now?"

The swordsman turned to Ranill, the younger of Talia's two footmen. "I don't know if I really want to make my life as a swordmaster but it was somewhere to go. So I went."

198

"Learn anythin' in Petrella?" The taciturn Arderton looked interested, for a change.

"I did. They fight a different style, here. It has to do with the amount of horse work they do. They keep their swords higher, and tend to attack the head and arms more. Also with a harder swing, because of those heavier chopping swords the Warlanders use. You might call that a weakness, that they tend to leave one area you don't have to worry about, but don't be fooled. Once you're lulled into that thought, they suddenly take a low swing or lunge and you're caught off guard."

"And were you ever caught off guard?"

The brown man smiled. "Only by Tadeo, and he's not even Petrellan. He actually played me for a fool, you know."

The circle around the table leaned in a fraction. Arvent looked pleased at the attention, for a change.

"Oh, yes, I know he did. He's a sly one, that Kyabran. I knew he was a master swordsman. They all seem to be. I thought I was ready for him, though. I'd been watching him, and I was all ready for those Weaponless tricks he throws in, you know?"

Several heads nodded. They had seen the little Kyabran in practice, and his versatility astounded everyone.

"But he came at me with the basic Petrellan attack, high and hard. I could hold him on that, no problem, but I was trying to figure out what he was doing. I threw in a few tricks of my own, and he responded with some of his, but then we were back up around the shoulders again. I had just figured out that he must be working on that style, and was starting to think about how to use that information, when suddenly he disappeared from in front of me. Before I knew it, he was down on the ground and had taken cuts at both my legs while my sword was still up in the air." He shook his head. "He dropped so fast, he actually disappeared from my view for a split second."

"Then what?"

"He bounced back up, gave me that serious smile of his, and saluted me politely, as if nothing had happened."

"What happened then?"

"Nothing, really. We opened it up a bit, trying different tricks on each other. Both of us got a few scores in, but that was because we were trying out new moves, you know. But I learned a lesson in that first go with him."

"What, never trust a Kyabran?"

"I trust them even more. I trust them to come up with something I never thought of. No, I learned never to judge a man by how he's fighting at any given moment."

They all nodded seriously.

"Who's better, you or him?"

Arvent took a moment to look at the younger mercenary, let him know that it wasn't really a worthy question. "In a contest, I'd probably take him two out of three."

Ranill frowned. "In a contest?"

"With rules. In a battle situation, I frankly have no idea. How can you rate your chances with a man who fights like he does? I tell you one thing. I'd have my chin-strap buckled tight."

They all chuckled, having seen Tadeo's favourite stunt of kicking an opponent's helmet off.

Pagris leaned back. "I am unhappy to travel with skilled fighters and not practise. It is time wasted."

Anine chuckled. "Wait till tomorrow. You'll get your chance."

There was a general hubbub of questions, to which she only answered, "We'll be at Lanil's Rock."

Talia sat up straighter. "At Sarha's inn!"

She nodded.

"It will be good to see them again."

Then the members of Talia's group had to tell Pagris and Arvent the story of the broken bridge, the cracked axle, Gavess's hat, and all that had gone into that cold, wet evening when Talia had discovered what conditions in the South were really like.

As Anine was doing her final rounds, she saw a slim figure standing in the inn yard. It was Arvent. It looked as if he was studying the stars.

"Anythin' good up there?"

"No, I just find them beautiful."

"I see." There was a pause. "Was that so difficult?"

"What?"

"Lettin' the others know your story."

"No, I suppose it wasn't."

She slapped him on the shoulder. "There ya go. You're startin' to act like a normal person."

He shook his head. "And to think I got sent here to learn spying."

She grinned. "If it was the Sivan who sent you, who says what you were sent for?"

He thought about that. "I see what you mean."

"Good. You made progress all over the place today. Well done."

His only response was a shake of the head. She continued her route, glancing back to make sure he went inside.

* * *

The next day, an enthusiastic troop pushed on through from Tsalk and made it to Lanil's Rock well before sunset. Jhanes and Sarha greeted them warmly at the inn. There was as much backslapping and rehashing of old tales as at any other mercenary reunion, and Anine, watching from the side with Pagris, noted how much Lady Talia was included.

Jhanes was not too surprised to hear about their intention to train that night.

"I'm really pleased to hear that. Would you mind the soldiers joining in?"

Lady Talia gestured to Anine. "Ask her. It was her talk about the training you're doing here that started all this."

Anine nodded enthusiastically and Frey, always listening, darted off towards the new stone buildings that nestled along the parade grounds.

A festive air began to develop on the damp clay of the village common, with the soldiers and mercenaries working with and against each other, and the villagers standing around watching and cheering. Soon, there was a table set out, and food began appearing: from the inn kitchen, the soldiers' mess, local homes.

Anine trained little, contenting herself with supervising the overall shape of the practice. Pagris was the centre of one group, demonstrating some of the Inari Weaponless, and Arvent was working with the others on fancier swordplay than anyone ever thought of using in a battle.

As she stood watching proudly, she became aware of the large presence of Jhanes at her elbow, and was reminded again of how silently the big soldier moved.

"So how do you like being an officer?"

She stared at him. "I'm not an officer!"

"You aren't? Then who's in charge?"

She thought about it. "Lady Talia...I guess."

He just looked at her.

"Well, isn't she? She's the one of noble blood. She's got her own retainers to protect her. Pagris, Arvent, and I are only along as extra swords in case of need..." honesty compelled her, "...and moral support once we get there."

He nodded judiciously. "So King Gerth sent his fiancée off on a dangerous journey in charge of a few mercenaries picked up by chance in the Inner Duchies, and dropped in a couple of extra swords, just to even the group up?"

"Well, I don't know..."

He looked out over the festive crowd thoughtfully. "You know, I never thought of Gerth as being an exceptionally stupid person..."

"What?"

"Aha. That got you. Come on, Anine. Think. Look over the capabilities of your troop like a mercenary. What have you got?"

She started thinking. "All right. I've got Lady Talia, who can defend herself if need be. Lateda is not one to take lightly in close quarters. She'll defend her mistress to the death. Then there's the three mercenaries she brought with her. Arvent's a superb swordsman. Pagris is older, more experienced in his own kind of battle, and a great scout. By far the deadliest of the group, I suspect."

"And...?"

"And me. That's it."

"All right. So, looking at that group, as a mercenary, who should be leading in a fight?"

She really began to think, then. "Well, it should be Pagris, but he doesn't speak Petrellan that well, and he doesn't know enough about the way we fight. Arderton is certainly a seasoned veteran, but he just doesn't seem to be the leader type, you know? I mean, he hardly speaks at all. The rest are too young, too inexperienced. Arvent has spent all his life learning to use the sword. He isn't really a military type at all, despite his experience."

"And that leaves?"

"Oh. Yes, of course."

"That's right, and don't you forget it. You're the only one in that group with the experience, the skills, and the intelligence to lead. You just watch. When an emergency comes, they'll all look to you. You be ready to tell them what to do."

"You think so?"

"Anine, are you questioning my experience?"

"Since you put it that way, no."

"I'm telling you. When I look at your troop, I see a group of fighters well chosen for fast escort duty for a lady. You have a skilled outrider, a superb bowman and two good fighters for the perimeter. Inside, you have one of the best young swordsmen I have ever crossed blades with, a fanatic with two daggers, a lady who isn't too bad with a sword herself..." he glanced down at her, "...and a leader who is strong, smart, and versatile, if a bit inexperienced."

She nodded. "I can see it, when you lay it out like that. So why didn't anyone tell me?"

He thought about it. "What do you know about leadership in the Inari?"

"Just the basics you taught us, summer before last. Their war parties have different leaders at different times. It depends on what's going on, depending on whose skills are the best for the task...I see."

"Right. Gerth couldn't tell Lady Talia that you were in charge. Remember, he's in love. And he didn't have to. Lady Talia is in charge of her own travel. It's only when the swords are out that you'll have to be ready to take over. Another point. Who did Zoysana brief on this? Talia?"

"Pagris and me."

"Exactly."

Anine nodded. "I'm glad you told me this."

"Why?"

"Because now it's official. Now, I'll be prepared. I'll be planning ahead, looking for danger, thinking what I'll do."

He looked across at her and grinned. "And what were you doing already? Whose idea was this?" His hand swept over the extended training session.

"Pagris. Well, he said he wanted to train with everybody. I figured this was as good a place as any."

"Perfect. You continue to take the advice of the experienced men in your group, and you make it work, just like you did this training. You'll do fine."

"I hope so."

"You have been, so far."

"So far, I've been lookin' pretty stupid, haven't I?"

His eyebrows went up. "That's not a word I'd normally used to describe you. Why?"

She waved a hand to indicate the group. "When you lay it out, it all seems so obvious. But it ain't to me. In a merc troop onea the worst tricks is sashayin' in an' assumin' command when it ain't bin assigned. I got no problem lendin' a hand where I got the talent and it's needed. But I don't assume I'm gonna give orders unless somebody official says I can."

He nodded. "I had the same problem at first, but not as bad as most mercenaries would because I was brought up by the Inari. Authority is much more fluid with them."

"Aye, and in this lot, half the time you're workin' with Inari, then you turn around and you're dealin' with some stiff-necked lord who's memorized the Codes and prays to them every night. I figger the trick is to find a middle ground to hold where you can cut fast in either direction without losin' your balance."

He gave a wry grin. "You find that middle, ground, let me know, will you?" He moved off to help one of the king's soldiers deal with Pagris, leaving her to think.

17. FARM

It was a different group that left the inn the next morning. There was a changed feeling: subtle, but evident to the experienced eye. A little more talk, the usual jests taking in a larger number of the party.

The silent Lateda was even a jocular target, as she had been persuaded to practise with the others last night. It was instructive for competent swordsmen to find themselves, time and again, tied in knots by a woman with two short daggers. They knew they could beat her with one good swing, but they also knew that with close-in fighting, a good swing came seldom. It was mostly hack and stab, and in that she was an expert.

The other benefit, Anine found in the days to follow, was that once the game was running, she didn't have to organize a specific time. Often, she would hear the men discussing some specific attack or parry, and then they would try it out at a rest break, or sometimes even on their horses.

She took the hint, and schooled the other women as they moved along. It took a great deal of practice for Lateda to be able to move closer to her mistress's back, yet stay out of reach of her sword. With some help from Pagris, she developed the ideal spot, with her horse's head just behind Talia's left elbow, pulled too close in to be struck by a low follow-through. Talia, in turn, practised guarding her right rear, as that would be the position she could be attacked from, with the intent of dragging her from her horse.

And so the next few days passed, and they approached the border of Petrella and Velikiii. The forest was rough here, and the hills pushed in closer to the road. Anine was more alert, and Pagris had casually pulled a few paces farther in front, but no one was worried.

They were jogging merrily along, and Anine found herself discussing a most unlikely topic – the length of women's gowns – when something in the way Pagris was riding caught Anine's eye. The Inari looked like a hunting dog on point. She stiffened. "What's wrong?"

"Battle ahead."

"Go!"

The stocky Inari heeled his horse to a gallop. Anine surveyed their immediate surroundings, but everything looked calm. Then she heard it, too. The clang of swords and the yells of men.

"Tight formation, quick trot. Lady Talia, I'll lead to your left. Lateda, you know your spot. Albier, outside Talia. Ranill, behind us." She glanced back to see that Gavess had already pulled in close, shortening the halter lines on the packhorses.

Everyone nodded and murmured acquiescence. They eased forward, meeting Pagris just before a bend in the road. He swung his mount around beside her.

"Merchants attacked. Two wagons."

"How many bandits?"

"Less than twenty. None mounted. No bows showing."

"How are they doing?"

"Overrun soon, Anine. Five men standing."

She nodded, raised her voice.

"All right. We don't know if this is a trap, but we can't let those people get killed, so we're going through once. Did everybody hear me? ONCE! We don't stop unless Lady Talia goes down. Arvent and Arderton, split left. The Lady and I go right. Ranill, I'm counting on you to stay behind, no matter what, and mind our backs. Also keep an eye on Gavess. Gavess, follow us and bring the pack animals through the best hole. No heroics, anybody. As close to the wagons as you can, sweep by. Don't stop to finish anyone off. Maximum damage, maximum speed, stay together. Got it?"

Those within her sight nodded. There was a chorus of assent from behind her. They approached the corner, and now she could hear the screams over the clatter of their horses' hooves. She drew her sword. "Full gallop. NOW!"

The exultation and power of a cavalry charge swept through her as they closed with the mêlée ahead. The two wagons had pulled together nose-to-tail, so the men on one wagon could protect the horses of the other. It had worked as well as possible, but now the milling mob of bandits had reached the horses and were starting to mount the wagons, where the five men still standing desperately fended them off with short spears and swords. She could see small figures huddled in the wagon boxes at the men's feet.

Such was the intensity of the battle that the bandits never noticed their doom riding down on them. She was among them, striking at unprotected backs before they even knew she was there. She swung again and urged her horse forward. The men on the wagons shouted in relief and counterattacked fiercely. The bandits, caught between two forces, broke and scrambled away.

Keeping an eye on Talia, Anine pressed her troop forward, noting Arderton staying even with her on the other side, his sword hewing methodically, red to the hilt.

Then they were free and galloping away down the road. She turned in the saddle to see the effects of their charge. Wagonmen standing, bandits running. Gavess and the pack animals gallumphing awkwardly behind, but keeping up. Good.

When she faced front again, Talia was yanking her horse's head around.

"Keep going!"

The lady shook her head, and continued trying to turn her galloping horse. "There were women and children back there. We have to make at least one…"

"No!" Anine grabbed the woman's shoulder roughly, pushing her forward, jamming the shoulder of her heavier horse against the leg of the other rider. As Talia's mount straightened, Anine whacked its rump with the flat of her sword, and was relieved to see it surge ahead.

"Pagris! Take the point. Arderton and Albier, a quick look and back to report. Don't stop. The rest of you, keep moving. Quick canter. Eyes open. We aren't out of this yet. Injuries?" Everyone was still ahorse, and none complained.

They loped ahead, every nerve tense. They were well away now, and the sounds of the battle, if any, were gone. Soon the two scouts returned, slowing their sweating horses beside her.

"They're on the road behind us, ma'am. Both wagons, full speed. Horses all look good."

"Fine. Go back and keep them in sight. Come forward if anything happens. We'll send help from Cdeile. I don't want to stretch our forces any further. There are too few of us, so we'll all go together. We'll slow to a medium trot now, but keep your swords out and your eyes open." She had a belated thought. "Two of you, string your bows."

"But if they have people injured…"

Anine stared across at Talia, then spoke, slowly and clearly. "Talia, when I say ride, you ride. You don't change your mind in the middle of a battle."

"Anine, I don't think you should be speaking to me like that."

Anine steadied herself as well as she could on a running horse. "Lady, the moment my sword comes out of its sheath, I'm your superior officer, and you're the least experienced member of my troop. You get that? My duty is your protection. You may not like it, but there it is. You follow orders, or you'll get some good people killed."

She glanced to see how the lady was taking this. The tightness around her lips was easing, so Anine continued.

"That coulda been a trap set up for you. Maybe there's a whole crowd of 'em in the forest waitin' for us to stop so they can attack us from behind, just like we did the bandits at the wagons. Those merchants knew what they were doin' when they came out here, and they chose to fight for their goods. They took their risks, same as everyone does. We can't jeopardize your safety, especially when one charge was all we needed. They still had five men standin', and the bandits were runnin'.

"And that's all beside the point. I said keep goin', and if I say keep goin', Soldier, your only question is 'How fast?' Got it?"

Talia rode silently for a several paces, and then a huge sigh went out of her. "I'm sorry, Anine. You're right. I just forgot for a moment, when I saw those children. I guess I'm really not a soldier."

"Yes, you are. And gettin' to be an experienced one. What did you think of your first cavalry charge?"

Talia looked over at her, then noticed her sword, which was red halfway back to the hilt. "Oh…"

Anine nodded. "Looks like you did your share." She watched the colour fade from the woman's face. *Is she going to faint?*

But Gerth's future wife was made stronger than that. She straightened in the saddle. "Do you think I…killed anyone?"

"Impossible to guess. However, infections bein' what they are, there's a good chance. Of course, if that lot is part of the same bunch that have been on this road all summer, they may have an experienced army surgeon to work on them." She smiled grimly. "He's going to be busy."

She raised her voice. "Gavess, I have a task for you."

208

"Yes, ma'am."

"I need a count from everyone. I want to know how many they think they put down, and how serious. I also want everyone's estimate as to how many there were in the attack. We'll talk to the merchants as well. The king and Loreline are gonna wanta know all about this."

"Yes, ma'am."

Lady Talia raised an eyebrow. "You seem to be getting cooperation from the rest of the troop."

Anine shrugged. "Somebody's gotta give the orders, and they all know it. Pagris or Arderton coulda done it just as well." She smiled ruefully. "Arderton wouldn't have forgot the bows."

"We all learned something today, then."

She glanced over to see if Talia was joking, but she seemed perfectly serious.

"I guess so. Those bandits certainly did."

Anine looked around. The forest was more open here, with little cover for an ambush. "All right, folks. There's a creek ahead. Let's clean off our swords and stand down. First half off the horses, second half make a perimeter, then switch."

They followed her orders with precision, and soon their swords were put away and the horses were walking smoothly along the road again, the wagons just behind.

There was a stir in the town when they approached, and a hastily erected barricade blocked the road.

"Stand and identify yourselves!"

Anine grinned over at Talia. "This ought to be fun." She stopped her troop with a gesture and paced her horse slowly forward.

"Zoysana's Clan on escort duty. We just broke up a bandit attack on two freight wagons back up the road. They'll be along any moment now. If you've got anyone with medical knowledge, you'd better get him ready. The teamsters were losing when we showed up."

A townsman in a mismatching helmet and breastplate stepped out from behind the barricade. "Where are the bandits?"

She shook her head. "Wherever bandits always go. Running as fast as they can, I hope. We didn't stop to ask. We have an important mission, and we don't have time to wipe the nose of every teamster who takes a risk he shouldn't have."

"But they said the bandits were gone."

Anine gestured her people forward, and they dismounted politely before complying. "I guess 'they' were wrong, as usual. Did you ever know a time when the bandits were gone?"

The man nodded. "I guess you're right. One of the lads from a nearby farm just came in, his plow horse all lathered up, to say there was a fight on the road, so we got ready. We can take care of ourselves, usually. We were just worried because of the size of the bandit groups this summer."

He was interrupted by the arrival of the freight wagons, their horses blowing and spent, children sniffling, one woman crying, one man moaning in pain. The townsfolk rallied around, pulling aside the barricade and hustling the wagons to safety.

Anine found a grateful teamster at her shoulder. "I have to say, I have never seen a charge like that, sir..."

He stopped when Anine pulled off her helmet, showing her full face.

"...I mean, ma'am. They almost had us there, I got to admit. I never been so close to losing everything. An' then you came around that corner at full gallop." He shook his head. "You saved our lunch, ma'am. Who am I to thank?"

"I'm Anine, of Zoysana's Clan. You're a lucky man. We just happened along at the right time. Now, I need information. Tell me about the attack."

While the man described the ambush, she noted with approval and not a little pride that Gavess was industriously copying down what he said. When he had finished, she asked a few questions, raised an eyebrow to Lady Talia and Pagris, but they could add nothing.

"All right. We'll get a good copy of that made up tonight and send it through to the castle by the next King's Messenger we see."

"You'll be staying the night, of course."

"We won't. We were planning our stopover in Dorbane, and I see no reason to change that."

"But I'm sure my fellow townsmen would like to thank you for removing this scourge..."

She cut off his speech with the swing of her hand that set the helmet back on her head. "We understand how grateful people are. However, we only bashed a few heads back there. The bandits are definitely not gone, no matter what 'they' say. Keep taking the proper precautions, and we'll look in on you when we come back through here."

She turned to her troop. "Everyone, I want the horses checked, nose to tail. Look yourselves over again, now that the heat of battle is over. You wouldn't be the first person to find out he's bleedin' and he didn't notice it."

There was a chorus of "Yes, ma'am."

"And you can stop that 'ma'am' business. The battle's over."

"Anine, if the battle is over, does that mean you're not my superior officer anymore?"

She glanced at the other woman, who was smiling. "I guess so."

"Then I think you should drop that last order."

"What?"

"I think it would be better if they keep calling you 'ma'am', like an officer. In the first place, as I have just found out, we are in more of a military situation than we thought. Most of our people are soldiers of one sort or other, and they would be more comfortable, and thus more effective, with a real officer in charge. Second, if word of us travels ahead for some reason, then a military troop with an officer in charge sounds like a party not worth bothering, don't you think?"

Anine shook her head. "I don't know, Lady Talia. I can't just appoint myself an officer."

The lady smiled. "Of course not. But I can."

"You can?"

"Certainly. Can you see anybody arguing? Anybody here, for example? His Majesty, my possible future husband, maybe?"

Anine stared at the woman, then burst out laughing.

"Why do you find that so funny? I thought you'd be pleased!"

"It's you. You are so good at that."

"At what?"

"Politics. Power. You've been doing it all your life, so you don't realize how good you are. Do you realize what you just did?"

"I obviously don't."

"I bet I'm not the only one who noticed. Pagris, you tell her."

The lady turned puzzled eyes to the Inari.

He smiled. "I think Anine says you just put her in place. She give you hard discipline, back at the fight. Now you must get back in

211

charge. So now you are, and how can she argue? You would be great Potentara, Lady Talia. Gerth very lucky. Very good queen."

It was Talia's turn to laugh, partly to hide her embarrassment. "And now, with your courtier-like compliments, you have just demonstrated your superiority to me in the arts of diplomacy."

Anine slapped her gauntlets against her leg. "Whether or not we have made any progress in straightening out the chain of command here, may I suggest that we get on the road?"

With a number of exaggerated, "Yes, ma'ams," they prepared to mount. When she was sure that everyone was in good travelling shape, she started out, to the waving and cheers of the townspeople and the grateful cries of the teamsters and their families.

She had to share a small grin of pride with Talia over that. "So now we're heroes."

The lady shook her head. "I certainly loved that charge. And the cheers at the end. I'm not so sure about the middle part, though."

"You get a sword stuck in you, you'd like it even less. How do you like fighting from horseback?"

"It wasn't hard, after the practice you gave us. You have to work at getting the sword out and up, so you don't cut your horse's ears off. But it certainly comes down easily." She shuddered. "So easily."

"There are some things you're better not to think about, my Lady."

"Why did we leave the town so fast?"

"I'm sure you can figure it out."

"You still think that may have been a trap for us? Isn't that rather far-fetched?"

She nodded confidently. "Aye. It's far-fetched and I'd like to keep it that way. I'm learning to read, remember? I've been practising on history and tactics. There are too many leaders who got caught celebrating when they thought the enemy was beaten. Actually, we'd probably be better off not stopping in Dorbane either."

"Because we told everybody we were going to?"

"Exactly. Do you think I'm being too careful?"

The lady shifted in the saddle. "I'll reserve judgment on that until I find out how much farther we have to ride."

Anine turned to Pagris, who had been riding at her shoulder, listening. "What do you think?"

He nodded. "Good idea. Dorbane too far to ride. Horses work hard today, too. We camp?"

"I'd rather not have to post a guard. I thought maybe we could impose on a farmer."

"What is the farmer going to think about that?"

She looked over at the lady. "It's good of you to consider him, but there's bandits around. I figure we'll trade a roof over our heads for our protection in keeping the roof over his head. Sounds fair to me. It's not as if he has to feed us."

At that they rode on and nooned comfortably where a stream crossed the road in an open meadow a short bowshot from any cover. After Gavess had passed out the food, Anine called for everyone's attention.

"With the mercenaries, it is standard procedure for the officers to get together after a battle to discuss what went right, what wrong. Since there is only us, I think we can all discuss it."

There were several nods, so she continued. "Any comments?"

Albier grinned. "Good charge."

Ranill nodded. "I liked that one. Did the job quick, nobody hurt. Went the way it was supposed to. Doesn't happen that often, ma'am. Good work."

She couldn't suppress the smile. "Thanks. You all did your parts well."

"I didn't."

"My Lady..."

"No, it has to be said." Talia turned from Anine and faced the group. "I didn't follow orders properly. I saw the women and children, and I tried to go back again to help. I shouldn't have done that. I know that now, and next time I will follow orders better." She leaned back, her face a bit flushed.

There were nods of approval all around, and Anine hoped the lady realized that they were for both the correctness of her admission, and her strength in admitting the error.

"Gavess, you had the hardest part. Any comments?"

The little butler shook his head. "I was worried at first, ma'am. I had no idea I would be leading my horses through a battle. I thought maybe I should go around. Then I saw the big hole you made through, and..." he paused uncomfortably "...well, to be frank, ma'am, you and my Lady are very easy to see in a battle."

They all chuckled.

"That was why I gave you the choice, Gavess. I thought that if you went around, the bandits would all be running, and you might come up against some of them. You were safer behind us, with the wagons covering your back as we left."

"You were right, ma'am. I'll remember that. And ma'am?"

"Yes?"

"I felt quite helpless out there. Will someone please find a way I can arm myself?"

Nobody laughed. She looked around the circle for advice on this one.

"Do you have any training at all?"

He shook his head ruefully. "Only in the kitchen."

Arvent raised his hands, palms upwards. "There you have it. Kitchen knives."

"Really?"

"Whatever you're familiar with is the easiest. Next time we practise, you show me what you have, and I'll show you how to work with it. Or Lateda will."

The butler nodded, and his frown cleared.

"Any other comments?"

When nobody said anything, she closed the conversation. "Fine. A good exercise, well carried out. We will be working with Lady Talia on saddle warfare," she grinned, "and Gavess on kitchen warfare.

"Ladies and gentlemen, shall we hit the road?"

They jumped up, tightened their cinches and mounted.

Later that afternoon, they found a suitable farm, and it turned out she had made one small mistake: the food. The big, fortified farmhouse where they pulled in contained three generations of a family of long standing in the area who had plenty of room, plenty of food, and a great deal of pride in their ability to host noble company, no matter if it came with a helmet covering its regal hair.

When a breathless rider turned up shortly behind them, a local lad anxious to spread the story of the fight, he was delighted to catch up with the heroes. Then the assembled farm people had to hear the whole story.

So, between the security and the entertainment they provided, Anine felt they repaid the farmers for their hospitality. She had just finished a last tour of the premises and was allowing herself to relax a bit for the night when a soft voice startled her from the shadows of a doorway.

"May I see your sword?"

"That depends."

"Oh." An uncertain pause. "On what?"

"On who you are and why you want to see it. You startle a soldier out of a dark doorway, you're likely to feel a sword before you see it."

"Oh. I'm sorry."

"That's all right. Just step out here and answer my...Oh."

The figure that stumped out from the doorway was shorter than Anine by only a finger, and probably outweighed her. It was like looking in a mirror at an image from five years ago. Wide, sloping shoulders, thick arms, huge hands roughened by farm tools all her life. Anine sighed.

"So, you think becoming a soldier will solve your problems."

"How'd you know?"

"How do you think I started out?"

"You?"

"That's right. Me. I got these arms from forking hay onto the wagons. From wrestling calves at branding time. From splitting wood, carrying water. I've been through it, girl."

"Then you think I should?"

"I didn't say that. You think you can run away from your troubles by becoming a soldier. You may be right. But my experience is, you just get another set dumped on you. You think I don't have troubles?"

"I suppose you do. But you have some control over them."

She laughed. "Sometimes I think I have less control than I did when I was your age."

"Oh."

"Tell you. You wait a couple of years. When you're old enough, and some young lad hasn't snatched you up, you come to the castle in Petrella, ask for Anine."

"Who's gonna snatch me up?"

Anine shrugged, a gesture lost in the darkness. "You never know. There's plenty of farm boys, good and bad, just like there's plenty of soldiers, same thing."

Another figure faded up out of the dim doorway. "What are you tellin' my daughter, Soldier?"

"More truth than she's likely to hear from anybody else, Farmer. I tell you like I told her. Give her a few years. If things don't work out here and she still wants to come, you let her go. I promise you one thing, I'll look out for her. I can't do better than that. She makes her own way if she can. Fair enough?"

The big figure relaxed as she spoke. "I guess you're right, ma'am. There ain't much place for a girl like Saira, here."

"Actually, there is. Thinkin' about it, if I'da had the chance, I'da made a darn good farmer. As it is, I think my next job is gonna be fixing roads for the king. So don't worry, Saira. It's a big world out there, and there's lots of places you might fit." She was about to walk off when another thought hit her. She turned back to the girl.

"Another thing. Don't you go moonin' about how you're gonna run off an' be a soldier and ignorin' the chores you're supposed to be doin' here and now. You work hard on the farm; get your muscles toughened up. You get a chance to learn with a sword or staff, you take it. You get a chance to learn to read or do sums, you jump on that. Get me?"

"Oh yes. I get you. I'm a real hard worker. You ask Dad, here."

The farmer chuckled. "She's right about that, I'll say that for her. Hardest worker on the place."

"Then her chances are pretty good at whatever fate brings her, aren't they? You come and see me if you want to, girl. If your luck takes you somewhere else, then go with my good wishes."

She strode back into the farmhouse, her step light, a warm glow in her middle.

18. Trouble on the Road

The following evening, Lady Talia looked around the common room of the inn where they were staying. "This is a big space without very many people."

Anine stared. "You think...?"

"We haven't had a sword training session since the Rock because of the horse work and the wet weather." The lady swung her long legs over the bench and rose to approach the landlord. After a quick discussion, she returned, a smile on her face. "He says we can use the half of the room away from the fire. I promised to pay for anything we break, so keep it under control, will you?"

They all chuckled as they enthusiastically cleared a fighting space. "Who's first?"

Albier, the quieter of Talia's two mercenary footmen, stood. "I'd like to try with the swordmaster, Anine."

She nodded. "All right. Do you want an official?"

Both shook their heads. Arvent stepped forward, bringing his sword into line. "No practice wands here, lad, so let's be gentle, shall we?"

Albier grinned and made a plain salute. "I don't think I'd have much of a chance if I tried to be gentle."

"Very well, then." The brown man seemed to shrink into himself, presenting a smaller target, his bright sword weaving slowly, hypnotically, in front of his face. The young mercenary tried several lines of attack, but each time he found his blade bound after the second or third move.

Finally, he dropped his point in frustration. "I don't get it. What are you doing?"

"Protecting myself. You seemed to think this was going to be a contest, so I'm practising my defense."

"I'll say. I can't even get started! How do you do that?"

When Arvent hesitated, Anine stepped forward. "That's what we're doing. Training. Will you show us those binds you're using? I haven't seen the third one before."

Arvent grinned. "Because I was improvising. The lad got closer to me than makes me comfortable, so I ran my corkscrew with his motion, instead of counter to it. It's dangerous with a strong opponent, because unless you come around faster than he does, you end up with his sword inside yours."

"Show me." She raised her sword and moved it at half speed in the same attack that Albier had used. He countered at a like speed, and his sword moved around hers in a tight circle, winding down towards her, to end jammed against her hilt.

"See how it works?"

She nodded. "Do it again."

Soon, all the others were anxiously waiting their turn on the floor to try the new moves.

When trouble came, Talia said afterwards that it had been bad luck. Anine called it stupidity.

She had noticed the young noble who strutted his way into the inn, flanked by two larger men, stopping in surprise when he saw what was going on. His eyes hardly left the fighters as he strolled across to a vacant table and sat. One of his friends said something, and he waved a hand negligently towards the bar, never losing his interest.

Once he was seated, drinking, she dropped him from her mind and concentrated on what Arvent was saying. It was half a candle later that a voice carried through a pause in the training.

"Is this a private party, or can anyone join?"

As all eyes turned to him, the young man rose and sauntered towards them. The first feeling of unease crept into Anine's throat. It was too close to a swagger.

Confronted with a row of surprised faces and no reply, he addressed himself to Arvent. "I mean it. Can I have a go? You seem to be a pretty competent lot. I've had some training myself. I'd like to match up with one of you. I don't mind which."

Anine slipped to Arvent's side. "Maybe not, Arvent."

He turned back to the interloper. "No, this is just a training session. We aren't competing."

The youth looked them all over, slowly. "I get it. The woman says no, and you all knuckle under."

Out of sight, Anine grabbed Arvent's belt and held it firmly, just for a moment. He stayed put. With a warning glance at Lady Talia, she stepped forward. "We were just practising, as the man says. We would be very foolish to let it get any farther, especially with strangers." She grinned. "Besides, we promised the innkeeper to pay for anything that got broken. Sit and have a drink with us."

He was having none of her diplomacy. "I see. You really are afraid. I suppose I expected that. You're over the border now, you know. You're not in Petrella, where you can run to the king's mummy and have your noses wiped."

Anine thought about this. She had been taunted before and had found that just saying nothing often had the double effect of spoiling the bully's timing and letting herself get a grasp on what was really happening. She thought, then she made her decision.

"I'm sorry, lad. We were just having a bit of a training session and we didn't mean to cause any difficulty. But I can't let you make a slight like that against King Gerth. You may apologize, have a drink, and we will forget all this."

The boy threw back his embroidered short-cloak, freeing his sword arm. "And if I don't?"

She sighed. "Then you win."

That stopped him. "What do you mean, I win?"

She shrugged. "You came in looking for a lesson in swordplay and manners as well. If you really want, we can give you both."

His handsome face scowled. "I don't take well to commoners insulting me."

"I suppose that's your answer. Arvent, would you oblige this gentleman? We didn't come here to make trouble. Know what I mean?"

Arvent nodded, spoke quietly. "Don't worry, Anine. I've handled plenty of these. I'll give him a good lesson and I won't hurt him."

"Good. All right, folks. Give them room." She drew her own weapon. "I'm going to officiate. Any silliness and I will break your sword in half. Do you follow?"

She was close enough that her bulk and the size of her sword impressed him, and she could see the muscles work in his throat. Then he pulled himself together, sneered, and nodded.

Arvent rolled his shoulders to loosen them. "All right, lad. I'll show you what the others were learning. Make a few passes at me."

"Oh, that I will!" Anine thought he sounded too eager by half, but she had to trust Arvent.

The first pass went exactly as it should have. The young noble attacked and found the tip of his blade driven into the floor. He tried again, and this time Arvent pushed his sword hand high and held it there. As they parted, Anine could see the blood of frustration rush into the man's cheek. She shot a warning glance at Arvent, but he had seen it, too.

"Do you want to know how I did that?" He spoke casually, no challenge, nothing to be angry at.

"I want to see if you can do it again!" the youth gritted out.

Arvent winced, then went on guard again. Three more times the youth attacked, each one more desperate. Finally, he rested, his face white with anger. Then he threw himself forward. Sensing a difference, Arvent made the bind on the first pass, but his opponent, instead of disengaging, fought against it. The two fighters made a half turn as they strove against each other, and Anine could see that the young lord had a dagger that had appeared from a drop-sheath in his sleeve, which he was about to jam into Arvent's side. She didn't have time to call out. Something in the offender's stance warned the swordmaster, and he shifted and spun. His free hand caught the dagger hand by the wrist, and he performed a smooth disengage from the bind which moved him forward, inside, and he jabbed the basket of his sword hilt sharply into the noble's face.

The lad went to the floor like an empty sack. He sat there, looking stunned, and then the blood began to run down his lip. Arvent moved toward the boy, but Anine motioned him back. She reached down, took the dagger from the unnerved fingers and stepped on it, breaking it cleanly. Then she picked up the sword and, using a technique Jhanes had taught her, snapped it with a flick of her wrists.

The noble erupted off the floor, blood sputtering from his damaged mouth. "My sword! You cow! That sword was ..."

He got no farther, as her hand closed on his throat, stopping his forward movement. She squeezed just enough to get his attention, lifted slightly, then spoke slowly and clearly. She wanted everyone in the inn to hear this.

"You're a very lucky boy. You woulda killed my friend with that nasty hideaway, just because he's a better swordsman than you. In return, all you got was a sore nose. Let me tell you somethin' about life, boy. You'd killed him, there'da been five swords in your throat before his body hit the floor. You're messing with people and you got no idea who. Don't be even more stupid. Collect your friends and walk out of here and be glad you're alive." She shook him once to emphasize each word. "Have. You. Got. That?"

She slowly relaxed her grip, and when she thought he could stand, let him go. He stood, rubbing his throat.

"Do you know who I am?"

She nodded. "You're the son of one of the lords around here. You think that means you can do what you like. Up to this point, every time you messed up your father has bought or bullied your way out of it. Not this time. You go home and tell your father that you made a mistake and tangled with Zoysana's Clan. If that means anythin' to him, he'll tell you how lucky you were."

She waited. "You can go, now."

He opened his mouth, but she flexed her fingers, and he closed it. He looked once at the grim faces confronting him. Then he grabbed his broken sword from the floor and stormed to the door. Just before he slammed it behind him, he turned back and shook his fist. "You haven't heard the last of this!"

They listened to the sound of hoofbeats, which started abruptly, then faded rapidly away.

Anine grimaced. "I'm sort of hoping we have heard the last of it."

Talia grinned weakly and slapped her on the shoulder. "You handled that beautifully, Anine!"

"No, I didn't. We don't want any trouble like that on this trip. We were supposed to keep our heads down and ride fast." She turned to Arvent.

"Thanks for trying. Until he pulled that dagger, I thought you were handling him perfectly."

It was the swordsman's turn to shake his head. "I'm sorry. I shouldn't have hit him. I'd just made a mistake, and I was angry. More with myself than him."

"You? You didn't make no mistake. If you'da made a mistake, you'd be dead now."

"Yes, I did. I could have read him better. I should never have given a weasel like that the chance to get a free hand behind me." He sat down, shaking his head. "I hate making mistakes like that."

She clapped him on the back. "Ah, you don't know what you're talkin' about. That kid was trouble the moment he walked in here.

221

The only thing you could have done better was to take his sword away from him on the first pass and spank his butt with it."

"I considered that."

"You did?"

"That's one way of dealing with that sort. But I decided not to, because it would just enrage him, and I figured then he'd do somethin' real stupid, like burn the inn down, just to get back at us."

Lady Talia met Anine's eyes. "Burn the inn down?"

"Sure." Arvent was inspecting his sword hilt for damage, wiping the blood off. "That sort of scum will do that kind of trick."

Anine slumped. "Great. Now we have to stand watches."

Arvent nodded. "Oh, I figured on that from the moment I saw him come in the door."

"You did?"

"We got a lot of those in the fencing schools. You had him pretty well pegged there, when you laid it out to him. He just might be back here with his daddy and thirty retainers."

While this conversation was going on, the rest of the party was putting the benches and tables back into position. When they finished, they all looked to Anine. She thought furiously. "All right. We need to know what we're really up against. I'm going to find the innkeeper."

"That won't be necessary, ma'am."

She turned toward the quiet voice at her elbow.

"Oh. Thank you. Who is that lad?"

The innkeeper shrugged. "Exactly who you said he is, ma'am."

"What do we expect? Would he come back and burn your inn down?"

"Probably," the man smiled wanly, "but only if you were in it."

"Don't worry, sir. We'll have guards posted all night, and we'll be out of here at first dawn."

"Thank you. I can show your men where the watch positions are."

"What about his father?"

The innkeeper took a deep breath. "You probably have less to worry about, there. His manor is some distance away, and by the time young Malaury gets home, it will be too late for him to do anything about it anyway. He's a fierce man, is Lord Ornaison, and has a blind spot for the boy. If you were to take my advice, ma'am..."

222

"That's why I asked, innkeeper."

"...I'd say you get out of here early and you just keep moving."

"You gonna get into any trouble over this?"

He shook his head fiercely. "This town doesn't owe anything to Lord Ornaison. We protect our own, and he knows it. Besides, I didn't do anything."

"Except witness the boy's embarrassment."

The innkeeper gave a 'what can you do' shrug and returned to his bar. Anine arranged the watches, refusing Lady Talia the duty.

"I know you'd like to, but that's a job for the professionals, my Lady."

"Don't you think I could do as good a job?"

"I don't wanta have to take the chance. You get a good rest, because tomorrow's roundin' up to have a lota ridin'."

The lady smiled. "You know, Anine, when you start being a soldier, all your new language patterns just fall apart."

Anine refused to return the smile. "I guess that just reminds everybody what I really am, don't it?"

Anine forced herself to go to bed because she knew she needed sleep. She took over the last watch just before dawn, and paced the area as well as she could in the growing light. But nothing stirred and, after a quick breakfast, the small troop was saddled and moving.

They were quiet as they rode along, which was understandable, considering the early hour. As the sun rose, Anine began to look around. A thought hit her. "Pagris, will you check our backtrail?"

He nodded and faded back through the troop.

"Point rider?"

"I was about to ask for volunteers, Arderton."

The man grinned and trotted ahead. Anine looked around. "Arvent, how is your horse doing?"

He glanced at her. "Fine."

"He looks pretty strong. Can he handle an extra run?" She tossed her head, pointing with her chin towards a rock that jutted out over the hillside up ahead. He nodded and spurred his horse off the road. Soon she could see him labouring up the side of the hill, and then, and only because she was looking for it, she saw the merest top of his head on the skyline.

He was back quickly. Too quickly, it seemed, to have made a proper survey.

"What is it?" The rest of the troop moved in closer to hear.

"I can't see any trouble ahead. Arderton's quite a way up the road, the ground's very open and there don't look to be any trails leading in, or ambush points."

"Good."

"That's real good, because the news behind isn't."

Her stomach dropped. "What have we got?"

"Large cloud of dust, just this side of the village. Sparkles in it."

"Like armour?"

He nodded.

"Well, folks, I guess it's ridin' time. I'll stay beside Lady Talia. Lateda, you follow right behind her. Gavess and the baggage horses after that. The rest of you spread out. You know how far. Close enough to help, far enough that we don't all get caught in a trap." She was about to kick her horse ahead when she thought.

"Any other ideas?"

Albier snickered. "We could stop and invite them for tea."

She looked back. "Do we have any tea, Gavess?"

"No tea, ma'am."

"Then I guess we can't do that. Thanks for the idea, though, Albier. I'll be coming to you for advice in the future." Then she kicked her horse into motion, a slow, steady canter that they could hold all morning if necessary.

At least two candles later, she glanced once again over her shoulder to see Pagris's horse approaching from behind. He overtook them rapidly, yet his horse was only breathing hard.

"What do we have?"

"Very slow, Anine. They are behind far. You may rest the horses."

She signalled a trot and they continued. "Anything more?"

He nodded. "One Warlander, one boy with sore nose. Twenty men, light horse fighters. Look good. Ride slow."

"Do you think that's because they want to wear us down?"

He grinned. "No. Warlander angry. He yell, they ride fast. Ten steps, they slow down. He yell, they ride fast. Like that. Tired men. Tired horses."

She felt the relief boil up in her. "They wore their horses out at the first. Do you think they can catch us?"

The Inari shook his head. "Only chance is ambush. I go check."

"Arderton is out in front."

"I will help." With a wave of his hand, he lifted his horse into that swift lope and was soon far ahead.

It wasn't long before they rounded a corner and found Arderton waiting for them. "Pagris said to wait for you. He says there's no way they can be in front of us, but he's making sure."

She nodded. "Thanks, Arderton. Good work."

Pagris did not reappear until noon, and then it was from behind. His beautiful horse was now lathered, its bay hide darkened with sweat around the saddle. As he pulled in beside Anine, it slowed gratefully to a walk, sides heaving.

"News?"

"Horse fall down. They go back."

"Which horse?"

The Inari grinned. "Big horse. Horse in front."

"The Warlander's charger wore out?"

"Not quite wore out. I help."

"What did you do?"

The stocky man shrugged. "Inari trick." He would not say more.

"Should we stop for food?"

He nodded at that. "Water ahead. Stop now. Ride far today."

"Tell you, we ride far today. I don't want that oaf sending a messenger ahead for some friend of his to grab us."

There was general agreement at this, and their nooning was short.

When the opportunity arose, Anine led the troop around the next town. Using a sweeping bend in the road and an outcropping of rock that screened them, she ran them in a shortcut through the farmers' fields, dropping and rebuilding a few stone fences in order to get by. Then they were out on the road again north of town, leaving any pursuers to scratch their heads as to how a troop of nine people and eleven horses could disappear into thin air. Pagris had dealt with their footprints at exit and entry, and the traffic of the day was enough that only a skilled tracker could read the road.

She knew that if their pursuers started questioning other travellers her precautions wouldn't make much difference, but the shortcut helped them get to the next town near dark. They set watches that night as well, and it was only after another uneventful day that Anine started to relax.

"Do you think we've lost them?"

Anine smiled over at Lady Talia. "Have you had enough of riding fast and hard?"

The lady smiled. "You're speaking properly again. We must be out of danger."

They both laughed.

"Well, we have one new rule in our training sessions."

"I'm sure I know what it is."

"No more locals."

"I agree wholeheartedly."

They were to break this rule within the next three days. They had been staying at inns through Velikiii, but now they crossed the border into the first of the Inner Duchies. On the second day past the border, Lady Talia suddenly pulled her horse to a stop. "I know where we are!"

"That is very good, my Lady. I have been sure that Anine was lost for several days, now."

She ignored Gavess' humour in her enthusiasm. "No, no, I've been here before. That crag over there, you can't forget it. It marks the end of my cousin's land." She turned to Anine. "We don't have to stay at inns every night, do we?"

"Of course not, my Lady. If you have a safe place you'd rather stop, we could all use a rest."

"A rest? Don't we rest every night?"

Anine raised her eyebrows.

"Oh. I'm sorry. You are all on duty, all day, all night, aren't you? Especially you."

"Well, not especially me, but yes, we are. We'd love a chance to let down a bit, if you really trust this cousin of yours. The boys'd like a chance to drink a bit too much, flirt with the kitchen girls, that sort of thing."

"And who will you be flirting with, Anine?"

She grinned. "Some rich farmer who can afford hired hands to do all the work while his wife just sits in her drawing room and gives orders."

"Somehow, I can't see that picture with you in it."

Anine sighed, only half joking. "I don't suppose I can either."

Sure enough, soon they were riding up a long drive, shaded on either side by a row of huge elms that met above them, creating a tunnel that was probably cool in the heat of summer, but at this season only served to make their road darker despite the leafless branches.

They were greeted with great enthusiasm by all the members of the cousin's household. He was a large enough man himself, but as he stood, dwarfed by the two women who confronted him, he laughed. "Well, Talia, you seem to have found good friends out there on the frontier."

Talia laughed as well. "Tell you, Tuchan, there's lots of big people out there. King Gerth makes me look positively dainty. And you ought to see Anine's superior officer!"

The lord looked his cousin up and down. "You've changed, Talia. I thought you were crazy when you went through here in that huge coach, headed out for adventure. I think maybe you found it."

"Oh, don't talk to me about that coach. I still don't know if it was a curse or a benison. It's a separate story in itself. At least it made me some good friends, despite the trouble it caused me."

"Well, that's better than I expected. I thought it would get you upside down in a river somewhere or killed by bandits."

Talia nudged Anine. "Did I tell you how smart he was?"

Her cousin laughed again and ushered them into the hall. "I'll have your men and stock quartered. I assume you want your maid with you. And the inimitable Gavess nearby as usual? What about your officer?"

Talia turned to Anine. "Wherever you put the mercenary officers, Lord Tuchan."

"You're a mercenary, are you?"

Anine's back straightened. "Not anymore, my Lord. I'm one of Zoysana's Clan, now."

He looked puzzled. "I'm sorry, ma'am, I don't know that troop."

Talia took his arm and pulled him into the main hall. "It isn't a mercenary troop, Tuchan, and if you haven't heard of them, you soon will."

Dinner at the Tuchan hall that night was a gala affair and Anine, freed of most of her concern for the safety of her charge, could put her mind to other things. She watched Arvent as he sat at a lower table with Talia's men. He seemed to be joining in more, and she

227

was glad of it. She hadn't forgotten her original charge, nor had her Clan Leader allowed her to.

Zoysana had tossed out a casual question about him near the end of the briefing, knowing that Anine would have no answer, and therefore sending the message that she was to continue to monitor him.

So, she was quite aware when a pretty serving girl who had been paying close attention to him all evening sat down beside him when her duties were done. Anine could tell from the stiffening of his pose that he was uncomfortable, and she watched, amused, to see how he would handle this situation.

He was given no chance. She had only leaned over to talk to him, one of those deep leans designed to reveal more bosom than necessary, when a young man appeared from behind her, grabbed her by the arm and lifted her physically off her seat. Anine couldn't hear what he said over the din of the other guests, but it didn't sound complimentary. Arvent had risen at the first sign of trouble and stood unmoving as the scene played itself out.

The girl was angry at the lad who had interrupted her fun and was letting him know it in no uncertain terms. They kept their voices low out of deference to their position, but Anine could imagine the derogatory nature of the exchange. She would soon find out if the youth was brother or lover.

It was lover. Unable to face the girl's tirade, he looked to take his anger out on another object, predictably Arvent. She could see the swordmaster smile and shake his head, try for a light reply, to no avail. She was just considering whether she should move that way, when it was all over. Another lad slipped up behind the swain and whispered urgently in his ear.

Relaxing, Anine could read the conversation in their postures:
"Do you know who that is?"
"Why should I care who that is?"
"He's the Swordmaster to King Gerth of Petrella, that's why."

She could see the youth's demeanour change as that shot went home. From then on, it was all face-saving bluster, and the lad stormed out, towing behind him a girl with a satisfied smirk on her face. Arvent glanced Anine's way, caught her eye, made a sweat-wiping motion across his brow and turned back to the rest, who were laughing and pulling him down for some good-natured ribbing.

Anine wondered how the reticent swordsman would react to this sort of publicity, exactly the kind he usually ran from.

On the road the next morning, she kneed her horse alongside him.

"All right, ma'am. Go ahead. I deserve it."

"Deserve what?"

"The dressing-down you're about to give me for that disturbance I caused last night."

She laughed. "You didn't cause anything."

"I didn't?"

"No. That girl had it all figured out. Did you see how satisfied she looked as she went out the door? I imagine there were a whole lot of sweet apologies going on right after that."

"Oh."

She glanced sideways at him. "I'm sorry if I deflated your opinion of your attractiveness."

"Least of my worries."

"Why is that?"

"That's the kind of thing I'm usually good at avoiding, for one."

"Yes, but I've been pushing you to get involved with people, and that sort of thing often happens with people, unpredictable critters that they are."

"You can laugh about it, but I'm trying to fulfill a purpose here, you know."

"Well, let's think about that, then. What would the Sivan say about last night's little interlude?"

"The Sivan? He'd say I messed up. He'd say I drew all sorts of attention to myself."

"I don't see it that way. After all, you did get out of it with no fighting."

"That's another thing. Did you see that fellow back off so quickly? His friend told him something about me that scared him."

"I assume he told him you were Gerth's swordmaster, or something like that."

"Exactly. Another thing the Sivan wouldn't like. I'm starting to become known. That reduces my effectiveness."

"Perhaps. But what would Zoysana say to that?"

He jogged on. "I have been at the castle for over six months, and I have long given up trying to figure out what Zoysana would say about anything. Or you, for that matter."

229

She grinned at the self-pity in his voice. "Well, I'll tell you. From what I hear, and I don't know the man, the Sivan always starts his pupils off with the most obvious point. They are supposed to think through the more complicated twists of the logic themselves. Zoe, being his best student, his most effective agent and a close friend, always jumps to interesting conclusions. Often the opposite of his, from what I have heard."

"And what is the obvious opposite you glean from this mess?"

She shrugged. "I don't have to be as wise as Zoysana to realize that you can't be nothing. Nobody can exist without being noticed. You have to have some sort of reputation. Swordmaster is a pretty safe one, I should think. A man of action is not often taken as the type to be a spy. And it got you out of this trouble, didn't it?"

"It did?"

"Of course. That girl was either really stupid or quite sly. If she was stupid, she just chose the prettiest looking guy she could find to make her boy jealous. Could have been a disaster. If she was smarter, and I think she was, she knew who you were and knew there was no chance he would get in a fight with someone of your reputation."

"So how did she know he would know?"

"Do you think it was an accident that his friend, whoever it was, knew who you were, in order to tell him before he did anything really stupid?"

Arvent again allowed his horse to move a few paces before he answered. "You know, when you work with the Sivan, you start to think that you are part of the elite, who are making all these incredibly complex plans and manipulating everyone. And then you see a classic bit of work like that, perfectly executed, and by who? By an uneducated serving girl who just wants to get her man's attention. It sets you back into the real world, it does."

Anine reached over and punched his shoulder. "Looks like you made some progress today, Arvent."

He nodded judiciously. "You know, I believe I did."

The incident made a difference to the rest of the mercenaries in their little troop, because she noticed him becoming more involved in the little jokes and ribaldry that helped their day pass.

As the journey continued and they pushed farther into the Inner Duchies, it was as if they were turning back the season. The weather warmed, the roads firmed, and the rain ceased.

The number of patrols they met, both mounted and on foot, increased. So did the number of towns and the spread of farms that bordered the road. When they reached the point where Anine felt their armament was attracting more attention as a potential threat than the protection they needed, she consulted with the others.

"What do you think, Lady Talia? We're more heavily armed than anybody on the road except the patrols. Will the local lords start objecting?"

Talia nodded. "I thought to mention it to you. I travel this road once or twice a year, usually with two footmen and a coachman, none of them of the quality of my present company."

"We're starting to present a spectacle."

"That would be the uncharitable way to put it."

From then on, Anine's helmet sat behind her on top of her bedroll, with her chainmail shirt rolled inside it. Her sword stayed where it was. The others likewise toned down their warlike look, except Pagris, who didn't really have any way to look other than he was.

When she thought about it, they were certainly in no danger. No private footpad would dare approach such a forbidding group, and they were close enough to Lesser Trenet that Talia's name would straighten out any lord incautious enough to object to their presence.

Of course, they had no way of knowing how the local politics were moving, so she kept good watch anyway. She wasn't about to deliver her charge into her own kingdom, only to have her kidnapped a day's journey from home by someone with more ambition than sense.

So, with her eyes open and her troop still on alert, they crossed the border into Lesser Trenet.

19. LESSER TRENET

There were no patrols at the border. It seemed that the Inner Duchies had no need to worry about their neighbours. The officer who raised a languid hand as they approached seemed only interested in what goods they were carrying. When Talia stepped forward she had no need to remind him who she was, and he welcomed her back, then sent them on enthusiastically, making her companions feel that they were the best thing that had happened since the sun rose that morning.

Talia shook her head as they left the border. "As you may guess, we have quite a large civil service here."

"Completely concerned with the politics of keeping their positions?"

Talia smiled. "Well, not quite. They do serve some purpose."

They were housed regally at a true castle that night, and approached Talia's home in the middle of a fine fall afternoon. Talia had sent a messenger ahead the night before, so they were officially expected.

That morning, she had taken charge. Calling them all together after breakfast, she faced them with an impish smile. "Would you like to have some fun?"

Curious nods.

"All right. Folks here at home have no idea what has happened to me this summer. But I have a good idea how they expect me to arrive. I have no intention of disappointing them.

"Pagris, do you have any finery with you? Ceremonial colours, that sort of thing?"

He nodded.

"Good. Put it on, will you? The rest of you, will you go back to full armour? Wear everything you've got. Anine? You know how you braid your hair before a battle? Could you do mine that way?"

"I hope you know what you're doing, my Lady."

Talia wrinkled her brow. "I don't know, Anine, but I'm not crawling in and trying to fit anymore. They accept me as I am, or screw them!"

"I hope you won't be talking that way in front of your mother, my Lady."

They all turned in surprise. It was the longest sentence they had ever heard from Lateda.

Talia let loose her usual peal of laughter. "Lateda, I know you don't want me to disappoint Mother. Don't worry. This is only a show for the rest of them."

So they rode into the main square in front of the castle of Lesser Trenet with a fully-armed Inari leading, his bronze arm-bands, upper and lower, shining, his horse's mane braided with mother-of pearl shells, and his shoulders mantled by a cloak of the varicoloured furs of every animal Anine could think of and some she had never seen.

Anine herself was dressed in her mercenary's best, which wasn't very flashy but was polished to its utmost shine. Both she and Talia had their braids wound in a cushion around their heads, but Anine's was covered by her helmet. The others followed in strict precision, two by two, with their weapons at the ready.

It was a fine martial display and the populace loved it. They cheered, they called out, and the children ran alongside, shrieking in terror when Pagris scowled at them. He was having trouble keeping a straight face.

The crowd parted naturally, showing Pagris their route to the castle gate, even though he had never navigated such twisting town streets before. When they had passed through the gates into the bailey, they were met officially by the castle bailiff, who mouthed ritual words of greeting while his eyes were bugging out of his head. He belatedly moved to help the lady from her saddle, only to find her already swinging down on her own, hitching her sword back into a comfortable position as he regained his poise.

Retreating into the safety of the ritual, he preceded them through the inner courtyard and into what Anine could only think of as a throne room. It was wide and lofty, with pillars that soared up to coloured clairstory windows high above. She resolved to look her fill later and concentrated on what was happening. She reminded herself that her task was not over. What if their reception was not what Talia confidently expected? Concentrating on her duty allowed Anine to move calmly through the unfamiliar ceremonies that followed.

As they passed through the carved double doors, Anine heard a giggle beside her. The corner of her eye registered two slim young ladies in pastel frills, hiding their faces behind ornate fans.

"Oh, my, my, my!"

"The Lady be praised, did you see that?"

"What a sight!"

"What does she think she's doing?"

Anine paused in her stride and turned toward the two girls. She did not speak, but looked down calmly at them. She knew what effect that had on people. The two froze in place, their fans sliding slowly downward, their eyes wide open, as were their mouths. Anine deepened her stare, and they melted away and were gone. She turned to Talia and winked. Talia gave a shaky grin and moved on.

Anine breathed a private sigh of relief when a tall, dignified gentleman, greying at the temples and dressed in ornate court robes, stepped forward to greet Talia. Once the girl was in her father's care, Anine's job was over. At least the easy part of it. Considering the two bitches in pink, she realized she wasn't going home just yet. She scanned the crowd for the next enemy appearance.

Once the formalities were over, the courtiers disappeared, and they were left with the duke. With a few words, he organized his retainers to take care of the other members of the party. Talia put a restraining hand on Anine's shoulder.

"Stay a bit longer."

"But your family..."

"I know. But this outfit..." she indicated her hair and gear "...it seemed like such a good idea when we started."

"And now you're feeling awkward in it, and you want me along to feel stupid beside you? Sorry. I can't do that."

"You can't?"

"How can I? This is how I dress for battle. It's me. Why would I feel stupid?"

Talia laughed. "Anine, you always put things into perspective for me!" At the duke's gesture, she led the way into the castle's family rooms, where Talia's father was finally free to embrace her, to be hugged firmly in return. He laughed, rubbed his side and reached out to touch a bump in his daughter's robe.

"That wouldn't be a hideaway dagger that inadvertently broke two of my ribs, would it?"

She laughed as well. "You sent me out into the world to learn about the world. What I learned was that a good hideaway is worth three pikemen if you know how to use it."

His smile dropped. "And I assume you do."

She matched his expression with a sad smile. "Yes, I do, Father. It is a rough place you sent me into. I wasn't quite ready for it," she placed a fond hand on his arm, "but you sent me to the right people."

"I did? Who?"

Then she really laughed. "All of them. Jhanes. Anine, the Petrellans, all of them." She paused. "Gerth."

A different look crept over his face. "Ah, yes. How are you and Gerth getting along?"

She looked at him longer than she needed to. "We're getting married, Father. Isn't that enough?"

For a moment his mouth worked, then his shoulders dropped, and he sat in the carved and polished wooden chair at the head of the table. "No, it isn't, Talia. I had hoped you would be happy about it, as well."

She held her frown until she could stand it no longer. "You deserved that. You deserved that and more. Didn't he, Anine? Didn't he deserve that, sending me out to marry me off to some barbarian he knew nothing about?" She flopped into a nearby chair and dropped her riding gloves on the table.

Her father stared at her, half in happiness at her joy, half in trepidation at her words. Then he turned to the only serious face in the room. Pagris.

"What is she saying?"

Pagris' face dropped into that mask that only an Inari bargaining for a particularly fine horse can achieve. "I do not know, my Lord. Inari girl chooses her own man. Father has no say." He shook his head. "No say."

The lord mimicked the movement. "I think I like the Inari way. If you have no say, then you have no responsibility, so you don't have anything to worry about, do you?"

He motioned, and Pagris sat. "The duke is a wise man."

"I didn't think so last winter when she was out there and I hadn't heard from her for months. Tell me, Talia, has anything changed since this summer? Are you happy?"

Anine could see that the girl was disposed to tease her father some more, and she stepped in. "She couldn't be happier, your Grace. She and Gerth act so sappy the rest of us just hide our heads sometimes. All your plans have come out as you hoped, your Grace, and more so."

He was immediately suspicious. "In what way more so?"

Looking to Talia and receiving an enthusiastic nod, she continued. "In Petrella, the thought is that you sent Talia out to marry Gerth, hoping to influence the way the Petrellan king dealt with the Inner Duchies. Unfortunately, at least for those plans, King Gerth and his advisers have used the information willingly provided by Talia, and they expect to influence the way the Duchies comport themselves. Have I got that right, Talia?"

"That's the way you were given the message, Anine. I was there."

The duke nodded. "So, this mercenary you have brought with you is also more than she seems. Why not? Are you expected to bring back an answer, Anine?"

"No, your Grace. Talia will be taking care of that. For many years to come."

He sighed. "I should not be surprised at where my daughter's loyalties lie. Our society here in the Inner Duchies has not exactly treated her with consideration. If she has found kindred souls in another place, it is understandable."

"But Father, this is all to the interest of Trenet as well."

"It is? From your point of view, I suppose so. I admit, things have changed. People have started to listen when I speak. Not much, but more than in the past."

"Believe me, Father, when the trade wagons from Kyabra start rolling through Trenet on their way to Petrella and the Inari, the rest of the Duchies will perk up their ears."

"Ah, so we are becoming traders now, are we?"

Talia gave a very unladylike snort. "As if we aren't already."

He sighed dramatically. "Anyway, here we are, and this is how things will go. I can't help but wish I had known a bit more ahead of time."

"Oh, stop playing self-pity, Father. You know you had some of the best information on Petrella that was available."

Anine realized this was her opening. "But did you ever question the motivation of he who gave you that information?"

Once more the duke looked surprised. "Why would I question his motives?"

236

"You don't know him as well as they know him back in Petrella." She paused. "And speaking of that person, I have instructions for him. I would like to convey them immediately."

"I don't know if that's possible just now."

Anine moved closer to the duke, towering over him. "Your Grace, I have my instructions. I am to give certain information to the Sivan. I am not to play games with him. The chances that he is somewhere else, at the very moment his plans are coming to fruition, are vanishingly small. He is either listening at this moment or one of his spies is. He is going to show up very soon, or I am going to go looking for him so noisily and so obnoxiously that no one will ever forget that he was here."

She stopped for breath.

"Those are my orders, your Grace. You have no reason to believe I will not carry them out to the letter."

"I most certainly don't. However, I will let the man speak for himself."

Anine turned at his gesture to face the figure that had appeared in the doorway. He was of average height, his shoulders stooped, and his hair was mostly grey. However, there was a sprightliness and energy about him that belied his apparent age. He stepped forward, a smile creasing the fine scars that crossed his cheeks.

"And this is the Anine I have heard so much about."

She held out her hand to clasp his arm formally. "I was not told you would try to get around me with flattery, sir."

"Then they sent you ill-prepared."

"Even the best minds can't think of everything."

He paused, frowned slightly, looked at her from head to toe. "I believe you have some information for me."

"No, sir, I have instructions for you. They are meant to be very forceful and very clear. I have been told to inform you that you have commitments to fulfill, and you are instructed to take the appropriate steps immediately. That is what I was commanded to tell you, Sivan, sir."

"Hmm. A cryptic message, soldier."

"No, sir. I was instructed not to let you weasel out of it that way. These are instructions of a personal nature, and they are not amenable to your usual political mati– manipulations. Sir."

A faint smile at her stumble. "You have received your instructions and followed them precisely, Anine."

"Which brings us back to the beginning, Sivan, sir."

"Ah, but now you are forewarned against my flattery."

"And your attempts to change the subject, sir. I am to inform you that there are only two possible answers. Yes and no. Which is it to be, sir?"

"Come, Anine. Surely there are more than two answers to any question. What kind of narrow-mindedness only allows for two answers?"

"This is a personal question, and not vulnerable to your...prevaricating, sir. Yes or no?"

"You seem to be performing your duty with an undue enthusiasm, even enjoyment, Soldier."

"Loreline is a friend of mine, Sivan, sir. And I believe we have already discussed your tendency to change the subject. Yes or no? I should warn you, sir, that no answer at all will be taken as a 'no' answer."

The spymaster turned to the duke, his hands held out beseechingly. "Was a man ever the subject of such a love letter? With such a delivery? By such a messenger?"

"Love letter?"

"Oh, make no mistake, your Grace. What you are listening to is a declaration of undying love, delivered with utmost precision by the one person whom my skills cannot deter. How can you prevaricate with the military mind? Yes or no. Two answers only. She has me tied up, sir. Tied up."

"Then what will be your answer, Sivan? I'm sure we are all anxious to know. That is," the duke dropped his voice, "unless you want to give your answer privately."

"Privately! Privately, he says. Do you think this juggernaut, this walking oak tree, will allow me the courtesy of a private answer?"

Anine took one precise pace forward and spoke in a calm, reasonable, voice. "Yes or no, Sivan?"

"Yes, yes, of course yes. If the answer were no, do you think I would subject myself to this ignominy? Of course the answer is yes. You may take that back to the lady. Are you satisfied?" He shook his head and spoke to no one in particular. "Ah, the inconveniences that emotional attachments put a man through!"

"Thank you, sir. I have my answer. Now about the timing…"

"What? I have given you what you want, and now you want more. How like a woman."

"Chauvinism aside, Sivan, sir, the lady says to tell you that stalling for any length of time will be considered a 'no' answer. She reminds you of the information you received this summer. Sir."

He threw up his hands. "All right. My objective has been achieved here, anyway."

"It has? What objective is that?"

The Sivan turned to the duke. "My one objective, that which was yours. It is completed. You heard the woman. I am called elsewhere. I now must regretfully sunder our association, your Grace. It truly has been a pleasure working with you."

Anine had the interesting experience of seeing the duke at a loss for words. "But…I thought you were working for me."

"Working with you, your Grace. Towards mutually beneficial goals. Have you any complaints on that note?"

"No, no, I suppose not. But what about all the other projects? Who is going to see them through?"

The Sivan treated the man to a faint smile. "Do you not feel yourself capable of that task? Surely I have indicated to you everything you need to do."

The duke sighed. "If you mean you have taught me all I need to know, I will swallow my pride and admit I have learned a great deal, working with you. How soon will you be leaving?"

The Sivan shot a glance at Anine. "Contrary to what our rather rigid-thinking young lady here believes, I do need a few days to put my affairs in order. However, I also have no desire to travel through Petrella in the winter, so I can definitely tell you that I will be gone within a month. Will that satisfy your conditions, Anine?"

Anine favoured him with her sweetest smile. "I'm sure you know the lady better than I do, sir."

He responded with a sour look. "I suppose you are going back to Petrella soon? Do you realize that some day you may be working for me?"

"I'm sure that would be interesting, sir. However, it isn't likely. Spying is not a line of duty I would freely choose."

"Oh, it isn't? And what is wrong with it?"

"As you have perhaps noticed, I do not take well to the subtle approach."

"I will attest to that. All right. I will see you in Petrella before winter falls, then. If you get there before I do, you may pass along my fondest regards."

"Love."

"What?"

"Love. I am waiting for you to send your love to Loreline. I believe you showed some understanding of emotional matters a while back."

"Yes, all right. If you must have my complete surrender. Yes, tell her I send my love, and all those sappy things."

"Thank you, sir. I'm sure she will be pleased. Especially with the sappy things."

"Pleased! Pleased? I certainly hope she'll be more than that!"

"The sooner you get there, the sooner you'll know, sir."

"You realize that I'm going to spend the whole trip planning my revenge on you for this."

She smiled again. "I have no fears in that respect. I'm sure that would be beneath you, sir."

He threw up his hands again and turned from her. "Your Grace, I hate to disturb your family moment, but time seems to be pressing. May we have a few words?"

"Of course, Sivan. I'll have plenty of time with Talia for a while now. I'll see you at dinner, dear. Please do something about your hair before then." He kissed his daughter's cheek, winked at Anine, and followed the spymaster from the room. Anine and Talia looked at each other, then burst out laughing.

"Anine! I couldn't believe that was you talking!"

"It wasn't. That all came from Loreline. With a whole lot of help from Zoysana."

"But the way you were speaking. I've never heard you talk like that."

"Oh, that wasn't me either. That was Gavess."

"What?"

Anine giggled again. "There weren't any words there that I didn't know already, except a few important ones Zoysana taught me, like 'prevaricate'. I've just been listening to Gavess the whole trip. You know he talks even more formally than you nobles do. I've been practising talking like him. Copying how people talk is a trick I learned from Ferlen. He's really good at it."

Talia shook her head. "Well, I've never heard anything like it. You sounded exactly like a lawyer presenting a case. The poor Sivan. He didn't have a chance."

"Aw, be fair to him. Like he said, the only reason he put up with it is because he's in love. If the answer had been 'no,' he could have given it easily, and then where'd I be?"

Talia laid a hand on Anine's arm. "I didn't dare tell anyone in Petrella that I knew him, no matter how they hinted. I didn't realize what an impact he had made there. How did you feel, meeting him after all these years and everybody talking about him?"

"I don't know. He was a bit of a myth, I suppose. It was only after I spent some time with Loreline that I got to thinking of him as a person. Younger than I expected. Handsomer, too. I can sorta see why Loreline's gaga over him. That and the mind thing."

"The mind thing?"

"You know, my Lady, you're going to have to stop repeating everything I say," she dropped into her own form of speech, "it ain't fittin'. I caught you usin' a coupla merc phrases lately."

"What mercenary phrases?"

"Oh, things like 'tell you" instead of "I'll tell you." You hadn't oughta talk like that. My Lady."

Talia reached out and clouted Anine's shoulder, hard enough to rock her balance.

"Now you're laying it on heavier than usual. Surely I don't sound like that." She mused a second. "Although it might be fun…" Then her attention came back to her friend. "What about Sivan's mind? And Loreline?"

"You know, they think alike. She's his match when it comes to remembering things. She doesn't have his sneaky turn of thought, I gather, but she knows stuff you wouldn't believe."

"I think that's really nice."

"A lot of the enemies of Petrella are going to think it less than nice when the two of them start working together."

"My Lady?"

They both turned at the unfamiliar tone in the maid's voice.

"Yes, Lateda?"

The woman merely nodded meaningfully towards the stairs.

241

"Yes, Lateda. I suppose I must."

Anine watched this interchange with fascination. She had never seen the maid impose her will on her mistress. This must be something to do with the mother, whom Anine had rarely heard mentioned.

Talia turned to Anine. "I now have the first duty I came back to Trenet for."

"Yes, my Lady?"

"Oh, don't be so polite. I have to visit my mother. We had a flaming row when I went to Petrella and she vowed never to speak to me until I came back with my ears pinned down. I told her in that case I'd never be back at all. Now she's ill and that sort of silliness doesn't seem so important anymore."

"You don't want me to come with you, my Lady."

"Of course I do, Anine, but I can't. This is one I have to handle all by myself."

Anine grinned. "Maybe it would be good politics to change your clothes, first."

Talia thought about it. "Do you think I should?"

Anine shrugged. "If you want to keep the battle going, show up dressed like that. If you want to tell her she has won, go put on your frilliest dress, or whatever she would most like you to wear."

Talia nodded thoughtfully. "But somewhere in the middle is a suit of clothing that says, 'I'm different, but not that different, and I don't want to fight about it'. You're so smart, Anine."

"Yes, well, you're pretty quick in that department yourself, Talia. Go make peace with your mother, and I'll check on the troops."

"Right as usual, ma'am. I will follow your orders to the finest detail. Lateda, we have some important decisions to make. Did you hear what Anine said?"

"Exactly, my Lady. I'm sure we can choose something her Grace will find acceptable."

Anine and Talia crossed glances with raised eyebrows. "And I'm sure you'll be a great help, Lateda. Come with me."

Anine gave a half salute and a hopeful grin as the two mismatched women started up the stairs. Then she turned to a page standing motionless nearby and instructed him to take her to her men.

20. MEETING WITH A WEASEL

Clang! The ringing of steel on bronze echoed through the arms room.

A stifled moan arose from the small group of watchers, but Talia merely shook her battered helmet back into place and countered strongly, driving Anine back a few steps while she regained her composure.

"Good work, Talia. When you're in trouble, the first thing to do is hit back harder."

The lady tried to grin. "When you can't see for the stars, you keep swinging until they go away."

"That's right." Anine attacked again, and Talia parried the heavy strokes bravely. "You had enough, yet?"

Talia spoke through gritted teeth, countering with an attack of her own. "If I say I've had enough...I know you'll just...attack stronger to prove...something or other to me."

Anine slid forward, binding her opponent's sword. They held like that, striving face-to-face. Anine then took her free hand off her sword and forced Talia's weapon, in spite of her desperate two-handed grip, slowly to the floor.

When the tip was firmly planted, Anine paused. "Now have you had enough?"

"If you say so."

Anine nodded. "I say so." She stepped back, wiping her forehead with her sleeve. "I've certainly had enough. I can't believe it's so hot, this late in the year."

They strolled over to a side table, laying down their practice swords and picking up towels. The small audience moved cautiously towards them. Three young ladies, dressed in fine lace and silk, and two young men, at least one of them equally frilly.

The tallest of the three women shook her head. "That was quite alarming, Talia."

The second girl, the one with the most lace, nodded. "You did that on purpose, didn't you?"

Talia frowned, puzzled. "Did what on purpose?"

"Took that frightful hit on the head."

Talia laughed. "The day I allow my wits to be scrambled by a whack from Anine just to impress my friends...well, let's just say my wits will truly be scrambled!"

"But she might have hurt you."

"Yes, she might. Not likely, though. In case you didn't notice, Anine is pretty much in control out there."

The third young lady, shorter and more plainly dressed, had not joined the conversation and was holding aloof. Finally, she spoke. "Doesn't it bother you to be...humbled like that?"

Talia turned to her, genuine puzzlement on her face. "What do you mean?"

The girl gestured towards the practice floor. "Well, you know. She is so obviously superior. Don't you feel embarrassed to be out there with her?"

Talia shook her head earnestly. "You don't understand, Leile. Anine doesn't humble me by working with me. She honours me."

The other girl took a moment to think that over. "In what way?"

Talia laced her fingers, twisting them. "It's this way, Leile. Anine is a professional soldier. This," she indicated the swords, the practice floor, "is her life. In fact, it could very well mean her life, if she did not keep in top condition. She and the others train often when we are travelling, and it is not play; it's deadly serious.

"Thus, if Anine is willing to step on the practice floor with me, I am honoured. It means she considers me a worthy enough opponent to help her keep at the top of her form."

Leile nodded. "I like that. It does credit to both of you." She faded back and said no more.

The taller girl frowned. "I am still trying to understand how you can be honoured by this woman who is obviously...not...of your class."

Talia shook her head, and Anine was pleased to see that the big girl was honestly sorry for the other. "You don't understand. You live such a different life, here. Do you realize that in the past year I have had to fight for my life? Twice? I had to be ready and able to kill someone in order to survive."

"You had to fight? To protect yourself?" The fancily dressed young man drew himself up. "What was wrong with your guards?"

"My guards were busy at the time. In both cases we were outnumbered."

"You say you were ready to kill? I find that hard to believe."

Talia merely held her hands up in surrender.

The girl in the frills folded her arms around herself. "Of course, it never actually came to that, did it? You never really had to fight someone and kill them!"

Talia's face blanched. Her glance slid to Anine, who eased forward to make her presence felt.

"In truth, my Lady, that is not a question that is considered good manners where I come from. I can answer you that, yes, Talia has fought in serious situations several times. Only braggarts boast about their kills."

It was the other woman's turn to pale. "She did, didn't she? You're telling me that Talia has actually killed someone."

"I am telling you nothing of the sort." Anine backed up a pace to include the rest of the party. "You want to know what kind of person Talia is in Petrella, what kind of reputation she has there? Let me put it this way. When we were on the road here, we came upon two wagons that were being attacked by bandits. The merchants were outnumbered about twenty to five. They had their wives and children with them. I had eight good fighters on horseback and the advantage of surprise.

"If I had been guarding you, my Lady, do you know what I would have done?" She paused to let them think. "That's right. I would have backed up, tiptoed away and gone around, found another route. It would have been too dangerous, and I would not have risked your safety. I would have left those men to die, their women to be raped, their children to...who knows what?"

She indicated Talia. "But I was guarding Talia, so we attacked. Talia held my right shoulder in the charge. When we reached the wagons, we split, half on each side. That meant it was Talia and me, alone in front. We were through and gone before the bandits figured out what was happening."

She eyed each one of the young people facing her. "Now, it was a quick attack, and nobody knows who killed anyone. But I will say that Talia did her share, she held her place, and her sword needed cleaning, just like mine."

The pale girl gulped. "C...cleaning?"

"That's right. Cleaning. So when I get a chance to practice with Talia, I take it. She's strong enough, she's experienced enough, and she's learning fast enough to make training with her worthwhile."

"Good for you, Talia." Leile took her friend's hand. "I always knew you had it in you."

"You approve?" Anine regarded the shorter girl. "Do you fight, my Lady?"

The young woman took a step backwards, her hands up in defence. "No, no, Anine, you're not getting me out there with a sword."

"In other words, you do fight."

"Not anymore!"

"But you used to?"

Leile shook her head firmly. "Not really. We all took the basic fencing moves in school because it was good for our body fitness and balance. But we never actually fought!"

Anine smiled. "You took training in school because once, long ago, it was thought necessary for children to learn to fight. Now your realms are so safe that you don't have to worry about defending yourselves, so the fighting has become a tool for physical training."

Her glance included the two young men, who both nodded. One shrugged. "We all took the training, but the only ones who continued were those who were going into the military." He shot a belated glance at the other lad. "Or something else like that."

Anine looked to the second youth, Orcan, who was dressed more soberly, and raised her eyebrows. He smiled.

"Merchants."

"Merchants?"

"Our caravans travel in some of the less civilized areas of the world. I need my fighting skills almost as much as you do, Anine."

She glanced around the group, but they all seemed to accept this statement at face value. "If you are a serious student of the arts of war, then please feel free to join us the next time we practice."

The young man bowed slightly. "Thank you, Anine. I would be," he shot a meaningful look at the taller woman, "honoured."

A light chuckle ran through the group, and even the subject of his drollery smiled.

This conversation was broken by the appearance of a small page, who arrived, breathless, skidding to a halt in front of Anine, looking up, then up farther, to see her face. "Excuse me, my Lady, but are you…" he gulped uncertainly, "…Anine?"

"That's right, youngster. I'm Anine. What can I do for you?"

"His Grace the duke is looking for you, my Lady."

"The duke is looking for me?" Anine glanced at Talia. Dukes do not go looking for anyone. "Where is he?"

"Right down the hallway, my Lady." The boy pointed.

"Well, then, I guess you'd better lead me to him, lad." She turned to the others. "You will have to excuse me. I think duty is calling."

They smiled and nodded, and she strode off, the little lad trotting ahead of her.

"Anine."

She stopped and turned.

"I think I'll come with you and see what Father is up to."

She nodded, and the two followed the page. They soon met the duke, striding up the corridor towards them. He paused to give the boy a pat on the shoulder. "Well done, lad. Back to your lessons, now."

The boy wrinkled his nose, but then grinned at the two women and trotted away obediently. The duke slipped between the two of them, a hand on the shoulder of each, and steered them back to the arms room, which was now empty.

"Anine, I have need of your services."

"Certainly, your Grace. What can I do?"

The duke looked around, apparently deciding that the middle of a large room was as private a place as any.

"You may have noticed that noble who came in two days ago? The stranger?"

Talia nodded. "You mean Teremsla, the self-styled Duke of Remence. He holds Petrella's northeast border. Doesn't get out of his demesnes much. I've never seen him before. Strange-looking fellow."

The duke nodded. "He's heard about some negotiations I'm having and wants to get in on them. Or something. It's the 'something' that worries me. He has been saying all the right things in the right places, but has let me know that there is something else he wants to talk about. Finally, it came out. He wants to meet me 'in private.' He says the castle isn't private, and he wants to meet down in the town. At an inn. He calls it 'neutral ground.'

"I don't like it at all. He wants me to come alone. I don't trust him that far, even in my own demesnes. I'd like to take you along, Anine. It will send him several messages at once if I show up with a Petrellan guard."

"Certainly, your Grace. Is one enough?"

"I'm coming, too."

The duke looked at his daughter in surprise. "No, you aren't!"

"Yes, I am. You said yourself that if I'm to help in the negotiations, I need to attend more of the meetings. If there's any agreement, I can be a witness. If not, well, he doesn't know me, and I can act like another mercenary."

Her father shook his head. "I don't know. What do you think, Anine?"

She shrugged. "It's up to you, your Grace. I don't really like going into a situation like that alone. I'd like to have one of my own people with me. Since, as Talia says, she has other reasons to be there, then she fits on both counts."

"All right. We'll leave after the third bell. Dress appropriately. Whatever that is." He turned and walked away, shaking his head.

Talia turned to Anine. "Do you really consider me one of your people, Anine?"

Anine raised her eyebrows. "I probably have that backwards, don't I? Once you marry Gerth, I'll be one of yours."

"That's right. Until your sword comes out. Then I'm just one of the soldiers."

Anine dropped into her normal accent. "A thing I like about ya, kid. Ya learn fast, and ya learn good."

Just at dusk, Anine and Talia, with short cloaks covering most of their armament, followed the duke down into the town. As they walked, they considered their plans.

"I don't get it, your Grace. Why is this guy playin' at spy stuff? Meetin's at dusk in a inn. Wantin' to talk 'private' where nobody else knows?"

The duke shook his head. "It is hard to say, Anine. There are several sets of negotiations going on right now, and just the fact that you have had a meeting with a second party may make a difference to the attitude of a third group. But this hide-and-seek business I don't understand. Perhaps the man has an overly dramatic side. Are you worried?"

248

"She's worried, Father. When she drops her posh accent, then she's all mercenary and no games. If she draws her sword, you do what she says without question. Do you understand, Father?"

The duke stopped dead in the street and looked at his daughter. "Yes, Talia. I understand. I understand more than you think." With that cryptic comment, he turned and walked on. Anine thought she caught a smile on his face, but it was hard to tell in the deepening darkness.

At the inn, Anine hesitated in the doorway of the common room. The small man at the table against the left-hand wall must be the duke. Dark brown hair fell across his face, darker eyebrows met in the centre of overhanging brows, his shadowed eyes impossible to read in the dim light. He sat hunched in his chair as if he was cold, looking like a badger she had watched once defending his den from a marauding bear. Her quick glance noted two hulking figures spaced at tables just the right distance on either side of him. One long stride and their swords would cover him. As Lord Trenet entered, she flicked her attention to each one, to be sure he knew. He nodded, then strolled across the room, his focus on his opponent. Anine and Talia took up positions on either side as he slid into the other chair at the duke's table.

"I told you to come alone." The voice was low, with a slight whine that put Anine's teeth on edge. If she hadn't trusted this man before, now she was certain.

Lord Trenet waved a languid hand at his protectors. "These two can be trusted not to take tales anywhere. What about yours?"

The man's eyes flicked inadvertently left and right, and Anine exchanged a glance with Talia. *Score one for us.*

Anine did not listen much to the conversation between the two men. It involved trading, boundaries, fees and things beyond her knowledge. She kept her attention on the room. She didn't like their position – backs to the other patrons – but she had to assume that the threat would come from the three in front. Still, she stood half-sideways, her attention divided.

It was only when she heard the word Petrella that she changed her focus.

"The famous Petrellans may not be such a force as you are expecting, Lord Trenet."

"And why is that?"

249

"That barbarian king, Gerth or whoever, is a young fellow. He thinks because he has solved some of his external problems he can work on his economy like any other peaceful merchant. I have a feeling he has a surprise coming."

"What kind of surprise?"

The man shrugged. "I wouldn't want to guess. But word is out in certain circles."

The duke considered this. "I see. Fine. So, assuming you are right, what does this have to do with Trenet and Remence?"

"The trade. You are thinking, are you not, of trade with the Petrellans, and through them, the Inari?"

"It would be an advantage."

"But if you can't work that way because of unrest and difficulties on the trade roads, you could do just as well to trade with us. Our routes lead safely through the Duchies for most of the way. I have contacts with the Inari as well. You can get the same deals from me more safely. There's still time to get your daughter out of the clutches of that barbarian. Perhaps one of my sons could be persuaded…you never know. Enough land, enough concessions. She could have a decent life in Remence."

Anine glanced over at Talia, who was holding her ground like a true mercenary. She scanned the room again, then returned her attention to the creature who confronted them.

The Duke of Trenet leaned back, making himself comfortable. "Let me see. You are suggesting that I fall in with whoever is plotting to disrupt the peaceful flow of trade to Petrella. You are suggesting that I break the marriage contract my daughter has with their king. You think I should trash all the negotiations with my allies, because you and your friends are going to make trouble for them. Then you will sell out your friends, I will sell out mine, and we can work together to make a lot of money."

"I wouldn't have put it in such terms, but yes. We will make a lot of money."

"And, after all this double-dealing, how will I know I can trust you to fulfill your part of the bargain?"

The man's smile became oily. "Well, now, it's a simple system, your Grace. Once you have allied yourself against people, you are sort of stuck with the people you have allied with."

"In other words, we blackmail each other, because neither one of us can back out for fear that the other will reveal to the world the skullduggery that has taken place."

"You have such an unfortunate way of stating the obvious, my dear Duke."

"You have such an unfortunate way of assuming that everyone else is as slimy as you are. I cannot believe you would actually present this kind of trash to me. No wonder you spend so much time out in your fortress in the rocks. Nobody in polite society will treat with you!"

His mouth twisting in a snarl, Teremsla snatched his glove off the table and slashed it across the duke's face. Lord Trenet began to rise, but his daughter was there before him. In one stride, she had the man by the front of his cloak, hoisting him bodily against the wall. His bodyguards started to rise, then froze in position as Anine's sword whipped out. She noted Talia's position. One hand on the victim, one hand free and hovering near her dagger.

Then the girl spoke, in a calm, conversational tone, deeper than her usual. "You shouldn't oughta done that, my Lord."

"Get your hands off me, you cretin!" The force of the order was weakened by the tight cloth binding his ribs.

"Oh, no. You're gonna apologize to his Grace there first. Or I'm gonna kick your arse so hard you'll be reachin' over your shoulder to wipe it."

The man's eyes twisted to the duke. "Any lord who needs mercenaries to defend his honour…"

Talia shook him, just once, to get his attention. "The duke, here, has a fine sword. Bin in his family for generations. He don't use it," here she hawked and spat a gob of phlegm on the wall beside the unfortunate man's face, "to shovel sheep shit. Apologize."

His face reddened, either with anger or because she continued to twist the cloth at his throat tighter and tighter. Finally, he wrinkled his lip.

"I apologize."

She stared into his eyes, as if considering. Then, with a final shake, she set the man back in his chair. Then she turned to her father.

"There, yer Grace. Now you kin get back to the talkin'."

251

She returned to her position at the duke's shoulder, but angled slightly so she could dominate the guard to her right. The Teremsla's eyes slashed to his men, but they sat, held in place by Anine's sword, swinging to the man on the left, now.

As Talia returned to her position, Anine was able to divide her attention to the room again, but nothing stirred. The few legitimate patrons were very clear about minding their own business, the bartender stayed safe behind his bar, and the outside door remained closed.

Talia's father rose. "I think our discussions are over. As is your time in my demesne. If you wish to plot with your filthy friends, do it on someone else's hospitality."

The man at the table sneered. "When word gets around that you negotiate by having your barbarian bodyguards rough up the nobility, how do you think your bargaining is going to go?"

Talia stepped forward, dropping the mercenary cant and the deep voice. "And when word gets around that the duke had to get his daughter to slap sense into a slimy toad, how do you think your plotting is going to go? I suggest you keep your mouth shut about this and get out of the city before you are laughed out. I can't say it's been a pleasure meeting you, my Lord," she dropped a presentable curtsey, using the hem of her cloak as if it were her dress, "but have as pleasant a night as possible, under the circumstances."

Then she spun and marched out, the duke following. Anine backed behind them, only sheathing her sword when the inn door was shut and they were clear.

As soon as the duke knew she had caught up, he hurried off along the street. They followed him at either shoulder, all eyes sharp, but there were no incidents on the way back to the castle.

Once they were inside and had shed their cloaks, the duke motioned them to follow him. There was no talk until they were sitting in his private study. Then he turned, allowing his smile to fall on his daughter. "Well!"

"Well what, Father?"

He shook his head. "Very well. You certainly have been spending time with the wrong sort of people, haven't you?"

"Oh, I know, Father. All that time on the road, with nothing but rough mercenaries to talk to. Have I changed so much?"

He laughed. "Yes, you have. I can't believe you actually spat on the wall! And where did you get that threat about the kicking?"

"Oh, that's one of Jhanes' favourites when he's training new recruits. The spitting was improvised."

The duke clapped his hands to his knees and laughed heartily. Then he sobered.

"Anine, what did you think of that? I need a Petrellan opinion."

She thought a while. "I think it went rather well. You were right to stay out of it and let us handle it. Lady Talia covered it perfectly. Watch your stance in the future, though, Talia. Stand a bit canted, and cross your upper leg in front to protect your crotch. Some fighters will put the knee in. It doesn't hurt us as much as it hurts a man, but it's still not a pleasant sensation."

"I'll remember that, ma'am."

She grinned at the girl. "Sword's put away, my Lady."

"And your speech is back to normal. I guess I mean not normal."

Anine returned her attention to the duke, who was smiling at this exchange. "One thing bothers me, your Grace. I sort of wish Lady Talia hadn't mentioned the part about keeping his mouth shut. That's what we want, all right, and so does he. You heard his plan to keep things hushed up. But you tell that kind of vermin what you want, he might find a way to do the opposite out of spite."

"Spite. Yes, he's got a lot of that." The duke rubbed his hands on his knees, as if to clean them. "We'll just have to hope he doesn't decide to blab, because it would be useful if no one knows that we, and Gerth, have the information which he so naively gave us. And that's what I really need your opinion on, Anine."

"On the information he gave you? I wasn't really listening, your Grace. Not until he started on about Petrella. I don't really have an opinion..."

"Yes, you do. You're just too diffident to express it. Look. You're an army officer who has spent months in the troubled area, if my information is correct?"

She nodded.

"You just heard someone talking about disturbing Gerth's realm and making the trade roads unsafe. What do you conclude?"

She shrugged. "Nothing but the obvious, your Grace. Somebody doesn't like Petrella getting rich on all this trading and is set to make it as difficult as possible. It fits with the so-called bandit problem we had this summer."

"Precisely. That is what I think, but if you came up with the idea yourself, you'll do a better job of explaining it to Gerth."

"Explaining what to his Majesty?"

The duke sat forward, inviting his daughter to listen closely as well. "This is how things are working out. Talia has to stay here for the rest of the winter. She and Gerth already talked about it. There is a lot of formality that has to be seen to, besides the planning of the wedding. When you are making an unusual alliance, it is much more important to follow all the etiquette perfectly so that nobody can fault you.

"You, on the other hand, are returning to Petrella. Soon. I know Talia would like to have your company for a while, but that's not going to be possible."

At Talia's nod, he continued. "I'm going to be sending this information by messenger, but as we all know, the messenger services are not as reliable as we hoped. So I am going to send very generally worded dispatches with them, and depend on you, Anine, to get the clear message through. We will be talking again, and I will fill you in on all the details of what the Sivan and I have discovered. The Sivan will be there soon as well, but nobody else knows that, and I want Gerth in the picture as quickly as possible.

"Besides, two messengers are better than one. Things happen on the road."

The thought that the famous Sivan might not get to where he wanted to go was a new one to Anine, and it made her even more serious.

"I understand, your Grace. Who will I be travelling with?"

"I have no suggestions in that regard. Whom do you want?"

"I think just the three of us: Arvent, Pagris, and me. Who is going to bother two mercenaries and an Inari on the road? A tough fight with no chance of any money. Mercs are all poor this year. No wars to speak of."

"Unless they thought you were carrying important dispatches."

Talia frowned. "Is there any reason for them to believe that?"

"The speed we're turning around and heading back."

"Nobody knows you planned to stay. You've done your duty, and you're returning before winter."

Anine nodded. "And if anybody has a sneakier mind than that, it can't be helped."

"That's true. You can't control what other people think, especially the type we are working against. I know you'll be careful."

"Aye, well at least I won't be gettin' into fights over pretty girls in taverns."

"How about pretty boys?"

"No fear, your Grace. I can concentrate."

"As your prophet Sarasha the Lame reminds us, fear is a great concentrator of the attention."

She nodded soberly. "It is that, your Grace."

21. CRISIS

"What's your dream, Anine?"

"My dream?" She glanced across to see that Arvent was perfectly serious, jogging along beside her through the pleasant fall colours of the countryside. "Whadaya mean, my dream?"

"The mercenary's dream. Everybody knows about that."

She tossed her head. "Huh! Everybody thinks they know about that."

"You mean it doesn't exist? Then why would everybody talk about it so much?"

Anine shrugged. "I dunno. I figure it's a way of makin' the merc understandable to the average person."

"In what way?"

"Well, a merc's gotta be different or he wouldn't be sellin' his life for pay. Most folks can't really understand that. So, they go lookin' for a way to see the mercenary that they can understand, 'cause that puts him in a familiar slot, you see?"

"I guess so."

"Everybody has dreams. The farm hand dreams of his own farm. The farmer dreams of a bigger farm. The lord dreams of – I dunno what lords dream about. But everybody has a dream. Folks figure a mercenary must have dreams, too."

"And do they?"

"Sure. Some of them do. They talk about them, anyway. A little farm, or a little inn, or a fishin' boat, or somethin' that don't involve puttin' your life on the line."

"What's yours?"

"Huh!" She slapped her gloves against her knee. "I'm more like to stick to the mercenary's prayer."

"What's that?"

"Lady, let me die quick in battle and never know what hit me."

He nodded. "I can understand that. I've seen men die from infected wounds. It wasn't a fun way to go."

"Or worse, live on, beggin' in the streets because they're blind or crippled. No, I'll take the merc's prayer any day."

She turned to Arvent. "What's your dream? You used to be a noble of some sort."

He nodded. "That's right. Used to be. Not that I've done anything to disgrace myself. If my brother were to die – and I hope he doesn't; I really like him – I'd be the Lord of Chavin. Just a little hamlet out by Deren Lake in Llandres, with a manor that's not much more than a big farmhouse."

"So that's your dream?"

He nodded slowly. "I think so. If I could have a place like that, without losing my brother to get it, I would be happy. I don't mind this swordmaster business. I like to travel, to see new places, meet new people, but it doesn't really satisfy me."

"How about spyin'?"

He shrugged. "That, I really don't know about. I haven't really done any of it. I'm supposed to be in training, remember?"

She laughed. "I guarantee you're not in spy trainin' at the moment!"

"Why are you so sure about that?"

"Because look who you got assigned to. I'm about the least likely spy you're ever gonna find."

"Maybe that makes you an even better spy. You're so obvious, nobody would suspect you."

"Aw, don't go all Sivan on me, with the backwards logic. I ain't gonna do no more spyin'. It's road work for me."

"Road work?"

"As soon as we get this bandit problem figured out, I'm back to fixin' roads."

"Oh."

"I got some ideas, and Zoe gave me some books with some more. I'da spent more time askin' around about road buildin' techniques here if we hadn't had to go home so quick."

"I'd been meaning to ask you, Anine. Why did we have the change of plans? I was thinking we would be a while longer in Lesser Trenet."

She looked over at him. "Oh, I imagine you know, all right."

He rode along in silence for a moment. "The rumour is that you're carrying some dispatches too important for the regular messengers."

"That sounds like a good enough reason."

"Are you?"

She shrugged. "I wouldn't be lettin' on, would I? Every good spy knows to keep her mouth shut about stuff like that."

"You're not going to tell me."

She stopped her horse, forcing him to do the same, and faced him. "Tell you, Arvent. Let's just say I was carryin' somethin'. All that means to you is that it's your job to make sure I get through to Petrella with that somethin'. Understand?"

He shrugged and kneed his horse forward again. "Sure, Anine. If that's the way it has to go. I'll do my duty, never fear."

They rode in silence for a while.

"Does Pagris know?"

"What?"

"Does Pagris know about the messages?"

"What messages?"

"Come on, Anine. It will help us work together if we know how the others are thinking."

"Pagris is Pagris. He'll do his best to get us through, messages or no messages. Pagris don't ask a lot of fool questions."

She pushed her horse ahead as a signal that the conversation was closed. As she rode, her thoughts darkened. *Where did Arvent get that information? Others have made the guess we had hoped no one would.*

Uneasy, she moved on, and he did not mention the matter again that day. However, the following day he rode up beside her again, and she had that cold feeling in her stomach.

"Why did you become a mercenary, Anine?"

It took her a moment to realize what he was asking, and register a touch of relief. "A matter of choice. I coulda bin a farm ox or a merc."

"That was it?"

"Sure. What else?"

"I don't know. Glory, money; what do mercenaries fight for?"

Anine shrugged. "We fight to make a living. Then we die. Not so much different from farmers, actually, though a farmer sometimes lives longer. Sometimes not."

"But don't some mercenaries make enough money to quit? I've always heard they get to loot the cities that they take, and sometimes they find some merchant's hidden stash, or a casket some noble put together and couldn't flee with. You'd be pretty set for life if you got a windfall like that."

She laughed. "Good word. Windfall. Do you know what it means?"

He looked puzzled. "Sure. You don't have to be a farmer to know that a windfall is fruit that the wind knocks off the tree, and you don't have to climb for it."

"That it does. But a windfall is also a tree that's been blown over by the wind. That means that the chance of a windfall like you're talkin' about comes around about as often as havin' a tree fall on your head.

"Plus, now that I think about it, my experience with windfall fruit is that it's usually got somethin' wrong with it, or it'd still be up there on the tree with all the normal fruit. No, Arvent, only the stupid mercs dream about that kind of luck."

"But if it happens…"

She shrugged. "If it happens, it happens. What's that got to do with life, anyways?"

He seemed to ponder this a while, but she could see that he was leading somewhere.

Finally, he decided. "These dispatches you're carrying…"

"The ones you say I am carrying."

"All right, say you are carrying some dispatches. You know, I picked up a lot of the gossip going around while we were up in Trenet. If I put together all I came up with, I can tell you for sure that there are some people who would be very happy if those dispatches didn't get through."

She looked at him with an alarm she didn't have to pretend. "Are you serious? Do you have any idea who?"

He shook his head judiciously.

"Well, that means we'll have to travel more carefully, doesn't it? Any ideas?"

"We can talk about that at nooning, if you like, when Pagris can contribute. That wasn't why I brought it up."

"It isn't?"

"No. What I wanted to suggest was, you may have one of those windfalls right there in your bags."

"What do you mean?"

"Think, Anine. If those dispatches mean a lot to some people, then they have value. A lot of value. Maybe you could sell them."

"I couldn't do that!"

"But why not? You're a mercenary. You work for pay. If somebody who comes along offers you more pay, wouldn't you go work for them?"

She just shook her head. "You know, Arvent, I'm beginnin' to understand why you got sent to Petrella. You sure got a lot of stuff you ain't learned."

"What do you mean?"

"You got no idea at all what it means to be a mercenary. Most folks don't, as we said yesterday."

"Where did I go wrong?"

She checked his face, but there was no irony apparent. "Fightin' for money. You think, as many do, that anyone who works for money should happily change employers and go and work for somebody else who offers them more money. If we were minstrels or somethin' like that, I would agree. But a merc don't dare do that."

"Why not?"

"Reputation. A merc company gets work based on its reputation. It would be a very short-sighted company that would change sides in a fight just because the other side offered more money. They'd never find work again."

"But you're talking about a company and their reputation. What if you could make enough money that you wouldn't have to go back to being a mercenary ever again?"

She shook her head. "You just don't get it. Besides all the practical things I mentioned, there's such a thing as loyalty. I'm not just a mercenary anymore. I'm a member of Zoysana's Clan. And even if I was only a mercenary, and I was workin' for the smallest landowner in Petrella," she stopped her horse and looked hard at him to drive her point home, "I did somethin' like that, there ain't enough money in the Arlyn Castle strongroom to buy back my self-respect."

She urged her horse on, and he followed. Anine considered the conversation closed, but she had a feeling he would try again.

The next morning, she contrived to be riding beside Pagris for a while.

"What bothers you, Anine?"

"Is it that obvious?"

"Yes."

A man of few words, Pagris. Of course, in her language, he didn't have very many.

"I don't know exactly how to put it…"

"Arvent?"

She almost sighed in relief. She nodded.

"Not happy clan where one must watch another."

"He isn't Clan, Pagris."

"True. He isn't Clan."

"What should I do?"

He shrugged. "You do what you do. I watch."

"You will?"

"I watch very well."

"I'm sure you do. Thank you, Pagris."

A few moments later, Arvent was there beside her. "What was that all about?"

In normal circumstances, she would have thought it normal curiosity. It felt different, now. "I'm helping him with his language. He's got a good memory, so he has a decent vocabulary. He just gets the words in the wrong places sometimes."

He nodded, seeming satisfied. She wondered if she had said too much. She knew that for a good lie you weren't supposed to give out any extra information. Then she shook herself. *I'm not a spy, I have no intention of being one, and I won't become a good liar for anyone.*

"I've been thinking about that dream. You know, my dream?"

"Aye."

"Aye. You know, a house, a small demesne, maybe a mill on it?"

"Sounds very nice."

"It is. But there's something missing."

"What's that? A princess to share it with?" She intended it to be cutting sarcasm, but he ignored it.

"Friends."

"Friends?"

"Yes. Don't look at me like I'm stupid or crazy. I really miss having friends. I've been trying for a year or more to develop a personality that works in this spying, and part of that, I have discovered, is not having any friends. If I could leave all this, I would have people around me. Good people. People like you."

"You consider me a friend?"

"Anine, you're the closest thing to a friend I've had since I left Pertin's. I can talk to you. You aren't always looking for some advantage, some way to turn our conversation to your own profit. You're just Anine. Take it or leave it. You have no idea how comforting that is."

She laughed. "Last thing a merc wants to hear, that she's the comfortin' sort."

"Anine, I'm serious. You know what I mean."

She looked over into his earnest eyes. *If you're going to make up a good lie...*

"Well, Arvent, I'll take that at face value. Thank you. I like the idea of bein' a good friend."

"So if I could find a way to get my dream, you could join me? As a friend?"

Anine sighed. This had gone far enough. She remembered something the duke had said to that weasel, Teremsla, back at the inn in Trenet.

"Look, Arvent, I know what you're gettin' at. Let's say for the sake of argument that these dispatches exist, and let's say there really is somebody who is gonna pay a great deal to get them. Let's say that allows us to buy you a little demesne that is all you dream about, and I can come and be your friend there, whatever that means."

"That's right. Whatever it turns out to mean, that's fine with me."

"What kind of friendship is that? If every time we look at each other and that land around us and know that we bought it with our honour? How can we trust each other when we have proven to each other that we are not worthy of trustin'? Sorry, Arvent, it just doesn't work. Not in my dreams, anyways."

He reined his horse away sharply, and she expelled a bit of breath. That had been a pretty strong rejection, and she knew he was going to come back with something to top it. Time for a quick word with Pagris.

About a candle later, she swung off her horse. "A good spot to spend the night, don't you think?"

Arvent shrugged and started setting up camp. When the fire was going, she stepped down to the creek and came back with water.

Arvent was just standing in the middle of the camp as if he was waiting for her.

"I sent Pagris off to hunt. He looked really pleased at the chance to shoot something. He won't be back for a while; game's scarce this close to the road."

He drew his sword. "I'm sorry it had to come to this, Anine. I really liked you, despite the fact that you were the one set to spy on me. Now give me the dispatches."

"What are you going to do when Pagris gets back? You aren't going to kill him that easily."

"I'm only going to destroy the messages. He won't care about that, and there will be no point in following me to get them back if they don't exist. If you make me take them from you, I'll say we were attacked, and I couldn't fight them off."

"And if I don't fight? It'll look a whole lot like murder. Can you murder a friend, Arvent?"

He grinned. "Oh, you'll fight, Anine. I know you. You're a fighter." He leaned forward earnestly. "This is for my dream, Anine. You know it. The mercenary's dream? This will get me what I want, finally. So, yes, if I have to, I'll kill you, because I want those messages. Give them to me or protect yourself. You might even beat me, Anine. You're stronger, with your big sword, your extra reach..." He lifted his sword and stepped back to give her room to draw.

Anine did not reach for her sword. Instead she sighed, raised her hand and made a chopping motion. There was the whirr of an arrow, and Arvent started to see a barbed Inari warhead sticking out from his chest.

As he toppled forward, Anine caught him and laid him gently on his side. Just before the awareness died from his eyes, she tried to explain. "You never understood, did you? It isn't the things you get. It's the people and the ideas they stand for. It's..." and then she knew it was too late.

Pagris stepped out of the brush. "All over?"

"I'm afraid so, Pagris." She could feel the tears burning. "He didn't understand. He was always outside, and he could have come in. Petrella had a place for him, just like it has a place for me."

The Inari nodded. "Me too."

She looked up, surprised. "You're going to stay in Petrella? I thought you were just travelling around to get to see the world."

He nodded. "It started like that, Anine. But soon I see…saw I like Petrella. I saw why Jhanes stays, works for Great Potentara Gerth."

He rolled the body up, snapped the arrow head off, drew the shaft out and wiped it economically on the brown leather shirt. As he spoke, he efficiently prepared Arvent for burial.

"Not so different from Inari, Anine. Zoysana knows this. Honour, friendship."

"I know. Arvent never figured that out. I thought he was going to, you know. He was really opening up, those last few days on the road up here."

"Yes, I thought it too. Someone in Trenet talk to him."

She nodded. "Yes, someone got to him. They must have offered him a lot of money."

"Land. He had dream, too."

"I know. But you can't take your dreams at other people's expense."

Pagris rocked his head in the Inari gesture. "Maybe. Maybe not. You cannot. I cannot. This is good."

"Well, now Arvent cannot either." She untied the mercenary's short-handled shovel from her saddle and started to dig, chopping fiercely at the roots with the sharpened side, stabbing the ground with the point. "I don't know whether that's good or not."

Pagris used his hands to work beside her. "Good, not good. Necessary."

"I guess so."

He stopped, forcing her to look at him. "Necessary. Always believe."

When she went to return to her digging, he touched her hand. "Think, Anine. I am one who killed a friend. Must believe necessary. Otherwise what?"

"But I gave the order."

"Thank you. Both killed a friend. Both agree necessary. Right?"

"Yes, you're right. It helps that we both agree that it was necessary. Thank you, Pagris. Let's finish this grave and ride on. I don't want to stay here tonight."

They put out the fire and left the lonely grave by the side of the trade road, marking it with an oval of stones. No one would ever know who lay there, and soon the grave mound would subside into the surrounding dirt, the stones would be kicked aside by grazing animals, and Arvent, swordmaster of nowhere, would cease to exist. The tears flowed freely as she rode, and she let them come. Pagris rode beside her, his quiet companionship the only consolation that he could give or that she wanted.

They travelled for two days like that, in congenial silence broken only by the necessary communication of the road, but each deep in thought. Finally, on the third day, the Inari pushed his horse alongside hers.

"Anine?"

She mentally shook herself awake, looked around for trouble. The road stretched ahead and behind, smooth and unthreatening. "What?"

He smiled. "No trouble, Anine. I want ask...I want to ask a question."

"Oh. Sure, go ahead."

"You speak well."

"That's not a question. But yes, I speak well. Not usually, but I can. I still make mistakes, but I can speak well."

He nodded. "You help me speak well?"

"You want help with your Petrellan?"

"Right."

"Why?"

"Why not? Maybe I stay in Petrella. Maybe I go back to Inari. Still, it be good I learn to speak well."

"It would be good if you learned to speak well."

"It would be good."

She shrugged. "There you are. First lesson. I guess that wasn't so hard, was it?"

He bowed slightly from the waist up. "The pupil thanks his teacher."

She reached out and tried to cuff his shoulder, but his horse chose that moment to drift out of reach, and her swing cut thin air. "Don't you get all formal with me. I couldn't stand that."

"Fine. No formal."

"No formality."

"No form...ality?"

"That's right, but I wouldn't bother to learn that. Why don't you talk to me, and I'll correct you?"

"It sounds good, Anine. What I talk about?"

"What do I talk about."

"What do I talk about?"

"You just said that."

"I know. I said it…"

"No, no, I was just making a joke. Forget it."

"Anine, what is your dream?"

"Better watch it, fellow. Last guy who tried that play is dead."

"I don't understand."

"It was another bad joke, Pagris. A 'play' is the words a man uses to get a girl to notice him. Arvent asked me that question, and all he wanted was to find out what I wanted, so he could bribe me."

"I think I see. Sometimes, when you talk fast, I understand not."

"I do not understand."

"I do not understand. Thank you."

"Arvent wanted to know my dream, too. He wanted to pay me with it."

"To give him the messages."

"Do you know about those, too?"

Pagris grinned. "Better hearing than most people."

"You heard all that? Between Arvent and me?"

He nodded. "Enough to be very serious when you tell me…told me? Yes…told me stay very close. Then when Arvent send…sent me hunting, I knew."

"Yes. I guess you did. Then you know about my dreams, or lack of them."

"Pardon?"

"I don't have a dream."

He smiled serenely. "Of course you do."

"How would you know?"

"Everyone has dream. You don't say yours to self."

"I have a dream, but I haven't said it out loud to myself?"

"I think so. Man or woman with no dreams is dead walking around."

"I'm not going to try to correct your speech on that one."

"Not my words."

"Whose words were they?"

"Famous Inari thinker. Rasha."

"Rasha? You don't mean Sarasha the Lame?"

"No, Rasha. Rasha the Wise. Inari Wise Woman. Said very good things. About life, about dreams."

They rode on. After a while, she turned to him again. "If you agree with that saying, then you must have a dream. Tell me yours."

He nodded. "My dream is live like good…ahhh, I always forget to put in the 'a'. My dream is live like a good Inari. Live with honour, die with honour."

She shook her head. "That may be true, but it's pretty general. Be more specific."

"What is general, specific?"

She did her best to explain. Finally, he nodded.

"I will be specific. I have much of my dream. A woman who loved me. Fine children. Success in the Circle of Stones. Now I have more of my dream. I see the world."

"I have seen the world."

"I have seen more of the world than all Inari. Now I need new dream, I guess."

"Your speech is actually getting pretty good. There's another dream you're realizing."

"I have…a…new dream."

"What is that?"

"Grandchildren. I dream I have grandchildren. Good Inari grandchildren. Girls grow up like Zoysana. Boys like Jhanes."

A shout of laughter bubbled out of her. It felt good. "Jhanes? You want your good Inari grandchildren to grow up like a Petrellan innkeeper?"

Pagris only smiled. "Tell you, Anine. Jhanes good better…no, best better…?"

"Much better, I think you're trying to say."

"Jhanes much better Inari than most."

"Jhanes is a much better Inari than most Inari? How do you figure that?"

He shrugged. "Inari need what?" He held up one finger. "Strong woman to keep tent. Inari trade horses, fight enemies, come home to well-kept, clean, honourable home. My wife like that. Sarha like that."

He held up a second finger. "Strong Potentara. Fighters know fight is honourable. Bring honour to Clan. But must win fights, yes? Zoysana is a good Potentara. Jhanes does strong deeds, makes honour for Potentara, for himself, for the Clan. Inari dream? Jhanes dream."

The idea struck her so forcefully that she did not correct her companion's speech. Jhanes a good Inari. What a joke! "Does he know this?"

The Inari shrugged. "I think he knows not. But he knows. Jhanes has very strong mind. Knows what he wants."

"Yes, he has a very strong mind. You mean he just hasn't said it out loud to himself."

That meaningful smile. "Like you, Anine."

"Like me."

"Like you."

"So, if you're so smart, tell me my dream."

He shook his head. "I do not know you long. I do not speak to you lot."

"A lot."

He nodded. "I do not speak to you a lot. Tell you, Anine. I watch, I talk, I think. When I know, I tell you."

She grinned. "Sure, Pagris. When you have me figured out, you let me know. You'll be a long way ahead of me, that's for sure."

He gave her a puzzled look.

"Never mind. It wasn't important anyway. By the way, that expression 'Tell you' that I use all the time? It isn't really proper speech. It's just an expression the mercs use. It's more like 'I'll tell you' or 'I'll make you a deal'. Understand?"

He nodded. "I see. 'Tell you' is merc speech I use with mercenaries. With others I say, 'I'll tell you'."

"Very good, Pagris. We keep this up all the way home, we'll have you speaking like Gavess by the time we get there."

"Not like Gavess!" The Inari did an imitation of the poor butler and his riding style, and Anine laughed again.

"Thanks, Pagris. I needed something to make me laugh."

He nodded soberly. "Me, too."

She looked over at him. "So why aren't you laughing?"

His expression never changed. He pointed at his breast. "Inside."

"You're laughing at me!"

His horse burst into a gallop, leaving her fist swinging at empty air. She made a show of trying to catch him, but she knew she had no chance. Still, it was good to have the wind in her hair and the horse straining smoothly under her and, as she reluctantly pulled back to a trot, she realized she hadn't felt so good in days.

22. Marel

They travelled on, up through the Inner Duchies, across Velikiii and finally home to Petrella, as the rains got heavier and the roads got worse. They paused in Lanil's Rock, but Anine had business at the castle and the sooner she got her messages delivered to Loreline the sooner she could put Arvent out of her mind.

Her hopes for an early release were dashed when Loreline was in a meeting, and the awed page asked her to wait until midafternoon.

Her mind spinning with the import of the tale she had to tell, she wandered down into the town, thinking to seek out the Mercenary's Rest. But when she got there, she didn't have the heart to go in. So she walked through the market, her mind a blank.

"Psst!"

Anine forced herself to turn slowly and move her hand away from her sword hilt, where it had jumped of its own accord. "Marel, you oughta know better'n to sneak up on me."

"Sorry, Anine." The boy peered around. "I din't want anybody to see us meetin'."

"Why not?"

He shrugged. "I dunno. Just 'cause."

"Well, it doesn't look like anybody's watching us, so I'll sit on this bench, and you can stand over there and pretend you're not talkin' to me if you like. What can I do for you?"

"Where's Arvent?"

"Arvent?" She considered. No reason not to tell him. "Arvent ain't comin' back."

"He ain't? He didn't tell me that."

"No, well...his plans changed, sudden-like."

"What changed his plans? He told me he was comin' back and he had some work for me to do."

Anine slapped the bench. "C'mere and sit down, Marel." The boy hesitated, then complied, perching on the farthest end of the bench, half-turned away.

"The reason Arvent's plans changed, Marel, is 'cause he's dead."

"Dead?" The boy turned, stared in her eyes, then turned away again. "Damnation."

He turned back. "What happened? Was he in a fight?"

270

Anine wondered what to tell the boy, settled on the truth. "No fight, Marel. He made a mistake."

"What kind of mistake?"

"He wanted to sell some messages we were carrying. King Gerth's messages."

"Sell them to somebody else?"

"That's right."

"He shouldn't oughta done that."

"That's right. He shouldn't."

"So you killed him."

"He would have killed me, Marel."

"Why did he do that? You were his friend!"

She shrugged. "He had a dream. That dream was more important to him than anything else."

"I know. He told me."

"He did?"

"Aye. He wanted a place of his own." The boy turned to her, his fists clenched. "But you don't kill your friends. What kind of dream is that, if you gotta kill your friends to get it?"

"Not much of a dream, I guess."

"Why did he have to do that, Anine? He was gonna help me. I had some plans…"

"You got a dream, too, Marel?"

The boy's face came around, and she could see tears brimming in his eyes. "I got a dream. And now…"

"Good for you. You know Pagris?"

"Older Inari fella? What about him?"

"He told me somethin' the other day. He said, 'A man without a dream is somebody dead walkin' around.' I liked that, Marel. A person has to have a dream."

The boy nodded. "It keeps ya goin' when the goin's tough."

"You keep to that dream, boy." She reached out and slapped the curved back, not hard, but hard enough that it wasn't a caress. She was startled by the way the bones pushed through the meagre flesh. "I gotta go, now. Got a meeting with Loreline, up at the castle."

"I know who Loreline is." The small face brightened. "She's the king's spy mistress."

"Somethin' like that."

"You spyin' for her?"

"Would I tell you if I was?"

"No, 'course not. I won't say nothin' to nobody, though."

"Thanks, Marel."

"See ya around." She glanced over, and the boy was gone. Shaking her head, she strode up the street towards the castle.

As she entered Loreline's office, she was startled by a difference in the woman. In the first place, she was smiling.

"Well, what's the news? I didn't think seeing me was going to be that pleasant an experience for you."

Loreline laughed. "Sorry, Anine, but no, it wasn't you."

"Got some good news, then?"

"You might say so."

"I was going to ask what, but then I remembered where I was. For example, if you were to receive news that somebody specific was about to show up, it might make you pretty happy. But you couldn't really share that with me, because that would mean letting on about somebody's whereabouts. And, as we all know, that specific somebody doesn't want that sort of information loosely floating around. How am I doing so far?"

Loreline controlled her smile. "A very good demonstration of analytical thinking."

Anine nodded. "A complicated life you lead. I'm just glad you're you, and I'm me, Loreline. 'Course, I imagine you feel the same, so isn't it nice it turned out that way?"

Loreline laughed out loud, then stared at the larger woman. "That was an uncharacteristic flight of poesy from someone who just came off the road after a day in the rain. Have you had some good news, too?"

Anine slouched onto the stool, stared at the floor. "No, the opposite, actually."

"Hmm. I saw Pagris in the bailey. Where's Arvent?"

"Well, that's part of the news." She gave a precise description of the situation.

When she was finished, Loreline sat, staring at her hands. "I guess we didn't make the progress Sivan hoped."

Anine shook her head firmly. "He didn't make the progress Sivan hoped. We gave him every chance. I gave him more chance than he shoulda needed."

The spy mistress smiled softly. "We did rather dump him in your lap. I can see why you're a bit down."

"Nah. Not really down. But it got me thinkin' about things."

"What sort of things? Life, and all that?"

"Aye. Life and all that."

Loreline folded her arms and leaned forward, a demonstration of patient interest.

"I saw Marel today, on the way through the town."

"That kid who hung around Arvent? What did he want?"

"To know what happened to Arvent, of course."

"Did you tell him?"

"I figured it was better he knew the truth. A simple version of it, anyways. He was pretty upset. Guess he set store by Arvent."

"Understandable."

"He just kept sayin' 'Why did he do that? I thought he was your friend. Why did he do that?' It really bothered him."

"Arvent dying, or Arvent trying to sell you out?"

"I think it was the lack of loyalty that got him most."

"Hmm. What do you think of the kid?"

"I dunno. He's quick, mind and hand. A good thief, if you want to know."

Loreline grinned. "In my business, that's no problem."

"You got an idea for him?"

"Just a thought. Next time you see him, send him up to me."

"He'd like that, I think. He knows who you are. He's got a dream, he said, and he's trying to make it happen."

Loreline nodded. "I can use people like that."

"I think Arvent was giving him jobs to do, so he'd probably welcome the chance to make a little cash."

"Hmm." Loreline pretended to search through the papers on her desk. "What's the stipend for an 'assistant spy'? I don't think we pay them very much. Maybe piece work?"

Anine chuckled. "I think that certain someone better show up pretty quick before our fabled spy mistress loses her mind completely."

Loreline immediately sobered. "Sorry, Anine. I didn't call you all the way up here for jokes. I've been looking at all the reports I've had in recently and I think I'm seeing a pattern…"

In spite of the gravity of the subject, it was pleasant to sit in the warm, dry room on such a nasty day and hear an expert talk about what she knew best. Anine leaned forward, elbows on the table, and listened.

When Loreline had finished her analysis, she and Anine tossed ideas back and forth for a while, but could come up with nothing more certain. It was possible that someone was scouting the area around Jaspen, but with the worsening weather and the lack of available troops, it was unlikely they could gain any more information before spring.

"They've probably gone home by now, anyway."

Anine nodded. "If they're going back over the mountains, they'd better go soon. There was snow on the peaks when I left Lanil's Rock."

Loreline shuffled her papers together and turned to place them in one of the many pigeonholes lining the wall behind her chair. "Well, it just helps firm up our plans for next summer. You expect the next infiltration to be farther west, and everything I see supports that. We'll be watching that creepy Teremsla, carefully from now on."

The meeting over, Anine left the castle, unsure of how she felt. It was good that her plans for the next summer had been accepted by Headquarters, but it wasn't so good that she had to make plans like that at all.

Realizing that she had forgotten to eat, she directed her steps towards the Mercenary's Rest and continued her conflicted thoughts.

She shook her head and resolved not to worry so much. She had plans to occupy her, now. Ferlen was out on his trapline, and she had to get the road crews set up in training for the winter, line up supplies, start the masons working on those long, narrow granite blocks they needed for the bridge over the west fork of the Caragata River…she realized that she was not alone.

She turned her head a touch, glancing down. He was half a pace behind her, just out of reach to the side. She smiled. "Decided not to surprise me this time?"

He grinned back. "I learn quick, Anine."

"Tell you, Marel, I'm goin' to the 'Mercenary' for a mug to warm my bones. You wanta come along?"

His eyes lit up, and he trotted even with her. "Sure, Anine. I never bin. They won't let me in there alone."

"It ain't a place for kids." She regarded him sideways. "Or don't they trust you?"

"Why wouldn't they trust me?"

"Don't give me that innocent look. You don't survive all on your own around here if you ain't more quick than fussy."

A small grin appeared. "I'm pretty quick."

"That's what I wanted to talk to you about."

"You want somethin' picked up?"

"No, I'm not after you to steal somethin' for me. I want to talk to you about...here, come in, sit down and I'll tell you."

The lad kept his eyes from bulging out of his head as they entered the inn. The huge common room was dark, even in midafternoon, and there were several well-armed men sitting at the tables, with mugs and bowls in front of them. Anine led the way to a table that was removed from the other patrons.

They were served by the owner himself, a lanky man with a limp and a scar across his left cheek. "Recruitin' them a bit young, Anine?"

She grinned. "Aye. We're gettin' real desperate, Barth."

"Desperate ain't the word." He regarded the boy, then turned to Anine. "What'll it be?"

She ordered stew for them both, a mug of hot punch for herself, and small beer for Marel. When they were settled, Anine took a pull from her mug and regarded the boy. He looked up from his bowl, and she held his eye. "Thievin' ain't the best way to make your life."

"It sure ain't. I do as little as I can get away with."

She grinned. "Ain't you got that backwards?"

He looked puzzled then answered her smile. "I see what you mean. Usually a thief steals as much as he can get away with." He became more serious. "But I ain't lookin' for a rep as a thief."

"From the look of Barth when he laid eyes on you, I think you already have."

The boy winced. "That ain't good, Anine."

"Why not?"

Again, he looked puzzled, thought about it. "You mean, how come I think it ain't good? Because once they think you're a thief, they'll never trust you."

"Sounds right to me. How can you trust a thief?"

The boy lowered his wooden spoon and looked anxiously at her. "Because it depends on why he's a thief."

"How so?"

"I see it this way, Anine. There's some folks are thieves from the get-go. They got this idea that everybody else owes 'em somethin' and they just gotta go and take it back."

"I gather you don't see yourself as that kind of thief."

"I sure don't. I know it's wrong to steal. But I gotta live. Usually I can scrape together enough to feed myself. I got a place to live that don't cost nothin' and nobody bothers me there. But sometimes, if somethin's just lyin' around, and I ain't got the price of a meal…" He opened his hands helplessly.

She nodded. "If you're that kind of thief, how can anyone trust you?"

"I only steal if I need to. Once I get myself established, I'll be gettin' enough to live on, and I won't have to steal. So I won't."

"Sounds pretty simple to me. I don't think it'll be that easy. Once you got the habit of pickin' up other people's stuff, you don't just quit, I don't think."

He shrugged. "I gotta think that, Anine. I can do it if I wanta."

"So how do you plan to get yourself established? What skills do you have? What can you sell?"

He hitched forward on the bench, spoke eagerly. "I know people, Anine. I made it my business to know everybody. What they're like, what they're doin', what they got, what they want, what they like, what they hate. If I find out somebody wants somethin', I know where to find it and what it's worth."

"And you get it for them, and charge a bit extra."

He sat back. "Exactly."

"Sounds like a merchant to me."

He considered. "I guess it does, you think of it that way." He leaned forward again. "That's why I don't like it if Barth thinks I'm a thief. If you're gonna be a merchant, people gotta trust you. Where do you think he got that idea? I ain't done no thievin' around here." He waved a hand around the room and grinned. "Too dangerous."

"Word spreads, kid."

"I guess so. I guess I better back off on that sort of thing."

"I woulda thought you'd say 'be more careful'."

"Naw. No matter how careful you are, somebody always knows. After all, you gotta sell what you take, don't you? No, it's best if I just pull in my belt and work harder on my legit stuff."

"I won't try to argue you outa that. Tell me somethin', Marel. When I told you about Arvent this mornin'. You was pretty upset."

"Aye. I had some plans, like I told you."

"But that's not all."

"No, I guess not. I'm…I dunno, I'm sorta mad at him, too."

"Why is that?"

"Well, it was a stupid move, you know? From what he told me, he's been treated pretty well, here. You and that Inari guy was friends of his. You don't go back on the man what pays you. 'Specially you don't go back on your friends. You do that, what're you left with? You got nothin'. Tell you, Anine, bein' alone ain't fun. I done it, and I don't like it."

"So you figure that in order to have friends, you gotta show loyalty to them?"

"That's it. You gotta prove you're worth it."

"I see. So if you had someone to work for, and he or she treated you right, then that person could trust you not to steal from them?"

The boy froze suddenly. "He or she? What're you talkin' about, Anine? No, don't look at me like that. This ain't just a friendly chat, is it? You hauled me in here to impress me, 'cause you're checkin' me out for some reason. You ain't asked me about what Arvent was up to, so I'm guessin' it ain't that." He peered up at her.

"So this 'he or she' bit is the key, ain't it? Let me figure. Anine talks to me. She goes up to the castle to meet with Loreline, the king's spy mistress. Then she comes back invites me to the 'Mercenary' and pries into my head about trust and loyalty."

He sat back. "So what kind of thing does the spy mistress want done? She wants somethin' stolen, I s'pose. Aye, that'd be it. All those questions about thievin'." A sneer wrinkled his lip. "Huh. So all those questions about right and wrong were just to see if I would take a thievin' job. I suppose it ain't so wrong if it's for the king?"

Anine grinned. "Good thinkin', kid. You even got some of it right."

"Some of it?"

"The first part. I was checkin' you out to see what you thought about loyalty and honesty. Loreline did ask about you. But she doesn't want you to steal anythin'. She's just interested in knowin' who you are, and seein' what service you might do for her."

Anine frowned. "But you are right about somethin' else, now that I think about it. When you start doin' things that are wrong, like lyin' or stealin', but you're doin' them for the right reasons, does that make them really right, or are they still wrong?"

The boy frowned back. "Is this some kind of trick question that I gotta get right or I don't get hired on?"

Anine laughed. "No, Marel, it isn't. It's a question everybody has to ask himself, and come up with an answer he can live with. And if you're gonna work with Loreline, you might need a good answer to that."

Marel nodded seriously. "That's true, ain't it? I guess folk think that spies don't know right from wrong. I guess some don't. I guess some spies must get to a point where they gotta decide."

"I guess they do. I sure don't ever want to be in that kind of situation."

"I don't either. But I guess I'll figure it out when it happens."

"I guess you will, or you'll worry about it all the rest of your life."

The boy looked doubtful, and she reminded herself that he was very young.

"Anyways, tomorrow you get yourself cleaned up and dressed in your best, and you head up to the castle. You tell them at the gate that Loreline wants to see you."

"You think they'll let me in, just on my say-so?"

"I don't know. Probably."

"Can I use your name, too? Can I say you sent me? If I use two names they know, yours and Loreline's, it'll sound more like it's real."

"A good idea. You tell them that. And if they don't let you in?"

He grinned. "I go back the next day, and the one after that. Sooner or later, somebody will think to ask Loreline, and she'll tell them to let me in."

"Good thinkin', kid. Tell you, I'll do somethin' else that might help." She beckoned to Barth, who strode over immediately.

"Somethin' else, Anine? Your young gen'lman want a brandy and cigar?"

"Naw, I think he's had enough with the beer. I just wanta tell you somethin'. You know Marel already, I guess."

"I seen him around."

"Well, you may see him around a bit more. Runnin' messages, askin' questions. He might want to come in here."

"You stand for him?"

"So does Loreline."

The innkeeper nodded. "That's fine with me."

"And don't worry, Mister Barth. I won't be takin' anythin' away with me that I ain't been given."

The man held the boy's eyes for a long stare. "I'd appreciate that."

Marel nodded. "This is a big chance for me, Mister Barth. I wouldn't mess it up by doin' somethin' stupid."

"That's a good attitude, lad. You come in here any time you got business."

"Say, Mister Barth, I got an idea."

"What's that, lad?"

"You got any need for errands run, messages sent, orders taken? I could do that for you. I know the city real well. I know where Kayle the winemaker is, I know where Jarl the butcher is, though you know, you'd get a better price from Treth. He gets his pork from a farm closer in, and it's in better shape when it hits the market."

"Would I now? And how do you know I don't buy from Treth?"

The boy grinned. "Well, now, Mister Barth, bein' I'm independent at the moment, I gotta keep information like that to myself. However, if you was to take me on, so to speak, then I'd be able to tell you all sorts of things."

The innkeeper reached out and cuffed the boy lightly behind the head. "You might be a bit too smart for yourself, lad."

"I hope not, sir."

"Don't lay it on too thick. I'm not 'sir', I'm Barth, and you can call me Mister until I know you a bit better. You drop round here regular-like, and I'll give you any work that comes up."

"Just after noon, when you do your orderin?"

"That'd be a real good time, lad."

The boy nodded. "I'll be here." He paused. "Unless I'm doin' somethin' for Loreline. King's business comes first."

Barth shook his head, rolled his eyes at Anine, and returned to the bar, laughing.

Anine got to her feet. "Well, you seem to have done all right for yourself, today. I gotta get packin'. Tomorrow I'm on the road. It's a long ways back to Lanil's Rock."

He jumped up as well, and held the door open for her. "I gotta thank you, Anine. You just put me in the way of a lot of business."

"I found you the chance, you took it, and it's up to you to make good on it, now."

"Don't worry, Anine. I won't let you down."

"Don't let yourself down either, and we'll all be happy."

23. PHILOSOPHY

She had been at Lanil's Rock less than a month when a messenger came with a summons to the castle. The winter cold had deepened, with less snow than usual, and she whisked through in good time on the frozen roads. It was a good thing, because she felt as frozen as the mud by the time she reached the warmth of the castle.

As she came up the stairs to the open doorway of Loreline's office, Zoysana's posture on her favourite stool was slightly different. Wondering why, she entered to find, not Loreline behind the big table, but the Sivan.

"Ah, our lady warrior."

She nodded to him. "Glad you got here, Sivan, sir. It's nice that all those threats I was forced to pass along to you had their effect."

He barked out a laugh. "Zoysana, surely you let her understand that such things mean little to me."

"I let her understand exactly what she chose, Sivan. I wouldn't dream of interfering."

"Ah, you have learned your lessons well, my favourite student."

"You don't have to flatter me, Sivan. I don't have anything you want."

"Not at the moment. As you know, I often like to prepare my way for future needs."

She slanted her head towards him in a mocking bow. "The pupil thanks the teacher for imparting wisdom."

Then she turned to Anine, all business. "So, how are things up at the Rock? Everything turning out as we hoped?"

"Yes, what's going on in the road repair business?"

She glanced at the Sivan, surprised at his interest. "I've found one good source of building stone. Right now, I'm scouting gravel pits near the road. At least, when the weather lets me. I have the information, if you want to hear it in detail…" *Do I wait and report to Loreline, or tell the Sivan and Zoysana now?* She glanced at her Clan Leader for a hint.

"There you go, Sivan. It's not good for the troops when they don't know who's in charge."

He made a dismissive gesture. "Of little importance. We can wait for Loreline before you go into detail. She's a great one for detail, Loreline is. I'd rather discuss your return home from Trenet."

She glanced to Zoysana, puzzled.

Her Clan Leader smiled. "Sivan just got here two days ago. We haven't had time to bring him up to date on everything. We thought we'd wait until you got here before dealing with problems concerning you. Please give him the complete story."

It flashed through Anine's mind that if the Sivan had only been at the castle two days, then the message to her, which she had thought came from the castle.... She dropped that line of thought for future consideration, and started her narrative.

"Oh, we had no problems. I think we got out fast enough that they couldn't catch up with us, because nobody followed us at all. The messages that came with the regular service weren't tampered with either, so it seems our speed and secrecy were wasted."

The Sivan twisted his hands together before coming to a decision. "I think it fair to tell you that the messages were tampered with."

"They were?" This came from Zoysana.

He turned to her. "Yes, I embedded certain phrases in the message that were written in certain ways so we could compare. Also, the mere act of opening the scroll would disturb them. Loreline knew what to watch for. Someone read several of the messages we sent. Unfortunately, they did not see fit to try to alter them."

"Why would that be unfortunate?" Anine stopped. "I can answer that myself."

She caught a glance from Zoysana to the Sivan, and steeled herself to make her Clan Leader proud.

"Knowing what we sent, and knowing what they changed it to, allows us to understand more of what they want. Especially if they aren't aware that we know, it may allow us to plant false information in other messages."

She looked to the Sivan to see if that was enough.

Apparently it was. "Such perspicacity should be rewarded with information. There was false information in those messages. We will be watching to see who acts on that information."

"Is it allowed to know how Loreline knew it was false?"

"The methods, no, because that code is only given to those who need it. The simplest technique, I should tell you. The information directly contradicted one of the messages you brought."

Now she recalled one point that Loreline had quizzed her on specifically. "And she was to believe my verbal message, not the letter from a Duke of the Inner Duchies?"

He truly smiled, now. "Isn't it amazing how matters of rank get jumbled where the good of the realm is concerned?"

Anine nodded. "Thank you, Sivan, sir. I have gained new wisdom today."

"And exhibited some of your own as well, my dear. And please, much as it does my heart good to be addressed with respect, most people simply call me Sivan. 'The Sivan' when I'm not around, and they can't think of anything worse."

"Thank you, Sivan."

He turned to Zoysana. "And now that Anine is here, we should discuss her protégée, my young friend Arvent. How is he getting along?"

Zoysana dropped her answer like two stones into a still pond. "Not well."

The old man nodded, his smile dropping as well. "I was afraid of that."

"You were?"

"Yes. He is limited."

"Limited?" Now her eyes flashed. "He was an idiot!"

The scarred hands made an open gesture. "I wouldn't have stated it so strongly, but obviously you have better information?" He raised his eyebrows expectantly.

"You sent us an agent whom you knew was flawed."

"I sent you a potential agent who needed training. I considered all the possibilities available and decided that you would afford him the best chance to develop in an appropriate direction, or fail. I gather he has failed. How badly?"

"As badly as possible."

"Oh. I am saddened. He did have talent. What was his error?"

Zoysana's smile did nothing to warm the soul. "He made a very poor choice."

"Zoysana, contrary to what you may believe, there are times when I have absolutely no information upon which to make decisions. Could you please just tell me what happened?"

She laughed bitterly. "The famous Sivan wants the straight truth? Not a chance. You tell me!" She leaned forward challengingly.

He sighed. "The reason I found you so appealing, from the very beginning, was that you were willing to challenge me at my own game. Now I pay the price." He settled back in his chair. "All right, it's my game, so I must play it. I assume he made an error of judgement." The pale blue eyes lifted to the ceiling for a breath or two. "I would expect that he misjudged someone."

"Correct."

"Ah. Arvent was always a bit too quick to judge. And he judged this man based on incomplete knowledge, and paid the price."

"Woman."

The pale eyes slid to Anine, then he nodded. "The situation becomes clearer. What? He played her for a woman?"

"Right."

"And it turned out she was...?"

"... a mercenary."

"Ah. He played her for a woman, and she acted like a mercenary. A simple mistake."

"Oh, no."

"Not so simple?" He leaned forward in interest, his knotted fingers woven together.

"I see. He played her for a woman. She reacted like a mercenary. So he played her for a man."

The greying head shook in amazement. "And she reacted...how? Let me guess!" His eyes again peered at Anine. Again, only her years of mercenary training kept her from twitching under that intense gaze.

"I've got it!" He slapped the table in glee. "Then he discovered he was dealing with a woman! Ah, the elegance of it all! He must have assumed that, because she allowed her mercenary training to overcome her womanly instincts, she would then continue to act like a man. But he was wrong, this much is obvious." His outstretched hand acknowledged her presence in the room.

"Got it. Honour. He assumed that, because she adhered to the mercenary code, and acted like a man, then she would act like an honourable man."

He cocked an eye at Anine and chuckled. "Oh, my. He didn't have a chance, did he? You cheated."

"I did not cheat!"

"Oh, didn't you?"

"I did not!"

"So you stood up to him, man to man, and beat him in a fair fight?"

She stared at the man. "You must be joking. He was one of the best swordsmen I have ever crossed blades with. I'm not stupid, you know."

"Yes, I do know that. Did Arvent ever figure it out?"

The intensity of the cold blue stare forced her to consider. "I don't think he ever did. Not really."

The Sivan laid both hands open on the table. "There you are. Because you reacted like an honourable man, he then assumed that you would fight him. Of course you didn't, because, as a woman, your loyalty overruled your personal honour."

Her mouth twisted wryly. "Plus, of course, he was playin' me for a fool. That made it real easy."

The Sivan laughed out loud, a cracking bark that coincided with the slap of his palms on the table. "Zoe, hang onto this one. She's going to be as bad as Kenna when she grows up!"

Zoysana turned to Anine and smiled broadly. "I think you've been given his greatest compliment. Kenna was always his nemesis, here in Petrella. In fact, I always figured that was why he left. He couldn't stand the competition."

The figure across the table suddenly lost its animation. He slumped in his chair, staring at the table between his hands. His voice dropped. "You are very right and very wrong, Zoysana. She was one of the main reasons I left. I could not allow myself to be placed in a position of opposition to Lady Kenna." He shook his head. "In fact, that is probably the main reason I left. I have never been especially attached to my pride. I have always found it to be a great impediment to the duties I perform. But the situation in Petrella I could not bear. It was necessary," his eyes focused on the woman across the table from him, "to leave the solution to someone else.

"I will be forever grateful, Zoysana, for your actions in that situation. I am fully aware of the cost to you. The fact that you acted completely on your own does not absolve me from the responsibility for placing you in the situation."

His face worked with some unknown emotion. "I have never said these words to a living soul, Zoysana, but I will say them to you. I am sorry. Not for what I did. That was necessary. I am sorry that it had to be you. I would have given anything in my power to save you from that choice. But I, myself, had few other options. Can you understand that?"

Zoysana's face twisted in a half-smile. "I am supposed to believe that the famous Sivan actually found a situation where he had only one solution?"

He shook his head sadly. "I didn't say that. You were just by far the best one."

Zoysana leaned forward. "I understand that part. What I don't understand is how you decide."

"How I decide what?"

"How you figure out how to act. Anine had a choice to make. It was easy, because she had her loyalty to guide her. My choice was more difficult, but I only had to understand that my loyalty to Petrella had to supersede my loyalty to Barent. Once I had that straight, there was no real choice, and I did what I had to do."

"Yes. I counted on that."

"What about you? You are as close to a free man as anyone I know. How do you decide? Where do your loyalties lie?"

"I don't choose to act upon loyalties. Not in the long term."

"You don't?"

"Don't misunderstand. Your young mercenary friend, here, will see what I'm getting at. As long as I worked for the Arlyns, I was completely loyal to them. As long as Barent was king, I worked completely for him."

"But that changed."

"Yes, it did. Loyalty is only the means to an end. Blind loyalty is a dangerous tool. If the employer starts to move against my personal code, as happened with Barent, then I must take myself, and my loyalty, elsewhere."

Zoysana sat back, cocking her head to the left. "I can understand that, but where do you get this personal code?"

He shrugged. "It is my code. I act according to the beliefs I have developed over the course of my life. No one can do anything else, if you think about it."

Anine couldn't help but break in. "But what about the craven who changes his loyalty the moment he is required to make some sacrifice? He isn't acting according to any code. Besides self-interest."

"Aha! She is listening. I expected no less. Of course he is obeying his code. The man you call a coward is a man whose code says that his own survival, perhaps even his own comfort, is the most important element of his world. He will act in the way that he thinks will achieve his comfort and safety. I find people of that sort comfortable to work with."

"You mean easy to manipulate."

He nodded. "Easy to predict, if you will. The rest of you, with your conflicting loyalties and moral codes, are much more difficult. In fact, that's what I take the most pride in: my ability to predict what any given individual will do in any given situation. Are you following this, Anine?"

She considered for a slow breath. "I think so. You have a basic ideal that you follow, no matter what. Everybody does, according to you. You just think yours is superior to everyone else's. Which we all do, come to think of it."

"Very well reasoned. You can come and be my student any day. But why would you? You already have a teacher of the first quality."

Zoysana tossed up a hand, as if to brush the compliment aside. "Wait. I'm thinking. That means that, somewhere, you must have one basic ideal. The very most important baseline, the one against which you can compare any action. I like that. It makes decision-making much easier." She paused to consider him. "What is it?"

"What is it?"

"Yes, oh great teacher. Give these naive, inexperienced students the wisdom of your perception."

"I'm supposed to tell you, just like that?"

"I think I have earned the right to ask."

He sighed. "Yes, I suppose you have. That's the trouble with apologizing to people. They use it against you for the rest of your life."

"Stop trying to duck. This isn't something we can arrive at through your question games." A thought struck her. "I suppose you really know the answer?"

He nodded slowly. "I think so. I have spent a lot of time considering it, you realize, but I've never had to explain it to anyone else. If I had to put it briefly…"

"Oh, please do."

"Don't interrupt. To put it succinctly, I judge my actions based on what will create the best results for the most people. No, wait. It's a bit more than that. The best results for the largest number of people for the longest time. Yes, I like that. Having said it aloud and heard it myself, I think that covers it."

Anine considered again. "You mean you do things because they're good for lots of other people. How about your own good? Where do you fit in?"

He gave a knowing smile. "Well, in order to do good for large numbers of people, I must first survive myself. I must also create situations where I have the power to act."

Zoysana placed a hand on his arm. "Is there a place in that code of yours for an act that is good for you and somebody else, but has no other use?"

"Ah, you mean Loreline?" He nodded. "Of course, one cannot fight the instincts that drive all men." He brightened. "In fact, one probably should not. One would find oneself making decisions based on emotional struggles that had no bearing on the decision at hand. Yes, I think it is better to attempt a normal emotional life, so as to be able to put all one's faculties honestly to work on one's duty."

"Hmph," a new voice broke in. "Doesn't he just drive you insane when he starts with that 'one should' and 'one shouldn't' line, to hide the fact he's talking about himself?"

They all turned as Loreline entered the room. The Sivan did not rise, but there was a subtle change in his posture as the woman slid behind him and rested her hand on his shoulder.

"What nonsense has he been spouting now?"

Zoysana laughed. "He was just managing to persuade himself that it really was a good thing, philosophically speaking, for him to come back here to you."

288

"Oh. Did he mention what a good thing it was, physically speaking, as well? Speaking of his personal safety, and the likelihood of him lasting more than a month should I have to come looking for him?" Now she had a hand on either shoulder, both creeping ominously towards his neck.

"No, he hadn't got that far, but I'm sure he considered it when he made his plans."

"Good." Loreline's hands dropped from her husband's shoulders, and she became all business. "Has Anine brought you up to date on the unfortunate Arvent? I'm sorry about him. He did have potential. Maybe he should have heard your philosophy speech a few more times."

"He never heard it. I do not make speeches."

"Oh, that's right. Too bad. Maybe you should. We're not all as bright as Zoysana."

"But some of us listen better. Fortunately."

Zoysana turned to Anine. "You don't really need to hear the family squabble going on."

"I don't know. I was sort of enjoying it. I've seen you two team up before."

"Really?"

"Yes, on the king." She let her voice thin, raised it in a posh accent. "Terribly improper. Bad for morale, if the troops found out. But you needn't worry, my Lady. Not a word passes these lips."

Zoysana turned to Loreline. "I told you she was good."

Anine immediately dropped the pose. "Don't let the idea even start. I'm not pretending to be anybody, ever again!"

They all laughed, she was relieved to note. She was a fool to let them know, and she mentally slapped herself for showing off. She really had to get back to her crew and her planning.

24. Wedding Trip

She spent the rest of the winter doing a lot of planning, because the weather didn't cooperate, and travel was difficult. In the evenings, sitting with Jhanes and Sarha at the inn, her thoughts, and sometimes their conversation, turned to Ferlen.

"How does he manage up there when it snows like this?"

Sarha shrugged. "Snowshoes, I guess. It doesn't really matter how deep the snow is, as long as you're walkin' on the top."

Jhanes nodded. "Cold weather's worse. The animals aren't moving around as much, so you get fewer furs, and there's more danger in case of an accident."

She shook her head. "I can't picture living alone like that. Anything goes wrong, there's nobody to help."

The innkeeper nodded. "But there's pride in managing. Doing something few others could handle."

Sarha chuckled. "And not getting your life messed up by anybody else. You'll appreciate that, Anine."

"Oh, yes. I guess that's why he was so mad last spring when Zoe saddled him with the road work."

"Oh, I don't know. He wasn't worried about doin' the job. I think he was most worried about takin' it from you. He knew what it meant to you."

Anine grinned. "Well, we've got that all settled out, now."

"You do?"

"Yep. A good working relationship. We'll do the best we can for the realm."

Jhanes nodded. "I'm sure you will." Then he turned and gave his wife a look that Anine couldn't read.

There's somethin' goin' on there. She gave a mental shrug. *If I need to know, they'll tell me. Must be nice to have someone like that. A simple look, and you both know exactly what's happenin'. Oh, well. Maybe someday. I got more important things to worry about right now.*

"Late spring will mean a late start to the road work."

Jhanes nodded. "But it will keep the bandits out of the bush as well, so it's not all trouble."

They fell to talking about schedules, and the private moment passed.

* * *

Two months later, the roads were dry and hard enough for safe travel, and she didn't need an order to know she was expected at the castle. So she saddled up her faithful horse and headed out.

There was no one on the road, and the wagons had not appeared to create the spring ruts, so she made good time and got her riding muscles hardened up as well. Sure enough, the day after she arrived at the castle she was called into the king's presence.

"Your Majesty, you sent for me?"

Gerth was sitting in his usual big chair in his mother's quarters, long legs stretched to the fire. He looked up lazily. "Anine. Come in and sit down."

She was becoming used to sitting in the presence of the king, but still she did not relax.

"You don't really suit that chair, Anine."

She looked down at the spindly seat that accounted for some of her careful posture. "It happens to me a lot, Sire."

He chuckled. "Me too. I had Mother bring this throne in for me. You seem to handle that one easily enough."

"Practice, Sire."

"Good. Want some more practice?"

There was no point in responding. He would tell her when he was ready.

Kenna's voice laughed from behind her. "Nice try, Gerth. You're never going to get a rise out of her."

"I had to try."

Kenna stepped forward and sat gracefully, despite her own considerable size, on a chair matching Anine's. "Don't worry. He'll get to the point when he's finished the games."

Anine smiled. "Yes, my Lady. He always does." She smiled, she hoped graciously, at the king and waited.

After a moment, he gave in. "How are the roads north, Anine?"

She considered this. "The last frost is gone, so they're a bit muddy at the moment. I came in from Jaspen with little trouble, although it took me an extra day. No rains for a week, so they'll be improving." She considered. "One big storm and they'll be impassable for a larger wagon."

"How about horses?"

"Slower or faster, depending on the weather. No problem getting through."

"Good."

She had expected this call. *He's anxious to bring Talia home as soon as he can.* "When am I leaving?"

"Pardon?"

Kenna gave a ladylike snicker, but said nothing. Anine waited.

Finally, Gerth sighed. "As soon as you're ready."

"How large a party?"

"What do you think?"

"It all depends on how many people Lady Talia will be bringing and their capabilities."

"Fewer than you might think. Her mother and father, a few friends, several officials from Lesser Trenet. The rest will be their staff and protection."

Anine nodded. "I'll have a chat with Sivan and Loreline about the political situation. I assume you'll be sending an appropriate escort from here?"

He shot a surprised look at his mother. "I had thought of it. What would you think appropriate?"

"Military requirements, Sire? Assuming we have safe passage through the rest of the Duchies and no worry of overt hostilities closer to home, I would think ten Warlanders would do. We'll also want a hand of Guides for scouting, and Zoysana can probably scare up a few Clan Inari. Their kind of information is worth a lot of weapon power. Who's going to be in charge?"

"Who do you think?"

"If you're sending ten Warlanders, I assume from your personal Guard, you'll have to send one of their officers. Since everything is quiet around here, you can probably spare Lukin. That would do the lady honour as well."

Gerth nodded. "Thank you, Anine. Those are good guesses."

"They aren't guesses, your Majesty."

"Aren't they?"

"No. They were my assessment of the needs of the situation. What, did you think I was guessing?" She shot a glance at Kenna, who seemed to be enjoying some private joke.

Gerth merely nodded.

"And did I pass?"

His brow wrinkled slightly. "Pass what?"

"Whatever test this was. You don't need my advice to set up this excursion."

"No, I need you for something else."

She waited.

"I need you for a rather special assignment, Anine. As you suggest, I have decided to send Lukin and five or ten Warlanders of the Guard, with the appropriate Guides as well. It is when you include the Clan that I have a problem. Talia has asked that they be included. Zoysana is still in Kyabra, dealing with our agents there." He grinned at his mother. "And incidentally spending time with her Guard of Life. Talia has also asked specifically for you, which is no surprise to anyone.

"The obvious solution is to send you along to liaise between Lukin, the Guard, the Guides and the Inari. The only way you can do that is if you are second to him."

She schooled her face to stillness while she considered this. "How will the rest of the Warlanders see that?"

Gerth grinned. "I don't think there will be any trouble from my Guard. They are quite in awe of your accomplishments. They also follow orders."

"Which the Inari do not."

"Yes. Lukin has not worked with Inari that much, so your skills might be very important."

"I understand, Sire."

"I think you do. Have you worked with Lukin before?"

"No, Sire. Our duties seldom cross. I have spoken to him only a few times."

"We will have to remedy that before you leave. Will you choose the Clan members for me? Also, talk to the Sivan and Loreline as you suggested. Unless they have anything new for us, we will go with the numbers you mentioned. Lukin will take care of the rest:

hostlers, cooks, teamsters, supplies. Do the Inari need anything special?"

"Clan Inari are happy to eat soldier's rations. They supplement it with whatever they pick up as they scout. We'll all eat well."

He grinned. "As long as they don't pick it up from the local farmers."

Anine smiled as well. "They have become relatively civilized over the past two years, Sire."

"I assumed so. You can meet with me tomorrow, and I'll get Lukin there as well."

She rose. "I'll get on it right away. Your Majesty, Lady Kenna."

The king nodded and Lady Kenna winked. Anine swung out the door, avoiding a few smaller knick-knack tables as she went.

The next afternoon she entered the king's workroom, just off the throne room. Lukin and Gerth were already deep in discussion, so she waited just inside the door. Gerth looked up and waved her to a seat.

"I don't think it will be a problem, Lukin. Lady Talia will have to bring an equal number of Knights back with her. With the kind of tracking and reconnaissance the Guides and the Inari can provide, you won't be surprised."

The grizzled old head nodded and turned to her. "I've heard good things about the Inari, Anine. How do you see them fitting in with the usual Guide scouting routines?"

She did not answer right away. That was a good question. "We won't get the same kind of patterns from the Inari, sir. They are more free ranging. How far ahead do the Guides usually push their point?"

"Depends on who they're scouting for. If it's all horse, which it looks like we have here, they stay closer in. Perhaps half a candle's ride."

She considered that. "The Inari like to cover a wider area. They move faster and track down anything that looks interesting, check on any ambush points, run out on all the intersecting trails."

"That's a less secure perimeter."

"It is, but you can't always cover everything. We give our Fighters the freedom to choose what looks dangerous. That uses the intelligence of our men to better advantage. I figure the Guides work that way as well. I know they range much farther than regular mounted scouts do for the mercs."

He nodded judiciously. "That's true. Of course, they always push out a little more for foot soldiers because infantry are so slow they are easy to find. If a mounted party changes direction, you can lose contact at a crucial moment. Do you think we can pull our Guides in a bit and let them cover the immediate vicinity tighter? Your men can do as you suggest, for an earlier warning of any danger. How about night duty?"

"Same thing. Inari don't stand guard at a post. They move in a large perimeter, using their own initiative."

"Any chance of them getting shot by one of our sentries?"

Anine chuckled. "If they do, it's their own fault."

"You mean that?"

She faced the king. "I don't, your Majesty, but they do. If I allowed it, they would have contests to see who could sneak through the other sentries when their watches were over."

Lukin's jaw dropped. "They what?"

Anine raised her hands helplessly. "They don't use passwords. When their turn on patrol is over, they turn around and try to sneak back through their own lines."

"Don't they ever shoot each other?"

"No. They wouldn't use an arrow on anyone in the dark. If they think there's someone there they go out after him."

The old Warlander shook his head with a slight smile. "Sounds like a bunch of kids."

"They are. Most of these Fighters are seventeen or eighteen winters. In their society, that's fully adult."

"How much Petrellan do they speak?"

"All Zoe's Clan speak it well enough to get by. You have to be careful, though. They know all the words for fighting. They can pass messages, talk tactics. But that doesn't mean they speak Petrellan well. If they have to talk about something else, they won't have the vocabulary. We're lucky, though. Mantinello came back early. He speaks better than I do."

"He does?"

"He's got a memory like a sponge. He's my aide-de-camp and he runs everything."

"A good aide is worth five spearmen."

"This one's worth ten."

The seamed face split in a grin. "I like an officer who stands up for his men."

"These don't need me to stand up for them, sir. You'll see."

"Anything extra in the way of supplies?"

"They all have two horses and they tend their own stock. I've got six Inari coming. When we're moving, we'll have five out on patrol, one with the remuda."

"We'll have five Guides out, one in, as well. That's more than usual, but we're guarding a more important party than usual."

Anine turned to the king. "Who will be in charge of the return party, Sire?"

Gerth frowned. "You'll have to work that out. Lord Trenet is obviously the one in charge of their people. I don't know what he'll want."

"That won't be a problem, Sire."

"No?"

"No. He'll take charge of the party. The moment a military situation arises, he'll defer to Lukin."

"Are you sure of that?"

"Yes, your Majesty. Lady Talia has him well trained."

Gerth nodded, a pleased smile on his face. Lukin nodded soberly. "I like a man who lets professionals do their duty."

There was a pause, and Anine took the chance. "May I ask a question, your Majesty?"

"Of course."

"Lukin, sir, how do you feel about me being second in command?"

He looked puzzled. "How do I feel?"

"I know you'll follow orders, but I'm a merc, I'm a woman, and I'm nineteen years old. How is that going to affect the chain of command with you and your men?"

The grey head nodded. "A good question, plainly stated. My men and I will have no problem with a mercenary. We're professionals as well, in a different sense. That also helps with the rest of it. If you act like a professional and do your duty as well as Gerth tells me you will, then there will be no problems with me or my men."

A small smile quirked his lip. "And your reputation won't do you any harm, either."

She covered her blush with what she hoped was a firm nod. "Good enough for me, sir."

Gerth slapped his leg. "Right, then. This is sounding like a good plan. I'm not worried about putting Talia in your hands, you two, no matter who Duke Trenet brings along."

"Thank you, Sire."

The old Warlander merely nodded.

"How soon can you leave?"

Lukin caught Anine's eye with raised brows.

"My people are ready now, Sire," she grinned. "They don't have much to pack."

Lukin took this in stride. "Two days more for us. We have wagons to load."

"Oh, Anine, did Sivan give you any information?"

"Nothing new, Sire. He says he discussed it with you last quarter."

"Yes. There won't be any serious bandit mobs in the Inner Duchies. If that bunch that gave the merchants trouble last summer is still in business, we don't think they'll be ready to match a force our size this early in the season. You'll have to keep your eyes open in Velikii."

"We'll keep our eyes open every step of the way, Sire."

"I'm sure you will, Lukin. You have served the Arlyns well all your life, and I know you will continue for a long time."

The weathered face broke into a grin. "I hope to, Sire. With all this trade and diplomacy going on, it doesn't look like there's much chance for an old Warlander like me to die on the field of battle."

"I'm really sorry about that, Lukin. Times change."

"I'm not complaining; I'd just like one more full cavalry charge, that's all."

Gerth's big hand dropped with a resounding slap on the old Warlander's unyielding shoulder. "I'm doing my very best to disappoint you, Lukin."

25. THE TRIP NORTH

It was Anine's idea that they train together on the road. "My Inari have never faced armour before, Sir. They could use some practice."

Lukin nodded. "It will help turn us into a single unit, as well."

"Yes. We don't have to work against you all the time. Maybe a couple of Inari could help a Warlander as a team of some sort."

Lukin pulled at his lip. "I can't see it, Anine, but let's keep open minds."

Mounted, the results were predictable and frustrating. No Inari could get anywhere near a Warlander. In turn, the armoured man couldn't get a good swing at the fast-moving Inari. On foot, Anine expected a similar situation, and she was as surprised as the Warlanders at the outcome. Against a fast-moving Inari, a fully-armoured Warlander had little chance. If he didn't connect with the first swing of his heavy sword, the Inari was inside or behind, his long knife seeking chinks in the armour or slashing at the leather straps that held the armour on.

Lukin frowned. "We have to do something about this."

Anine agreed, but she said nothing. She knew the solution. Lukin's frown deepened and he pulled at his lip. Finally, he strode into the practice circle they had laid out. "Let me have a try."

Anine nodded to Mantinello, who stepped forward. The Warlander stood watching his opponent, then reached up and tossed off his helmet. Mantinello faded back a bit.

Lukin smiled a ghost of a smile, and held his sword at the ready. Mantinello started a slow stalk, moving to the right. The big sword tip stayed pointing at him steadily.

The Inari tried a direct attack, starting with a two-handed beat against the larger sword, but Lukin circled his weapon tightly, gaining enough momentum to push the lighter blade aside.

Then Mantinello seemed to slip, and the Warlander jabbed forward. The Inari regained his footing easily and grinned. Lukin grinned as well. A bluff tried and called.

As they resumed, Anine noticed the sword tip of the Warlander slide sideways. Mantinello continued his slow circle, but Lukin did not seem to be following perfectly. Anine saw what was coming, but she did not interfere.

When Lukin's sword point was half a body-width off line, Mantinello made a sudden dive to the opposite side.

Instantly, the sword described a quick half-circle, dropping precisely where Mantinello would have been if he had pressed home his attack. Second ruse called and countered.

Mantinello stepped back. "I need a different weapon."

Lukin nodded, grounding his sword to wait. The young Inari sprinted to his tent, coming back with something balled in his left hand.

As Lukin raised his sword again, the Inari held his knife out as usual, but his left hand circled above his head, swinging something on the end of a string. He again stalked his opponent, the strange instrument starting to whistle as it gained speed.

As the whistle became a full hum, Mantinello suddenly let go. The object flew to Lukin's left and, just for a moment, the sword wavered towards it. Mantinello darted in and froze, his long knife a hand's-breadth from the Warlander's throat.

There was a moment's pause, broken by a surprising chuckle. "You beat me, fair and square, lad. Never thought I'd be fooled like that."

Mantinello shrugged. "I knew I couldn't get past your sword, sir, if I couldn't get you to swing." He walked over to pick up his bolo. "This is good for small game. As much good as my knife against an armoured Warlander."

Lukin nodded. "Fine. But it still doesn't help you much, does it?"

Anine stepped forward. "It's obvious that one-on-one is hard to work. Everybody think about it, and if you have any ideas, come up with them next practice session. Perhaps it might be more useful to find ways in which Clan might support the Warlanders."

They set out in groups, trying different combinations, on foot and mounted. No one came up with anything startling, but many possibilities appeared. Once the Guides were invited, a certain camaraderie grew up. Most of the Warlanders were younger sons of nobility, not much older than the Inari. The three older men saw themselves as mentors to the younger ones of both cultures. In their turn, Anine could see the younger ones of both grouping together because of common interests and feelings.

There wasn't much time to practice, though, because the footing was soft, the going was tough and the light failed soon after they came off the road each evening. It was hardest for the supply freighters and their teams, although Lukin had made sure the wagons were lightly loaded. Sometimes the whole band would have to dismount and help the wagons up a slippery pitch. Again, the high spirits of the young carried them through, with laughter and pranks in the mud.

Once again, as they moved into the Inner Duchies, the weather warmed and dried, the roads firmed, and they made better time. They rolled into Lesser Trenet clean, dry, and sharply turned out.

As they entered the castle, they were met by a squadron of foot soldiers, rank upon rank, arms polished to blinding, flanked by twenty Knights in full armour. Talia stood alone in front to greet them, her father up on the stairs with a tall, gaunt woman who must be her mother.

Swinging down from her horse, Anine found herself crushed by Talia's embrace.

"I'm so glad you came, Anine. Your men look wonderful. Mantinello! Good to see you!" She greeted each Inari by name, then turned more formally to the Warlanders.

"Lukin. It is a great honour that you came yourself. Welcome, you and your men." She turned to her parents, urged them forward.

Duke Trenet strode down the stairs eagerly, greeting Anine in friendly fashion, and treating Lukin with the respect his daughter showed. The mother waited at the top less enthusiastically, although when she moved to greet them, her step seemed firm. When she was introduced to Lukin, he gave her the full honours of the Codes.

"It is a pleasure and an honour to meet a member of a family held in such high regard throughout the region, my Lady."

Somewhat mollified, the lady gave him a gracious bow in return, but one that demonstrated no status to the one honoured. Upon her daughter's urging, she turned to Anine.

"Mother, this is Anine. I've told you all about her. She's my best friend in Petrella. She taught me all my sword work, and my mounted work," she turned to her mother, "and saved my life a few times."

Again, the lady gave an indeterminate bow. "I am pleased to thank you for the time and patience you have shown our daughter. If you have saved her life, you have our undying gratitude. Be welcome to our home."

With this formal speech, the lady turned and sought her husband's arm. Talia slipped her own arm through Anine's and urged her forward.

"Your men will be taken care of. Come on inside. Please join us, Lukin. I'm so glad you came."

Warmed by her enthusiasm, the old Warlander smiled and matched their strides. Inside the main reception room, an officious major-domo placed them in strict order and they were introduced to a number of higher-ranking nobles of Trenet. During this ceremony, Talia was having a quiet but firm word with her mother.

Suddenly, the girl pulled her mother's arm, and allowed her voice to rise a bit. "You don't understand, Mother." She stopped in front of Lukin. "This is the Captain of the King's Guard. He has loyally served the last four kings of Petrella. He is known throughout the realm as the first friend of the Arlyn dynasty. They have no diplomats, Mother. They have no courtiers who make their lives from gossip and manipulation. Gerth has no one he could send who honours me more. Each of the Warlanders escorting me is a representative of a major household of the realm. That covers the diplomacy."

She turned to Anine. "Look at Anine, Mother. Do you see how she stands? Did you see her move? Do you see how naturally the armour clings to her, how the sword swings with her step? Now look at me. Don't you understand that when I try to be like her, I become me? The person I want to be? You look at her and you see how it is possible for me to be the Queen of Petrella, Mother. Do you understand?"

The keen eyes rose to meet Anine's, and she could see the lines of pain that pinched the pale lips. "I can see why you would find such an image appealing, my dear. It has certainly changed you. And I now see that these people live by a different standard than we do. If you say Gerth has sent his best, then I must accept that." Her eyes flicked around at the weapons surrounding her.

"At least, I have little fear of trouble on the road."

Talia grinned. "You're right there, Mother. And you haven't even seen the Inari at work."

"An experience I'm not sure I look forward to. May we return to the ceremonies?"

"Oh! Of course. I didn't mean to monopolize you."

The elder woman smiled. "Since you are the reason for the whole affair, I suppose you could be forgiven."

Talia grinned over her mother's shoulder as they returned to the Duke's side. Anine stayed beside Lukin, taken aback by Talia's words. Had the other girl really looked up to her that much?

"You seem to have made a great impression on our future Queen."

Anine shook her head. "I don't quite know how, sir. It just happened."

He nodded. "Not unusual. Good for her, I'd say." He lowered his voice. "Lady Trenet has been ill, I gather."

"Very. Word going around is she hauled herself out of a terrible decline by sheer willpower to attend Talia's wedding."

"Which means that when it's all done..."

"Either she'll stay better, or she'll..."

"Hmm. Go back to where she was at the beginning."

"That's what they say, sir."

"I've known it to happen both ways. Shall we join the others?"

He offered his arm, and as she took it she clashed her vambrace against his sword hilt. He quirked the corner of his mouth at her and led the way forward.

There was a banquet that night, of course. Anine was not too surprised to find herself placed strategically below any titled nobility, but above the rest of the guests. Lukin, resplendent in court clothes she had never seen him wear, took a place of honour at the head table. She couldn't hear what was being said, but obviously he kept the attention of the Duke and Talia. Lady Trenet did not attend.

The food was marvellous but rich, and the wine, after a dusty day on the road, was tempting, but Anine held back and was clear-headed the next morning for the first council.

Lukin was looking at a long list. "This triples the number of people in our party."

The Duke nodded. "I thought it might."

Lukin nodded. "How many of these can fight?"

"All of them, if need be...I know. That's not the answer you want. You have brought twenty-two fighting men and ten retainers. I am adding ten more real fighting men, ten guests, and twenty retainers who, as I say, can defend themselves." He glanced over at Anine. "Even Gavess."

302

His gaze returned to the old soldier. "Is that enough protection?"

Lukin shook his head. "You can never have enough, your Grace. If I had not seen Anine's Inari in action, I would be concerned. However, with the kind of scouting we have, we will not be surprised on the road or caught in a trap. If there is trouble, we have plenty of strength to hold the road while the royal party flees to safety."

He glanced at the Duke. "If that suits your Grace."

Trenet grimaced. "It doesn't suit me at all, but my wife is ill and my daughter too important to sacrifice to my personal pride, so I will follow your recommendations, whatever they are."

"That is a good point, your Grace. We discussed this with his Majesty, and he said it would be up to you to decide who was to lead."

Again, the Duke glanced at Anine. "I believe we have that straight already."

"Anine did mention something like that, your Grace."

The Duke grinned. "Yes. I'm in charge until the swords come out. Then I'm just baggage."

Lukin raised his eyebrows. "I doubt that, your Grace. But you will become one of my soldiers?"

"Most certainly. I was once counted good with a sword, but I have not practised the military sciences for many years, so I will place myself in your capable hands. I have no doubt in Gerth's choice of escort."

Lukin nodded. "That's very good, your Grace. It will smooth things out. I note you said ten guests. Who are they?"

"I include my own family in that number. The rest are friends of Lady Talia and two or three relations, coming along to make sure everything is done according to the rules."

"How will they travel?"

"Most on horseback. We will need two carriages. We have good carriages: sturdy but comfortable. Good horses for them as well. ...oh, I know, Anine. You're thinking about that huge old thing Talia chose to take with her. Most of ours are much more practical. I gather you managed to get it to the castle?"

"Yes, your Grace. It's sitting outside the gates, fully protected from the weather."

"I'll be thanking someone for their kindness. That carriage has carried my kin to their weddings and their graves for four generations. I would not see it come to harm."

"No harm, sir, except some of the trim removed."

The duke laughed. "I heard about that. All that extra gold trim had nothing to do with the original design. I gather it went to good use."

"The results speak for themselves, your Grace."

"That they do."

Lukin rolled up the list. "Are there any ceremonies yet to be completed?"

"No, I believe we could leave tomorrow if we really wanted to. The day after would be most convenient."

Lukin glanced over at Anine. "I think tomorrow would be better, sir. The sooner we get on the road, the less time anyone has to prepare for us."

The duke shook his head. "I keep forgetting. You talk like folk in the middle of a war. How serious is it?"

Lukin snorted. "There's no war, your Grace. At least, not a declared one. Our enemy is a small group of sneak-arounds who don't want to see prosperity come because it threatens their little castles of glass."

"My sources concur. However, they still pose us a danger, and I would like to minimize that. We will leave tomorrow and travel as fast as possible."

Anine nodded, pleased, but then another thought struck her. "Will it make it difficult for Lady Trenet to travel in those conditions?"

The duke shook his head. "She seems to be in reasonable shape. As long as she is comfortable in the carriage she should be all right." He smiled sadly. "Of course, if she isn't, she won't let on, so we won't know."

26. LADY TRENET

Because of the swift departure, Anine didn't get to know Talia's friends until they were well out on the journey south. She had to admit, the lady's analysis was fairly accurate. The two cousins, both in their final year as squires, were upright and straightforward fighting men, who could turn a phrase, a dance step or a lady's head with equal ease. Anine was more interested in Talia's two friends, the only non-relatives in her party. Orcan, the merchant lad whom Anine had met on the last trip, was nobility as well; it was obvious from his carriage and his way of speaking. However, there was a no-nonsense toughness about him that made him seem much older than his contemporaries.

He insisted, without making a show, on taking his turn at night watch. He covered a great deal more of the road than the rest, his eyes constantly alert to their surroundings. She put that down to his caravan experience and was glad of his presence. As *Haskel's* said, a rider with a sharp eye was worth five heavy infantry, slogging with their heads down.

She also found Orcan comfortable to be around. He had no need of chatter, and seemed quite happy to sit or ride in her company for a candle without speaking more than a few words.

The other friend Anine had also met, but as the days went by, she found the young woman more and more fascinating. At first glance, Leile seemed exactly the opposite of the person Talia would have chosen for a friend. Small, graceful and pretty, she eased through the social life of the party without leaving a ripple, with a friendly word to everyone but rarely more. Intrigued, Anine watched the girl as the days went past. Often, she would ride beside Talia, and while the smaller woman did not say much, Talia seemed to blossom in her company, speaking with more animation, her gestures larger.

Initially, Leile attracted the attention of a few of the young Warlanders in Lukin's Guard, but while she seemed unfailingly polite and friendly, their interest soon dwindled. Anine watched this with curiosity. *How does she do it? Does she get rid of them on purpose, or is it by mistake?*

"Well, have you figured it out yet?"

Anine started. Her horse, sensitive to his rider's reaction, skittered a few steps sideways. She straightened him out, then looked down at the other woman, gliding along on her palfrey. "Figured what out?"

"Me."

"What do you mean?"

Leile snorted. Somehow, she made the sound ladylike. "You've been watching me the whole trip."

Anine never allowed herself to be rushed. She let her horse jog on for a few more steps before answering. "I watch everyone. It's my duty."

"How is that?"

"I have to figure out as quickly as I can how every member of the party will react if we have to fight. Or if we run into some other problem. So, I watch everyone and try to figure them out."

"But you've been watching me."

"Don't flatter yourself."

"Don't change the subject."

"I didn't. I'm still trying to get a handle on everyone. Some, it's easier than others."

The small girl grinned. "By which you mean you're still working on me."

"I gotta admit."

Leile nodded. "That's fine, then."

"It is?"

"Oh, of course. I just wasn't sure."

Anine thought. "But you, on the other hand, have me pretty well pegged."

"I think so."

"At least well enough to realize that the best thing to do was ask."

"Exactly."

"So far, so good."

"Hmm."

They rode along in companionable silence for a while. Then a disturbance ahead of them caught Anine's attention. She rose in her stirrups to see better. A horse had shied off to the side of the road, its rider fighting for control.

"Excuse me. Duty calls."

Leile raised a hand and dropped it forward in tacit permission, and Anine spurred her horse ahead.

By the time she got there, the problem was over. At least, for the moment. She couldn't be sure whether the squire's horse had spooked out of high spirits or had been helped by one of his friends, but it was under control, now. The lad was abashed by Anine's attention, but she said nothing. She knew that her presence was often enough to settle the troops. She gave a meaningful glance to the other squire, which he answered with an innocent smile. She held his eye a moment longer, then reined her horse away. If there was further silliness, they had been warned.

Not that there was really any problem. This was a wedding party after all, and a certain amount of high spirits was expected. Feeling the need for some action herself, Anine trotted forward to join Lukin.

"What was that?"

"Squires and their games."

"Thought so."

"They've been friends for years. Nothing out of the ordinary, I wouldn't say."

"Good."

They chatted for a while about their progress and plans for the evening's stay. There were no manor houses nearby of a size that could accommodate them, so they were overnighting in two separate inns in the next town, a feat that required a certain amount of organization. When they were both satisfied with the details, Anine reined her horse aside and watched as the procession passed her.

But a hand beckoned from the window of Lady Trenet's carriage. Pulling alongside, Anine leaned nearer. "Yes, my Lady?"

Lateda's face appeared at the window. "My Lady would like to know if you are staying in the same inn as we are tonight."

"I believe so, unless something changes once we get there."

"In that case, my Lady asks, would you dine with her?"

"Of course."

There was a murmured conversation, and the maid's head appeared again. "My Lady says don't worry about dressing up. Just an informal supper at an inn."

"I'll do my best."

That brought the ghost of a smile. Lateda knew full well that Anine had little to dress up in, so the conversation was needless. However, it was thoughtful of Talia's mother to mention it. Lateda withdrew into the carriage, and Anine let it move ahead of her while she mulled over this development.

That evening, Anine made an effort to clean herself up, splashing most of the road dust away in the basin in her room, finding a clean blouse in the bottom of her pack and wearing a bit less armament than usual. She attended Lady Trenet at her room and was surprised to be asked in. Lateda curtseyed as she made the invitation to put Anine in the picture. Anine nodded. *The informality is a matter of degree*. She squared her shoulders and entered.

Lord and Lady Trenet had the largest suite of rooms in the inn, if a bedroom and sitting room could be called a suite. There was evidence of enhancement of the usual decor, with bright carpets and curtains of a quality which had never graced that room before. A table had been set for two. Her pause was ever so slight, but the bright eyes of the older lady picked it up.

"Please come in, Anine, and sit down. I have been looking forward to getting to know you better."

Anine took her usual refuge in silence. She sat carefully on the small chair, glad she had left her longsword off her belt. She looked with what she hoped was polite interest at the face of the woman across from her. The warm candlelight eased the pallor of the skin, but drew fine lines around the mouth and eyes, lines that could have been caused by pain. The lady signalled Lateda, who poured a deep amber wine into a glass that disappeared in Anine's hand. Observing the other woman's actions, she shifted her grip to finger and thumb.

Lady Trenet raised her glass. "To my daughter and her new husband."

Anine nodded, raised her glass, figured out that she was not meant to touch the other's rim, and drank a sip. The wine was good, probably better than she had the tongue to tell, and it slid down beautifully, leaving a smoky flavour in her mouth. She sipped again, savouring the aroma.

"Do you like the wine?"

"I do, my Lady. It's not a variety we get in Petrella."

"You don't? That's good to know. It is called Trenet Bisro, and it is from our own vineyards. Lateda, did we bring enough?"

"There's never enough of the Bisro, my Lady."

The lady raised her eyebrows. "Just make sure some gets spread around once we get there." She gave Anine a look that on a lesser person would have been a grin. "We must not miss the opportunity to show our wares."

"I'm sure it would sell well in Petrella, my Lady. Especially in the heat of summer."

"That's fine. Don't feel you have to hold back. We have enough for tonight."

"I won't overtax your cellars, my Lady."

"Never really off duty?"

"That's right, my Lady."

The lady nodded as if approving, and glanced at Lateda, who immediately served the first course, an appetizer of small morsels of some kind of white meat, folded in leaves of lettuce. Anine waited to see which fork her hostess used, then tried a bite. Then she looked up.

"Are you expecting my comment on everything you serve, my Lady?"

The lady chuckled. "Only if you find something very good or very bad. I didn't invite you here to experiment on you."

Again, Anine felt that a response was not needed, and she concentrated on enjoying the appetizer. She felt comfortable with people who didn't need to fill every moment with talking.

It was during the main course, a stew from the inn's kitchen, perhaps with some help from northern spices, that Lady Trenet broached the reason for the invitation.

"It is good to spend some time with you, Anine."

"Thank you, my Lady."

"You are perhaps wondering why I invited you?"

"No, my Lady."

"Are you not the curious type, Anine?"

"I save my curiosity for where it's needed, my Lady. I consider it reasonable for you to wish to learn more about me."

"Because of your relationship with my daughter."

"That's how I saw it."

"So did I."

The older woman nodded. There was a moment of silence, which Anine used to enjoy a spicy biscuit that had never come from the kitchen of an inn. She looked up to see the other's eyes upon her.

A smile quirked Lady Trenet's lip. "Silence is a useful tool, is it not?"

"I hadn't thought of it that way. I just don't find it useful to talk if I have nothing to say." She paused, regarded her hostess. "And, like right now, it's an invitation to the other to give more information. What would you like to know?"

This time, the older woman laughed out loud. "What I want to know about you has nothing to do with questions and answers. It would be useful, though, for you to fill me in on what life is like in Petrella, from your point of view."

"And you can draw your conclusions by what you observe about me while I talk."

The lady's face became serious. "I wish to draw no conclusions about you, Anine."

"This isn't about me."

"Correct. It's about my daughter."

There was another pause while Lateda cleared their plates away and deposited a platter of cheeses and fruits between them. Once again, Anine took advantage of the lull to enjoy the food. They had always eaten well at home and her mother had been a formidable cook, so she could appreciate the subtleties of the flavours.

"This goat cheese is very good. Do you make that?"

"Unfortunately not. It is a favourite of mine as well, which I import from Kyabra when I can get it."

"Thank you for sharing it with me."

"Your appreciation is the only thanks I need."

Anine glanced up at her hostess. "Are you beginning to understand about Talia?"

The lady looked at her sharply, then relaxed, ever so slightly. "Yes." She shook her hand in a negative gesture. "Oh, the obvious part I knew even before she left. The frontier is the place for someone like her. I believe I even envy her. She is big and bold and moves too fast. There is no space for her in our dainty drawing rooms. That part was a chance we took, and it has paid off."

Lady Trenet looked at Anine, then leaned closer. "It is the rest of it that I need to know about."

310

"What rest of it, my Lady?"

She tossed up her hands. "It is hard to explain. Let me put it this way. I know about the meeting with Lord Teremsla."

"I see."

Another smile quirked the pale lips. "Yes, my husband took great pleasure in telling me every detail. He was so pleased." Again, she leaned forward. "My question for you is this. As her commanding officer, what is your opinion? Did she do well?"

Anine shrugged, grinning. "You can't argue with success, my Lady. From what I gather, Lord Teremsla disappeared from town the next day, couldn't get over the border fast enough."

"We have made an enemy."

"It's not my place to say, but I don't think what Lord Trenet said or what Talia did had any effect on the situation with Lord Teremsla, my Lady."

"I have to agree. He could never have been an ally."

"As far as her actions went, it's hard to call them, too. No mercenary could have stepped in as she did when her lord was challenged by another noble. However, Talia wasn't a mercenary, so she could, she did and it worked. Talia follows orders, but she can think for herself. I've said it before, though I don't suppose it will help you any," she grinned, "but I'd have her in my troop any time. She'd make a good soldier and a better officer."

Lady Trenet leaned back. "It does help me, Anine. It helps me to see that Talia can truly function in this environment. She isn't just a silly girl, banging naively around in a situation that she enjoys."

"There may have been a bit of that at first." Anine rocked her hand back and forth. "We got that bashed out of her pretty quick."

"I gather."

"It was necessary, my Lady."

"I'm sure it was. Now I have another question."

"Yes, my Lady."

"She killed a man."

Anine waited, but there was no more. "That's not a question, my Lady."

"Excuse me. There is no doubt that she killed him?"

"No doubt at all, my Lady. Umm...did you hear the details?"

"I was told they were attacked, and she had to defend herself."

"And that's all?"

"That is why I am talking to you, Anine. I do not wish my tender sensibilities protected."

"All right, my Lady. If you really want the details. We were attacked, and it was an uneven fight, six on four. Two of our guards were forced into desperation moves that left them defenceless. Her cousin Varlinden was down at her feet, in trouble. She blocked the knife of her opponent with her forearm guard, and took a swing at the man who was attacking Varli. A big swing. My Lady, she...uh...she took his head off."

"She what?"

Lateda started forward, but her mistress forcibly settled herself back into her chair, gesturing the maid away. She stared at Anine. "She took a man's head off? With one swing?"

"She was in a great hurry, my Lady, and she swings a heavy sword."

"I see." There was a pause while the lady took this in. "How did she handle it? Afterward."

"Tears, horror, about what you'd expect."

"What you would expect from whom?"

"From any decent person who isn't crazy to fight and kill people."

Lady Trenet nodded grimly. "Does she have to learn to fight?"

Anine shrugged. "Whether she has to doesn't matter, my Lady. She wants to."

Another slow nod. "That's always been true. If Talia really wants something, very little else matters. Is she any good?"

"Not yet, but she will be. She learns fast and has a strong wrist. And the right attitude."

Lady Trenet leaned back, and Anine could see the stiffness falling away from her spine. After a moment, the duchess motioned to Lateda, who served fine glasses of spiced tea. She took one sip, then turned her attention back to her visitor.

"Anine, I would like to thank you for coming this evening, and for everything you have done to help my daughter cope in her new life. In return, I will tell you something.

"I was like Talia when I was young. I was big, I was impulsive and I bumped into people. Physically and socially."

Anine nodded.

"But I was not like Talia. I decided to fit in. I made up my mind to cope with my life. Of course, I succeeded. But I lost something of myself as well."

"I can understand that, my Lady. It's difficult to become someone you really aren't."

"That's right. So, when I brought up my daughter, I think I nurtured the part of her that I was missing. The rebel, the one who was different. I didn't do it on purpose, but I did it, all the same."

"I see. And when she determined on this crazy journey, you thought it was your fault. You thought you had brought your daughter up wrong."

The older woman nodded. "I was worried sick. Yes, sick. I don't know how much of my illness was caused by my own mind or how much my worry weakened me, to allow the real illness to fester. But I was worried. What if she had died out there? It would have been all my fault."

Anine smiled. "You know, my Lady, we have some books in Petrella that you ought to read. Old, old books, not the originals, but copies made of copies, from centuries ago. There's a woman called Sarasha the Lame, and she says some funny things, and some right things. She has something to say to you."

"Oh? And what would this Sarasha the Lame from centuries ago have to tell me about bringing up my daughter?"

"Something like, 'Once a child has grown, it's too late for blame.'"

"Whose blame?"

"Sarasha doesn't tend to explain herself. I guess both ways. The child's responsible for what she does, and she can't blame her parents for it. Nor can they blame themselves, for the same reason."

"Well, that may be easy for Sarasha the Lame to say, but when you've just driven your daughter out into the wilderness where she may die, it's a bit harder."

"Utter nonsense, my Lady."

"Pardon me?" The steel was back in the spine now. Lateda stepped forward, ready for action.

Anine looked from one to the other. "That is pure melodrama, my Lady, and you wouldn't put up with it from your daughter or from anyone else. You didn't drive Talia into the wilderness. She went

313

because she wanted to go. You say you couldn't stop her; how could you have made her go?"

The wrinkled mouth twisted, and the eyes held Anine's. "You may be right. You certainly are an outspoken woman."

"My Lady, Talia is my friend. You're her mother. If I see you making a mistake, I feel it is my duty to correct you."

"You feel responsible for me?"

"Of course. If I saw you about to put your foot in a hole, shouldn't I warn you?"

"This is a bit different, I think."

"I don't see it that way. In the mercenaries, we looked after each other. Sometimes we might have been a bit rough about it, but we took care of our friends."

"And you consider calling my concerns melodramatic nonsense 'a bit rough' do you?"

"Did you want me to pat you on the back and say, 'there, there,' my Lady? What good would that have done?"

The older woman sighed. "My life has come to a pretty pass when a young woman can call me a fool to my face and I have to thank her for it."

"You're welcome, my Lady. Think of it as coming from Sarasha the Lame. I gather she was a bit outspoken herself."

Lady Trenet sat back again. "A quality I will probably see more of as we move into the south."

Lateda moved forward quietly, and a signal passed.

"Yes, Lateda, I am tired. I do not wish to be rude, Anine, but I do thank you for joining me. Perhaps we may repeat the occasion at some future time?"

"I would be honoured, my Lady." She grinned. "I could even promise to mind my manners, if you like."

"Oh, don't do that. It would make for such a boring time."

Anine had risen to leave, but the duchess called her back. "Just one more point, Anine, before you go."

"Yes, my Lady?"

"I want you to hear this. Lateda, come here."

The maid stepped forward. "Yes, my Lady?"

"Do you remember, Lateda, that we have some friends who are good friends? Friends who are to be protected?"

"Yes, my Lady."

314

"Anine is such a friend, Lateda. Do you understand?"

The wiry maid looked up at Anine, her eyes narrowed. "I thought so already, my Lady, but now I know."

"Good." The duchess turned to Anine. "Lateda sometimes misses the subtler nuances of society. It's best to say things straight to her."

"Thank you for clarifying the situation for her, my Lady." She winked at Lateda. "I'll sleep better."

The maid nodded seriously. Anine could not remember ever hearing her laugh.

Lateda glided over and opened the door. Anine paused at the entrance, bowed formally, then turned away. The door closed silently behind her, and she paced back to her room, deep in thought.

27. LEILE

There was, as usual, a lot to do, so she was still tossing ideas back and forth in her head on the road the next morning when Talia nudged her horse in beside her.

"Didn't see you at dinner last night."

She glanced over, raising her nose a touch. "Don't you find it boring, mingling with the common rabble? I prefer to dine in solitude with the nobility. So much more enlightening."

Talia chuckled. "Now, that was pure Gavess."

"He's very good at things like that. Better than you are, actually. I wonder why that is?"

Talia shrugged. "I never had to try, I guess. Never wanted to."

"I think that speaks to your strength of character."

"I certainly hope so."

"Take the compliments when you can get them, kid."

"You certainly did all right."

Anine refused to rise to the bait. After a few more paces, Talia gave in.

"Mother says you're a natural."

"Whatever that means."

"She said you don't really know much etiquette, but you manage to follow it anyway."

Anine grinned. "She means I don't know her etiquette."

"What do you mean?"

"Don't you think there's etiquette in a merc troop? They don't call it etiquette, but it could save your life if you follow it."

"I never thought of it that way. Of course. The Inari have their own customs, now that you draw it to my attention."

"As do the farming people I come from. It's just different. Once you've had to live in a few different cultures, you learn how to cope."

"How do you cope?"

"I don't know. Mainly you just take your time, don't rush into anything. Watch people and copy what they do. If you mess up, smile." She considered briefly. "If you're with truly gracious people, there's always plenty of hints. That covers most of the problems. If it doesn't, there's always this." She slapped the sword hilt at her side.

"Anine! You don't mean that."

Anine shrugged. "It's always there. People tend not to call me on small slips I make."

"Does that include my mother?"

"No. She didn't call me because she's a lady and it would have been beneath her to notice." Anine rode in silence for a while. "I like your mother."

"You do?"

"Is that so strange? I like you. I respect your father. Why wouldn't I like her?"

"But you're so different."

"Not completely. We were just brought up different. She made herself into something she didn't start out to be. I have the opportunity to do that, but I'm not sure I want to."

"Something she didn't start out to be? Whatever are you talking about?"

Anine glanced across and grinned. "That was a private conversation. If you want to know, ask her."

"I just might do that."

"You just might be pleased you did."

Anine raised a hand and turned aside to check yet another disturbance back down the line of march. It still surprised her, when she had time to think about it. She had often thought that being on the road was boring. Candle after candle of trudging, trotting or slogging with nothing to break the monotony. Being in charge changed all that. Once you knew you were responsible, every small hiccup in the day's progress shouted out to you, and there were many of them.

Having ascertained that in this case, the recalcitrant mule had been re-harnessed to prevent him from loosening his traces, she cantered alongside the line to the head and then sat to watch them all pass, a small degree of pride burning inside her.

Then her eye caught another anomaly. There, in the line of riders, was an empty saddle. She waited until the unladen horse approached and saw that someone was leading it. Walking. Curious, she waited until the pair got close enough to identify the walker. Leile.

The girl glanced up with a friendly smile as Anine swung in beside her.

"Problem?"

"No."

"You like walking?"

"Yes."

Anine thought that over. Several responses occurred to her, but she discarded them. If the girl wanted to walk, why shouldn't she? If she couldn't keep up, she could get back on her horse. There would be no difficulty. Unless...

"If there's any trouble, get back ahorse as quickly as you can."

"Certainly. Are you expecting anything specific?"

"No. It's my duty to expect something in general, and you on foot in the middle of a battle is not my idea of helpful."

"I'll keep my eyes open."

"Fine."

She held her position for a while, noting that Leile paced out with a fine, long stride, keeping up to the horses' travel gait easily. There was a slight wind from the east, so the dust did not bother her.

After a few bowshots of walking, something seemed to occur to the girl. She swung lithely into her saddle again and moved next to Anine.

"Who is that?"

Anine looked ahead, to where two of the Inari scouts had just pulled up to report to Lukin. "Which one?"

Leile merely raised her eyebrows.

"Ah. Him. He isn't just one of the regular scouts. That's Mantinello, my aide-de-camp."

"Can he speak to us?"

"In Petrellan, Kyabran, Chinotuk, or Inarituk?" Anine grinned. "Want to meet him?"

"Not necessarily. I just noticed him. He seems to be around a lot. You know. More than the others."

"Sort of like I am."

"Now that you mention it."

"He functions for the Inari like I function for the rest of you. He's the one who passes along the instructions, sends information to whoever needs it the most. He's a very bright lad."

She glanced at her smaller companion. "Handsome, too."

"Hmm."

On an impulse, Anine whistled, once, briefly, and not loud. Up ahead, Mantinello's head came up. He glanced back at her, raised a hand briefly, and continued his discussion. However, he soon broke away and pulled his horse out of the line, waiting for Anine to approach.

"Anything I need to know?"

He nodded his head politely to Leile before replying. "Not our problem, I think, Anine. Three dead sheep. Wolves."

"You tell anyone?"

"Best to let someone more..." he grinned over at Leile, "...normal speak to the local people. Not polite to frighten them."

"Very thoughtful of you. Mantinello, please be known to Talia's friend Leile. Leile, I present my aide-de-camp Mantinello."

He nodded again, the only gesture the Inari ever used to acknowledge anyone. "Ah. The Lady of Manners. I am honoured."

Leile had copied the nod, smiling pleasantly, but his comment brought her up short, frowning. "Lady of what?"

His smile was more open and friendly than usual. "The lady with the perfect manners. The others have noticed."

Leile raised her eyebrows. "What others?"

Mantinello turned in apparent confusion to Anine. "I have made a mistake? It is not polite to say a lady has good manners?"

Anine laughed.

They both looked at her.

"Mantinello, you can try to bamboozle Leile with your 'poor foreigner who doesn't understand' act, but don't try it on me."

He shrugged, turned to Leile. "I saw you before. It is good to walk sometimes."

Leile hesitated, and Anine wondered if she was going to let him get away with the quick change of subject. She was.

"Yes, I find a whole day on horseback is not good for me. I cannot move so well at the end."

He nodded. "My people are known here, below the Edge of the World, as riders of the Great Prairies. They think we ride everywhere, but every day we also walk. It is good for the horse, and it is good for us."

Anine had often felt that the amount of time the Inari spent on the ground was more than necessary for tracking, and this confirmed it. "How do you know when to walk, when to ride? Are there rules?"

He shook his head. "When we feel like walking, we walk. When we feel like riding again, we ride."

Leile gave Anine a 'so there' look, and Anine grinned. "I've just been warning her to get back in the saddle if there's any trouble."

"A good idea." He looked over at the smaller girl. "However, if there is a battle and you lose your horse, look for our remuda. They are at the back of the march."

"Why your remuda?"

"Inari horses are used to being ridden without saddles. If you grab a mane and swing astride from either side they will not throw you. They will also stay with the other horses, so you will not get lost. Also, you will be safer."

"Why is that?"

"If my Lady wishes, I could tell a lesson."

"I'm hardly a lady, Mantinello. I'm barely more than a commoner. Please call me Leile. What kind of lesson do you wish to teach me?"

Receiving a nod from Anine, he continued. "Well, Leile, it is a thing with horses that perhaps you have noticed. Perhaps not, in these tame lands. When danger threatens a herd of wild horses, the weaker members move to the centre and the stallions and younger mares confront the enemy."

"I can understand that, but how will that protect me?"

"If a horse has a rider on his back, he is slower. He feels less free to fight. If you do not guide him, he will be uncertain. Thus he will go to the centre of the remuda. You will be safe."

She nodded. "Very logical. Thank you, Mantinello. I do not plan to be caught without my horse, but if I am, I will consider your remuda."

She paused. "And now you will tell me about the Lady of Manners."

He rode in silence. He did not shrug, but Anine could see the set of his shoulders change. He glanced over at his new acquaintance, just once, as if assessing her mood.

"It is a thing with people who are visitors to watch the manners of their hosts carefully, to keep from making mistakes, yes?"

She nodded.

"So, we notice you, because your manners are so perfect. First one notices, he tells others, then we all notice. We watch you, to learn good manners."

She looked at him, he waited, but she did not look away.

Again, the unseen shrug. "And the others notice as well. They have...other interpretation."

"And these others are...?"

"Lukin's Guard. The young lords of Petrella."

"And what is their interpretation?" Her voice was level, perhaps a bit too even.

"It is only young men, talking about girls, Leile. It is not meant in harm."

"But...?"

"I think..." he paused as if to consider. Anine knew it was an act, but she hid her grin and watched.

"I think they see the manners as a wall, a protection."

"In what way?"

"In the way that manners are always a wall between people." His head suddenly came up, and his demeanor changed. "Excuse me please, ladies. I do not have the leisure to speak further." With a glance to Anine for permission, he urged his horse to a quick trot and was soon lost in the dust towards the front of the procession.

"An interesting fellow."

"I suppose."

Leile frowned up at Anine. "I thought he was your aide? Don't you like him?"

Anine laughed. "I like him fine. I just don't always like what he's doing."

"What was he doing?"

Anine looked down at the smaller woman. "All right. I have divided loyalties, Leile. Mantinello is Clan, and my officer, and I normally wouldn't tell you this. But he's a boy, and you're a girl and a friend of Lady Talia's at that. So I'll tell you."

"Tell me what?"

"Don't trust him."

"What? You're telling me not to trust your most trusted aide?"

"Exactly. Let me tell you something else. Mantinello is the slickest politician I have ever met. He never makes a mistake in manners. He never says anything if he isn't sure exactly the effect it will have on anyone."

"So?"

"So if you think that all that 'oops, have I made an error, please excuse me' act was for real then you've been taken in, and I'm sure there will be more to come."

"You're serious?"

"Never more. Just think how fast he came up with that line. What does that tell you? Think it through."

Leile mused a while. "I suppose, if what you're telling me is true, that he had it already planned. It means that he had already noted me, and was just waiting for his chance." A thought hit her, and she twisted in the saddle to look directly at Anine. "Should I be flattered?"

"Probably. Also a little bit afraid."

"Of what?"

"In the two years that I've known him, I've never seen him turn his skills on one of the local women."

"And I should be afraid…?"

"That he's serious."

"Oh."

They rode in silence and Anine watched the emotions play across Leile's face. The thought of Mantinello's attention obviously did not displease her, but then a more serious idea came. There seemed to be some sort of conflict there, because when Anine gradually slowed her horse, the other did not seem to notice.

Well, she had done her duty. The woman had been warned. Anine shook her head. Mantinello had succeeded in surprising her again.

The next day, she took advantage of the chance to talk to Talia. "Tell me about your friend, Leile."

"Certainly. Not exactly my type, is she?"

"It wouldn't seem so, at first, but I have seen many such unlike pairs of friends."

Talia nodded. "She looks and acts like the others, but inside, she isn't."

"The Clan call her the Lady of Manners."

"Is that good or bad?"

"Mostly good. I figure you've been friends for a while?"

"Since school. We were sort of thrown together. I was…well, I was me, and you know what that meant in a bunch of teenaged girls. She was different as well, and she's not very high in the social scale."

"And that didn't endear her to them."

"No. However, her family is rich, so there she was."

Anine ripened her vowels. "Nothing worse than uppity new money."

"Precisely. We became friends, and now we might become more than that."

"How so?"

"Well, you know dear cousin Varli is getting to an age…"

"She's going to marry Varli?"

"Not necessarily. But their fathers have business interests together and his old family with her new money would make a good match."

"If they like each other."

"Exactly. I know it seems like the children of nobility get married off for mercenary reasons…oops, I guess I shouldn't use that term in a negative way, should I? And sometimes we do. Usually, though, we get some say in how it works out."

"Hence you and Gerth?"

Talia shrugged. "I was considered…less tractable than most."

"To your credit."

"Thank you."

"She's coming along on this trip to check out the new, grown-up Varli. I hope she deserves him."

"Clan loyalty?"

"Sure. But personally, I like him. He's a great diplomat in his own way, and I think he'll do well. He won't be an easy husband, but his wife will never be bored."

Talia laughed. "Have you heard the old Historian's Blessing?"

"What's that?"

"Something like, 'May the gods bless you with a life in a boring era.'"

"Sounds like the Mercenary's Quandary. 'May my children grow up in a time when their father is out of a job.' I think that's another from Sarasha the Lame."

"Actually, it's from Haskel's *Code of the Mercenary*."

"Are you sure? I could have sworn I read it in that old book in the castle library, you know, the one with all the quotes."

Talia grinned. "Maybe it's in both of them."

"Interesting coincidence."

"Not if it's been around as long as Haskel's *Code*."

"Aye, but I don't think Sarasha talked about mercenaries much."

"You know something about her?"

"Zoysana told me. There's a lot of legend about her, to go along with the books. Apparently she was some sort of genius, led our people through some terrible time or other, no one knows what. Died a hero's death, sacrificed herself so the king could live, or something like that. You know legends. One says she took on a puma with her bare hands, one says she stopped an avalanche. How she did that, I can't figure.

"She really was lame, apparently, from some terrible battle wound. Never married."

"Because of the lameness?"

"Maybe she couldn't find anyone who wasn't afraid of her tongue."

"I've read some of her quotes. She certainly didn't take time to be polite."

"Zoysana used the word 'incisive.' Like a sharp knife, she said."

"That pretty well sums her up." Talia sighed. "I hope being different doesn't always have such a tragic ending."

Anine clapped her friend on the shoulder. "Don't worry. I figure as long as you don't push it in people's faces, they'll usually let it ride. If not..." she slapped her sword in that familiar, comforting gesture. "After all, you're going to be the queen. I doubt if you'll have any problem."

The other girl looked doubtful. "I don't know, Anine. I grew up as the duke's daughter and it didn't seem to help me much." She grinned pointedly at Anine's sword. "I think I better keep up my arms practice."

"Well, that'll never do you any harm, anyway."

They shared a comfortable smile, then jogged along peacefully together.

28. Night and Rain

The day wore on and the clouds moved in. Anine looked over her shoulder at the sky to the west, where the tops of the nearby hills were becoming misty and indistinct. She muttered an imprecation to the weather gods and tugged her slicker from behind her saddle. Once it was draped around her, she moved her horse along the line, making sure that everyone was prepared. When she reached the head, she swung in beside Lukin. "What's it look like to you?"

He grimaced. "You're the farmer. You're supposed to know about these things."

She snorted. "Farmers know about praying for good weather and complaining when it's not."

"What are you doing at the moment?"

She shrugged, rustling the oiled cloth about her shoulders. "Preparing to complain a lot, I guess."

He nodded. "I'm afraid I agree. Can we make dry camp tonight?"

She passed her mind over the road ahead. "We were planning to stay with Lord Chiesa tonight, but if the road gets slippery, we won't make it. Second choice is the inns at Talbigan."

He considered. "I'd say wait a candle. If it's still raining, we'll send somebody ahead to arrange for Talbigan."

She nodded and pulled her horse back down the line to where one rear wheel of a wagon had slipped into the ditch because of careless driving on a corner. She dressed down the teamster for his error, but not too seriously. His accident was only the first of many to come, if the spring weather in the South showed its usual temperament.

And so it did. For the next five days the sky was dark clouds one moment and bright sunshine the next, but the road was always wet. Schedules were adapted and re-adapted as the mud took its toll on the straining horses. Tempers wore thin and clothing remained muddy, despite the best efforts of the maids at the inns and manors where they stayed.

On the sixth night, the leaders met in the common room of the biggest inn of the smallest town they had been stuck in yet. Lord Trenet looked around the table. "We are getting far behind schedule. Is this a problem?"

Eyes centred on Lukin. "Not necessarily, my Lord. The only problem might be if our friends from former years decided to take advantage to catch up with us. We left Trenet in good time, but mounted messengers could pass us easily in conditions like this."

"You don't think our enemies are following us?"

"No, they'd run into the same problems we have. The only possibility is if they have troops already in front of us and all they need is a go-ahead message."

"What do you suggest we do about this?"

"Nothing specific, my Lord. We maintain our safety shield at all times. There is no sense in weakening our men by putting them on double watches after a long day of slogging through the mud."

"What if we're attacked?"

"We're counting on our scouts to warn us. Between the Guides and the Inari, we have the best coverage I have ever seen. I have no worries that any force big enough to give us serious trouble will slip through their net."

"But they don't have to give us serious trouble, sir."

"Why not, Anine?"

"These people don't have to wipe us out or even give us a decent battle to accomplish their ends. All they have to do is demonstrate, once again, that the roads are not safe."

Lukin and Trenet exchanged a look. It was the soldier who continued. "What do you suggest, Anine?"

"Thinking like an Inari, sir, there is only one solution."

Lukin grinned. "Attack, I suppose."

"That's right, sir."

"Even if we are outnumbered?"

"As you have just suggested, we probably won't be outnumbered. Unless they can pull in a lot of local help..." Her voice trailed off as the thoughts hit her. "Once we get to Velikiii...?"

The soldier nodded. "That would be the place. Plenty of disaffected nobility, ready at the drop of a glove to give the Arlyns a slap in the face."

"Velikii in four days, sir. Five at the most, even in this weather. They wouldn't attack right away. Let us get into their territory, is my guess."

"Then six or seven days to be thinking about what we can do." Lukin looked to the duke for a nod of permission. "Spread the word. Any ideas, we're listening."

The meeting broke up on that grim note.

For the next quarter the party moved slower, taking pains to keep in proper order, eyes sharp, swords loose. Equipment was checked carefully every night. No teamster wanted to break down in the middle of a running battle. The Inari took special care of their mounts, each man breaking out the small bundle of special food that his clanspeople had developed to keep the horses at their best form in tough conditions. The Knights and Warlanders saw to their weapons; the squires checked their masters' armour and horses.

Even those who were merely passengers showed their concern. Lateda flagged Anine down one afternoon, and she pulled her mud-caked horse to a grateful walk beside the carriage. Lady Trenet herself pulled aside the leather curtain.

"This seems to be a very orderly progression, Anine."

"We're doing our best, your Grace. We will not be surprised."

"I assume not. What do you expect of the non-combatants in case of an attack?"

"Your best spot is in the carriage, your Grace. No arrow can pierce the sides, the windows are small, and it is easily recognized and defended."

"Also easily recognized by the enemy."

"Unfortunately true. I see no ruse to help that which does not involve you on horseback."

A new set of wrinkles appeared briefly at the corners of the Lady's eyes. "If it were not for the gravity of the situation, I might find that image humorous. I will stay in my carriage."

"Thank you, your Grace. You will be well protected. Half of your Knights and half of our Warlanders are assigned to your defence."

"What? A full half? And the others are left to defend the whole rest of the procession? I find that flattering, but hardly good tactics."

"Not just yourself, your Grace. The other carriages and the supply wagons as well."

"Good. I should have known I wasn't worth that much."

"Oh, you are, your Grace. The others are just an excuse to mass our power here."

Lady Trenet waited while the wagon jounced along a few paces, her eye never leaving Anine's face. "Do I detect a note of sarcasm?"

Anine suppressed a smile. "Oh, no, your Grace. That would be highly unbecoming for one in my position, and would demonstrate a complete lack of appropriate respect for one of your status. Levity of that sort would be of no use to either of us. I must respectfully suggest that your Ladyship is in error."

"Hmm. My daughter has told me about you and your accents. They always mean something."

Anine merely inclined her head gracefully. "Is your Ladyship satisfied with the arrangements?"

Her Ladyship snorted in a very unladylike manner, and waved Anine away. "I'm sure you have more important things to do than reassure an old woman of her safety."

Anine bowed as respectfully as one could from a saddle and wearing a bulky rain slicker. "Always happy to be of service, your Grace."

The curtain closed on another cynical snort, and Anine pushed ahead, chuckling to herself.

She wasn't chuckling that night when they had to bivouac on a small farm, with the nobility commandeering the farmhouse and the rest the barns and storage sheds. She was making her usual rounds when a clamour of loud voices from in front of the cowshed brought her sprinting.

As she rounded the corner there was a hissed warning and the tableau froze: one of the squires and one of her Inari, facing each other across naked blades in the firelight. At her appearance, their weapons wavered, and both heads turned towards her. Too late. She pounced on them, a hand on either neck, and shook them until the weapons dropped to the mud. When they were both limp in her grasp, she dropped them, and they staggered for balance.

"I'm not going to ask what that was all about, because I don't care."

"But he…"

She took half a step forward. "I said I'm not going to ask, Squire, and that means you don't want me to ask. You wouldn't like the answers I found. We are in a tight situation here, and we all know it. The last thing we need is squabbling among ourselves. The way I see it, if anyone can't keep himself under control in this situation, it's because he is afraid. Get that? Afraid." She added the Inari word, to make sure they both understood. They did. An incredulous look crossed each face, and she could see them both puffing up like roosters.

"I know, I know. You're going to tell me you're not afraid. If you're so brave, keep yourself under control. If you're so brave, pick up those weapons and get out on patrol until midnight. The two of you go together. And stay together. If you don't come back together, don't come back at all." Her voice had dropped to the grate of iron on stone, and they leaned forward to hear her.

"Do you understand?" This last blasted them back on their heels, and both nodded frantically, scrabbling for their swords in the dirt.

"And one more thing!"

They froze.

"Both of you dropped your guard and turned away from an opponent with a drawn weapon. If it wasn't for the fact that you might need your swords any moment, I'd break them! Now get out on patrol!"

They scrambled away and she turned her stare to the other boys. "And the rest of you. How could you let this happen? You are supposed to be looking after each other." She waved a hand in disgust. "No, don't tell me your excuses. Mantinello!"

"Yes, ma'am."

"I want a full report in half a candle."

"Yes, ma'am."

She strode away, moderately satisfied. It was bound to happen, with this kind of pressure on youngsters, even experienced fighters like the Clan. The waiting game was the hardest, and neither Petrellans nor Inari were very good at it. No harm done, a bit of steam blown off and authority re-established.

Anine pushed through the farmhouse door and reported the incident to Lukin and Lord Trenet, who were occupying themselves by the dim light from the fireplace.

"Which squire was it? I'll deal with him in the morning."

"I'd rather you didn't, my your Grace."

"Why not?" Trenet frowned. "He is trained to do better than that."

"No, your Grace, he isn't."

"Pardon me?"

"What you mean, your Grace, is that you have tried to train him to do better than that. If he doesn't do better than that, then you didn't train him to do better, did you?"

"Don't play logic games with me, young lady. That lad has besmirched his honour and betrayed the trust placed in him."

Anine straightened her shoulders. "And he's bin dealt with in the way he shoulda bin. We're gettin' into a military situation, your Grace, and this here's a matter of military discipline."

The duke was about to rise when his daughter's voice stopped him. "Did you hear it, Father?"

"Did I hear what?"

Lady Talia merely nodded towards Anine. "I told you."

"Oh." He sat back and looked at Anine, whose puzzled glance went from father to daughter and back.

"Oh." He relaxed more, and a grin began to form. "She did, didn't she? Just like last time."

His daughter nodded. "Just like I said. And you know what it means."

"Yes. I understand." The duke turned to the stunned woman. "I'm sorry, Anine, you are right. It's a military matter, and I'm sure it's better for the two of them that you handled it the way you did. Come to think of it, it's better for the whole troop if you treated them equally. I bow to your judgement."

Lukin leaned forward in his chair, as puzzled as Anine. "Have I missed something?"

Talia laughed. "Probably. It's Anine. I warned my father already. You have to listen to her grammar."

"Her grammar?"

"When she loses her posh accent and starts sounding like a mercenary, it's a military matter, and time to listen to her."

"Oh." The old soldier looked from one to the other. "Well, I don't pretend to understand, but it seems to have solved a thorny little problem. We're all honed too sharp and stretched too thin, and I'm glad we got through this with nobody hurt."

"A little spat like this, handled well, is good for their morale, sir. Sharpens 'em up."

"I agree, Anine." He glanced towards the duke. "Begging your pardon, your Grace, but saving her Grace's presence, I'd be happy

330

if they did attack. We're at top readiness for battle. We'll never be better prepared."

"I'd have to agree. What do you think? Some time in the next two days?"

"If our analysis is correct. We crossed the border this morning."

"Then I'd better go sharpen my sword."

"Again?"

The duke paused in the doorway. "Anine, have you been watching me?"

"She watches everyone, Father."

"I suppose she does." He turned up the stairs to the loft.

Lukin and Anine exchanged a satisfied look. The old Warlander nodded, once, and returned to the job he had been doing when Anine entered. He, too, was sharpening his sword.

* * *

Mantinello, slid in beside her on his mud-spattered horse. "Right on schedule, Anine."

"Found them?"

He nodded. "They're waiting a few candles ahead. Placed carefully, just this side of Leoning. If we push ahead to the town, they surprise us on the road. If we camp before then, they hit us at night in tents."

"Any danger close by?"

"No sign. We have discouraged their scouts, but they are going to be aware of us sooner or later."

"Fine. Let's go see our leaders."

They trotted ahead to Lord Trenet and Lukin, and Mantinello repeated his news. To his credit, Lord Trenet said nothing, merely looking to Lukin.

"They have an ambush prepared?"

"Yes. It is a well-chosen spot, and they would cause us a lot of trouble there."

"How many men, what sort?"

"About forty foot soldiers, ten mounted Knights. A few scouts. Less now than before."

Anine felt it necessary to explain Mantinello's satisfied smile. "Our Inari have been discouraging their scouts."

"I see. Are they well armed?"

"The Knights are, though not so well mounted as the Petrellans. The foot soldiers are armed, but not heavily. I think they are local levies. I have no reports of any mercenaries to match Anine's old troop."

Lukin nodded. "Any chance of an attack?"

The Inari lad shook his head in disappointment. "There are too many. If we took our main force ahead, we would not leave enough protection for the baggage train."

"If we wish to choose the ground we must camp and wait for them."

"I would agree, sir."

Lukin's eye swept the group, received nods from everyone except Anine, who spoke.

"Suggestions, anyone?"

"If you wish a good defensive spot," Mantinello pointed, "that ridge is perfect."

"I detect no enthusiasm."

"It would solve nothing. They could not attack, so they would wait. We would have to wait until help came."

Anine took in the indignant look on the duke's face. "I think we will not be looking for help, Mantinello. You have another spot?"

"Yes, two. The first would be the safest, yet they would still attack us. The second would be more interesting."

"Interesting?"

The Inari looked around. "You must see to understand. I have set a very close watch on this area, both Guides and Clan. It is safe to ride ahead and show you."

Again, the leaders exchanged glances and a decision was made. Just before they moved ahead, Lukin reined his horse back. "Rear guard out?"

Mantinello smiled and nodded. The old soldier gave his single, sharp nod and rode on.

As they moved up the road, the Inari explained his thoughts. "The first position is, as I say, the safest. We could stop, set up camp, and spend our time with what fortifications we could throw up. They would know we had seen them, accept our challenge, and come to attack." He pulled up at a sheltered meadow where a creek crossed the road.

"It is defensible."

Anine nodded, pointed. "A few tree trunks there, there, and over there. Coaches backed together under those trees, freight wagons against that rock. Yes, we could defend this against the force you mention. However...?"

"It would solve nothing. But there is a chance we can reverse the trap. Another spot, much closer to their ambush. They do not know they have been discovered. We could ride to the second spot, which looks like a poorer position, then stop quick, as if we just noticed them, and set up fast defenses. Come, I will show you."

Interested, the party moved forward for several bowshots.

"Here."

The leaders sat their horses, staring at the small field before them.

"You are right. It looks much less defendable. Our horse would be hampered by the rocks and a lack of room for a charge. Foot soldiers could move up through those low trees, and we couldn't get at them."

Anine peered around. "Where is the 'however', Mantinello?"

The lad waved a hand and moved off the road. He pushed his horse among a stand of poplars and disappeared. Puzzled, they followed him.

The trail opened immediately into a small bowl surrounded by steep rock walls. Almost opposite them, it ran out again through another stand of poplars. Mantinello sat proudly in the middle, pointing.

"Two archers, there and there, could protect the entrances. A fire at those two points would provide enough light in a night attack. Carriages can back against that wall for protection. Mounted can move through, sweep the flat and out again, to attack those on the road."

Lukin pushed his destrier out through the screen of trees, and was soon back through the first opening. "I see what you mean."

Anine had not moved. "Mantinello, have their scouts come anywhere close to us?"

"I think not. We have been very careful and not polite."

"They don't know how many we are."

"From a distance, yes. Exactly, no."

"Then we can hide our non-fighters in here with half our horse. Put up a smaller camp in front with a good number of wagons and tents. When they hit the front camp, it's full of fighters. Then the horse troop comes out from over there and surrounds them."

"I had thoughts like that."

Lukin's eyes darted around the clearing. "Mantinello, go back to the carriages. Pull all the Guides and Clan. Put squires on the Clan remuda and the Guides' spare horses. All your men out to keep this area from being scouted. I don't want them anywhere close enough for a count until our decoys are in place. Anine will signal you when we are ready. Then you can allow their scouts a restricted view. Got that?"

Mantinello nodded, a single, curt gesture that matched the Guard Captain's, and lifted his horse to a gallop back down the road.

"Anine, will you scout the archers' positions? The fire spots too. It will be a night attack. That or early morning." He turned to the duke. "Any ideas, my Lord?"

Trenet shook his head, smiling wryly. "This is where I find the advantage in allowing the professionals to do their task."

"Fine. Let's you and I ride around a bit, look for problems and vantage points."

They rode away, and Anine dismounted and scrambled up the rocks, her eyes roaming as she climbed.

Two candles later, as dusk approached, Anine and Lukin sat their horses at the entrance to the hidden dell and surveyed the camp outside.

"Looks quite normal, don't you think?"

"If you don't get close enough to see that there are no women moving around."

"In this weather, they'd be inside."

"Ah…that's something else, sir."

"What?"

"Do you remember your comment about farmers?"

The Captain slapped a mosquito on his neck and nodded. "What does your weather sense tell you, farmer?"

"Mosquitoes."

"I know. They seem to be pretty bad here. Glad we're not staying long."

"That's not it. Just before a big rain, the air feels different. The mozzies know it and they come out in swarms."

"Can you feel this?"

334

"Can't you?"

"I'm not sure. It's colder, damper."

"That's the feeling. There's going to be a real dump of rain tonight. It'll make everything more difficult."

"Any chance they won't attack?"

"It only makes it cold and wet for them. All they have to do is find our fires and our tents. We have to find them in the dark."

The old Warlander sighed. "Nothing more fun than a fight in the rain at night: can't see anything, can't get up a good gallop, and it rusts the armour. I'll take a good, straight charge on flat ground any day."

She grinned. "Dreaming, sir?"

"I'm beginning to think so. Let's do the rounds again and make sure we're battened down for a solid night of rain."

The evening meal went without incident and the rain increased gradually as darkness fell. By bedtime, it was a steady torrent. The paths between the tents were slick with running water. Those in the carriages had it a bit better, but there was scarcely room to stretch out. They had decided to keep the horses harnessed to the hidden wagons so that they could break out quickly if things went wrong. The horses slouched in their traces, ignoring the rain, munching from their nosebags.

Anine had left her sword in Lady Trenet's carriage, preferring a pair of Inari long knives for night work. Her helmet, at least, was waterproof. She blessed again the forethought of the armourer who had rolled the front edge above her eyes so the water poured to either side instead of over her face.

As far as they could tell, the enemy scouts had found the bait, and the foot soldiers were moving in. The Inari floated out and back, bringing reports, silencing enemy scouts, and even picking off the odd straggler. Unknown to the enemy, their supply wagons had been raided the moment they were far enough away not to hear the screams, and the horses had all been spirited off up the road some distance to await the coming of their new masters in the morning. The Inari refused to miss out on the chance to pick up a few good horses.

She had to hand it to the enemy leader. The soldiers rolled in with a huge gust of wind that covered their sound and a blast of rain that hid them. The first Anine knew of the attack was when one of the perimeter tents went over in a rush of dark shapes. There was a short moment of milling around while the soldiers slashing at the canvas realized that there was no one underneath, and then the battle was joined.

No one ever did put the whole of the battle together afterward; it was simply too confused. At the attack, the Knights and Warlanders who had been standing to their steeds mounted and rushed the foot soldiers. Lukin's hidden troop charged out from their concealment, taking the enemy horse from behind. For those on the ground, it was a confused mess of water and heaving bodies. No one knew how many went down under the swords of friends.

Anine paced in her position, resisting the temptation to move into the mêlée. Men she was responsible for were dying around her, and she stood in the dark and did nothing. She was responsible for the defence of the carriages. Her post was the first entrance to the hidden valley, to signal the fire lighters if the valley was attacked and drive off anyone who tried to enter. This was the easier task, as only three of the enemy came in her direction. If they had not come all together it would have been even easier, but as it was, one was down before he knew she was there, the second got in one cut before she removed his sword hand, and the third gave her a short go-around before she disarmed him and ran him through.

The carriage horses behind her became restless and she heard voices. She strained her eyes into the darkness, wondering if she should go back there, but she was loath to leave her post. Soon everything settled, and she stuck to her position. She stood in the rain and the dark, her eyes peeled for movement down among the campfires, but by that time there was very little. Firelight flickered on the tents, unmoving blobs showed the fallen, and everyone else seemed to be elsewhere.

When she was as sure as she could be that the enemy had withdrawn, she had a thought. She whistled, hard and long, the signal for "Follow." She thought she heard an answer from the night, but only one. She whistled again, twice, and left it at that. Then she went into the main camp to see how everyone had fared.

29. LINEAULT

Someone was throwing dry brush on the fires, and soon the area was lit. People were dragging the bodies of the wounded and the dead into the light, and she was gratified to see that the large pile seemed to be the one of enemy dead.

Then Mantinello was at her elbow. "Problem, Anine."

"What?"

"They went for the remuda."

"Damnation. Did they get them?"

"I do not think they meant to take them, just drive them away."

"Take a couple of men and go look for them, then."

"I heard your whistle. I sent most of our men to follow the retreat. The rest we need here."

"Double damnation. What do we do, then?"

"We wait. Our horses are well trained. They will not run far. Perhaps the other animals will stay with them. Perhaps not. In any case, much time will be wasted in the morning..."

She nodded, and they continued tidying up.

Some time later, Mantinello stopped and his head went up. "Horses. Many horses."

Her hands went to her knives. "Where?"

"Not Warlanders. Horses moving slowly. No hurry. Maybe..."

He was cut off by the appearance at the edge of the firelight of a small golden pony with a slim, dark figure astride. The horse wheeled and snorted, and several larger shapes back in the darkness stopped and stood there, heads low, waiting. Behind these, again, steam rose from a mass of dark backs.

Then the rider in front slid from her horse and stood there, holding tight to the mane, staring around the camp.

"Leile?" Anine strode forward. The girl turned to her. "What have you been doing? I thought you were back in the carriages."

The girl untwisted her hand from her mount's mane and made a short, staggering step forward. The horse moved forward as well, snuffling at her rider's shoulder. Leile shook herself and stood straighter. "I was in the carriages when the battle started. Then there was a big uproar. Somebody snuck in and was messing with the carriage horses. Lady Trenet sent me to get you and sent Lateda out to deal with the intruders. Talia stayed with her father and mother. I saw you, but I couldn't get to you because you were fighting. Then I got cut off, and I couldn't get back to the carriages."

She turned to fix Mantinello with a hard stare. "Then I remembered what the genius, here, said, so I went into the remuda."

"Oh, no!"

"Leile, Lady, I am so sorry. I would never have told you to go to the remuda if it were Inari attacking. They always take the horses. I didn't think these people were that smart."

"Well, I guess these people were. Somebody was shouting and smacking horses, and they started milling around. I was worried I was going to get stepped on. Then I saw this one, and she was smaller than the rest. I jumped on. At least that part worked."

She turned and patted the gold horse's nose. "But then they all started running, and guess what she did, genius again?"

"I don't know, Leile. What did she do?"

"Well, she didn't go to the centre like she was supposed to. She went straight to the front! There I am, charging back down the road with thirty huge horses pushing me from behind, pitch darkness ahead, and me clinging on, bareback with no control, in the mud and the rain."

"What happened?"

She shrugged. "After a while, I realized that they weren't really stampeding, just running. I remembered there was that big field down the road, and we were just passing it, so I thought that if I could just turn them into it, you know...

"I started to nudge her to the right. There was this big horse running beside us, out at the front, and she tried to turn, but he just kept running. I nudged her again, she nudged him, and he still didn't change.

"Then she got mad. She screamed and nailed him, shoulder to shoulder, squashing my leg between them. Oh, did that hurt. She bit him in the neck, and she hit him again. He swung away from her, and she pushed ahead of him and swung him around again. The rest followed. We just rode in a big circle around that field, back onto the road, and started home. By this time they were only trotting, and soon we were walking, us in the lead, everyone else following. The big one was there, too, but he kept back."

She turned and pointed. "I think that's him, there. The one with the star on his forehead."

"Oh." Mantinello was quite pleased about something. "That one? She shouldered him, she screamed at him, she bit him on the neck and then she pushed him off the road, and then he followed her home?"

"That's about it. She's some horse. Whose is she?"

"She's yours."

"What?"

"She's yours." He appeared to think of something. "*Linealt,* of course, but yours."

"What do you mean? You can't just give someone somebody else's horse! And what's this Lineal thing?"

"*Linealt* is…" For once, Mantinello seemed at a loss for words. He turned to Anine. "Will you explain it to her?"

"Why can't you explain it?"

"I have made a mistake about this culture once tonight. Perhaps she will not understand. Perhaps she will find it," he regained a faint smile, "unmannerly."

Anine grinned. "I see. All right," she turned to the girl, "this horse belongs to Mantinello. It's not one of his usual riding horses. He did some trading while he was in Trenet and he got hold of this little beauty for some reason. He wants her for his breeding stock. However, that's all he wants. So he's decided to give her to you. You own the stock, but you don't own her breeding rights. It's not uncommon in the Inari."

"It's pretty uncommon where I come from. What if I breed her, or she gets bred by herself?"

"He still owns the offspring. It is better manners to consult him on the breeding, of course."

Leile smiled. "Of course." She turned to Mantinello. "I understand. I will have no problem following your custom. But why are you giving me such a valuable horse? What did I do?"

He grinned. "You probably saved us three horses injured in a stampede and two candles of horse-hunting tomorrow morning, when we really need to be travelling. Those two candles of travel time could be the difference between being attacked again or not, so you might have saved some lives as well."

His grin widened. "And there is something else. You see that big horse there?"

"Yes. The one she bit. Who owns him? Is he going to be mad at me?"

"Oh, no. That stallion belongs to King Gerth. He's a wedding present from the herds of Trenet. He's far and away the dominant male in the remuda. All the others stay out of his way. Until tonight, so did she. But with you on her back, she is suddenly a different horse. She is the *untelune*, the Lead Mare. The dominant stallion gives way to her, follows her. This is of some importance to me, because there is a small amount of status in being the owner of the *untelune*. However, it is not with me riding her that she becomes this great horse, it is with you. So you must own her. The status must go where it is deserved."

"I think this is getting complicated."

Anine slapped the girl lightly on the shoulder. "Don't worry. I'll make sure you don't make any serious mistakes in etiquette. Do you want me to look at your leg?"

Leile took a few hesitant steps. "I don't think so. I'll probably be bruised down the whole side, but no real damage."

"Fine. You go back to the carriages and let Lady Trenet know you're all right. Mantinello, you'll want to check the horses. Go ahead. I'll take the rest of the battle numbers as they come in. Get a scout's report together when they're all back. Gerth is going to want to know which dens these rabbits ran to."

Anine removed the grin from her face and went back to her usual after-battle tasks. The numbers looked very good. They had several wounded, but only two deaths, at least so far. There were twelve bodies in the enemy pile and seven too badly wounded to run away. If odds went as they usually did, that meant there would be two or three out in the forest too wounded to go farther, who could be picked up at daylight. There would be a good number of walking wounded making their slow way back to wherever they lived. The Inari would kill a few of these and let the rest lead them to whoever had formed this plot.

Then Gerth could come down and rattle a few chains, replace a few traitors. *If it was my decision I'd give their names to Werlen, the new lord, and let him deal with them, giving him full support if there was any trouble. Of course, Gerth will think of that. Or Lady Kenna. Don't matter.*

She toured the camp, seeing to everything she could think of. Lukin, his Warlanders and the Knights from Trenet continued to patrol outside the perimeter and for a long way up and down the road. "As long as your Inari are out of the picture, we don't dare let our guard down," was Lukin's only comment. The Guides, too, were all out on picket duty.

Anine saw to it that the wounded from both sides were taken care of and all was secure, then made her way back to the hidden carriages. Once the danger was over, tents had been set up in the little dell, and a cheerful fire was roaring over the patter of the rain. In the main tent, Lady Trenet was reclining in front of a glowing brazier, a hot drink in her hand. Lateda, looking more cheerful than usual in spite of a huge bruise on her cheek and suspiciously wet hair, was standing behind her. Talia and her father sat nearby, neither looking quite as happy.

"Your Grace. I gather you shared the excitement."

The elder lady shook her head. "I had to regretfully decline the opportunity. Lateda took care of it for me."

"Who were they, Lateda?"

"Inari."

"What Clan?"

The maid shrugged. "I don't know their braiding patterns well enough. Check yourself; they're out there in the pile. None of ours, glad to say. I'm beginning to like these boys."

"I'll tell them. I'm sure they'll be scared stiff." She sobered. "How many of them?"

"Just two. I don't think they had figured out what was going on. They just found some horses to steal. I found them."

"Looks like one of them found you."

Lateda's hand touched her cheek. "It was dark. He was lucky." She paused briefly. "Not too lucky."

"You're sure there were only two?"

"Can't be sure of anything in the dark and the rain. If there was another, he got lost pretty quick."

"We'll keep a good guard about tonight; don't worry about that."

"And I'll keep a good guard as well."

Anine smiled at the smaller woman. "I'm sure you will." She turned to the duchess. "Sleep well, your Grace."

"As well as I can, Anine."

Two wet, cold candles passed, and there was no evidence of any further attack, so Lukin stood most of the horsemen down. The Petrellans had incurred no damage in the fight, although one of the chargers from Trenet had slipped in the mud, dumping his Knight in an unceremonious pile. The horse seemed sore but not seriously injured, and only the Knight's pride was hurt.

It was near midnight when Anine got the call to attend Lukin at Lord Trenet's tent. She expected a face-to-face meeting but, when she arrived, the tent was full: the whole Trenet family, Lateda, Leile and Orcan. Mantinello slipped in behind her and Lukin rose from the camp stool where he had been resting.

"We need a quick discussion of the fight, Anine, in case there's anything we missed that might matter before morning. Do you want to start?"

She shrugged. "I didn't do anything. I was guarding the passage in here, and only three tried to come through. Two are on the pile out there; I guess one made it away."

Lukin nodded. "I led the charge. We took their horse from behind with superior size and numbers. They crumbled and many went down. After that, it was one-on-one in the dark. Those who stayed to fight were killed. The leaders probably slipped away immediately. I hope your Inari will find out where they went."

"Given a choice, they will follow a mounted Knight first, foot soldier second."

"I assumed so. Now, most important, what happened in here?" His glance invited Lord Trenet to answer.

"We were snug and safe until the horses started acting up. We couldn't see a thing, but we assumed someone was trying to steal them. I knew Anine was at the mouth of the trail, so I sent Leile to find her, let her know what was happening. Lady Trenet sent Lateda out to deal with the intruders," he made a face, "while we sat here, safe and dry."

"Lateda?"

The maid stepped forward reluctantly. "They were after our horses, sir. I went out and Lord Orcan was there. I sent him one way, and I went the other. He drove them to me, and I killed both of them."

"That account leaves several questions unanswered, Lateda."

The maid stood silent, a questioning look on her face.

Lukin's breath exploded in exasperation. "You went out into that mess out there, found two dangerous men and killed them? How did you do that?"

The girl remained mute, casting an anxious glance at her mistress.

Anine took pity on her. "Lateda, it is important that we understand this. You know how all the fighters talk in the evenings, telling stories, comparing techniques?"

The maid nodded.

"Do you think we do that for fun?"

"Yes. But you also learn."

"Exactly. Now it's your turn. You have something to teach us. What you tell us might save our lives some day. It also might allow us to save your mistress. So it is your duty to tell us."

The woman swallowed, glanced around the room and, after one last, despairing plea to Lady Trenet, took a deep breath and faced Anine as if she were the only one in the tent.

"Darkness is a matter of point of view, ma'am."

"Point of view?"

"Yes, ma'am. Whether you think like prey or think like a predator."

"Please explain."

"If you are prey, the night is your enemy. Every shadow holds fear."

"But if you are a predator?"

"The night is your friend. Every shadow is a place to hide."

"I see." Anine took a moment to digest this idea. Then a thought struck her. "And how does Orcan fit into this picture? You said you sent him somewhere?" When Lateda was slow to answer, eyes turned to the young merchant.

He grinned. "I don't know anything about it, Anine. I was guarding the carriages. When the horses started putting up a clamour, I couldn't see a thing. Then Lateda appeared, pushed me to the left, and said, 'Go get them.'

"I went. I never saw anyone, and I never did anything, but after a while the horses calmed down, and that was it. Lateda appeared, gave me the 'all clear,' and went back in the carriage. I stood guard until the fight was over."

Anine turned back to the maid. "I guess I have to ask again. Where does Orcan fit into your little scheme? Predator? Prey?"

The maid's posture drooped and she turned, apparently in some distress, to Lady Trenet. "You see, your Grace? I try to help, and now I must pass judgement on a noble. It is not fitting, your Grace."

"Nor is it necessary. I know what her answer must be."

Eyes turned to Orcan.

"It is obvious, is it not? She sees me as prey. If it was predator, why would she be afraid to speak?"

Lateda's face went deathly white. The words came, spaced evenly, from between gritted teeth. "I am not afraid, my Lord."

"No, no. Pardon me. I mean you are too polite. But now I must know. Why do you consider me prey?" He looked around the group as if for support. "Anine, do you find this amusing?"

She stopped trying to suppress her grin. "Like any riddle, Orcan, once you know the answer, it's all very simple. What does your family do?"

"Pardon?" He sat back in his chair, thrown by this change of topic.

She spread her hands. "Here you are, out on a wedding journey with friends, but you stand guard, you're always armed, you cover more ground than anyone except me. Where does a young lordling from Trenet learn that sort of attitude?"

"From escorting my family's caravans."

Anine raised both palms. "Caravans. And your duty?"

It took him only a moment. "Of course! The caravan is the prey of the thieves. I try to make the prey too dangerous to attack. But still prey."

"So, you think like prey."

"I suppose I must." He turned back to Lateda. "But how did that work tonight? Did I still act like prey?"

"Yes, my Lord." The maid had relaxed visibly during this exchange. "You acted exactly like I knew you would. You went out into the light, looking for a good view and your own ground. You made a big fuss and a big show. The Inari…"

"Aha! I get it. They are predators. They saw me out in the open and they went into the shadows. Where they found…"

Anine couldn't help finishing it off. "…another predator."

Lateda nodded, glanced from Orcan to Anine to her mistress, and considered their smiles permission to withdraw to her usual place.

Anine stopped her with a gesture. "Where did you learn tactics like that, Lateda? It doesn't sound like any training school I ever heard of."

A ghost of a smile. "No school, ma'am. When I was little, I was afraid of the night. A…person…told me about predators and the dark. It helped."

Lukin slapped both hands on his knees. "Predators and prey, is it? There isn't a day goes by that I don't learn something new, but that takes the prize for this month. I don't think I'm going to ask her where I fit in. I might not like the answer."

His look took in everyone. "The remuda has been returned, thanks to Leile, with only one of our horses missing. It was well trained, and I fear a mishap. There are three dray horses gone as well, but I imagine we'll find them in the morning. The Inari have not returned?"

"No, sir. They will come in when they come in, no telling when. If they bring important information I will let you know. Otherwise, we have set a good watch, and everyone can sleep easy."

Lukin nodded wryly. "Except you and me."

Anine did not respond, merely rose, made a Deference to All and faded out through the tent flap, Mantinello at her shoulder. Together they made a full round of both camps, then she sent him to his bed and went to check the remuda.

In spite of all her duties, Anine snatched a few hours of sleep in a damp bed and was up at dawn. She had expected the Inari back during the night but, true to form, they had slipped in and gone to their bedrolls without telling anyone. They knew their information was not urgent and they were tired.

The wedding party broke camp late that morning, having spent enough time to make sure everything was neat and tidy. Even shiny; the duke had been insistent.

"This is too good an opportunity to waste. Everybody in the whole area knows that force was here and why. If they attack us, and the next day we go marching down the road sharp and spruce, in fine formation, what message does that send?"

Anine and Lukin had agreed, so every horse was curried, every wagon tarp was scrubbed and all armour polished. Fortunately, the sun cooperated, so it was a cheerful group that filed onto the road south. A straggle of unhappy prisoners rode in the back of the last wagon, to be dropped off at the next town for safekeeping.

Anine chuckled as she rode up beside Talia and Leile where the road widened. "Having a pleasant ride?"

The smaller woman grimaced. "She was much easier to handle in the dark and rain. He never told me she wasn't broken properly to the bridle."

"You didn't expect the Lead Mare to be docile, did you?"

"No, I guess I didn't. Don't worry, we're getting everything straightened out," she pulled on the reins, "and you will *not* snack on any piece of grass you have a mind to!"

Anine turned her attention to the silent Talia. "A bit glum this morning, my Lady?"

Talia shrugged. "Not really. I know there are times when you get to fight and times when you don't, but I had to sit in that carriage and do absolutely nothing! Can you imagine how I felt?"

"Considerably drier than the rest of us, I'd say. You're valuable cargo, Talia, get used to it."

The big girl sighed. "I know." Then she grinned. "I'm not half as upset as Father. He was absolutely certain he was going to go out there and get involved. Mother had to really put her foot down."

"You're joking!"

"No. It got to the point, just after Lateda went out to settle the horse thieves, when I figured Mother was going to ask me to sit on Father, and I was wondering who to obey!"

Anine chuckled, then had a sudden thought. "Who would you have obeyed?"

Talia shook her hair back from her face. "Mother, of course."

"Why"

"Because she was right. That kind of battle was no place for any of us, and we had to stay safe in order to make your task as easy as possible. I was even worried about sending Leile out, but someone had to go."

"That worked out well, too. Sort of." They paused to watch Leile's mount dance sideways a few steps until her new owner hauled her back on the road again.

After a while, Anine moved ahead in the line to speak to the duke.

"Your Grace, I'd like to thank you."

"You would?"

"Yes. You gave the rest a good example last night."

"Hmm. Not a very good example, I'm afraid. It was very difficult to sit in that carriage while my men were protecting me with their lives."

"Think if you'd gone out and been killed and your daughter had to cancel her wedding plans because of it."

"I hadn't looked at it that way. In any case, I didn't go out. I'm ashamed to admit it was mostly the thought of having my daughter sit on me that brought me to my senses."

"You mean she really did threaten to sit on you? I thought she was joking."

"So did I, but I didn't want to call her bluff. My dignity would never survive."

Anine trotted forward again, pleased to report to Lukin that all their charges were in good spirits.

He nodded judiciously. "Same thing after any successful battle. We'll have to be a little more on guard for the next day or so."

"Because we're still in enemy territory."

"And having just won a battle, we might get a bit too full of ourselves and make a mistake. Especially the younger ones."

"Good point. I'll keep my eyes open. When I see someone slip up, I'll come down hard."

"I have every confidence that you'll do that, Anine."

"Thank you, sir."

"And don't worry about your part in the battle."

"My part? What did I do?"

"That's my point. You didn't do much. Does that bother you?"

"A bit." She grinned. "Not as much as it bothers the duke."

"Sometimes you get to be the hero, sometimes you do your part and it comes to nothing. Take solace that your men performed their duties perfectly, Mantinello's plan worked perfectly..."

"...except for the remuda."

"Thirty horses stampeded in a rainstorm and only one broken leg? I'd call that pretty good luck. Except it wasn't luck. I know Leile wasn't part of the plan, but who told her to go to the remuda? Mantinello did. I hear he gave her the horse."

Anine explained the intricacies of *Linealt* and he shook his head. "I'd be worried, some handsome young fellow started giving my daughter horses."

"I guess she's old enough to take care of herself. Word has it she's come out to check over Varli as a potential husband."

"Young Varlinden would be a fine catch indeed, if she could keep up to him."

"Until last night, I wasn't sure she could."

"After last night, he may not get the chance to find out."

Anine shook her head. "Mantinello's just playin' around."

Lukin mimicked her headshake. "That boy doesn't play around."

Anine winced at the accuracy of the statement.

The old Warlander sent her a piercing gaze. "Neither do you."

She raised her eyebrows, uncertain whether a response was necessary.

He nodded. "When Gerth sent you along, I had my reservations, but I trusted his judgement. You and Mantinello and the rest of your Clan have made this trip as smooth as it could have been." He shot her another glance. "Gerth got plans for you?"

She slouched. "I hope not."

The corner of his mouth twitched. "For someone doing as well at her duties as you are, that's a strange response."

She faced him directly. "It seems that what I want to do and what I'm good at don't quite jibe. The king has this idea of what I'm good at, so he keeps sending me to do it. And I keep proving him right, because the only other choice is failure, and I can't do that."

"Ah. I know how that goes."

"You do?"

He glanced at her. "Oh, yes. Until I was fourteen, I was bound and determined I was going to be a balladeer." He regarded her stare, then smiled. "Truth."

"I don't know if that makes me feel better or not."

His mailed hand clashed against her vambrace. "Then you'd better take advantage of every chance you get to do whatever it is you want to do, and do it even better than everything else."

"Aye. Thanks, Lukin. I already knew that."

"I was sure you did." He raised his rein hand, and his warhorse slipped into a trot and forged ahead, leaving her to think.

30. SPRING WEDDING

For the next few days, Anine tried to keep track of Mantinello's contact with Leile, but found it increasingly difficult. As the wedding party moved into Petrella, travel became more complicated rather than less. It was a good thing the danger of attack had waned, because a lot of Anine's effort was taken up with forcing their way through crowds of cheering people at every village and town. People with no idea of protocol and no interest in learning.

She sat her horse beside Lukin's charger, watching the mêlée one afternoon, shaking her head. "Where do they all come from? There's only about a hundred people live here."

The old Warlander nodded towards the village green, scattered with tents and cook-fires. "A lot of visitors."

"I don't remember this ever happening."

He tilted his head and smiled. "Popular king, beautiful princess, just like in the children's tales. The realm needs occasion for joy."

She shrugged. "Well, they deserve it. What with the weather improving, at least we're making decent progress."

Lukin raised his eyebrows. "If Lady Talia didn't insist on stopping the whole procession to show her parents the setting for every event that happened on her journey here, it would help."

They reached the edge of the town and the company picked up the pace again. "The next village is Lanil's Rock, and if she stops to tell them everything that happened there, we're going to be camping out in the forest tonight." She jogged ahead to ride alongside Talia and managed to slide her mother's comfort into the conversation.

Talia was instantly concerned. "Do we have a long day today?"

"That's sort of up to you, my Lady."

The other woman frowned across at her. "You're being too polite. What have I done wrong now?"

"Nothing. It just might be advisable not to stop quite so often."

"What...? Am I talking too much? But it's fun to tell them ..."

The dismay on the girl's face was rather comic, but Anine kept a sober look. "I was just thinking, my Lady, that your friends are a rather intelligent group of people. I'd wager they can ride along and listen just about as well as my Lady can ride along and talk. Without stopping...that is, without stopping the riding part."

"Anine, you may practice your witticisms on my future husband. I forbid you to try them on me...oh!" Her eyes lifted towards the road ahead.

"What is it?" Anine was instantly on the alert.

"This is it. This is the bridge our carriage went through, isn't it?" The lady frowned. "No, I suppose not. It all looks so different in the sunlight."

Anine grinned. "No, this is the right place. Ferlen put in a new bridge last summer. You rode over it on the way north and didn't even notice."

Talia grimaced. "Well, that's one story that won't hold the procession up very long, will it?"

* * *

Their reception at Arlyn Castle was a different story. The people crowded the streets of the lower city, kept in line by a cordon of soldiers clad in their spick-and-span shiniest. Up on the parade ground before the castle stood rank upon rank of footsoldiers, each regiment led by a Warlander in full panoply, fierce helmet glowering at the festive air.

Gerth, too, was in full armour on Pelex, although he had foregone the helmet. The huge warhorse pranced forward as Talia's coach arrived and then spun to lead the procession through the main gate.

In the bailey, the guests descended from their coaches and dismounted from their horses to be guided by lines of footmen, maids and other domestic staff up the stairs and into the castle.

At that point, Anine lost touch with them as her duties, at least as she saw them, were more attuned to the unlading of baggage and the billeting of the escorts.

Sooner or later she would be expected to show up inside to cushion the clash of cultures, and in the back of her mind she knew she was putting that duty off as long as she could.

No formal banquet was scheduled, so she ate with the Guides and other Clan and turned in early, satisfied at a job well done, and wondering what duties she would be posted to next.

* * *

Anine managed to escape anyone's attention and took advantage of the time to iron out the small details of her life until early the next afternoon, when one of the older pages knocked on her door. "Lady Talia's compliments, ma'am, and would you attend her at your convenience?"

"You said that very nicely, lad. What does it mean?"

"Pardon me?" He stopped in the act of turning away.

"At my convenience. That sounds pretty loose. What if I don't show up for a couple of candles?"

"I...I don't know, ma'am. She...uh...she didn't look very anxious or anything."

Anine laughed and slapped him gently on the shoulder. He staggered but held up manfully. "Just trying to make you think, lad. You go back and tell her I'm coming right now."

"Thank you, ma'am."

She reached out and stopped him. "How soon should 'right now' be? I don't want to rush her."

The boy's eyes went up to the left. "I think...about a quarter candle would be correct, ma'am. We are always told that to rush is unseemly."

"Unless you're a page, and then you have to rush all the time."

He grinned. "That's right, ma'am. They tell us one thing and make us do the opposite. We're getting an education."

"And you've learned something, haven't you? Off you go."

With a crooked grin, the boy scrambled back down the stairs and clattered out of sight. Anine finished folding the clothes she had just brought in from the line and followed at a more leisurely pace. She found the lady in her 'sewing room,' giving the same page some instructions. She looked up as Anine entered.

"Oh. Here you are, already."

"Came as soon as I could, my Lady." She winked at the page, who winked back and scurried off again.

Talia took both of Anine's hands and towed her over to a bench, pushing her down and sitting opposite her. "Now, Anine, we have to plan where you're going to be in the wedding party."

"The wedding party."

"Yes! You were my first friend here, and I want you to be in my wedding party."

"Lady Talia, there isn't a place for someone like me in the queen's wedding party."

"There isn't an official one, so we'll have to make one."

Anine pulled back her hands, placed them on the table firmly. "No, Talia. There ain't no place for me in your wedding party. Think what your father said about when you're doin' somethin' unusual. You keep it as traditional as possible, to keep the fuddy-duddies happy. Me in your weddin' party is not gonna make anybody happy, especially me."

"But Anine! You're my friend, and I want to honour you!"

"Fine. I'd be honoured to be a guest at your wedding. You can seat me wherever you like. I'll even make a speech if you want a laugh. But I won't be in the party. It just wouldn't be right."

"Why?"

"Think on it, Talia. How did you picture me? In a dress? Not likely. In armour? I'd stand out even more."

"You could wear a dress. You're not much bigger than me."

"Right. And you've been wearin' dresses like that all your life. Can you see me in a fancy one for the first time? No, you don't want a scene like that takin' attention away from those who should rightfully have it."

Talia paused, looking at her friend. "Anine, you're not afraid, are you?"

"Afraid? No, I'm not afraid. Oh, sure, I'd be out of my depth, but I could handle that. If I had to wear a fancy dress for my duty to you or the king, I'd wear one and do you credit if I could. But this ain't necessary. You'd realize it the moment you saw me, and it would spoil the day for you. Don't do it."

A grin crept across Talia's face. "I could order you to. I'm going to be your queen."

Anine raised her eyes to meet her friend's stare.

"All right, that's a bad idea, I was only teasing. I'd have you glowering in a corner the whole time. That would really spoil my day!"

They laughed a bit, but then Talia became serious. "Then what are we going to do with you?"

"Tell you, Talia. You put Gavess on it. Have him talk to Varli. Between the two of them, they'll figure something out."

"Varli? You'd trust Varli with something like that?"

Anine balled up her fist and stared at it meditatively. "Oh, I trust him." Then she dropped her hand. "Actually, I do trust him. He's Clan."

"It's that important?"

"Sure. He'll tease me, insult me, play tricks on me, and get into all sorts of trouble I have to pull him out of, but he'll never let anything happen that would harm my honour."

"You feel that strongly about him?"

"He's a good friend."

"More than a friend?"

Anine dropped her hands to the table, then remembered to close her mouth. "This weddin' stuff has softened your mind, Talia. You gotta understand how it is. He's a companion at arms, a fellow soldier. He's Clan. There's a trust there that goes deeper'n friendship. But it don't mean anythin' else. Lady's sake, he's a noble, and he's half my size!"

Talia snorted. "Don't think that stopped them from lining me up with any number of twits they thought might be desperate enough to marry me."

"Aha! So that's why you came out to the wilds. You were running away!"

"There's some truth in that, Anine."

Anine shook her head slowly. "Well, that's a problem I won't be havin', Lady be thanked."

"But Anine, surely you'll get married some day."

"First Varli, now you, tryin' to get me all het up about bein' married, like I was some ugly cousin you hadda get rid of." The unfairness of it all clogged her throat. "What's with you lot, anyways?"

"But Anine, we just want you to be happy."

Anine found herself on her feet, her fists clenched. "Who says I'm not happy? At least I would be, if I could get out buildin' roads like I want to and not runnin' errands for everybody who can't do nothin' for themselves."

With a disgusted snort, she turned and stomped out of the room.

Five paces down the hall she slowed, stopped and turned back. When she reached the door, Talia was still sitting there, a shocked expression on her face. Anine stepped inside, held up her hands in surrender.

353

"All right. That wasn't fair. My trouble with my duties to the realm's got nothin' to do with your weddin', and I sure don't want to spoil it for you. You know I'll do whatever you like. Just say the word."

Talia did not respond at first. Then she got up and placed her hands on her friend's shoulders. "No, Anine, you are right. It's your life, and your friends don't have any right to be pushing you where you don't want to go…"

"It's not that I don't want to, Talia…"

"No, I said that wrong. We just shouldn't be messing with your life."

Anine grinned. "I know. You're getting married yourself, and you're so happy, you just think everybody else would be happy if they got married, too. I hear a lot of young brides are like that."

Talia looked at Anine, her head cocked to one side. "You know, I've never seen you get angry before."

"So, you learned something."

"Yes. I learned that I don't want to be across from you when you are angry. I was very relieved when you turned and went out the door."

"Why?"

"Because you are quite scary, Anine. Your face goes all white, the cords on your neck stand out and you look about twice as wide as usual."

"Oh. I'll remember to be careful about that. What man is going to want to marry someone twice as wide as me?"

"Anine! Save your sarcasm for my future husband. He appreciates it. I do not."

Anine sketched a courtier's bow. "A mere jest, my Lady."

* * *

Anine straightened from the book she had been poring over. Had that been a noise at her door? She waited, but there was no repeat. She leaned back over the book. *Why do these people have to use such long words? What's wrong with the short ones that everybody uses for speaking?*

Her head came up again. That was definitely a noise. A very gentle tap. Puzzled, she got up and strode to the door, her hand near the sword belt that hung there. She opened the latch and looked down into the staring eyes of Oren, Kenna's newest page. He said nothing, merely gaped up at her.

"What is it, lad?"

He blinked, seemed to come awake. "Oh! L..." his eyes scanned up to the side as he searched his memory, "...Lady Kenna s-sends her respects, my Lady, and r-requests that you attend her."

"I thank you, sir. And when does Lady Kenna ask that I attend her?"

"Uh...in half a candle, my Lady."

"All right, then. I will attend Lady Kenna in half a candle."

He stood, still staring at her.

"Oren?"

"Yes, my Lady?"

"When you're talking to a military person such as me, you don't use 'my Lady'. You say 'ma'am'."

"Oh. Thank you, ma'am."

"Now you can run along and tell Lady Kenna that you've done your duty."

"Oh. Right. Thank you, ma'am." He gave her the slightest twitch of a smile, then scooted off back down the corridor.

Anine pondered this request. It sounded rather formal, so she'd better change her shirt. The short dress sword instead of her usual hand-and-a-half, of course. Not that her dress sword was anything but a weapon. She had no time or money for the fancy, useless blades that people wore for show.

She 'attended' Kenna at her suite of rooms promptly as asked, and halted in the doorway. Lady Trenet was there. The page ushered her in officiously, more at ease on his home ground. Although the weather was mild, the room was warm and the duchess was cosied up to a small brazier of coals. Anine entered and nodded to Lateda, standing behind her mistress as usual.

Kenna was seated opposite, looking comfortable in a sleeveless gown. "Come in, Anine, and have a seat. We have just been talking about you."

"Not good news for a soldier, my Lady. The brass are talking about you, you're in for some extra duty, every time."

Kenna laughed. "A good guess, Anine."

Anine sighed. "What is it this time, my Lady?"

355

"Don't look so put-upon. This won't be onerous, I hope. Lady Trenet was just saying that she is short of attendants here, and suggested that perhaps you could stand in when required."

Anine immediately became serious. "That would be an honour, your Grace."

"Good." The older lady nodded slowly. "It will be useful to have someone familiar with the amenities."

Anine chuckled. "I'm afraid you have the wrong person for that. Of course, you could always use me like Talia does."

"How is that?"

"She hopes I'll mess up first, then she won't look so bad."

"And how does that work?"

Anine put on her best Gavess accent. "I endeavour to disappoint her consistently."

The two ladies exchanged a glance, and both smiled. *The mothers of the wedding couple are getting along. That's a relief.* They were both strong women, and if they struck sparks the result could be a conflagration.

At some unseen signal, the page stepped forward with a loaded tray. Kenna nodded encouragingly as he placed it carefully on the table. "Thank you, Oren."

She turned to Anine. "We were just about to have tea. Would you like to serve?"

"A pleasure, my Lady."

As she busied herself with the apparatus, she thought furiously. She only knew two modes of service. Sarha had started to teach her last winter at the inn, but Jhanes had interfered.

"That's 'hostess to client' style, Sarha," he had objected. "Anine can't use that."

He had insisted on teaching her the simple Warlander's mode he had learned from Zoysana. It suited her better, anyway: fewer fancy movements and complicated meanings.

So she laid the places in her own style. If Kenna asked Anine to serve, then she would be happy with Anine's serving. As she ground the leaves, she wondered how Kenna knew that she knew how to serve tea. It certainly wasn't a skill you found in Haskel's *Code of the Mercenary*. With a mental shrug, she concentrated on the rite. Kenna always knew.

She was thinking so hard about what she was doing that it took her a moment to realize something was wrong. Once she was aware, it was clear. *Lady Trenet has no idea what to do.* She slowed her movements and began to adapt the steps. Unless it was absolutely necessary, she began to serve Kenna first. The duchess would not be offended since she had no idea what was supposed to happen.

The two older women chatted comfortably at the appropriate moments, using the polite conversational skills they had practised since they learned to talk, and the ceremony continued without a hitch. When the last drop had been emptied and the page came to take the tray away, all three women sat back with a sense of accomplishment.

The duchess spoke first. "That was an interesting experience."

Kenna frowned, ever so slightly. "You have not seen a tea ceremony before?"

"No. I have heard of them, of course. It is a cultural trait shared, strangely enough, by only yourselves and the Kyabrans."

Anine laughed. "Not so strange, your Grace. We have many things in common, notably this realm."

"What do the Kyabrans have to do with the Kingdom of Petrella?"

"According to Tadeo, Zoe's Kyabran guard-of-life, we invaded and threw them out of here about four hundred years ago."

Anine watched as the duchess absorbed this. Finally, the older woman nodded. "Yes, that would explain a lot of things. Including the present situation, I suppose."

Kenna was not to be put off her topic. "But Lady Trenet, I did not get the impression that you were unfamiliar with the tea ceremony."

Lady Trenet caught Anine's eye and smiled. "The ability to cope with the elements of another culture is a skill I have had little chance to acquire. However, on this journey I have been learning from experts."

"I see."

"The technique is to watch others and take your time. I have also been told that if you are dealing with truly gracious people, there are always plenty of hints as to your proper behaviour."

Kenna smiled. "It is a clever diplomatic trick, to place someone in a position where she must accept a compliment."

"A clever trick indeed, and not my own."

Kenna followed Lady Trenet's glance to Anine, who merely smiled.

Lady Trenet sat up straighter. "I am feeling especially energetic today. I believe there is an informal reception this afternoon?"

Kenna nodded. "There is, but I'm sure no one expects you to show up."

"I think, then, that I shall have to surprise them." She made to get up, and Anine beat Lateda by a heartbeat to lend an arm. "Thank you, my dear. I hope you will aid me on the stairs. This castle has more levels than I am used to."

Attended by Anine and Lateda, the two dowagers descended gracefully into the reception room. Gerth noticed them but, at a gesture from his mother, stayed where he was. The two older women took chairs at a spot that commanded a good view of the proceedings, and observed.

Talia, her back to them, was obviously in fine form. Her laughter rang out frequently, and once she reached out and clouted Varli hard enough to send him reeling. Or at least pretend to be reeling. With Varli, you could never tell.

After some time, Lady Trenet shook her head. "I find this difficult to believe."

"What is that?"

"My daughter."

Kenna raised her eyebrows.

"She is a different person here. Look at her. She's bright, talkative, personable. Even self-assured."

"Yes, that's how she always is."

"I don't wish to speak ill of my daughter, but where is the surly, sulky and stubborn?"

Kenna laughed. "The stubborn part we know about. The other two," she raised empty hands, "maybe she grew out of them."

The girl's mother shook her head. "And to think I was so happy a few years ago when she quit growing."

"Perhaps she had a different kind of growing to do."

They sat in silence for a while longer, watching the young people. Then the duchess straightened, as if to ease a stiff back. "I have made my appearance. Perhaps that is enough for one day."

When Anine stepped forward to help her, she waved her away. "No, no, Anine. You stay here and enjoy yourself. I do well enough going up stairs. Coming down is what bothers me."

Taking Lateda's arm, she moved slowly away, with a grace that suggested a stroll rather than a hobble. Kenna matched her pace as if it were her normal stride.

Anine waited but there was nothing to keep her, so she decided to slip away. But not quickly enough, it seemed.

31. The Social Swirl

Varli dropped into the chair beside her. "Can I talk to you?"

"Any time, Varli."

He sat, observing the gathering. "You get along with Leile pretty well, don't you?"

She smiled. "Aye. We seem to think alike."

"You do? I've never seen two people so unalike in my life!"

"Strange, isn't it? I guess you're right. I've never met anyone like her before. She's completely unmilitary, nothing like any farmer I ever met. If I had to compare her, it would be to the Inari."

"The Inari? A pleasant little thing like that?"

Anine laughed. "I know what you mean. She doesn't seem like an Inari at all. But she thinks like one."

"In what way?"

Anine thought about it. "Well, you know how they don't really care what other people think about what they do? As long as the deed is honourable, that's all that counts. She's like that. She has some system of her own to decide what's right, and she doesn't really care what anybody else thinks."

"I see."

"I was also thinking she's a bit like Arvent."

"And that's bad."

"I think so. You can't just withdraw from people like he did. Somewhere, sometime, you have to let down your guard, let people know you. Otherwise you get...I don't know...too different. You start out keeping away from people by choice, but after a while you don't know what's really right, or how to come back. You have to keep in touch with people. Other people. I don't know any other way to explain it."

"You explained it pretty well, Anine. Even dumb old Varli could understand."

She nudged him, gently she thought, with her elbow. "So, are you going to marry her?"

He recovered his seat and looked over at her. "I just met her, Anine. How should I know?"

She shrugged. "I hear with some people it's just as easy as that. You meet them, and wham!" She clapped her hands together. "You know."

"Well, that didn't happen this time. Her either. I could tell. So I'll just have to wait and see." He turned and faced her. "But she's so different. Don't you have to find somebody who's like you to marry? Otherwise you fight all the time."

"You're talking to the wrong person, Varli. I don't know anything about marriage."

"You think you'll ever get married, Anine? I mean, if you don't mind me asking."

"No, I don't mind you askin'. I doubt I will."

"Why not?"

"Aw, I dunno. I mean, look at me. I'm a mercenary. I'm big, tough, bossy..."

"...and plain."

She swung to face him. "Hey, I didn't say that!"

"No, but you were going to. And you're wrong. You have a nice face." He grinned. "Not right now. When you glower like that, people tend to duck. But most times it's a face people will trust. And whether you're plain or not, I think that's a pretty poor reason to make a decision like that."

"Do you?"

"I do. I'm going to throw your own words back at you, Anine. You have to keep in touch with other people."

"I keep in touch with other people! I got plentya friends."

"I'm talking about a different level, Anine. Just having friends isn't good enough."

"All right, that's what I said. I guess I just haven't found anybody that made me think about gettin' married. When I meet the right man, then maybe."

"I wish I had that kind of freedom."

She nudged him again. "Well, that's the problem with being born noble and rich."

"...and handsome. Don't forget handsome."

"Aye, you got a tough life, Varli."

The squire didn't answer. She glanced over at him. He was gazing at the girl across the room. She was standing perfectly

361

still, as if posing for a portrait, a look of pleasant interest on her face, only her eyes moving to each person who spoke. She never intruded into the conversation, but twice when she was addressed she responded instantly, and once her riposte set the whole group into laughter.

Anine nodded. "She has her own set of rules, and she follows them."

"So how is that different from Arvent?"

"I don't think he really had a set of rules. He was just floating. I don't think he knew who he was, what he wanted. She knows exactly who she is. She's just different from everybody else, and doesn't worry about it."

"Like you."

"Me?"

"Sure. Do you know anybody like Anine? I doubt it."

"Somehow that doesn't sound like a compliment."

"It isn't meant to be. It's a truth. From what I see, you live with it pretty well. You know who you are and what you want, and you're going to get it."

"I wish it was that easy."

"I'd say you're doing pretty well. Look at you."

She glanced down at her new uniform, specially designed for the wedding. A mercenary officer's tabard, modified with an Inari sash in Zoysana's colours. "But Varli, this isn't what I want to be!"

He frowned up at her. "Well, if it isn't, you're doing a great job of achieving something you don't really want. Are you sure you don't really want it?"

Her mouth opened, but nothing came out. She closed it.

He tipped his head and, with a quick grin, faded into the crowd. She hardly noticed that he was gone.

She spent the rest of the wedding ceremonies in a strange stage of self-awareness, looking over her own shoulder, so to speak. Noticing how good she was at so much of this. Her notoriety gave her access to every conversation, and she knew she held her own. It became easier and easier to speak in modulated tones, to keep up with the wit.

So how do I answer Varli's question? Why am I so good at this? And the answer came to her. *Because it's easy.*

* * *

The wedding itself was a complete blur to Anine. Festivities and ceremonies, guests from the Inner Duchies and Kyabra, small evening socials with all sorts of people and a huge gala at the end. And all the while she skirted the edges of society. Whenever possible, Talia had her in attendance, sharp and dignified in her new dress uniform. And always, underneath, the negotiations and meetings. Under that, the plots and schemes. And probably another layer beneath that, which she was glad she could leave to Sivan and Loreline.

It was enough to keep track of the legitimate levels. During every conversation she had to be aware of who she was talking to, what that person knew, what they were supposed to be told.

And then the king would call on her, and the tension would notch up another level. But then Talia would give him a sharp elbow, and he would grin and turn to someone else. Talia would wink, Anine would pretend to mop sweat off her brow, and the party would continue.

Once it was all over, she breathed a sigh of relief and began to plan her spring activities. She lay on her bed one evening, taking great pleasure in going over the training schedule for the new masons, making sure that it was comprehensive.

Until she heard the knock. It was unlike the knock of anyone she knew. Sharp, but soft. A strange blend of confidence and subtlety. She almost wondered if it was the Sivan. When she opened the door, there was Lateda, her face in its usual placid form.

"Good evening, Lateda. Would you like to come in?"

She thought she detected a faint smile. "No, thank you, Anine. My mistress would like a moment of your time."

"Of course. When?"

"Whenever it suits you, ma'am."

"You mean, like, right now?"

"If that is suitable."

"All right. Step in while I put on a better blouse."

"My mistress has seen you in your work clothes. She would not object."

Anine looked up from her buttons. It was the first personal comment she had ever heard from the maid. "I don't mind showing respect."

Lateda nodded, once.

As they crossed the bailey, Anine looked down at her companion. "Can I ask you a question?"

"Certainly."

The even tone of voice showed no enthusiasm, but Anine forged on. "What do you sound like when you talk normally?"

A small frown wrinkled the other woman's brow. "Just like this, of course."

"But you didn't always speak like that."

Lateda glanced up. "Neither did you."

Anine smiled. "So here we are, the two of us talking to each other in voices that aren't ours."

"Yes. Interesting."

There was nothing more to say, and they continued up the stairs to Lady Trenet's suite in silence. When they arrived, the lady rose to greet Anine and indicated a rather sturdy chair. Her sigh as she sank into it brought out a wintery smile.

"I thought you might appreciate that."

"Oh, I do, your Grace. You are very thoughtful."

The elderly woman shrugged. "I am used to managing a castle. Here, I find smaller tasks to busy myself."

Anine regarded her hostess. "If I may comment, you are looking well, your Grace."

"Yes, I believe I am." She motioned to Lateda to pour amber wine into fine crystal glasses. "The mountain air seems to agree with me."

"And other things as well, your Grace?"

"You are perceptive."

"You gave me the information I needed. I imagine it must be wonderful to see your daughter have such success."

"More than you could ever dream."

Anine considered. "Your Grace, I've been thinking on that topic."

"And what conclusions have you drawn?"

Anine sipped the Trenet Bisro with appreciation. "I have come to think that all this marriage and parenthood and such may not be so bad, after all."

The duchess grimaced. "There have been times when I would have disagreed with you."

"But now?"

"Now, I would not be so quick to judge." The lady sipped again. "And is there some handsome young man who needs to be concerned about his independence?"

"No, not really."

The old eyes narrowed. "I make no comment."

"Which is a comment in itself. Am I that obvious?"

"Yes. In a very refreshing manner, I might add."

"If what you said is a compliment, thank you, your Grace."

Again, the quirk of a smile. "Let us consider it such."

They sat in silence while Lateda refilled their glasses. "My husband must return to our demesne, but I am staying here for a bit longer."

"I'm sure Talia will be happy to hear that."

"She is. She gets so much entertainment from showing off how wrong I was about her."

"I'm sure that has little to do with it. There isn't a mean bone in her body."

"It is not meanness. It is the rightful enjoyment of being right. I do not begrudge her the joy."

"Especially when it brings you such joy as well."

"It is the one time in my life when I was glad to be wrong."

"How long will you be staying?"

"I believe the traditional New Queen's Procession takes place forty-nine days after the wedding ceremony. Do you have any idea why forty-nine? Is there something wrong with a nice, round, fifty?"

"Absolutely none, your Grace. We haven't had a new queen since long before I was born. I don't know who remembers these things."

"In any case, the Procession traditionally stops at C'deille, which is on my way home. I plan to enjoy my daughter's triumph that far and then take the road north."

"In your beautiful coach?"

"Yes. I may be needing it for a shorter and less pleasant journey in the near future."

"Perhaps not."

"You are an accomplished young woman. Perhaps you are also a doctor or a seer?"

"Do you recall a comment I made once about your daughter's strength of character?"

"Yes. I quake to think what you will come up with, this time."

"Not at all, your Grace. I merely observe that if you were able to force yourself into such a decline through guilt about your actions, surely you have an equal ability to rebound, since your actions have proven so successful."

"Hmm. I would like to share your optimism."

"If I might make an observation?"

"You're going to, anyway. Please continue."

"You are a woman who does what she likes most of the time. Why not now?"

"Ah. Quite so. I can't have it both ways, can I?"

"Not if you are honest with yourself."

"So, last time we spoke I was nonsensical and melodramatic. Now I am self-deluding. Do you practise this style of diplomacy often?"

"Quite often, your Grace. His Majesty King Gerth is good enough to aid me."

"Yes, I have observed that. To good purpose, I might add."

"I much prefer you, your Grace." She glanced at Lateda. "The audience is less critical."

"But better armed, ma'am."

"Yes, Lateda. I get the message. And I remember the Inari camp last year."

Lady Trenet cocked her head. "What happened in the Inari camp?"

"Lateda performed her duties with great enthusiasm. The Inari were impressed."

"I had not been informed of this." She turned to look directly at her maid.

"I did not see the need, your Grace. I was protecting Lady Talia to the best of my ability."

Anine nodded. "I don't know what you have been told, your Grace, but, from what I saw, Lateda has been more than protection for Lady Talia. Her emotional support was invaluable."

The old lady reached out and took the maid's hand. "Another deed that has turned out far better than I ever dreamed. I am doubly blessed."

It was dim in the candlelight, but Anine swore she saw a brief glisten in the young woman's eye. Then the maid turned away to bring a plate of biscuits, and the moment passed.

They chatted about less important things for much longer than Anine had expected, and through several of the small glasses of wine. *Yes, I think Lady Trenet is on the mend. Or determined to go down fighting, at least.*

Anine returned to her rooms in a warm glow, wondering at the resilience of the human spirit.

32. To Work Again

Anine looked back at Arlyn Castle, the festive flags still streaming in the early spring breeze. Then she looked at her travelling companion. "Tell you, Ferlen, I am glad to get out of there."

He tilted his head. "You were having a good time. All those parties and receptions, and there you were, half your time standing beside the new queen. I was wondering if we'd ever get you back."

"Huh! Don't get the celebrations mixed up with reality. The wedding's over, and the roads are still full of holes. By my calculations, we've got seven culverts and two small bridges to replace before we can even think about letting a heavy freight wagon cross the border. Not to mention whatever tricks the bandits have dreamed up over the winter."

"And that answers my concern. You're back."

"No choice." She glanced at him. "You ready to hit the trail running?"

He nodded. "I am. It was a slow winter, and I spent a lot of time thinking about how to make things go smoother this summer."

She glanced at him. "Did you? Any specific ideas?"

"As a matter of fact..." As the discussion ran on, his enthusiasm rose, and she saw a side of him that rarely showed. She didn't know whether to be happy or not. *Certain, it's great to have him so keen. But does he still want to keep to our bargain? What if he sees this as his opportunity, like I see it as mine?* She cursed her suspicions, but listened for the thoughts behind what he said. As far as she could see, it was the same old Ferlen.

The following day, however, she wasn't so sure. He was the one who started the conversation. "Strange, isn't it. Here we are, out on the road together."

"Just like last time."

He raised an eyebrow. "Except we're not married this time."

She shrugged. "Now we're business partners. Sort of the same thing."

"Aye. But it's easier." He chuckled. "We don't have to worry about sleeping in the same bed."

They rode in silence for a while. She knew him well enough by now. *Something's going around in that brain.*

He glanced over at her. "We still working under the same deal?"

Aha. Now it comes. "Aye. As far as I'm concerned. You work the summer, I take over..."

"No, not that one. The original one."

"The...oh. That one."

"Aye. We've gone a few miles together since then. I just wondered..."

"Oh...oh, aye. Certain. I don't see anythin's changed. We got a fine workin' relationship. Whatever's changed is only for the better. Look how well we done."

He glanced over. "You've gone back to your mercenary's accent."

"Huh? What's that got to do with it?"

"Nothing. No, that's just fine. I was just checking. We've got a good working relationship. That's what I wanted to hear."

He said no more, and she rode on at his side, her head spinning. *What's going on? This is Ferlen. He never talks in riddles.*

Finally, she got up the nerve. "Ferlen?"

"Aye?"

"What's goin' on?"

He glanced over, frowning.

"What was that all about?"

His face cleared. "Oh, that. That was me getting anxious. Just ignore it."

"You? You're the least anxious person I know. What do you have to worry about?"

He shrugged. "You know. The wedding and all. You looked pretty comfortable, up there with all that nobility. Talking to the king and queen, and them listening and laughing at your jokes. You looked natural, Anine. Completely natural."

She laughed. "Well, I've got you to thank for that!"

"Me?"

"Certain. You're the one that got me started off learning to talk like other people. I just copy how they talk, and then I sound like one of them." She dropped into her normal speech. "It ain't hard, y'know?"

369

He gave her a full grin, and clucked to his horse to move on quicker. She glanced over a while later, and the grin was still there.

Well, that's just fine. I remember what he's always telling Sarha. If he found the right woman, he'd get married. But that won't come between us. We've got a good working relationship, and nothing's going to change that.

A warm glow that didn't altogether come from the spring sunshine filled her, and she began to plan the sequence of culverts that needed to be replaced.

Her optimism carried her through the next few weeks, until it came crashing up against the realities of the world.

* * *

Anine hauled her flagging horse to a standstill, her feet hitting the ground before he had fully stopped.

"All right, Mantinello, what's goin' on?"

He straightened. "Everything as usual, Anine."

"How did the last patrols turn out? Find anything?"

Mantinello winced. "No fun there, Anine. We swept that whole valley and didn't find even a track. If they came in, they didn't come in that way."

"We know they came in. We know they went out. They attacked a pair of wagons five days ago and disappeared. I don't know how."

"What would you like to do, Anine?"

She smiled sourly. "I'd like to take a quarter off and go fishin'. That's what I'd like to do. Or just get on the trail of those bandits, Inari style, and track them down and have a good, old-style battle and thrash 'em good. That'd make me feel even better." She twisted back towards her tent.

"But I don't have time for that. I've got to get things straightened around here and go back down to Jaspen tonight. Ferlen's got some problems with his crew on the road north and he don't even know it, 'cause he's off lookin' at a new quarry."

She ran a hand through her sweat-slicked hair. It had started out to be such a good summer. They were so well prepared, with their crews well trained and eager to go. The new Inari recruits who showed up were much better primed than last year's, having spent the winter listening and learning from the stories of last year's bunch.

They had mapped out their areas, built the rough road, set up their camp and started their patrols.

Then reality had hit them with a bang. Somebody on the other side had been thinking over the winter as well. When the Clan went looking, they found no one. Then a wagon would be hit, the teamsters killed and the tracks would fade into the forest. Besides a few real bandits who had been rousted out, there had been no kills, no battles and a whole lot of frustration. The Inari were taking it well, knuckling down and trying harder, but Anine knew the signs. Too much failure was bad for a troop's morale. For the Inari, even a battle they lost would be better than this.

She pondered her options as she took a fresh mount and loped back down the road, the horse's hooves thudding on the newly graded earth. This problem of Ferlen's was just going to have to wait, unless she could scare up somebody at the work site in Jaspen tonight. She was headed over to Lanil's Rock for a talk with Jhanes.

His response, when she pounded into the inn yard the next afternoon, was to swing her bodily onto a bench, pour her a large mug of cider, and settle his bulk down on the opposite side of the table.

"All right, Anine. What possible trouble could have you stomping in here with your mouth moving before you're off your horse?"

He held up a big hand to forestall her response. "No, drink. Breathe. Unless there's a war band of Inari coming down the road, it'll keep that long."

She took a deep swig of the cool, tart cider. She took three long breaths. She tried to relax, to marshal her thoughts.

"I know it don't look good, Jhanes. I know I'm supposta take care of my own problems and you've got your own to worry about."

He raised his empty hands and glanced around the well-kept common room of the inn. "I hadn't been thinking about it, but I really can't see any problems hanging over me right now. Innkeeping can be a boring job, sometimes."

"Ah! Give me a bit of boredom! Tell you, Jhanes, I think I'll push for a post standin' guard over the Royal Library next winter."

He chuckled. "Yep. You've got your first case of 'No time to do anything.' What's got your tail in a knot?"

"What're you laughin' about?"

He chuckled some more. "You. You think you're the first new officer who suddenly had so much going on he couldn't handle it?"

She sighed. "I suppose. Thanks for puttin' it into that kinda perspective for me." She sat for a while. "I still need help, Jhanes."

"Maybe. Like I said, what's the main problem?"

She mulled it over. "It's the fake bandits we're supposed to be chasing. We didn't have any problem with them last summer. Our Inari did exactly what they were supposed to do. We wiped them out. But this summer, we can't seem to lay a hand on them. I don't know what I'm doin' wrong."

"Probably nothing."

"So why can't I find a bunch of stupid bandits?"

He shrugged. "Because they aren't?"

"Whaddaya mean?"

"Who said the people behind these bandits are stupid? You had some success last summer because you came up with a good idea. It worked. Think of it from their point of view. They got thrashed last summer. They've spent the winter figuring out how to keep that from happening again. What did you spend the winter doing?"

"Planning our road crews."

"So?"

She sat in silence before glancing up at him. "Are you pullin' Zoysana's tricks with me?"

He grinned. "Probably. They seem to work."

"All right," she sighed. "Figure it out myself. So, from what you pointed out, it seems that my enemy has come back with a bunch of new ideas and I been sittin' still."

"Could be."

"What do I do? Don't answer that. That's my problem. I've got to come up with some answers."

He held up a hand. "Not necessarily. If I can think of anything, I'd be glad to help. What are you going to do?"

She considered a long time. "I guess the first step is to figure out what they're doin' that's new. Well, that's easy. If they're there and we can't find them, then they're doin' a better job than last year of hidin' their tracks."

"That's pretty logical."

She nodded. "Then we gotta figure out how they're doin' that."

He merely nodded, waiting.

"I guess I said it. They're coverin' their tracks better. That means one of two things. Either they've got a bunch of new bandits who are all very good at this sort of thing, or else they've got the same old bandits or maybe a bit better, and somebody who's takin' care of their tracks."

"Which do you think it is?"

She shrugged. "Don't really matter at first, does it? Whichever it is, they're doin' a better job and we gotta do a better job of trackin' them. Once we've solved that problem and we start findin' them, that's the time to figure out who they are."

He frowned. "I guess. But knowing who you're trying to track makes a lot of difference. For example, if I was tracking Zoysana, I'd expect her to do a lot of things differently from, say, one of your Inari."

"Oh? Like what?"

He shrugged. "I haven't really thought about it. I've spent so much time with the Inari I'd know how to track one of them pretty well. Zoysana would be different for two reasons. One, she's Kyabran and was brought up by her grandfather, living in the bush. Two, she's very smart and is always coming up with something you don't expect. So if I was tracking somebody and he was brushing off his tracks and walking over solid rock and doubling back on his own footsteps, I'd figure I had an Inari in front of me. Zoysana? To give you an example: I've seen her walk her horse down to a water hole, into the water, then back him up right beside her inward track. To the casual eye, it looked like two horses walked into the water and didn't come out. The point is, who can you think of that can fool some young, but decent, Inari trackers?"

"I dunno, Jhanes. I mean, those kids are pretty good. They can find just about anybody except the best of the Guides the Sivan trained before he did his disappearin' trick. Who's better than an Inari in the bush?" She pondered. "Nobody's better than an Inari."

Jhanes grinned. "I think Zoysana said once that once you've tossed out all the impossibilities, whatever's left is the truth."

Anine slapped the table with both hands. "Dammit, Jhanes! You told me the moment I stepped out of the saddle!"

"I did?"

"You said somethin' about a pack of Inari on my tail. The question ain't who is better than an Inari; it's who's better than my young Inari."

"Ah!"

"Damn right. It's an older Inari. Those bastards from the Inner Duchies have been stealin' my ideas! They've found themselves some renegade Inari and hired them to cover the tracks of their fake bandits."

"Any chance the Inari are the ones doing the raiding?"

"Don't think so. There has been more killin'. Like they don't wanta leave any witnesses. But I gotta think. I seen some of the bodies. Didn't look like Inari weapons, to me. Swords and regular steel war arrows. No barbed Inari ones."

"I'll have to ask the boys once I get back, but I don't think the Inari are doin' the dirty work."

"Want me to come out and have a chat with your bunch?"

She gave him a level look. "Jhanes, I hate to ask for help, but I seen too many officers let their pride get in the way of doin' the job right. Would you mind?"

"Not at all. Like I said, I was gettin' bored around here anyway."

"That's for sure." Sarha appeared at the bar. "He's been wanderin' around like a bear that woke up in the middle of winter. Take him out and run him around the bush for me, would you?"

Jhanes grinned up at his wife. "You been listening behind doors again?"

"This is my inn and you're my husband. You talkin' to a pretty young girl and you think I don't have the right to listen?"

Anine surprised herself by blushing.

Jhanes laughed. "There you go, Sarha. You've embarrassed the leader of a hundred frustrated Inari. It's a good thing King Gerth doesn't have you up at the castle advising him."

Sarha moved into the room. "Well, it's a good thing he hasn't got you. You'd have him in the middle of a war in no time, just to keep your hand in." She turned to Anine. "I mean it. Get him out there and make him feel useful. You'd be doin' me a favour."

Jhanes held his hands out, palms up. "There you go, Anine. You've heard it from the head of the pack. I'll get my horse saddled and be with you in short order."

374

He jumped up, and was gone so quickly that the bench was still rocking as the door closed. The two women shared a smile. Then Anine sobered.

"He'll probably be coming out tracking with us, you know."

Sarha shrugged. "I long since figured there was no use in gettin' upset about that. I married a soldier, even an old washed-up merc. There's gonna be danger, and there's nothin' I can do about it. I'm sorta proud of him, too, you know. He wouldn't be him if he wasn't doin' this stuff. Take him out and watch his back like I know you will."

Anine nodded. "I'll do what I can." There was nothing else to say. There were no guarantees in this business that couldn't be voided by one stray arrow.

Once she and Jhanes were back in camp, things started moving. Sort of. He and Pagris began having informal discussions with anybody who came in off patrol. Even for Anine, used to the kind of reports the Inari came back with, the whole thing seemed strange. There would be a bunch of Inari sitting around, trading what sounded like inane stories of trees and trails and waterholes. Jhanes would pop in a question once in a while and sometimes it would be answered, but just as often it didn't seem to be.

After one of these encounters, Anine turned to him, shaking her head. "I don't figure it. You were talking about the trail between here and the water hole under that ridge out west. Then you started talking about the ridge. Then you quit. What was the point?"

"It's a standard Inari practice to find another path, parallel to the regular trail. You wouldn't notice it if you were to cross it, but it's there. If it's Inari that are scouting for the bandits, they'll be using that path to get back and forth, so they can wipe out tracks on the main trail, lay false trails and still catch up with their troop. I managed to remind the boys about that and I'm sure they'll be watching that ridge more carefully the next time there's a raid in the area."

"But you didn't actually ask them if there was a trail, or tell them to patrol the ridge."

"No need. We all knew what we were talking about."

"Except me."

"And now you know, too."

She grinned. "Sorry. I was feelin' a little left out, you know." She regarded him, her head to one side. "You're different when you're with them. I never noticed it, the other times."

"Am I?"

"No question. You're less forceful. You don't give any orders, you don't pull rank on anybody, you just sit around and talk, and give them tea, and talk some more."

He grinned. "Aye, it's fun, you know? This summer, I can act like an Inari Elder. Never thought that was going to happen to me.

"I'm not their officer. You are. I'm just an older guy they can chat with, discuss their ideas and get hints. It's the way they're used to learning. Back in the tribe, they go to some older person that knows something they want to learn, and they hang around and help him and he tells them or shows them what they want to know."

She sketched an Inari gesture of respect. "Oh, Venerated Elder, what information do you have for this beginning officer?"

"I don't know. You'll just have to hang around and drink tea with me and maybe I'll think of something. What do you want to know?"

She threw a cushion at him. "You know very well what I want to know. You've spent the last three days gossiping with my troops, and I want to know what you've come up with."

"I haven't come up with anything."

"What?"

"I never thought I would. I didn't come up here to solve your problems. I came to help you solve them."

She sighed. "There you go with the Zoysana stuff again. Can't you tell me anything straight?"

He nodded. "Maybe. I've been trying to think like an Inari for three days, and it's hard to go back to thinking like a mercenary officer. I can give you an idea of what I've been doing. I'm figuring like there are Inari out there against us. I'm just reminding the boys of what they should be looking for. They should have a better chance of success. We'll just have to wait and see."

"Great. Sounds very Inari, but it doesn't make me feel any better."

He shrugged. "I'm working with Inari, and I figure we're chasing Inari. How else do you think it should sound?"

She shook her head. "I know. Everything you say makes sense. It's just hard to sit here with nothing happening, and do nothing."

He laughed. "So, quit complaining. Three days ago you had too much to do!"

* * *

Anine had no choice but to take his advice, although it tried her patience. One thing that became apparent was a new purpose that filled the camp. The men moved quicker, surer, and their voices were softer. Horses were groomed better and the sound of sharpening weapons slipped through the camp like the underhum of bees in a hive.

Results began to come in. The Inari scouts were starting to pick up traces of their opponents. Mantinello explained it to Anine. "It's quite simple, really, because we all have the same lore. We know what length of trail you have to sweep to persuade most trackers that the trail has not been used. Up to now, we were searching like most trackers. We know that our enemy knows he is being tracked by Inari. So he will be brushing his trails farther. Now, we look farther than that."

Anine nodded. "How much farther?"

He smiled. "Enough. We went back and picked up a set of tracks, six bowshots away from one of the old attack sites. We couldn't follow the trail because it was too old and it rained since, but it proved that the tracks were there. Now we know where to look."

"I see. All we have to do is wait for another attack and we have a better chance of picking up the trail of the bandits."

"I think so, Anine."

She thought about it. "In order to have the best advantage, we need to know as soon as we can when the attack has taken place."

He nodded. "That is logical, Anine."

"Right. Let's double up on the patrols on the wagon roads. We've got four Castle Clan here this quarter. I'll send them out to all the farms along the road and remind everyone how important it is that they let us know if they hear anything, see anything."

She turned to Jhanes. "I'm going to go down to Jaspen to the road camp. They can step up their patrols as well, and put their faster horses and better riders out. If it slows down the road repairs a bit, it can't be helped."

He nodded. "Sounds like a good plan. What do you want me to do if a report comes in while you're gone?"

She grinned. "Nothing. You don't have any status here, remember? If you feel up to it, go along. Just do what you're told, and remember, the boys will be moving really fast."

33. ARROW

Anine strode along the rocky path, moving as quietly as she could while still making time. After all, she wasn't the tracker and hunter in this outfit. She had plenty of Inari for that. She had other problems.

Until she came around the corner of the rock and faced him.

It was an older Inari Fighter, also rounding a corner about forty paces away, and he seemed as startled as she was.

In the eternal heartbeat it took for the sing of her sword-draw to fade away, she had time to notice how fast he had an arrow nocked. She stared along the shaft at his eye, coldly regarding her.

She held her sword straight in front of her. The skill of deflecting an arrow had never been one she felt she would ever need. Still, she had practised, well-padded and with blunt arrows, until she could usually deflect an easily shot arrow from about twenty paces away.

Zoysana could use her bare hand to turn away an arrow shot from forty paces, but that was more difficult. She had to hit the side of the shaft at exactly the moment it reached her. All Anine had to do here was set her sword at an angle to the arrow's path and it would hit the steel and deflect away. Many bruises from the practice field had taught Anine how difficult this was.

Today, failure would bring more than bruises.

As she drew, she slid into a sideways position, holding her sword a touch to the left, leaving just a shade more target on the right-hand side. He was aiming for a chest shot, probably the armhole of her chainmail. Gambling on the fact that he had not had mercenary training, she would slant her sword to the right as her enemy loosed, hoping he chose that side, and letting her reflexes take care of the rest.

She did not make the mistake of watching his eyes: they would tell her nothing. Instead she watched his hand on the bowstring. When his fingers began to release, she moved. She could actually see the arrow spiral as it approached her.

Then there was a shock to her sword arm, a tug at her shoulder, and the arrow was gone. She felt a moment's exultation. She had actually done it!

She moved two steps closer, her sword still forward. He had another arrow on his bowstring immediately, but now she was ready.

Then, from either side of the trail, two more Inari appeared, their bows half-drawn.

She drew her lips back in a snarl. She wondered, in a distant way, how far she could make it with three arrows in her. Two if she was quick. Maybe even one, if she was lucky. But then she would be among them, and they would be defenseless, still holding their bows.

It would be a fair trade. She slipped another precious step forward, her back foot gripping the rock for that first, crucial leap.

No one moved.

She heard the wind rustle the trees, and a bird call, clear and sweet. The sun was warm on her back, and she felt good. She knew she was strong. She could feel her face relax into a real smile. If it was time to die, this was a good time.

But the bows stayed half-drawn.

The first Inari glanced right, then left. He lowered his bow part way, and she realized that he had taken a breath to speak.

"What Clan do I have the honour of facing?"

"Zoysana's Clan."

His eyes widened at hearing Inarituk from a mercenary of Petrella. Then he nodded to his two friends, and they all stepped back.

"Pregota gives Zoysana the number of one. Do you witness?"

The other two grunted in affirmation. The leader's eyes bored into hers.

Did she witness? Ceremonial question. *How am I supposed to know the proper answer? Easier if he just shot another arrow.*

"I witness what has happened here today."

He nodded. "That is enough."

He faded back into the brush, and then there was nothing but the wind in the trees and the song of the bird, glorifying the joy of life.

She eased her sword down and listened, peering around.

Nothing.

Shaking her head, she sheathed her weapon and turned back along the trail to camp. *Somebody's got a lot of explaining to do.*

* * *

"You did what?"

Anine held up her hands helplessly. "What was I supposed to do? He shot an arrow at me. I deflected it."

Chéu, one of the Castle Clan, nodded. "It's possible. I've seen the mercenaries practice. They use blunted arrows and an undersized bow."

Mantinello winced. "But this was one of our full-sized bows? From forty paces? What happened then?"

"Well, nothing. I don't know if he was going to shoot again, but then two of his buddies showed up. They kept their bows half-drawn, though. If one of them had drawn fully, I was going to charge. I figured if I got the jump on them, maybe one would miss. I might even deflect another arrow. I didn't figure one arrow was gonna stop me before I did some serious damage."

"But they didn't shoot?"

"No, the first one gave some kind of signal, and they all stood easy. He asked me, in Inarituk, what Clan he had the honour of facing. I said it was Zoysana's Clan. Then he said something like, 'Pregota gives Zoysana the number of one.' Anybody know what that means?"

Pagris nodded. "Yes, it means that you have made a great impression on them and gained status for your Clan. The next time our Clans meet in battle, one of their best Fighters must stand aside. Only by winning in this way will their Clan be able to regain equality."

"Oh. That's good, then, I guess. Then he said, 'Do you witness?' and I had no idea what that meant, so I just said that I witnessed what had happened there. That was good enough for him, and they all just disappeared. I waited, nothing happened, so I turned around and came home. It didn't seem at all so important to get through to Drecker anymore. It was only after that I started to shake."

They all laughed, although she could see meaningful glances being exchanged.

"All right. Will somebody please explain what all of this means? I mean, I can figure out the basics, but fill me in on the details, will you?"

Pagris nodded. "Certainly, Anine. Of course, you realize that you have made a great deal of progress today."

"I can see that. I've proved for sure that we're dealing with Inari. Older Fighters. Younger than you, Pagris, but much older than the rest of our guys. I also know that I've scored some major coup on their tribe. The Pregota. Which tribe is that? I remember the name from last summer."

"The Pregota are one of the tribes that did not join in with the Great Potentara Chuko last spring when he began the trading with the Great Potentara Gerth. The Potentara Callar of the Pregota is the father of Lamanare, killed because of his lack of manners by Tadeo Priya two years ago."

"So that explains why they're helping our enemies."

He nodded slowly. "Yes, but it might make a large difference in the situation. If the Fighters of the Pregota are helping our enemies because of Callar's anger at Zoysana, your brave and honourable actions towards the Pregota Clan mean he must re-think his anger."

"He can re-think his anger? Those two words don't really belong in the same sentence, do they?"

Pagris chuckled. "I understand. I mean that Callar must think about his anger. Thinking about anger is the first step towards controlling it. If the Potentara Callar thinks that his anger is bringing his Clan into dishonourable conduct he will re-think his anger or he will not long be Potentara of his Clan."

"I see."

Pagris nodded wisely. "You understand, Anine. Leadership is sometimes moving forward and everyone following in your direction. It is also sometimes looking back over your shoulder to see where everyone is going, and then leading in that direction."

Anine could see the puzzled looks among the younger Inari, but she nodded and grinned. "Around here, sometimes I have to look all around me to see if anybody is even on the same trail before I take a step."

Pagris looked even wiser. "Ah, Anine, you have truly made progress today."

"If bein' alive is makin' progress, I'm doin' fine. Tell you, Pagris, I used to laugh at the guys when they practised that arrow stuff and tell them they was showin' off. Not anymore!"

And then nothing happened. Life in her Inari camp went on as usual. There were more triumphs and fewer defeats, but not many, and Anine started to believe that her brief meeting had meant nothing.

Until Jhanes showed up just before dark ten days later. He pulled into camp on his big horse, tossing greetings to the Inari he knew. He dismounted and strode to her tent, where she waited to greet him.

He grinned and sat on the chair she offered, accepted the glass she poured and regarded her as he sipped. "Well, you really put a weasel in the henhouse, Anine."

"I did?"

He grinned. "Oh, did you ever. Do you know who that was that shot the arrow at you?"

"I don't know that many Inari just to look at. I figured by his age he might be somebody important. But if he was important, what was he doing down here?"

Jhanes took a sip of his ale and leaned back. "Let me tell the whole story.

"Eight-nine days ago, a messenger showed up at the inn, horse all sweated up, said I was to go to the castle, quick as yesterday. Said an Inari was coming, and they wanted me to translate. So I went, fast as I could.

"I got to the castle, and Zoysana was waiting for me. They'd got word that some important Inari was coming down over the mountain and had asked for her and me specifically. No idea why, but it was the Pregota Clan. As you know, they're one of the main opponents to the trading, so if one of them wanted to talk, it sounded good.

"Zoysana and I went up to Broken Boulder Gap to receive this guy with all due ceremony. Which isn't much, but we've got some of the Clan stationed up there still, so there were enough of us to put on a show.

"Well, down he comes over the Pass, and it's Callar, the Great Potentara of the Pregotas himself. Remember, he's the one whose son got in Tadeo's way when we went up there the first time. He's got a few of his men with him, but not many. Just his Designated Fighter and his brother, Guadan. Turns out that's your friend with the bow. A couple of older heads as well. Looked like serious talk.

"We set out the cushions and we sit down to find out what they want. Of course, Zoysana doesn't really need me to translate anymore, but Callar doesn't know that. I figure he's surprised when she starts out in Inarituk, but he hides it pretty well.

"He starts talking, and I could see it wasn't fun for him. He tells us what happened this summer.

"It seems that certain nobles of the Inner Duchies made contact with the Inari over to the east during the winter. They said they were looking for allies in a battle against those who wanted to make changes in the way the world had always been.

"At this point, Callar stops and throws up his hands, a sort of helpless gesture I've never seen an Inari make in a formal speech. Then he says, 'Be wary of he who tells you what you want to hear.' It's an old Inari saying."

"Sarasha the Lame said that, too."

"Then he goes on. The reason the Pregotas went against the trading with Petrella was that they're traditionalists. Callar himself is one of the strongest. They don't like these changes happening, and they truly believe that the old ways are the good ways.

"He's a man with a problem, Callar. You see, he's a decent leader. He's really got the good of his Clan in mind, not his own power. So, when he sees that times are changing and the old ways just aren't going to work anymore, he's really got trouble. He doesn't want to change but he knows he has to.

"When these guys came to him with this proposal of theirs to turn back to the old days, he hoped it might work. Plus, of course, he was still upset about losing his son. Again, he admitted, a good leader doesn't let things like that get in his way.

"He agreed to help them, in turn for them helping him close off the trade with Petrella. He sent ten of his best men, with his brother in charge, down to do the scouting for the bandits. A bunch of his allies followed.

"By the time you ran into Guadan things were already getting tense. Guadan wasn't happy with the way the bandits were acting. Not dealing with honour, stepping on all the Inari traditions. It was harder and harder to keep his men from taking chunks out of the ruder bandits.

"Then your little incident occurred. Guadan isn't stupid, either. He's a traditionalist as well, and when he realized that his opponent was acting with more traditional Inari honour than his allies, he figured his Potentara would want to know. By the rules of the debt he owed Zoysana, he had to pull one of his men out of the battle, so he decided that man would be him. He went hotfoot over the

384

mountain and told Callar what was going on. So Callar came himself, in the proper traditional manner, to try to solve the problem with the Potentara of the other Clan: namely, Zoysana.

"From there it was pretty simple. As I said, he's a traditionalist, looking for a way out of a tough spot. He'd spent the summer dealing with people who had a loose interpretation of honour and he was tired of it. Once he got talking to Zoysana and I gave her a hand with following the traditional forms, he could see that, given a chance, she was by far the best choice to work with.

"After all, we don't want much. We'd like the youngsters to stop raiding down over the mountain. If they want to fight among themselves, they can go right ahead. All we want from Callar is no interference with the trading. He can stay up there on the plains and do what he wants. It won't solve all his problems, but it gives him room to set up his people for the changes that are coming, but on his own terms.

"He went back over the mountains a much happier man."

Anine took a moment to absorb this. "What will that mean to us?"

"I think he's going to pull his Clan Fighters out of here. It might make quite a difference because he had sent some of his best. There will still be Espola there, and maybe some minor Clans, but it ought to help."

"How long will it take for him to get word to his men?"

Jhanes rubbed his cheek with a forefinger. "Say two days to get back to his own ranges. Then another four or five to get a message down the mountain. Took me four days to get here."

"So in three days, we ought to start rounding them up?"

He nodded. "I'd say our chances of catching someone will get a whole lot better about then."

She stood up. "All right. I'd better get our boys prepared."

"Are you in a hurry?"

She turned back to him. "I guess not. They're all out doing regular patrols at the moment. We don't need to make any changes for the next couple of days."

He grinned. "That's good, because I have another message for you."

"From who?"

"From my dear brother-in-law, Ferlen. I ran into him on the road down."

Her shoulders sagged. "What's the problem now?"

His eyes snapped to her face. "Why do you think there's a problem?"

She passed her hand over her eyes. "Just a guess. We were doing too well earlier in the summer, and we put too many men on patrols against the bandits and the bandits got worse, so we got behind on the roads. There's some problems we have to solve before the winter rains; we're trying to make up time and it's causing a lot of trouble. Some of the fighters don't mind working, and working hard, but fighters aren't exactly the kind to do six days a quarter, month in, month out, so some of them are gettin' antsy.

"Then there are supply problems. Once word got around that the king was paying for all this and how much work he was planning, the prices started rising. Now we can't get enough dressed stone for what we're working on, we can't get enough men to do the work and we're stretched too thin on the patrols."

She passed a hand through her hair, and smiled ruefully. "Sorry to bother you with my tale of woe, but you did ask."

"That would explain Ferlen's message, then. He wants you to pop over to Alderly and take a look at a source of stone."

"Pop over to Alderly? That's a long day's ride each way. And why does he want me to go? He's the one who knows what he needs."

Jhanes grinned. "He said you'd ask that. He's going up to the castle to talk to Lady Kenna. She knows about your pricing problems and she's got some ideas."

Anine relaxed. "Any ideas that come from Lady Kenna are likely to be useful and a pleasure to put into action. All right. I'll take a little holiday ride over to Alderly to look at stones before I go back to hunting bandits. If anybody comes looking for me with another problem, tell them I went fishing."

He laughed. "Don't worry, Anine. Things will work out. You're doing pretty well, you know."

She responded with a grim smile. "I don't know where you see the evidence of that. I don't have much to show for either of my duties, and the summer's moving on."

"It happens."

"But why to me?" She stood up. "I better hit the planks. Long day tomorrow."

He nodded. "I'll ride back to the inn with you tomorrow. Do I bunk in with Mantinello as usual?"

"As you wish."

"He's always interesting to talk to." He turned at the tent flap. "Sleep well."

"I might need the rest."

He nodded and turned out into the night.

34. FINAL BATTLE

It was early afternoon three days later when Anine jogged up to the inn leading a limping horse. Jhanes stepped out the door as she panted to a halt.

"Nice day for a training run."

"Tell that to the damned horse."

"Lamed?"

"Aye. Don't know what for. Started limping when I left Alderly yesterday. He can move without my weight but I bin doin' the merc's pace since. Stayed at a farm last night but they didn't have any horses that could make better time than I do. You got a horse for me? I gotta get back to camp."

His eyes lingered on her sweat-stained shirt, her red face. "I don't think so."

"Whattaya mean? We talked about it before I left. In three days we figured I could put out a big sweep and pick up a bunch of bandits without hittin' any of our new allies. I gotta get up there and get goin'. We got work to do."

Jhanes shook his head. "I think you'd better take a rest."

"I don't have time for a rest."

He stepped in front of her. "Anine, I'm going to pull rank on you. You've pushed yourself too hard. Wait here tonight; go up to the camp tomorrow."

She pushed him aside and led her horse towards the stable. "What kind of rank can an innkeeper pull on me? Where's that big horse of yours? He'll get me there."

His voice cut into the haze of fatigue. "If you go up there and stagger into camp after three days on the road crammed into two and go out with the troops, you're going to be too tired to do anything and you're going to make mistakes that could cost lives. Think about it."

She thought. "I suppose."

"You suppose right. Besides, that's an order. You stable that horse, you come in here and sit down and you drink a large mug of cider. And then you drink another. After that, you can tell me what the stone is like out at Alderly, and what you plan to do to chase down the bandits."

She was in the middle of the first mug when Sarha sat down opposite her. "Hear you're in the thick of it, as usual."

"Oh, aye." She brought her focus back from where it had been ranging over her problems. "Wasn't for your dear brother keepin' his part of the deal goin', we'd be chasin' our tails round in circles."

"He seems to be enjoying it."

"He is?"

"Oh, he never says anything, but I can tell. Most summers he used to just loaf around, do some fishing, laze in the sun, but I could tell he was bored. Now he's bustling about like somebody important. I guess he is somebody important, come to think of it."

"Oh, he's important, all right." She looked down into the empty mug. Sarha swiped it from her hand and refilled it. Taking another sip, slower this time, Anine nodded. "Credit to him. Don't know how he does it. Thought he was a trapper, a hunter. Turns out he knows how to work stone as well. Who'd a thought it?"

"Oh, he's been working stone all his life."

"He has?"

"Sure. You ought to see the cabins on his trapline. I used to go up there in the summer, years ago before Pa died. You ought to get him to take you some time, Anine."

"Sure. Some summer when we don't have a hundred Inari, fifty road workers and Gerth's political problems on our shoulders."

"How about the fall?"

"And take a chance of gettin' snowed in for the winter?"

"That might be fun."

Anine snorted. "For the first two weeks, maybe."

"Well, anyway, you ought to see those cabins." Then Sarha's face grew serious. "You hear him talking about selling that trap line, you don't let him."

"Me? Why would he listen to me? Why don't you tell him?"

"I'm his sister. He never listens to me. You, he listens to."

"When we're talkin' road work or fightin'. I somehow don't think he'd take it so good, I started interferin' with his life."

"Well, somebody has to. If he sells that trap line, the cabins go with it. I spent some wonderful times up there. It's so beautiful.

389

Mountains all around, rocks peeking up through the moss, flowers everywhere."

Jhanes appeared, sliding another mug of ale in front of Anine. "My wife seems to have a romantic side I'm just starting to notice. Maybe we should take a holiday up there some summer."

"And who'd run the inn?"

"Ferlen, who else? He is part-owner."

"Aye, when Anine turns him loose from fixing roads and chasing bandits."

Anine shook her head. "If only I had the choice."

"Change the topic, Sarha. The idea was to get her mind off her worries."

"No, that's all right. I'm feeling much more relaxed now. I can talk about business."

"As long as you quit before we have to light candles. You need your sleep, and summer nights are short."

The next morning, as she set out on a fresh horse with a good night's sleep behind her, she had to admit his advice was good. They had discussed tactics for an hour or more and she was much more ready to start their final attack on the bandits. As the horse loped up the new road, she finalized her plans.

When she approached her camp, however, those thoughts were chased from her mind. More than the usual number of people were moving around, and the noise was much louder. She kicked her horse into a trot, ignoring good manners, and rode straight into the middle of the clearing. Sitting there above it all, she surveyed the scene.

Most of her Inari were in camp, milling around, sitting outside their tents, looking satisfied with themselves. Some had injuries, but not many. Sitting off to one side and looking much less pleased were a number of strange Inari in different Clan colours. Last, there was a disgruntled officer in an ornate uniform, torn and dusty, a couple of uniformed subordinates hovering around him.

"Mantinello!"

At the sound of her voice, quiet descended on the camp. Unused to such attention, she held her horse still and waited. Her aide came running from the command tent.

"Anine! Welcome back!"

She made a point of surveying the camp, then stared down at him. "There seem to have been some changes since I left."

He grinned up at her. "Oh, you mean all those extra people?"

She swung off her horse. "That might be a good place to start. Where did you pick them up?"

He shrugged nonchalantly. "Pretty much all over the place."

"I see. And the one in the pretty costume over there?"

Mantinello grinned. "You'll have to ask Pagris about that one. Here he comes now."

Sure enough, the older Inari came striding out of the command tent. "Good afternoon, Anine. I hope you had a pleasant journey."

She dismounted, slapped him on the shoulder and spun him back towards the tent. "All right, you two. You've got some explaining to do. I don't want to get tough with you in front of all these people, but we're going in there and we're not coming out until I know what's going on. If you're gonna win the war while I'm gone, at least you coulda warned me."

Grinning, they led the way into the command tent. The map, formerly full of pins, was almost empty. A thick, red line surrounded most of their area of operations.

"Tell me. How did you manage this?"

They each looked at the other, then Pagris spoke. "We did some thinking, Anine. You weren't here, but we decided you would agree."

She sat down. "Well, since it was obviously successful, I guess I agree. What did you decide?"

"Well, you told us that we should be looking for Inari. So that's what we did. We all went out on our usual patrols, trying to think what an Inari would do in this or that terrain. Soon we began to find traces. We followed the traces and found some camps. The Inari were mostly camping away from the bandits, so we just rounded them up."

"You rounded up the Inari?"

"Yes. It was much easier than we had expected. Then, once the Inari were taken care of, the bandits were simple to find. We still have a few patrols out picking them up, but we got the officer in charge already."

"And where are the rest of the bandits?"

Mantinello rubbed his neck ruefully. "Well, Anine, we had a bit of a problem, there."

"Yes?" She put all the skepticism she could into that one word.

"Well, there was another attack. The bandits cleaned out a small family trader, only two wagons with his wife and kids. Killed them all. There was no chance. It was the largest group of bandits, about forty of them, and there wasn't even a fight. They just murdered them. The boys were a bit upset, and when they found the bandits…"

Pagris continued. "…Mantinello had a tough job saving the officers. The rest are out in Vico Canyon, feeding birds."

"I didn't think that kind of thing would bother the Inari."

"We love our children."

"Ah." She rose, looked once more at the map. "It seems you have covered things rather nicely. Let's take a look outside."

They followed her out and she approached the strange Inari. They were in three groups. The largest group was sitting straight, looking ahead bravely. The second group, six of them, were lounging around in what Anine could tell was forced detachment. The third group, an older Fighter and two younger ones, sat stiffly separate, and they looked angry, rather than afraid. She indicated the trio. "Pregota?"

Pagris nodded.

"Good." She walked over to them and spoke as formally as she could remember. "Zoysana's Clan welcomes visitors from our friends the Pregota Clan. Please be free with the hospitality of our tents. It would probably cause the least disharmony if you were to wait for us to arrange an escort back to your Clan territories, but that is your choice."

As she spoke, the three rose slowly to their feet. The eldest regained his poise faster. He saluted her formally as well, a satisfied grin on his face. "The Pregota Clan is pleased to accept the hospitality of the honourable Zoysana. We are impressed by the valour and virtue of her young Fighters. Do you have word for us from our Clan?"

She nodded. "Nothing specific, but I have news which will please you, I am sure. Perhaps you will honour me by guesting at my tent once the sun has fallen half-way."

They saluted again, and returned to their place to sit with satisfied expressions.

She turned to the larger group. "I see members of the Espola Clan here. Have you given your parole to my Fighters?"

There were several surly nods, but one older Fighter stood. "Yes, Anine of Zoysana's Clan. We have been bested by an honourable foe. We freely give our word to obey Zoysana and you in any way you wish, within the codes of our people." He turned to his companions and made a curt gesture. Immediately those in Espola colours were on their feet in formal poses of attention.

Anine nodded to him. "I accept your parole. I am pleased to find that some of the Espola have not forgotten the codes of your people. Perhaps you will find occasion to visit my tent later, and we shall discuss the fate of your Clan members."

"I thank you, Anine of Zoysana's Clan. I will attend you at any time you wish."

She gestured, and the Espola Clan members sat. She waited and, slowly and reluctantly, the others in the group rose.

"Which Clans do you represent?"

This group took their cue from the Espola elder, and each spoke firmly and clearly.

"Tibera."

"Didera."

"Rivola."

She nodded. "And you have all fought honourably, been bested fairly, and have given your paroles as well?"

Most of them nodded, but one young lad stood forward. "No, Anine of Zoysana's Clan. We did not fight honourably. We were mistaken in our choice of allies and we aided in a dishonourable cause. We will give our parole if you will accept it, but we understand that we have given you no cause to do so. If I, like those Seonga over there," he indicated the small group lounging separately, "had come here without the sanction of my Potentara, I would demand that your Designated Fighter meet me in the Circle and I would accept my fate."

She looked the young Fighter up and down. He fairly bristled with anger, and she could see a tremor of emotion in his arms. She glanced to Pagris for a proper response.

"The ability to admit one's mistakes in the presence of a foe is one to be admired."

She nodded, turning again to the boy. "There have been enough errors made this summer that it would be a cause for disharmony for one Fighter to pay for all. It is required that someone carry this information back to the Clan Potentaras personally. Perhaps you might be willing to perform this service for your Clan and mine?"

The young man nodded stiffly. "I am at the command of Zoysana for the rest of my life. She has only to speak."

She allowed a small smile to curve her lip. "Another ability to be admired is that of tempering one's passion to the reality of the Clan's need. An excess of zeal can cause disharmony even in pursuit of honourable action."

The Inari bowed his head in acceptance and did not speak. She turned to the last group. They merely sat and looked up at her. She waited, unspeaking.

Then Mantinello was in front of her, his voice lashing them into motion. "When the representative of Zoysana approaches, you will show due deference. You are slaves to Zoysana's will, a fact you will never forget. Anine will have you in one line NOW!"

They startled into a ragged line, all except one, who came to his feet slowly and slouched towards Anine, a sneer on his lips. He stood in front of her, looked her up and down casually, and took a breath.

Before he could speak, a throwing knife buried itself in his throat. As his body toppled, two arrows pierced it. There was silence in the camp. Anine did not turn to see who had dealt with her problem for her. She waited, then addressed the suddenly straight line in front of her. She spoke quietly, conversationally, as if reviewing facts that everyone knew.

"It seems that some of us have been caught up in a political situation which we could not control. Mistakes have been made, from the highest to the lowest level." She indicated the body in front of her. "This should not be taken as an excuse for disharmony, a lack of honourable behaviour, or the opportunity to kill for dishonourable reasons. Do you understand me?"

There was a series of nods, and someone mumbled, "Yes, ma'am."

"Good. I find it interesting that these honourable Clan members, who are now Zoysana's slaves, do not wish to associate with you. I take this as evidence that you have not acted in the most honourable fashion. Could this be true?"

There was considerable shuffling, and none would meet her eye.

"I see. Then I must deal with this unfortunate situation, while causing as little disharmony as possible.

"Listen closely. You will be escorted to the border of Falticeni. From that point, you will make your way back to your family Clan. There, you will report the results of this summer's actions. You will then hold yourselves ready, at any time, to do Zoysana's bidding. You will not aid your Clan in any warfare. You will take no opportunity to increase your status. You are the slaves of Zoysana, and your only task, until she might decide to free you or give you another, is to remind your Clan of the results of your dishonourable actions."

She started to turn away, then spun back to their startled faces. "But you will return to your Clans. If you do anything else, go anywhere else, speak to anyone else, your life is forfeit, as well as your honour. Do you understand?"

"Yes, ma'am," was choked out of five throats. She nodded and walked away.

"Come over to the tent, Pagris and Mantinello. I've been spinning on the point of my sword for the last candle. I hope I did that right. I don't know exactly what the proper forms are, but I figured we had to get it straight."

Pagris fell into step beside her. "I think that was quite correct, Anine. They were all impressed, and I think most of them will obey."

"And I want the names of the three who took care of the surly one for me." She grinned. "I bet the knife belongs to Glock. Tell the archers they are too slow. He beat them by at least half a breath."

35. Ambush

"I learned a new word today, Zoysana. Pessimistic. Do you think I'm too pessimistic?"

The Kyabran woman looked up from the map of the new Free County she was studying. "Not any more than your average mercenary."

"That's too bad."

"How could not being pessimistic be bad?"

"Because if I'm too pessimistic, then we don't have any trouble."

"Ah. But if you aren't?"

"I've been looking over these maps and matching them up with the number of Inari we pulled in, and the number of attacks we had lately. They don't add up."

"In what way?"

"The boys made good progress because they went out and hunted down the Inari. Then they found the main force of so-called bandits and wiped them out after they massacred that family. But with Gerth and Talia coming, I got to thinking. I've never been completely happy with the numbers, and now it comes to me. What if we didn't get as many as we should have? I figure the number of Inari, compared to the number of soldiers, and the way they divided up, there could be another fifty soldiers, easy, hiding out somewhere."

"Or hightailing it for the border."

"Maybe, aye. But what if they're not?"

"There haven't been any attacks. What could they be doing?" Zoysana stopped, one hand in the middle of a gesture. "Oh."

"That's what I'm worried about. How many people know about Gerth and Talia coming?"

"You don't keep something as big as the New Queen's Procession quiet."

"So, anybody could know about it by now."

"I think so."

"How many Warlanders do they have with them?"

Zoysana shrugged. "About twenty. It's not supposed to be too big a party because of the 'delicate political situation' in the Duchies. If Gerth showed up at the border with a hundred, they'd be right back where they were a year ago, with rumours of an invasion."

"So Gerth and Talia are riding through here with a medium-sized escort and there could be as many as fifty enemy soldiers unaccounted for. Plus, she's got her mother along in that big carriage. Am I being too pessimistic?"

Zoysana thought about it. "No, not by half."

"What do you mean?"

"You think there might be fifty soldiers out there. What if you underestimated? What if they've been slipping more in while we've been chasing the first bunch? We pulled most of our patrols off the northeast border because there have been no attacks there. There could be a hundred or more by now, just hiding out and bothering nobody, waiting to ambush Gerth and Talia."

Anine smiled grimly. "Now, that, I call pessimistic."

Zoysana returned the smile. "I don't. Not if we know about it."

"True. What do we do? I figure we need more information."

"Right. Let's send out a lot of small parties, two or three men each, your best trackers. Let them slip through the whole area north from Lanil's Rock to the Velikiian border, very low profile. Meanwhile, I'll head back south, meet the procession and discuss it with Gerth."

"The boys'll love this."

"Good. Be very sure they understand that there's to be no fighting."

Anine shook her head. "I'm not worried. When I explain what's going on, they're going to jump right in. They'll start a competition to see who can get out and back the fastest without being seen."

"Sounds like the Inari, all right."

"I'll send one Clan with each group, just to make sure. Three's traditional. One to stay, one to report, and one to cover for whoever gets killed."

"Very practical. Get that organized, come daybreak."

"What's daylight got to do with this?" She strode to the tent door. "Mantinello! Get everyone out here."

As soon as they had formed the usual horseshoe, she started. "Somebody tell me. How big a party can one good scout hide the tracks of?"

Numbers between five and ten were called out.

"Right. So it's arithmetic time again. How many enemy Inari did we bring in? About thirty. At five-to-one, that means a minimum of a hundred and fifty enemy soldiers out there." She waited until uncertain frowns appeared on some faces. "That's right. I can account for less than a hundred. Where are the others?"

An uneasy hum arose from the fighters.

"Exactly. There could be as many as two hundred enemy out there." She explained about Talia's Procession.

"We have a new task. It will be a hard one, but we have the skills. These are only soldiers, and a big group of them. Their Inari have gone back above the Rim of the World or been captured. We will find them."

She outlined the plan, and allowed them to organize themselves into groups of three, some of four, each with a member of Zoysana's Clan.

"We need to get this information with nobody knowing. Not the enemy, not the Petrellans who live near. The fox must not know that you passed his den. The doe must not be aware that you stepped over her fawn. You must move through the country like a mere breath of wind, noticed by none."

Their eyes glowed with enthusiasm as they lined up at the map for their sweep assignments. Then she sent them out, at different times and by different routes, using the roads, the smuggler's trails and every animal path they had mapped out over the past two summers. By morning the camp was near empty, and eighty Clan were ghosting through the forests of northern Petrella.

When Gerth and Talia reached Jaspen three days later, the reports were in.

Anine reported to Zoysana. "There are a hundred and twenty, more or less. Regular soldiers, from the look of it, better armed than we saw during the summer. They've got two camps a half-day's ride apart, just north of here. There's a low pass nearby, several good ambush points along the river. No indication which one they'll use. Mantinello left two trios there to keep an eye on them. They'll be sending reports, morning and night. What does King Gerth say?"

Zoysana smiled. "He says leave them alone."

Anine took a moment to think, then she nodded. "Good. And then?"

"We have ten of his best Warlanders, led by Lukin. Twenty footmen from the Castle Guard. Ten more of the nobility, fighters all. We've got a hundred Inari."

"And thirty road crew."

"I'd forgotten about them." The Kyabran woman mused. "They'll come in handy, because they can move around without causing suspicion. Where are your mercs?"

"They're all in the road camp outside town. We'll just pick them up along the way. It'll be a nice change for them. They don't complain about the road work, as long as they get a bit of a fight every couple of quarters."

Zoysana nodded. "That sounds like enough, but not much. Somebody in the Inner Duchies has planned this very carefully and isn't going to risk failure. These will be some of the best troops they've got. Evidence? They've managed to stay around for three quarters at least without a whisper of their presence getting out. That's skill and discipline. I think we'll have to be ready for anything."

Anine nodded soberly. "I need to have a chat with the Clan. These boys have never been in a pitched battle with real soldiers. We'll need to keep a hit-and-hide going, or we'll get flattened. Pagris will know."

"Pagris isn't with us."

"He isn't?"

Zoe shook her head. "He said he didn't need all the pomp and ceremony. He had a different task. He took Leile and Orcan up to the Great Prairie."

"Ah. Orcan would be looking for trading opportunities. But why Leile? As if I didn't know."

The Clan Leader grinned. "Young love will have its way, I suppose. I was just as happy to split her off from Mantinello for a while." She pulled the map closer. "Back to business. Any horse in the enemy ranks?"

"Thirty-five of the men are mounted. Good-looking horses, according to the boys: big, but not up to Petrellan standards. Plate armour. Most are probably Knights from the Duchies. A few squires, and the rest lancers on lighter steeds."

"Fine. Gerth and Lukin will make the plans, but he'll want to keep his Warlanders together in squads like Barent trained them. At least the King's Guard. The nobility might charge off on their own as they usually do. We'll have about half your boys mounted, harrying, and the others on the ground for scouting and containing their pickets."

"Sounds like a good start."

"And there's a special job for you."

"For me?" Anine didn't like the twist to Zoe's lip.

"Yes. You get to ride in Lady Trenet's carriage."

"That thing?"

"Of course. We're going to take advantage of your similarity in size, as we've done in the past. You'll ride in the carriage with Lady Trenet, and Talia will be mounted, with Gerth, in Warlander's armour."

Anine grinned. "Glad Lord Trenet went home last month. I wouldn't want to have to sit on him." She shrugged. "I'm better off without a horse anyway. I can use my proper sword, then." She considered. "They'll probably attack with the horse first, try to draw the Warlanders away. Then they'll swarm the carriage with the infantry. Do you think they want prisoners?"

"We looked at that. Probably not. Gerth is too dangerous, mainly for his ideas, apart from his fighting ability. Talia would be a good example for anybody who thinks of siding with us. No. We think they're aiming for a massacre."

"Let's make sure they get one." She rubbed the pommel of her big sword.

"We'll have to keep an eye open for the leaders. This is too big an operation to send out with a lackey in control. Those in charge will be very close to the actual plotters, so we want them. Alive if possible."

"We'll do our best, ma'am. But it is a battle."

"Yes, it will be."

There was a reception that night in the lord's palace, but Anine, Jhanes, and Zoysana were much too busy with their preparations.

The next morning, Anine reported to Talia's apartments carrying the modified Warlander's gear for the queen. Talia opened the door herself, smiling broadly. "Oh, good. We were just finding something for you to wear."

Anine grimaced. "Just remember I have to fight in it."

Talia laughed. "Lateda thought of that. We found this." She held up a gathered travelling robe. "Plenty of material to cover your armour, and it's a wrap-around, so you can get rid of it in a hurry. However..."

Anine's heart sank at the queen's mischievous smile.

"...it's belted, so you will have to pull in your waist a bit."

The dress was frilly and gathered in at the waist. "Oh, no! You're not getting me into that!"

"Sorry, Anine. It's your duty to the realm. Take off your jerkin."

"Couldn't I just go out and capture mountain lions with my bare hands, or something easy?"

As an added touch, Lateda checked the trunks and came up with several gold-embroidered tabards with the Trenet crest on them.

"Perfect for Talia's mercs and the fellows from our road gang."

Ferlen came by as they were dressing. "Nice duds. Got an extra?"

Lateda wordlessly dove into a trunk and came up with an even more resplendent one.

"Fine. Officer stuff. Singles me out for attack." He put it on. Then he turned and looked musingly at Anine.

She felt completely exposed in the frilly dress. "What? What's wrong?"

He shrugged. "I just noticed what Varli was talking about."

"What? When?" But he had turned away and was discussing tactics with Talia's personal guard.

The procession wound out of Jaspen on the road north to Renalk buoyed by the cheers of the people. As they left the town, the audience thinned, and finally it was only the workers in the fields who left their toil to watch the royals pass.

First on the road came the mounted Guard with the king and queen in their midst. Then sixteen infantry Guard marched in good formation, keeping easy time with the horses. Anine and Lady Trenet came next in the big, black carriage, surrounded by the liveried mercs on foot. Then two luggage wagons with servants, all armed, front and rear. Following came another six infantry, with the ten mounted nobles at the end. An unseen web of Guides screened the perimeter of the group. The Inari ranged far and wide. Of Zoysana, Patu and Jhanes, there was no sign.

When the road was wide enough, Ferlen rode on Anine's side of the carriage. He chatted with her a bit, although she knew that his every sense was alert.

"We're into tough country, now."

"I can see that." The hills had closed in and the road wound above the river. In places, the rock pushed them onto causeways with the water lapping at their left side. An Inari on a sweating horse pulled up beside Gerth, spoke briefly. The king responded, and the boy galloped back to the carriage.

"The Clan Leader says they are at next bridge, Anine. Gerth says let rear guard cross bridge, then pull in against rock. Zoysana and Hidden Twig go to the forest to find leaders."

Nodding, she lifted a hand to the king. He responded, then trotted his destrier ahead, loosening his sword as he rode.

They approached a bridge and the mounted Warlanders clumped across. As they ascended the small rise on the other side, Anine saw Gerth looking back anxiously.

Ferlen stiffened and jogged his horse ahead. He watched carefully as the infantry marched across the bridge, then turned his horse hot-foot back to swing in alongside the coach. "There's something wrong with that bridge."

"What do you mean?"

"I wouldn't take this heavy coach out on that bridge. It looks wrong. I think somebody's tampered with it."

"Then the ambush point is on this side." She stuck her head out the front of the coach. "Pull up, Arderton. The bridge is weakened. Trumpeter, can you sound 'Monarch in Peril?'"

The man leaned a worried face closer. "Well, yes, my Lady, but the Arlyn kings don't use that signal."

"Do I look like an Arlyn king? The only ones who will understand what it really means are those who know that Talia isn't here. The enemy will think she is. Sound it now, and sound it loud. Arderton, swing the coach over beside that clump of trees so they can't get at us from both sides. Ferlen, remind the mercs we want the leader. If one of them gets close, let him through."

The moment the trumpet blared through the morning air, the forest came alive with soldiers. A troop of mounted Knights stormed around the last corner of the road behind them and the rear guard of Warlanders wheeled in good order and formed up to meet them. The

402

foot soldiers who had just crossed the bridge had stopped when the carriage did and they rushed back to form a perimeter around Anine and her charge. Their big shields locked together, and they stood fast, awaiting the attack.

The enemy soldiers pressed in, but there was little room for all of them, so their numbers were hampered. The shield wall held, spears and swords bristling from it. Arrows whirred over her head as Ferlen and Arderton loosed from the protection of the baggage on top of the coach.

Fuming with impatience, Anine moved from window to window of the carriage, her sword drawn. Back in the forest, her Inari ghosted from tree to tree, their barbed war arrows piercing unsuspecting backs.

"Like to be out there, would you?" Lady Trenet looked amused.

"Tell you, I would, but we gotta keep the ruse going as long as I can. Gerth and Talia are on the other side of the bridge. We might need to cut the road so they can get away to the north if they have to. If we do, I'll pull the carriage out on the bridge. That'll block it, whether the bridge goes down or not."

Then a third troop of horse thundered out of the forest opposite and charged directly at the carriage. She shouted over the sound of the battle.

"Spandrel! That's the one. Let him through!"

The thick trees divided the new charge, and the foot soldiers were able to divert most of the riders. However, the centre came on: four Knights led by one in fancy black armour.

The mercenaries fell back, then split, and the Knight in gold-chased plate pulled his destrier close beside the carriage.

"Do you know him?"

"Lord Glosla of Plasamin. Pretty armour, but the gorget's too low. Kill him."

"But we…" She glanced at the icy face in front of her. "Yes, your Grace."

The old woman nodded. "He has needed it for a long time."

"Talia" peeked out through the leather curtain. Sure enough, the Knight's armour had a low neckline, probably to facilitate his head movement. A lunge from below…

"Better come out, Lady Talia. We've got you like a pigeon in a trap."

403

Anine grinned at Lady Trenet as she shucked off the dress, then tightened her helmet strap. "In for a surprise, isn't he?" Talia's mother tilted her head and raised an eyebrow.

Flinging the door wide, Anine stood up. "Nice trap, Lord Glosla. Wrong pigeon."

He only had time to say "Oh, shit..." before her lunging sword took him through the throat. The mercenaries and infantry closed in on the three mounts behind him and tore their riders down.

Anine turned back into the carriage. "That's it, then. Bar the door and stay inside with Lateda. Will you be all right?"

The older woman gave a thin smile. "I might be dying. Given the choice, I'd rather go on the field of battle and not know what hit me." Her hand motion chopped Anine's response. "Go out and kill the whole pack of them."

"Yes, ma'am!" Anine saluted and swung to the top of the coach. Most of the battle had deteriorated into a full mêlée, with small groups fighting in all directions, but the carriage perimeter held firm. A third of the enemy horse was still engaging her rear guard. Another third was trying to keep Gerth from returning across the bridge, and the rest were still attacking Anine's footmen around the carriage.

She watched a mounted Clan Fighter tempt a Knight to chase him, luring the heavier rider into an ambush by several other Inari. It was a good trick, because the only way the enemy learned about it was by dying. She called out suggestions in Inarituk, and was pleased to see them followed. Her perimeter was getting ragged, and she shouted at them to trim it up.

Then Gerth broke through: Talia stuck to his right side, Varli at his left, and two of his mounted Guard behind. They thundered over the bridge, and Anine could see it shake. Unfortunately, the five were cut off and immediately assailed by horse and foot.

Gerth, high on Pelex, kept a wide swath clear in front of him as he mowed towards the carriage. Varli and Talia clung to his flanks, protecting him from encirclement. The two Guards were valiantly keeping the south end of the bridge clear, but were seriously outnumbered, and Gerth was forced to slow his charge to protect their backs. They were holding their own until six of the enemy horse from across the bridge saw the situation and charged after them, attacking from the rear. One of the Guard went down, and

404

Varli turned to help the other, leaving Gerth's left flank unguarded. The foot soldiers closed in, darting forward to stab at the horse's flanks at every chance.

It was looking grim enough that Anine was preparing a desperation charge when a single Warlander burst from the other side and charged across the bridge. It was Lukin, and he didn't pause to fight. He simply threw his huge destrier at the tight-packed enemy Knights, and they all went down, the old Warlander on top, his sword hewing methodically.

It was a heroic move, but the shock was too much for the weakened bridge. With a groan and scrape of rock, the roadway crumbled. The whole group, horses and men, disappeared from Anine's sight, the rest of the bridge tumbling after them.

Now Gerth's position was looking grave. With no escape route, he allowed himself to be pushed back against the ruined bridge, with Talia under the protection of his sword and Varli back on his left. Soldiers swarmed around them, closing in.

"Anine!" The shrill female voice cut through the battle noise.

She turned to the carriage. Lateda stood in the open doorway, heedless of her own danger, pointing. "Pelex! Spear to the shoulder!"

Anine waved her thanks and turned to regard the king's position. The charger reared and pawed at his enemies, and bright blood spattered from a flow down his left shoulder. He landed with a lurch, his leg almost giving, but he rose gamely and fought on.

Anine slipped back to the coach. "Your Grace, Gerth and Talia need me. You'll be all right once we take the pressure off."

A firm voice echoed from the interior of the coach. "I'm an old lady. They're the future. Do what you have to."

"Yes, your Grace."

She dropped her buckler and picked up a larger shield someone had lost. The little shield was versatile enough for open-field work, but she needed brute force now. At the same time, she started calling out orders in Inarituk. She could see Varli translating for Gerth between swings, so they knew what she was going to do. Twenty Clan appeared from the grove beside the carriage and she swept them out to her flanks, worried about their ability to handle the press of armoured soldiers.

She called out to the soldiers holding the line. "There's only one way to do this, boys: the hard way. I'm taking the point." They gave a roar and jammed around her, and she started to break through to Gerth. It was rough going, but she fought grimly through the press, step by slippery step.

She felt an easing of the pressure on her left. A heavy figure slid up beside her, sword hewing: Jhanes. He and Zoysana were covering her, the small woman working down between her two larger friends. Patu, kitted out in ceremonial fighting gear, was snarling at her hip, darting forward to slash or grab at any undefended flesh. With this protection, Anine raised her attack confidently and began to rain heavier blows down on those who confronted her. Her arrowhead became a widening front as the enemy foot began to give way.

The line in front of her dissolved so suddenly that she stumbled forward, and she found herself looking up into the fearsome visage of Gerth's helm.

"Anine! Jhanes! Even Zoysana and her Clan! I seem to have friends all over this battle!" She could tell from his voice that he was enjoying himself.

"We can set up a line from the bridge to the carriage, your Majesty. Backs to the river."

"Do it. What about those on the other side?"

"No problem, Sire. The Clan is taking care of them."

Many of the enemy horse, trapped on the opposite side of the river, were trying to get across, but any Knight scrambling up the bank was swarmed by a group of Inari, who dragged him off his horse and dispatched him. The rest of Gerth's Guard pushed the enemy to the edge of the ruined bridge.

With Clan horsemen nipping away at stragglers, the beleaguered rear guard finally finished off their attackers to move in on the central conflict from behind, and soon it was over. Anine's longer line firmed, then held. Trapped between two implacable forces, the enemy foot was rounded up and disarmed, the Knights were unhorsed and placed under guard, and the cleanup began.

36. Anine's Choice

Anine was calling out orders when she realized that the king and queen had dismounted and were standing watching her. She stopped, confused, but Gerth motioned her to continue.

"You've done fine so far. Why stop now?"

"What do you mean, Sire?"

He grinned. "Correct me if I missed something — I was a bit busy — but all through the fight I kept hearing this woman's voice calling out orders, half the time in a language I don't understand. Then Varli's telling me that we have to push left because you're coming out to meet us. So, I do what I'm told, and there you are, and the battle's over. Isn't that how it went?"

"I suppose, your Majesty. Most of the troops were mine, so I was telling them what to do. I knew if I used Inarituk, Varli would tell you, and the enemy wouldn't understand."

"Don't worry, Anine. Talia has already put me in the picture. Don't sheath your sword yet. As long as everybody continues to do what you say, you're in charge."

It took a moment for the idea to sink in, and then she squashed her immediate reaction. *When the king promotes you, you don't tell him you'd rather not.* She firmed her shoulders.

"Right, your Majesty." She caught Talia's wink as she turned away. "Jhanes? I saw Lukin go down with the bridge. Took six of them with him and he was on top. Could you look for him? Ferlen? We need to cross the river somehow."

The big soldier turned on his heel and she motioned three nearby Inari to follow. Ferlen nodded and disappeared. Mantinello and the other Inari had already formed a line of wounded and were tending them in their rough fashion, aided by Zoysana. Lady Trenet had Lateda and Ranill opening trunks to find cloth for bandages while she supervised from the window of the carriage.

A shout from the riverbank caught their attention, and then a group staggered up the slope, carrying the still form of Lukin.

"How is he?"

"Breathing. No serious wounds. Helmet's dented, though."

Anine glanced up at Jhanes, frowning. "Let's get it off carefully."

407

They laid the old Warlander out on the ground and eased his helmet free. Sure enough, a trickle of blood ran from the side of his head. Zoysana probed carefully through his hair. She winced and shook her head.

"There's a depression. He must have taken one of the big rocks when the bridge went down. Listen to his breathing."

There was silence, except for the snoring of the wounded man's breath. "That's a bad sign. His skull is probably broken in. He's deeply unconscious. Nothing we can do."

"Put him in here. There's room, and I can make him comfortable."

There was no denying Lady Trenet, so the injured man was stretched on a bed across the capacious seats of the carriage. Lateda brought cool water from the river and the lady bathed his head while they gently removed his armour.

Anine gazed around as order was restored. "Mantinello! Numbers?"

He appeared in front of her. "It was a bad fight, Anine."

She nodded soberly. "I never intended to put you up against armoured Knights."

"We lost seven, Anine, and ten wounded bad enough that they can't fight."

That reminder jostled her mind, and she started up, only to see Zoysana sending out scouts, foot and horse, and setting pickets. Reassured, she continued. "The others?"

"The foot soldiers lost more. Five of the King's Guard and eight road crew. Twelve wounded."

She nodded. "The enemy?"

A satisfied look crossed his face. "Twenty-five good horses captured."

She grinned, glancing over at Gerth. "And we'll see that you keep them, although they're a bit big for your uses."

"We'll trade them for proper ones."

"Fine. And now that the important facts are dealt with, could I have the numbers on the enemy dead and wounded?"

"Oh, of course. Twelve of the mounted ones dead, five injured. Fifty-two foot soldiers dead. Seventeen wounded. Five escaped, one on horse. They will be back soon."

Gerth whistled. "Fifty-two foot dead, and we only lost twenty?"

"They were getting in each other's way, your Majesty. That's why I pulled the carriage over by the trees. The smart ones that tried to sneak up behind ran into Clan Fighters back there. We also handled anyone who moved outside the battle zone."

Varli stepped forward. "And we took a lot of them between us when you attacked. They were really hemmed in. Couldn't run, couldn't fight, and you just kept coming. It was something to watch. I've never had a chance to see a wedge of foot soldiers move like that. It was like nothing could stop you!"

"I had good help."

Jhanes and Zoysana laughed. "We just followed in your wake."

The big soldier looked around. "Where's that bunch in livery? They held your right all the way."

Anine stood to full height and scanned the battlefield. The group in the bright tabards was huddled around a figure on the ground. She strode over. It was Strinde, one of the archers. He was swearing in a steady, low, voice while the big black-skinned man worked over a sword slash on his thigh. As Anine approached, the group opened for her and he looked up.

"Sorry, ma'am. I never should have tried for that last shot."

"What? Don't tell me you missed?"

He looked indignant. "Of course I didn't miss. The bastard fell on me with his sword out."

She looked at the others. Espere, the other archer, nodded. "True, Anine. We set ourselves up on the left flank of the wagon, and this big swordsman split the line and charged us. Strinde put an arrow right through him, but the guy had his sword up and he just sort of dropped it as he fell, and caught Strinde on the way down."

"Any permanent damage, you think?"

Ouida looked up from his task. "No, ma'am, it's not even very deep. I'll have it sewn together in a moment."

"Well, take your time. It's only my leg."

"I just want to do it right, or I'll never hear the end of it."

Anine joined in the general laughter. "Jhanes says you did well on that last charge."

"We just followed you."

"Figured you knew what was goin' on, so the safest place would be right behind you."

"Safest place? Are you turning into a road builder on us?"

Ouida shrugged. "Roads don't swing back."

"I just thought I'd let you know. Jhanes mentioned your work, and the king was listening."

Spandrel nodded. "Fair enough. Thanks, Anine."

"Say, can we keep these? They're sort of pretty." Espere was fingering his embroidered tabard.

"You just take that straight back to the carriage and give it to the young lady there."

"The one that doesn't talk?"

"That's her. Don't even try to wash the blood off. You'd probably shrink it or something. You want clothes like that, you gotta learn a whole different way of life."

He shrugged out of the tabard, stroking it again. "A guy could get used to stuff like that."

Anine laughed. "You don't think much of yourself, do you? Here I tell you that your chances of signing on in Petrella are improving, and next thing you're pushing for livery in the Duchies."

"If you're gonna get ahead, you gotta think about stuff like that."

She assured herself that Strinde's wound was properly cleaned and sewn, then rose. "Well, boys, you did good work, and the king knows it. One of you stay with the poor victim, here, and the rest help with rounding up the prisoners for the march."

"Yes, ma'am," came from five voices, and the men moved sharply to their duties.

She returned as Gerth and his new queen seemed to be having their first public spat. Talia was standing, hands on hips, and glaring at her husband. "Tell you, Gerth, it was because you were in the front. You couldn't see what he was doing. He was right with you the whole way, and he matched you swing for swing."

"And you had time to observe this?"

"Tucked under your wing like that, with everybody watching out for me?" She held out her sword. "Look at that! I only made three good bashes in the whole battle!"

Gerth gently moved his wife's sword away from his throat and regarded the edge. "I'd say you did better than that. Five definite notches, two with blood." He let the sword point drop. "And I saw you run over several foot soldiers. You're getting good with that horse."

She grinned. "He likes a bit of excitement, you know." She looked at Gerth suspiciously. "You saw all that?"

The king laughed. "I watch everything in a battle. If Anine hadn't been running this one, I'd have been in charge. Not that I'd have been much use, on the other side of the river. So, yes, I watch. And I saw what you did. Varli!"

The squire appeared at a jog. "Yes, your Majesty?"

"I have one more use for my sword. Is it clean?"

"Yes, your Majesty."

"Perhaps you'd prefer it sharpened up a bit..."

Varli regarded Gerth before the light dawned. "Oh, no, your Majesty. I think it will be fine just like it is."

Gerth laughed and drew his sword. "Then stand straight, lad." He looked at his sword musingly. "You know, there were times when I didn't know if I was going to be using the edge or the flat of this sword on you. But you have done well for yourself. You held your place like a true Warlander in this battle, and my queen and I," a meaningful glance at Talia, "want you to have the honour permanently."

As Varli stood stiff and straight, Gerth ran the edge of his sword gently along the side of his neck, just above the rim of his breastplate. A trickle of blood flowed from the jagged cut.

Varli spoke the words of the Oath of the Warlander, followed by his Allegiance to Gerth and Petrella.

Then the king turned his former squire to face the assembled soldiers and lords. "Behold the new Warlander. May his friends remember his face."

A cheer rang out. Gerth placed the helmet on Varli's head.

"Behold his helm. May his enemies fear its visage." Anine led the cheer this time.

The Clan grouped around to congratulate the new Warlander, and Gerth stood back with one arm around Talia, a satisfied smile on his face. He turned his head to Anine.

"What do you think, Anine?"

"He'da made a good merc, your Majesty."

"High praise."

"He grew up a lot, the last few years. What are you going to do for a squire, now?"

Gerth rolled his eyes. "That's something I hadn't thought about."

"I've got a candidate, Sire."

"You do?"

"Aye. Mantinello."

"Your Inari aide?"

"Aide, squire, same thing. I hate to lose him, but he'd be perfect."

The king nodded. "I caught the bit about the numbers at the end of the battle. Does he do that all in his head?"

"That's right, your Majesty. I've been teaching him to read and write, but he still does it by memory."

"Impressive. Bring him over here, and we'll have a chat."

She hardly had to raise her voice, and the Inari lad appeared. "Yes, Anine?"

"King Gerth would like to talk to you, Mantinello."

The boy turned and made a very presentable bow. "How may I be of service, your Majesty?"

Gerth shared a glance with Anine. "I was wondering what your plans were for the winter. Are you going back to the Roof of the World?"

"I think so, Sire."

"You think. Do you have something else you would like to do instead?"

"Yes, your Majesty. I would like to stay here, and learn more about the Lowlands."

"I see. Do you understand the duties of a squire?"

The agile face turned up to the king for a startled moment but then the smile faded. "No, your Majesty. It wouldn't work. I've never even been a page. It would cause disharmony to choose an outsider for such an important position as the king's squire. There must be a candidate who would be more politically useful."

Gerth's brows furrowed. "Are you advising me on protocol?"

"Yes, your Majesty. It is the duty of every Clan member to give his knowledge for the use of the Potentara for the benefit of the Clan."

Gerth snorted. "Well, you're starting to sound like my mother. I'm not so sure that this is a good idea after all."

Mantinello bowed again. "I am pleased that your Majesty sees fit to hear my words."

"Oh, no, you're not going to get out of it that easily. If you're going to be my squire, that means you have to listen to what I say."

"Yes, Sire, my understanding of the Codes says this is true most of the time."

"Most of the time?"

"Yes, your Majesty. It is the duty and honour of the squire to obey the Warlander in every way."

"But..." Gerth rolled his eyes heavenward.

"...but it is also the duty of the squire to do what he thinks is best for his Warlander. It is possible that these two duties may conflict. If that happens, the squire must make the right choice, the one that will bring the most honour to the Warlander and the Clan."

Gerth shook his head and turned to Talia. "My dear, you have been listening to this. Are we in a bargaining session?"

She laughed. "It sounds like you are getting the terms of your new relationship straight."

"In other words, bargaining."

"He's Inari, dear. They get everything straight before they commit to a course of action. It could take days."

Gerth raised his hands helplessly. "Well, we've got days. We can't get across this river, so I guess we'll have to take a detour."

"I don't think so, your Majesty."

Gerth turned to Anine. "What do you have in mind?"

"You've forgotten, your Majesty. You have your road crew here. Ferlen is already checking out the ford."

"Ford?"

"Yes, Sire. Most of these bridges have only been here a hundred years or so. Before that, there was a ford. Paved with stone, if we're lucky."

"If there was a ford, why didn't those other Knights come across and attack us after the bridge went down?"

Anine laughed. "Because, your Majesty, every time one got across, the Clan grabbed him and stole his horse."

"I missed that. So, when do you think we can cross?"

"If the ford is safe for the carriage, as soon as you like. I think you should get the important people on the road again soon, so you can make Renalk before dark. It's not too far, but we've spent a lot of time, and everybody is tired."

She stopped. "That is, if that suits your Majesties..."

They both laughed. "Yes, Anine, it suits us very well, I'm glad you're thinking ahead. We'll take Jhanes and Zoysana and the able

413

Petrellan horse and foot. I suspect your Clan will have no problem with the prisoners and the wounded?"

"None at all, Sire. Especially if the prisoners carry their own wounded."

"Your Majesty! Talia!"

Gerth's head came around. "Yes, Lady Trenet?"

"He's awake. He wants to talk to you."

Gerth strode over and mounted the carriage carefully. As he leaned inside, a silence descended, as everyone strained to hear the words.

"How are you, Lukin?"

"Not good, Sire. But I want to thank you."

"For what?"

"I always wanted one more charge like that. It was just like back in the old days with Barent."

"Anine tells me you took down six of them."

"That was Marathren, Sire. He is a truly superior animal. How is he?"

"Limping a bit. I don't think you're supposed to use your horse as a battering ram."

"Had to get them off your back, Sire."

"Well, you did that, Lukin."

"What happened then, Sire?"

"You don't know?"

"No, Sire. I guess I got the mercenary's prayer answered."

"I hope not. How do you feel?"

"Weak. Head aches like fire...." His voice trailed off, then returned. "Good battle to go out on. Never had a woman commander before. Something new every day. Good battle...like the old days."

Here, his voice faded. After a moment, Gerth reappeared. "He's asleep again. Or unconscious. Is it safe to move him?"

"We've used it for wounded before." Talia reached out to rock the carriage. "Smooth ride."

"When can we leave?"

Ferlen appeared at the king's shoulder. "Any time, your Majesty. We tossed all the loose rock out and the ford's clear. We'll take the big carriage through slowly and the rest can follow. It's no more than knee deep, this time of year."

"Good enough." Gerth raised his voice. "We'll move out immediately. Anine and the Clan will bring the prisoners and the wounded. Mount up."

There was a general bustle and soon the king's party was moving up the road to the north. As they departed, Anine lined the prisoners up and stood in front of them.

"We have a lot of work to do, and I don't want any trouble. You see those three bodies over there? They tried to get away and they wouldn't stop when my men asked them politely. I want no paroles. I don't need them. First, we bury the dead. Then we make stretchers for the wounded. Then we walk to Renalk. If you work snappy, you don't walk in the dark. If you work, the Clan will help. If you make trouble, the Clan will have to guard, they won't be available to work, and it will take longer. Your choice."

Mantinello called assignments and Ferlen handed out shovels from the equipment wagon. Soon, the former battlefield was back to normal, if you ignored the torn turf and the bloody spots. *A week of rains and no one will ever know a battle took place.* Except for the burial mounds, large and small, and the broken bridge.

A candle later Anine's command trudged up the road, but without Ferlen and two of his stonemasons. They were already surveying the damage and making plans for the repair of the bridge. There would be merchants wanting to move their goods tomorrow.

When they tramped into Renalk it was dusk, but still light enough to see the road. A squad of Lord Tischen's soldiers took over the prisoners, and the wounded were brought to the infirmary. Billets were prepared for her party, although the Inari opted for a sward of grass beside the stream and set up their tents.

By the time all were settled, Anine had little leisure to dress. She merely splashed water across her face and hands, hoping it got most of the blood off, and changed her jerkin.

When she reached the main hall, the banquet was already in full swing. The story had been told and the toasts had been drunk, because the noise was increasing as she stood in the doorway and watched. A huge crowd jammed the hall, and she stayed in the shadows. She tried to spot Ferlen, but he must be still coming in from the bridge, because he was nowhere to be seen. Maybe there was a place for her at the lower tables. However, Gerth somehow spotted her, and his voice brought an immediate hush over the crowd.

"Anine! The hero of the battle has arrived."

Wild calls and cheers lifted her towards the head table, where Talia motioned to an empty chair beside her. Anine found her cheeks hot and ducked her head. Then she somehow regained her composure and strode forward.

As she slid into the seat, she leaned close to Talia. "That was more difficult than charging through the battle today."

Talia laughed. "You certainly seemed like you were enjoying yourself more this morning."

Gerth raised his flagon. "The story has been told. If not for Anine's forewarning, if not for the Clan scouting, we could easily have been surprised on the road today. When I was divided from the battle, she called the strategy, led the main charge, and generally won it all single-handed."

That brought Anine to her feet. "Your Majesty!"

"Yes, Anine?"

She put on Gavess' best accent. "Much as it pains me to disagree with my liege in public, I find your last statement a gross exaggeration!"

He roared with laughter. "You see, my friends? This woman has courage to spare. She throws the truth even in the teeth of royalty." He raised his drink again. "To Anine, one of the best military minds in the kingdom!"

Then they were all on their feet, and Anine found herself standing, her face flaming hot, unable to think of anything to say. She raised her own flagon.

"I drink to Lukin. He got the Mercenary's Prayer today and died a hero, saving his king!"

There was a moment's silence, then everyone rose and toasted the old Guard Captain, who had slipped deeper and deeper into unconsciousness as the afternoon progressed, and died soon after reaching the castle.

Gerth rose. "I, too, mourn the loss of the first friend of the Arlyn Dynasty. He lived as he wanted, with honour and with dignity, and he died happy. You know, he kept begging me. 'One more charge, your Majesty. Just one more full frontal attack, like the good old days.' Well, he made his charge. Straight into six of them and he

416

took the whole lot of them down, him on top. It took a bridge falling on him to kill him."

The king raised his flagon, and everyone drank again.

"And I would also like to drink to all our defenders: Warlanders, foot soldiers, and Inari. They fought well today, every one of them!"

Again, he drank, and the court followed suit.

"And by the way, Anine?"

"Yes, Sire?"

"What was that you shouted, just before your final charge?"

She thought about it. "Oh, that was just something in Inarituk, Sire."

"I assumed it was Inarituk, Anine. I just wondered what it meant. It certainly brought a cheer from your men."

"Oh. Well, it's hard to translate, Sire…"

"But…?

"Well, your Majesty, it means something like, 'Time for some fun'."

After the roar of laughter died away, Talia pulled her arm. "You can sit, now, Anine. You've done enough for today."

"Thank you, my Lady."

Gerth leaned across his wife. "So, Anine, I would not prove myself ungrateful." He spoke quietly, and the rest of the crowd turned back to their meal. "What reward would you like to claim for saving the king and queen's lives?"

Anine wrinkled her brow. She felt hesitant. "Can I…go build roads?"

"What?" The king sat bolt upright. "Roads?"

Queen Talia made a slapping motion towards her husband's ear. "Don't pretend to be surprised. You know that's what she's been trying to do for two years now, and you keep hauling her away to chase bandits."

The king looked perplexed. "I know, but Anine, you have done such a wonderful job on your military tasks. I wasn't exaggerating. You have a fine military mind, and a wonderful touch with the men in your command. Do you want to lose all that?"

She considered this. "It might seem strange to you, your Majesty, but that's my request. I didn't become a soldier because I wanted to. I chose the mercenary life because it was better than being a beast of burden on a farm. Building roads is something I chose because I

417

wanted to, not because I had to, or because I wanted to get away from something else. I think I can use the same skills you just mentioned in running the road crews. Especially since we are using them to control the bandits.

"Your Majesty," she leaned forward, "if it wasn't for this political interference from outside, we wouldn't need all the Clan Inari. We would need only a few more men and our road patrols could keep the roads safe and in good condition."

Again, Gerth's laugh rang out, echoed by his wife. "So already you're bargaining for more men."

"Word's out, Gerth. Some day she'll be as bad as Lady Kenna."

The king grimaced. "Thank you for that advice, my dear. I shall have to take steps to protect myself." He sat, thinking. Finally, he spoke, his voice slow at first, then quickening as the ideas came.

"First, I'm going to leave you under the direct supervision of Lady Kenna." He spoke aside to Talia. "That means I won't have to deal with both of them at once."

"I am also going to relieve you of your duties with the Inari, except for what Zoysana requires of you as a Clan member.

"As you know, there is a new demesne to be awarded. The person who takes control of the road building must have noble status. It will be a different kind of demesne, because it will not be defined by the amount of land it contains. It will be a demesne defined by the duties that it performs."

He leaned forward, ticking off points on his thick fingers. "You will, however, need a centre to work from. You will need living quarters, work quarters and staff quarters. You will need temporary housing for your workers as they pass through. You will need storehouses, workshops, a smith, a cartwright..."

Anine couldn't hold herself back; "...a stonemason's shop and a storage yard for gravel, stone and timbers. In fact, we could save the realm a lot of money if we quarried our own stone and felled our own timber."

"If you're going to keep up your military duties, you'll need a practice field, an armourer and a parade ground."

"I can't see placing this just anywhere, your Majesty. With the kind of work we're going to be doing, we'll have to have a mill."

They became aware that Talia was slowly passing her hand up and down between their faces. "All right, you two. You can talk

418

business tomorrow on the road to C'deille. In case you forgot, there's a banquet going on. We must pay some attention to our host and our guests."

The two looked around. Gerth turned to the lord on his left. "What do you think, Tischen? If I give such huge responsibility to this young woman, will anybody be upset? Will the other lords think it unfair?"

Their host was a large man, leisurely in his speech. He thought, passing a long look over at Anine. "From what I've been hearing, if you don't give her something pretty substantial as a reward, there's going to be a whole lot more trouble. I took over this demesne when I wasn't much older than her. My father got thrown by a bad horse, hit a fence post. It happens. I handled it. It looks like she can.

"As far as most of us are concerned, your Majesty, Anine's the main reason the roads are safe, and she and that Ferlen fellow are doing a pretty good job of making them smooth as well."

Then he leaned in and lowered his voice. "Also, your Majesty, the Lords would probably be happier if our king didn't have such a fine military mind in his forces. We'd rather have her out on the roads protecting us than heading the King's Guard, keeping us under control."

Gerth laughed once more. "Well, that's frank speaking, Tischen, and probably true as well. Once again, the all-powerful king finds himself doing what will keep his subjects happy, whether he wants to or not.

"So, Anine. It's the road-building demesne for you. We'll think up some kind of official title. You can start looking around for a place for your headquarters. I suspect you'll cause less *disharmony*," he used the Inari word and grinned proudly "if you look in the Free Counties. You won't be taking land from one of the other demesnes that way, and as long as you don't take any good farmland, whatever town you choose will be happy to have you."

Talia nodded. "I should think so. Look what happened to Lanil's Rock when Zoysana set up there. The town's almost twice the size it was two years ago."

Anine could hardly think. "Thank you, your Majesty. I don't know what to say. It's good of you to relieve me of my other duties, but what about the bandits?"

419

"I don't think we're going to have those problems again. I've already had a chat with some of the Knights we captured. There are going to be a few red faces in the Inner Duchies when news of this gets around. Most of the nobles there are in favour of trade, and anybody who goes around killing merchants will not be popular. That man you spitted, Lord Glosla, was one of the main instigators. With him gone, I think their little alliance will fall apart. But remember, you're still responsible for any bandit problems."

"Of course, Sire." She leaned over and caught Zoysana's eye. "I'm sure the Clan will always be at our disposal. In fact, we better have a campsite for the Inari somewhere nearby."

Talia slapped the table. "You're bargaining again. Back to the banquet."

Obediently, Anine sat back, lifting her drink to her lips. But her mind was still turning.

37. END OF SUMMER

Anine and Ferlen stood in the slanting autumn sunshine, enjoying the look of the warm yellow sandstone on the new bridge over the Kernagata River.

"Not bad for a couple of amateurs."

She kicked a small stone off the finished roadway. "After the little ones you worked on all summer, this was the next obvious step."

"I guess so. We'll know how we did when the floods come next spring."

"Or the next, or the next after that. This bridge had better last longer than you and me."

"Speaking of floods, there's one last wagonload of rock to be put off on that protective wall, there. Who do we have available?" He was looking around the site at the workers, busy to a man.

Anine stretched her shoulders. "You know, Ferlen, I haven't had a good workout in ages. Wanta help me unload those rocks?"

His usual slow grin. "Sure, Anine, as long as you do twice your share of the work like you always do."

She grinned back. "Just back her alongside the wall, there, and I'll hand them up to you. You only have to stack them."

He jumped up on the wagon seat and skillfully manoeuvered the team into position.

"You're getting pretty good at that. Maybe I'll hire you on for next year."

He didn't respond, and she wondered if she'd said something wrong. *Oh, well, with Ferlen, if something's wrong, he'll soon enough let me know. He's a man of few words, but he makes the most of what he says.*

She started handing up the big, flat rocks and was soon sweating in the pale fall sunlight. He seemed even more silent than usual. She waited him out.

Sure enough, soon he stopped. "Anine, I'd like to talk."

"That's a switch." Then she sobered. "Sure, Ferlen. What's the deal?"

"You know the agreement we made last fall? How have you liked it?"

She looked around at the new bridge, the firm roadbed leading up to it. "I've been real happy, Ferlen. You got me out of a spot last year, and I'm not likely to forget it. I like the way it worked out this year after the fightin' stopped, with me doin' the road work and you buildin' the bridges and walls."

"So, you're happy with the deal as it stands?"

She shrugged. "Sure. Aren't you?"

"Well, actually that's what I wanted to talk to you about. With you having the responsibility for the demesne and all that, I was thinking the agreement would have to change."

Disappointment coursed through her, then surprise that the loss was so keen. "Well, sure, Ferlen. The deal was for the summer, and summer's over."

"Aye. And the deal was that when summer was over, I'd hand it all back to you. Well, the king's done that already."

"Forget what the king says, you're still you and I'm still me, and nothin's changed. Our deal still holds."

"You really mean that?"

"Of course. Summer's over. You fulfilled your part, and more. Like I said, I ain't likely to forget it. If you want to go back to trappin', you can consider the deal well completed."

"No, no, that's not it. I'd like to stay."

"What?" Her glance shot to his face.

"Anine, I found something out this summer. I like to build. I like doing this bridge work as much as anything I've done, even laying out my trap lines in the fall. I know I said I'd step back when the summer was over, but now...well, I really hate to ask it, Anine, because I know how much this duty means to you. But now I'm going back on the deal. I still want to be part of it. Could I stay and...just build bridges, or something?"

Anine had been holding a rather heavy stone in her arms, and the strain was making them ache. She passed the rock to him to cover her confusion. "Well, Ferlen, I gotta say, that's the longest speech I ever heard you say. It must be important to you."

He gave a weak smile. "I sort of practised."

"Oh. Well, let me get the gist of it. You like doin' road work. You especially like buildin' bridges. You don't want to break our bargain. You want to extend it."

He brightened. "I hadn't thought of putting it that way, Anine, but yes. I'd like to extend the bargain."

"How's that gonna mix with your trappin'?"

He tossed the next rock on the wall. "I've been thinking about giving up trapping for some time, now. Last winter finished it." He rested one foot on the rock pile, his elbow on his knee, and looked down at her.

"I didn't have so much fun, last winter. As I said, laying out the lines and setting things up perfectly has always been my favourite part. I'm all set up. I've got my lines the way I like them. There's nothing new. In fact, I was pretty bored, last winter, thinking about all that was going on down here. Actually...lonely, as well. I've never found it lonely before.

"I've got a man wants to buy a half share in my trap line, and I'm thinking seriously of taking him up on it. Depending on what you say."

She grinned, mostly in relief, and passed him a joke along with the next rock to cover her confused feelings. "Another long speech. You practise that one, too?"

"No. That one was ad lib."

"Hey, you're getting to be a real talker."

She paused again, rested the next rock on her knee. "So, you'd like to extend our contract. You gonna spend the winter down here gettin' organized for next year's work?"

He nodded. "If you need me."

"Like a partnership."

"If you don't mind. I know you wanted this to be all your own duty. Actually, the king made it your duty. I don't really come into it. I hope you don't think I'm doing this just because...you know."

She laughed. "You mean greasing up the new power? Don't worry, Ferlen. It's like I said. You're still you and I'm still me. Nothin's changed."

"That's real good, Anine."

"Of course, I'll have to check it over with Lady Kenna, because she's in charge. But you know I'd be glad to have you. If things go as planned, we'll still be using the Inari, and I'll have to be responsible for them. Not as many, you understand, and Pagris and a couple of the other Clan will take over most of it. But I've still got to spend some time patrolling. And we got a lot to do next summer.

I could really use some experienced help. In fact, if we do that bridge over the Panjhali out west we was talkin' about, remember those extra big stones with the rounded corners we wanted? Somebody's gonna have to supervise the masons quite a bit on that, and..."

"There's something else, Anine."

She stopped. "There is?"

He nodded, wincing. "Yes."

She gave an exaggerated sigh. "So now that you've got an in, you're askin' for more. What we gotta have, a bargaining session?"

"Anine, I didn't practise this one. I tried, but I couldn't, so just let me get through it, will you?"

He seemed deadly serious, so she laid the stone back down and stood facing him. "All right, Ferlen. I'm listenin'."

"Well, it's about the duration of the partnership."

"You want it longer?"

"Actually, more than that. I thought maybe we should make it permanent."

"A permanent partnership? That's pretty unusual, isn't it?"

"Not between a man and a woman, it isn't." He looked down at her puzzled expression and threw up his hands in frustration. "Anine. You are so literal. I'm not talking about making roads!"

"What? You mean all this talk of contracts wasn't business at all? Ferlen, you are the last man I expected to dance around anythin'. How am I supposed to figure out what you mean?"

"All right, Anine. I'll say it straight, if that's what you want. I think we should get married."

She stood stunned, looking at him. Then she remembered to close her mouth. She tried once, cleared her throat, but her voice still came out weakly. "...Married?"

"Yes. We get along so well. We complement each other's skills and personalities. We...we work together so well."

She snorted. "Sounds like you're pairin' up a team of oxen."

He was plainly uncomfortable now. "I know, I know. I'm supposed to be talking about love and things like that. But I don't know how, and I don't know what love is anyway. I do know that I like being with you. I know that when you walk into the room, or onto the work site, I get a certain feeling like everything is...better. I see you lift a big rock, or figure out a problem, and I get this feeling of pride, you know, that it's you that's doing it, and doing it so well."

She laughed and jumped up beside him. "That's as good a definition of love as I ever heard!" She wrapped her arms around him and gave him a kiss. She had never had a kiss before, but she had heard about them and it seemed all right. After a startled moment he responded, and then it was much better.

Whoops and cheers erupted around them. They broke off. Every workman on the site was watching. She regarded Ferlen, looked back at the workers and shrugged.

"Fine! You all saw it! We're gettin' married. A big hoo-ha, and you're invited to th' party." She swung her arm to indicate the work site. "Get back to work. We got a bridge to finish!" There was another good-natured cheer, and the men and women bent to their tasks.

She jumped back down on the cart. "And you and me, Partner, got a wagon to unload."

With a light heart, she chose the biggest stone and hoisted it up to him.

The End

If you enjoyed this book, do a favour for the author and other readers and go to one of the online sources and give it a review.

ABOUT THE AUTHOR

Brought up in a logging camp with no electricity, Gordon Long learned his storytelling in the traditional way: at his father's knee. He now spends his time editing, publishing, travelling, blogging and writing Fantasy, Sci-Fi and Social Commentary, although sometimes the boundaries blur.

Gordon lives in Tsawwassen, British Columbia, with his wife, Linda, and their Nova Scotia Duck Tolling Retriever, Josh. When he is not writing and publishing, he works on projects with the Surrey Seniors' Planning Table and is a staff writer for <indiesunlimited.com>

www.ingramcontent.com/pod-product-compliance
Lightning Source LLC
Chambersburg PA
CBHW051242270626
47162CB00001BA/110